"Riveting, exciting ... ⟨rs⟩ want." —Conn⟨...⟩or

"Pamela Clare is a ⟨...⟩ly written, fast-paced t⟨...⟩ici-pation. She creates h⟨...⟩ease of a master that draw the reader irresistibly into the story, making them part of the pain, the fear . . . and the passion."

—Leigh Greenwood, *USA Today* bestselling author

Praise for the MacKinnon's Rangers Novels

UNTAMED

"Captivating . . . Clare's detailed attention to the history of alliances forged and battles fought near Fort Ticonderoga adds authenticity, and the characters evolve and change with a realism that readers will love."

—*Publishers Weekly* (starred review)

"Magnificent . . . You need only to read the first page to know that you are beginning another historical romantic masterpiece by Pamela Clare, a master storyteller who always delights readers . . . *Untamed* will leave you breathless and cheering with its attention to historical detail, characters you can almost reach out and touch, a story line that's deeply riveting, and a love story that will melt your heart as only these MacKinnons, Highland warriors, Scottish brothers, can do . . . You must always keep a Pamela Clare book on your keeper shelf. She is not just a read, she is a reread."

—*Fresh Fiction*

"Riveting. Clare cleverly combines history and fiction to bring us a tale full of drama and sensuality, with well-drawn characters and continuous action."

—*RT Book Reviews*

continued . . .

SURRENDER

"[A] lush historical romance . . . Believable characters, scorching chemistry, and a convincing setting make this a worthy read."
—*Publishers Weekly*

"Be forewarned that this is not a book you'll put down lightly. Once you start, you'll be hard-pressed to do anything else but travel along on this journey filled with action, danger, fantastically vivid historical events and written in almost liquid prose: nonstop and ever-flowing words that blend together in a lifelike portrayal of colonial times and the people who stood up to almost unimaginable hardships, written only as Pamela Clare can write them . . . *Surrender* is a must-have . . . I can't recommend this book highly enough." —*Romance Reader at Heart*

"An astonishing story. All you need to do is open the cover and read page one to know you're being taken on an incredible journey and beginning one of the most exciting books ever written. *Surrender* is nothing short of genius, a work of art, written by a master storyteller. Pamela Clare pens a story so gut-wrenching, so intense, so deeply moving that you can barely put it down. There are wonderful one-liners that make you laugh along with the most beautiful words of love you'll ever read. It's an intense drama with unforgettable characters and a hero and heroine you'll hold in your heart forever. Surrender to *Surrender*." —*Fresh Fiction*

"Trust me, you do not want to miss this exciting and HOT start to what promises to be a fabulous new series. I have loved all of Pamela Clare's novels from the first one and this is one that I hated to see end . . . Great plot and characters as well as some very memorable supporting characters . . . If you love historical romance, be sure to pick this one up soon!" —*Night Owl Romance*

continued . . .

"This is fantastic historical romance that uses the backdrop of the French and Indian War to tell a terrific tale of love. The story line is action packed . . . and never slows down until the final exhilarating climax . . . Fans will treasure this keeper and look forward to more MacKinnon thrillers."

—*Midwest Book Review*

"Engrossing . . . This is a book to savor."

—*The Romance Reader*

"Ms. Clare writes a compelling story that I found difficult to set aside. I was totally submerged in the characters and the story through the very end. I'm anxiously awaiting the next two novels where we will learn more about Iain's brothers."

—*Once Upon A Romance*

"[Surrender] has its fill of adventure . . . The author evokes her setting wonderfully . . . Readers looking for a passionate romance and plenty of adventure will likely enjoy this story."

—*All About Romance*

UNTAMED

Pamela Clare

BERKLEY SENSATION, NEW YORK

THE BERKLEY PUBLISHING GROUP
Published by the Penguin Group
Penguin Group (USA) Inc.
375 Hudson Street, New York, New York 10014, USA
Penguin Group (Canada), 90 Eglinton Avenue East, Suite 700, Toronto, Ontario M4P 2Y3, Canada
(a division of Pearson Penguin Canada Inc.)
Penguin Books Ltd., 80 Strand, London WC2R 0RL, England
Penguin Group Ireland, 25 St. Stephen's Green, Dublin 2, Ireland (a division of Penguin Books Ltd.)
Penguin Group (Australia), 250 Camberwell Road, Camberwell, Victoria 3124, Australia
(a division of Pearson Australia Group Pty. Ltd.)
Penguin Books India Pvt. Ltd., 11 Community Centre, Panchsheel Park, New Delhi—110 017, India
Penguin Group (NZ), 67 Apollo Drive, Rosedale, Auckland 0632, New Zealand
(a division of Pearson New Zealand Ltd.)
Penguin Books (South Africa) (Pty.) Ltd., 24 Sturdee Avenue, Rosebank, Johannesburg 2196,
South Africa

Penguin Books Ltd., Registered Offices: 80 Strand, London WC2R 0RL, England

This is a work of fiction. Names, characters, places, and incidents either are the product of the author's imagination or are used fictitiously, and any resemblance to actual persons, living or dead, business establishments, events, or locales is entirely coincidental. The publisher does not have any control over and does not assume any responsibility for author or third-party websites or their content.

UNTAMED

A Berkley Sensation Book / published by arrangement with the author

PRINTING HISTORY
A Leisure Book mass-market edition / December 2008
Berkley Sensation mass-market edition / January 2012

ISBN: 978-0-425-24581-1

BERKLEY SENSATION®
Berkley Sensation Books are published by The Berkley Publishing Group,
a division of Penguin Group (USA) Inc.,
375 Hudson Street, New York, New York 10014.
BERKLEY SENSATION® is a registered trademark of Penguin Group (USA) Inc.
The "B" design is a trademark of Penguin Group (USA) Inc.

PRINTED IN THE UNITED STATES OF AMERICA

10 9 8 7 6 5 4 3 2 1

For Amy Vandersall,
who has always believed in me.

Acknowledgments

Special thanks to Catrìona Mary Mac Kirnan for once again lending her expertise in Scottish Gaelic to the MacKinnon Brothers and to Stephanie Desprez for correcting my French. *Tapadh leibh! Merci beaucoup!*

Much gratitude to Natasha Kern for her support and encouragement and to Cindy Hwang for allowing me to keep this series alive—and for caring about the historical details.

Additional thanks to Mike Terenzetti of Pontour Tours of Lake George for taking me to the magical waterfall on the eastern shore of Lake George and showing me the lake from the Rangers' point of view; to Christopher Fox, the curator at Fort Ticonderoga, for the tour of the fort and its collections; to Dr. David Starbuck for sharing his insights about his excavations on Rogers Island; and to Eileen Hannay of Rogers Island Visitor Center for being so patient with two people who didn't know when to stop asking questions.

Love and thanks to my sister, Michelle, and to my good friends Sue Zimmerman, Kristi Ross, Libby Murphy, Ronlyn Howe, Suzanne Warren, and Jennifer Johnson for their tireless support and loving friendship.

And, as always, thank you to my family, especially my sons, Alec and Benjamin. I love you.

PROLOGUE

July 8, 1758
Fort Carillon (Ticonderoga)
New France

Amalie Chauvenet straightened the gold braid on her father's gray uniform, trying to hide her fear. "I will be fine, Papa. You've no need to trouble yourself on my behalf."

In the distance she could hear the dull thud of marching feet and the scrape of metal against metal as thousands of British soldiers surrounded the fort's landward side and prepared to attack. Certain *les Anglais* would capture the fort in a matter of hours, her father had come to escort her to the little chapel where he felt she'd be safest.

"If the fort should fall, stay close to Père François." Papa's dear face was lined with worry. "I will come to you if I can. If aught should befall me, Père François will take you to Montcalm or Bourlamaque. They will keep you safe."

"Nothing will happen to you, Papa!" Her words sounded childish even to her own ears—a measure of her fear for him.

It had become the custom in this accursed war for both sides to shoot officers first in hopes of leaving the enemy leaderless and confused. But Amalie could not abide the thought of her father in harm's way, a mere mark in range of some British soldier's musket.

Papa lifted her chin, forced her to meet his gaze. "Listen to me! You are an officer's daughter, Amalie, but in the rush of victory, even disciplined soldiers are wont to rape and pillage. Do not allow yourself to be found alone!"

She heard her father's words—and understood the unspoken message beneath them. She was an officer's daughter, but she was also *métisse*, her blood a mix of French and Abenaki. Though most French accepted her, the British were not so kind. In their eyes, a woman of mixed blood was little better than a dog—or so she'd been told. If the fort should fall, her standing as a major's daughter likely would not keep her safe without a high-ranking officer's protection.

"Oui, Papa." Dread spread like ice through her belly. "Is there no chance that we may yet prevail?"

"The British general Abercrombie commands a force of at least fifteen thousand, easily four times our number—and Mac-Kinnon's Rangers are with him."

Amalie's dread grew. Everyone knew of MacKinnon's Rangers. There were no fiercer fighters, no warriors more feared or reviled throughout New France than this band of barbaric Celts. Unmatched at woodcraft and shooting marks, they had once crossed leagues of untamed forest in the dead of winter to destroy her grandmother's village at Oganak, ruthlessly killing most of the men, burning the lodges, and leaving the women and children to starve. The French had put a bounty on the MacKinnon brothers' scalps—but the Abenaki wanted them alive so they could exact vengeance in blood and pain.

Some amongst her mother's people said MacKinnon's Rangers could fly. Others claimed to have seen them take the forms of wolves or bears. Still others claimed they feasted upon the flesh of their dead. The stories about them were so astonishing that some believed these MacKinnon men weren't men at all, but powerful *chi bai*—spirits.

But there were other rumors, stories of Rangers sparing women and children, tales of priests and nuns whom they'd shielded from British Regulars with their own bodies, accounts of mercy shown to French soldiers and enemy Indians alike.

But which stories were true?

Amalie did not wish to find out.

"Why did you not stay at the convent?" Her father's brow folded into a frown. "At least there you would be safe."

She smoothed a stray curl on his gray wig. "I came because you needed me, Papa."

She'd journeyed all the way from Trois Rivières in April to care for him when he'd fallen ill with fever. He was her only true family. Though she had cousins and aunts amongst the Abenaki, she barely knew them. Her mother had died in childbed when Amalie was not yet two, and her father had parted ways with his wife's kin, preferring to shelter his only child amongst the Ursulines than in the wild. And although Amalie was grateful for the care she'd received at the abbey, she had long chafed at the strict rules and rigid routine that shaped convent life, longing to see the world beyond the abbey's stifling walls.

"Beware of seeking adventure," the *mère supérieure* had warned her when Amalie had announced she was leaving. "You might not be prepared when it finds you."

Amalie'd had no idea what the *mère supérieure* had meant— until yesterday, when hundreds upon hundreds of British boats had landed to the south on the shores of Lac du Saint-Sacrement, what the British called Lake George, disgorging thousands of soldiers dressed in blood red. Now battle was imminent, and only God knew what this day would bring.

Yet, despite the peril, she did not regret her decision to come to the frontier. She'd never spent more than a few weeks at a time with her father, and the months she'd lived by his side were amongst the happiest and most exciting she could remember. She'd found joy in nursing him back to health, cooking and cleaning for him, mending his uniform, heating his bath and filling his pipe, as any devoted daughter would do.

But there was more.

They'd laughed together, read Voltaire and Rousseau, discussed the latest ideas of the day, notions about society and liberty she'd not encountered at the abbey. Her father had let her speak her mind, even encouraged her to do so, never chastising her for asking questions as the *mère supérieure* had so often done. She'd come to know him as a father, to admire him as a man, to respect him as an officer. She'd come to love him.

She could not bear to lose him.

She pressed her palm to his cheek. "If the strength of our army should fail, it will not be long before the British reach Trois

Rivières and Montréal. Then abbey walls will make little difference. I would not trade these months with you for something so small as safety."

His gaze softened. "Ah, my sweet Amalie, I do need you. You have brought such sunshine to my life. If I had but considered it, I would have taken you from the abbey long ago. But if the breastworks cannot withstand Abercrombie's artillery . . ."

His voice trailed off. Then he smiled and drew her close, surrounding her with his reassuring strength and his familiar scent—pipe smoke, starched linen, and brisk cologne. "It is in God's hands, *ma petite caille.*"

My little quail.

And so Amalie went to await the outcome of the battle in the chapel, swallowing her tears and forcing herself to smile when her father took his leave of her to return to his duties at the breastworks.

"Be safe, Papa," she whispered as he walked away, so smart in his gray uniform.

She knelt down with her rosary beside Père François and had just begun to pray when the battle exploded. Like thunder it seemed to shake the very ground, the din of cannon, musket fire, and men's shouts almost deafening. She'd never been near a battlefield before, and her hands trembled as she worked her way through each bead, fighting to remember the words, her thoughts on Papa—and what might happen to all of them should the fort fall.

The soldiers would be imprisoned. Her father and the other officers would be interrogated and traded for British captives. And the women . . .

In the rush of victory, even disciplined soldiers are wont to rape and pillage.

"*Notre Père, qui êtes aux cieux . . .*" Our Father, who art in heaven . . .

She hadn't been kneeling long when Père François was summoned to the hospital to comfort the wounded and anoint the dying. Impatient to help and mindful of her father's warning not to be found alone, Amalie, who'd tended sick and injured women at the convent, asked to come with him.

"Are you certain, Amalie?" Père François looked down at her, doubt clouding his green eyes. "This is war. It will be gruesome."

She nodded, braiding her long hair and binding the plait into a thick knot at her nape. "*Oui,* Father, I am certain. I have seen death before."

But she'd never seen anything like what awaited them at the hospital.

The dead were so numerous that there was no room for them inside. Their bodies lay without dignity in the hot sunshine, moved hastily aside to make way for those still living. The wounded lay on beds, on the floor, against the walls. They muttered snatches of prayer, groaned through gritted teeth, cried out in agony, waiting for someone to ease their suffering. Monsieur Lambert, the surgeon, and his men worked as swiftly as they could, but there were so many. And everywhere, there was blood, the air thick with the stench of gunpowder and death.

Surely, this was hell.

Amalie thrust aside her childish fears and her tears, donned an apron, and set to work, doing what the surgeon asked of her. Outside, the battle seemed to come in waves, building until she feared the very sky should fall, then fading to silence, only to begin anew.

A soldier clutched at her skirts with bloody fingers. She took his hand, sat beside him, and knew the moment she saw the wound in his chest that he would perish. If only she could give him laudanum, ease the pain of his passing, but there was not enough. She'd been told to save it for those who at least stood a chance of survival.

He seemed about to speak, struggled for breath.

And then he was gone.

About her age, he'd died before she could utter a word of comfort, before Père François could offer him last rites, before the surgeon could tend him. She swallowed the hard lump in her throat, muttered a prayer, then drew the soldier's eyes closed.

Another blast of cannon shook the walls of the little log hospital, making Amalie gasp.

"Those are French guns, mademoiselle." The soldier in the next bed spoke, his voice tight with pain. "Do not be afraid. As long as they fire, we know the breastworks stand."

Ashamed of her fear, Amalie covered the dead soldier with a blanket, a signal to the surgeon's attendants to remove his body. How could she, who was safe behind the fort's walls, allow herself to cower at the mere sound of war when all around her lay men who had braved the full violence of the battlefield?

"It is I who should be offering you comfort, monsieur." She moved to sit beside him and checked beneath the bloodstained bandage on his right arm. The musket ball had passed through, but it had broken bone. Monsieur Lambert would almost certainly have to amputate. "Are you thirsty?"

"You are the daughter of Major Chauvenet, are you not?"

"*Oui.*"

"You are just as beautiful as the men say. I have never seen such long hair." Then his eyes widened, his face pallid. "I hope you take no offense at my boldness. The battle seems to have loosened my tongue."

Though she'd been at Fort Carillon for more than three months, she still hadn't grown accustomed to the attention of men. Uncertain how to respond, she reached for her plait, which had somehow slipped free of its knot, its thick end touching the floor when she sat. Quickly, she bound it up again, lest it trail through the blood that was tracked across the floorboards. Then she pulled the water bucket close, drew out the ladle, and lifted it to the soldier's lips.

"Drink."

The wounded soldier had just taken his first swallow when there came a commotion at the door and Montcalm's third in command, the Chevalier de Bourlamaque, was brought inside, bleeding from what looked to be a grave wound in his shoulder.

"How goes the battle?" someone called.

An expectant hush fell over the room.

Bourlamaque sat with a grimace, his white wig slightly askew. "We are prevailing."

Murmurs of astonishment and relief passed through the crowded hospital like a breeze, and Amalie met the injured soldier's gaze, her own surprise reflected in his eyes.

"For whatever reason, Abercrombie hasn't brought up his artillery." Bourlamaque gritted his teeth as a soldier helped him out of his jacket. "We are cutting down the enemy as swiftly as they appear, and their losses are grievous. Four times we have repulsed them. None have even passed the abatis to reach our breastworks."

"Abercrombie is a fool!" one of the soldiers exclaimed to harsh laughter.

Bourlamaque did not smile. "That may well be—and thank

God for it!—but his marksmen are laying down a most murderous fire upon us from the cover of the trees. We have pounded them with cannon, but we cannot root them out."

"MacKinnon and his men?"

"*Oui.* Their Mahican allies are beside them." Bourlamaque wiped sweat and gunpowder from his brow with a linen handkerchief. "The lot of them shift from tree to tree like ghosts and will not relent."

"And they call themselves Catholic!" A soldier spat on the floor.

But Bourlamaque held up his hand for silence. "Listen! They are retreating again."

The sound of shooting died away, replaced first by the distant beating of drums and then by an oppressive, sullen stillness. So many times now the battle had ceased, only to begin again. Amalie dared not hope, and yet . . .

Barely able to breathe, she bent her mind back to her work. Whether the battle was over or not, these men needed her help. She bound the soldier's wound in fresh linen, gave him laudanum, prayed with him, then moved to the next bed and the next. She'd gone to the back room to fetch more linen strips for bandages when she heard the drums beat afresh.

Her stomach sank, and her step faltered.

"Curse them!" a soldier shouted. "Do they not know when to withdraw?"

There came a roar of cannon, and again the battle raged.

More dead. More wounded.

But not Papa. Not Papa.

Holding on to that hope, Amalie went where she was needed. She carried water to the injured men who lay on the bare earth outside, cleaned and bandaged their less serious wounds, offered what solace she could. She did not notice the sweat trickling between her breasts or the rumbling of her empty stomach or her own thirst.

Then the cadence of the British drums changed again, and once more the battle fell silent. And then—was she imagining it?—cheers. The sound swelled, grew stronger, and all heads turned toward the northwest, where soldiers stood upon the walls, their muskets raised overhead, their gazes on the breastworks and the battlefield beyond.

A soldier ran toward them, his face split by a wide smile. "They are retreating! The British are fleeing! The day is won!"

Relief swept through Amalie, leaving her dizzy. She closed her eyes, took a deep breath, felt a gentle squeeze from the soldier whose hand she was holding.

"C'est fini, mademoiselle!" he said, a smile on his bruised face. *It's over.*

Amalie opened her eyes, smiled back. *"Oui, c'est fini."*

But even as she said it, she knew it wasn't true. For the men who lay here and those inside, the fight was far from over, life and death still hanging in the balance. She threw herself into caring for them with renewed strength, refreshed by the knowledge that no more need die today and grateful beyond words that her father did not lie amongst the injured or the slain.

But if she'd expected the end of the battle to stem the tide of wounded and dead, she'd been mistaken. Carried on litters or hobbling, they arrived by the dozens, some scarcely scathed, some terribly wounded, some already beyond all but God's help. Most had been hit by musket fire, holes torn into their flesh by cruel lead. Others had been pierced by shards of wood or burnt by powder.

"Be thankful they never had the chance to use their bayonets or their artillery," said a young soldier when she gasped at the terrible wound in his shoulder. "Have you ever seen a man with his entrails—"

"That is quite enough, Sergeant."

Amalie recognized Lieutenant Rillieux's voice and glanced back to find him standing behind her, his tricorne in his hand, his face smeared with gunpowder, sweat, and blood. One of her father's officers and a tall man, he towered over her where she knelt on the ground.

He bowed stiffly.

"I pray you are not wounded, monsieur." She stood, wiping her fingers on her bloodstained apron.

It was then she noticed the pity and sadness in his eyes.

The breath left her lungs, and her heart began to pound, the sound of her pulse almost drowning out his words.

"Mademoiselle, it is with great sorrow that I must report—"

But she had already seen. *"Non!"*

Two young officers approached the hospital, bearing her father on a litter.

Heedless of soldiers' stares or Lieutenant Rillieux's attempt to stop her, she ran to him. But it was too late. Her father's eyes were closed, his lips and skin blue, his throat torn by a musket ball. She didn't have to check his breathing to know he was dead.

"Non, Papa! Non!" She cupped his cold cheek in her palm, then laid her head against his still and silent chest, pain seeming to split her breast, tears blurring her vision.

Over the sound of her own sobs, she heard Lieutenant Rillieux speak. "He was slain by one of MacKinnon's Rangers during the first assault. He toppled over the breastworks, and we could not reach him until the battle ended for fear of the Rangers' rifles. You should know that he fought bravely and died instantly. We shall all mourn him."

And in the darkness of her grief, it dawned on her.

Everything her father had been, everything he'd known, everything they might have done together was gone. Her father was dead.

She was alone.

Chapter 1

April 19, 1759
Ticonderoga
New York frontier

Major Morgan MacKinnon lay on his belly, looking down from the summit of Rattlesnake Mountain to the French fort at Ticonderoga below. He held up his brother Iain's spying glass—nay, it was now *his* spying glass—and watched as French soldiers unloaded kegs of gunpowder from the hold of a small ship. Clearly, Bourlamaque was preparing to defend the fort again. But if Morgan and his men succeeded in their mission tonight, that powder would never see the inside of a French musket.

Connor stretched out beside him and spoke in a whisper. "I cannae look down upon this place without thinkin' of that bastard Abercrombie and the good men we lost."

Morgan lowered the spying glass and met his younger brother's gaze. "Nor can I, but we didna come here to grieve."

"Nay." Connor's gaze hardened. "We've come for vengeance."

Last summer, they'd had no choice but to follow Abercrombie—or Nanny Crombie as the men had called him—to a terrible defeat. An arrogant bastard who paid no heed to the counsel of mere provincials, Abercrombie had ignored their warnings that Ticonderoga could not be taken without artillery. He hadn't believed that the hastily built abatis—the barrier of felled trees and branches that had been piled afore the walls—could hinder trained British

Regulars and had ordered his men against the French breastworks
with naught but muskets. Soldiers had become ensnared like rab-
bits, cut down by French marksmen afore they could reach the
walls, victims of their own loyalty and Abercrombie's overweening
pride.

On that terrible day, the Rangers, then under the command of
Morgan's older brother Iain, had taken position to the northwest
together with Captain Joseph's Muhheconneok warriors and had
fired endlessly at the French marksmen, trying to dislodge them.
But the French had turned cannon upon them and pounded them
into the ground. So many had been lost—good men and true, men
with families, men who'd fought beside them from the beginning.

'Twas here they'd lost Cam—and dozens more.

Dead for naught.

When Abercrombie had finally sounded the retreat and the
smoke had cleared, the fort had stood just as it had afore.

Never had Morgan seen such senseless death—and at the age
of seven and twenty he'd seen death enough to sicken a man's
soul. For nigh on four years, he and his brothers had lived and
breathed war. Forced by that whoreson Wentworth to choose
between fighting for Britain or being hanged for a crime they had
not committed, they'd taken up arms against the French and their
Indian allies, harrying them with ambuscades, seizing their supplies, fighting them in forest and fen. They'd slain fellow Catholic and heathen alike, burying their own dead along the way.

Morgan had never imagined that he, as a MacKinnon, would
fight the French, traditional allies of all Scotsmen still faithful to
Church and Crown. During the Forty-Five, the French had aided
the Highland clans, including Morgan's grandfather—Iain Og
MacKinnon, laird of Clan MacKinnon—in their vain struggle to
drive the German Protestant from the throne. Then, after the disas-
trous defeat at Culloden, the French had given refuge to many an
exiled Scot, saving countless lives from the wrath of Cumberland. Even now France sheltered the rightful heir to the throne,
bonnie Charles Stuart. Every true Scotsman owed the French a
debt.

Aye, it was a devil's bargain that had spared Morgan and his
brothers the gallows. Father Delavay, the French priest Iain had
kidnapped last year when he'd had need of a priest to marry him

and Annie, said the sin was not theirs but Wentworth's. And yet absolution stuck in Morgan's throat, for it was not bloody Wentworth who pulled the trigger on his rifle, but he himself.

If anything gave him peace, it was knowing that Iain was now out of the fray, settled on the MacKinnon farm with Annie and little Iain, the firstborn of a new generation of MacKinnons. Wentworth had released Iain from service, not because he'd wished to spare Iain, but because he was besotted with Annie. Whatever the cause for Wentworth's mercy, Morgan was grateful. He'd never have found the courage to face Annie had Iain been slain in battle—or worse—taken captive.

Morgan saw something move in the dark forest below, heard the slow click of rifles being cocked around him, and felt a warm swell of pride. He rarely needed to give orders. Having fought side by side for so long, the Rangers thought and moved as one. There were no better fighters in the colonies, no men better suited to the hardship of this war. 'Twas an honor to lead them, as Iain had done afore him.

Morgan closed the spying glass, raised his rifle, cocked it. But it was not French scouts who emerged from the green wall of forest, but Captain Joseph's warriors, eighty men in black and white war paint moving swiftly and silently through the shadows. They'd been watching the Rangers' west flank on the long march northward and had gone on to scout out the French sentries while Morgan and his men surveyed the fort from above.

Morgan lowered his rifle and whispered to Joseph in the Muhheconneok tongue. "You thrash about like a randy bull moose. We heard you coming from a league away. You might have been shot."

Joseph grinned. "There is more to fear in a bee's sting than in your muskets. My blind granny has better aim."

Bonded by blood to Morgan and his brothers, Joseph Aupauteunk was the son of a Muhheconneok chief and a fearsome warrior. He and his father had come to the MacKinnon farm, bringing gifts of dried corn and venison that had helped Morgan and his family survive their first bitter winter of exile in the colonies. Though Morgan's mother—God rest her soul—had at first been terrified of Indians, a lasting friendship had grown between Morgan's family and the Mahicans of Stockbridge. 'Twas Joseph and his uncles who'd taught Morgan and his brothers to track, to fight, to survive in the wild. As for what Joseph's sisters had taught them, Morgan was too much of a gentleman to say—without a gill or two of whiskey in his belly.

Morgan switched to English so that those amongst his men who did not speak Muhheconneok could understand. "What does Bourlamaque have waitin' for us?"

It was time to plan their strategy.

A malie picked at her dinner, her appetite lost to talk of war. She did her best to listen politely, no matter how dismayed she felt at the thought of another British attack. Monsieur de Bourlamaque was commander of a garrison in the midst of conflict. It was right that he and his trusted officers should discuss the war as they dined. She did not wish to distract them with childish sentiments, nor was she so selfish that she required diversion. And if, at times, she wished her guardian would ask to hear her thoughts . . .

Her father was the only person who'd ever done that, and he was gone.

And so Amalie passed the meal in silence much as she'd done at the abbey.

"We must not let last summer's victory lull us into becoming overconfident." Bourlamaque dabbed his lips with a white linen serviette. His blue uniform, with its decorations and the red sash, set him apart from his officers, who wore gray. "Amherst is not a fool like Abercrombie. He would never have attacked without artillery."

Lieutenant Fouchet looked doubtful. "Surely he will think twice before attempting to take us again. The British lost so many men!"

Amalie had heard that British losses exceeded fifteen hundred men. She could not imagine so many deaths. In all, the French had lost a hundred with another three hundred wounded, and that had seemed devastating. And yet, Amalie had overheard Bourlamaque call those casualties light.

Lieutenant Durand took a sip of wine. "How can they dare to plan another attack after having been defeated so resoundingly?"

"That resounding defeat is exactly why Amherst will attack." Bourlamaque fixed both Fouchet and Durand with a grave eye.

"For the sake of British pride, he will try to capture the fort this summer."

Lieutenant Rillieux leaned back in his chair, his face a wide grin. Alone amongst the younger officers, who favored their natural hair, he wore a powdered wig, the white a marked contrast to his olive skin and dark brows. "Let him do his worst."

Amalie stifled a gasp. How could he tempt fate in such a way when it meant the deaths of his own men? He'd do far better to pray for peace!

But Lieutenant Rillieux didn't seem to realize he'd said something thoughtless. "We shall drive Amherst back into the forest just as we did his predecessor. My men are ready."

"Were they ready when MacKinnon and his men attacked that last supply train?" Bourlamaque raised an eyebrow in clear disapproval. "We lost a fortune in rifled muskets—not to mention several cases of my favorite wine. No matter how well you prepare, the Rangers seem to stay one step ahead of you."

Amalie's belly knotted, as it did anytime she heard mention of MacKinnon's Rangers. They seemed to be everywhere and nowhere, these men who had killed her father. Although Papa had reassured her that there was no such thing as *chi bai,* she'd begun to wonder if her cousins were right. Perhaps the Rangers weren't men after all.

Lieutenant Rillieux's nostrils flared, and he bowed his head in apology. "My regrets once more for your loss, monsieur. The MacKinnon brothers are formidable adversaries, but we will break them."

"Let us hope so. Perhaps now that the eldest MacKinnon has been released from service, the Rangers will fall under poor leadership."

"I doubt that, monsieur. Morgan MacKinnon is every bit the woodsman, marksman, and leader that Iain MacKinnon was. It would be foolish to underestimate him. But arrangements have been made. As I said, my men are ready.

Amalie wasn't ready. She hadn't forgotten last summer's battle and feared the prospect of renewed bloodshed. Her grief for her father was still keen, her dreams filled with musket fire and the cries of dying men.

If only the accursed war would end! Life would be free to blossom again in New France. Sails would fill the harbors, bringing not soldiers but men and women who wanted to build homes and raise families here. The towns would bustle with hay wagons and applecarts instead of cannon and marching soldiers. Farmers would return to their fields and orchards, trappers to their forest trails, wives to their gardens and their weaving.

And what will you do, Amalie? Where will you go when the war is won?

Bourlamaque, who was now her guardian, believed that it was past time for her either to take vows and serve Christ or to marry and serve a husband.

"I would see you safely settled," he often reminded her. "It is my duty to your father, whom I greatly admired, despite his politics."

But Amalie had no desire to return to the dreary life of the abbey. It seemed to her that she'd drawn her first real breath when, after sixteen years, she'd left its walls. There she'd felt listless, as if some part of her were trapped in slumber. Here at Fort Carillon, in her father's company, she'd been truly happy. She'd felt alive.

She supposed she ought to marry, and yet in her grief she had not the heart for it. Bourlamaque assured her that a husband and children were the answer to her sorrow, and she knew he believed a swift marriage would be best for her. Still, she had hoped to make a love match as her parents had done. Women were expected to perform certain duties in marriage—to lie near their husbands and to bear their children—and Amalie knew from Sister Marie Louise, who'd taken vows after her husband and children had died of smallpox, that these wifely duties—did a man really mount his wife as a ram mounted a ewe?—were onerous even when one felt affection for one's mate. To hear the good sister speak of it, childbirth was akin to the tortures of hell.

"I'd rather spend my life kneeling on a cold stone floor than suffer such agony again," she'd whispered one afternoon as they'd tended the herb garden together. "God demands far less of a woman than does a husband."

What little Amalie knew of birth seemed to prove Sister Marie Louise's words true. It was not uncommon for a young girl to be left at the convent to bear a child in shame, and more than once Amalie had been awoken by the piteous cries that marked the throes of labor. Hadn't her own mother perished in childbed? If

Amalie were ever to suffer so, it would be on behalf of a man she loved. She wanted a husband who cherished her and whom she cherished in return, a man who, like her father, would value her opinions more than her obedience, who would see her as more than a helpmeet and the mother of his children, who would truly see *her*.

Certainly, Lieutenant Rillieux, while possessed of many admirable qualities, was not such a man. After her father's death, he had begun to show an interest in her, pressing his suit with her guardian despite her insistence that she did not wish to be his wife. He did not seem to understand that his disregard for her opinions was the very proof she needed that they would *not* make a suitable match. And so she had pleaded bereavement, feigning confusion over which path to take—that of a novice or that of a wife—and Bourlamaque had relented in his efforts to find her a husband.

Yet she knew her reprieve wouldn't last. Neither Monsieur le Marquis de Montcalm nor Monsieur de Bourlamaque wished her to remain at Fort Carillon any longer than was necessary, insisting that the frontier was no place for a woman without a husband. If it hadn't been for MacKinnon's Rangers, whose lurking presence made the forest around Fort Carillon perilous, Bourlamaque would have sent her back to Trois Rivières when Montcalm had traveled north to Montréal. But the destruction of several supply trains and the loss of almost thirty soldiers to the horrid Scotsmen had convinced him that she was safer for the moment staying at the fort.

What will you do if the British prevail and the war is lost, Amalie?

She could not journey to France, for she knew no one there. Nor would she seek out her mother's kin, whose customs and language were strange to her. From two different worlds, she seemed to belong in neither.

The thought doused her last spark of appetite. She set her silverware aside.

"You haven't eaten a bite, Amalie." Bourlamaque frowned. "Are you feeling ill?"

Amalie had come to feel affection for Bourlamaque, the sort of affection one might feel for a favorite uncle. She did not wish to seem spiteful. "I fear talk of another battle has ruined my appetite, monsieur. Forgive me."

"There is nothing to forgive." He smiled indulgently. "We soldiers must do better to govern our tongues in your company."

Lieutenant Rillieux took her hand, stroked his thumb over her knuckles. "You have nothing to fear, mademoiselle. There is not a soldier at Fort Carillon who would not fight to protect you. Is that not true, messieurs?"

"But of course!" Fouchet and Durand insisted, almost in unison.

Amalie pulled her hand free, tucked it in her lap. "I am not afraid for myself, messieurs, but for the soldiers. Almost two hundred have perished since I arrived last spring. I would hate to see more crosses planted in the earth."

Lieutenant Rillieux chuckled. "Your concern is to be commended, Amalie, but they were soldiers. It was their honor and privilege to die for France."

Amalie felt heat rush into her face, and the words were out before she could stop them. "That does not mean France should be wasteful with their lives."

Lieutenant Rillieux's smile faded, his gaze boring through her. "And what can a young mademoiselle who was raised in an abbey tell us about the complexities of war? Do go on, for I am most eager to hear."

She lifted her chin, was about to speak, when Bourlamaque held up his hand.

"Your point is well taken, *mon cher lieutenant*," he said, "but let us speak of something else. In Paris, we would never be forgiven if we were to persist in speaking of so dismal a topic in the presence of ladies."

Lieutenant Rillieux bowed his head again. "Ah, quite right, monsieur. I do apologize."

But Amalie did not miss the flush beneath his olive skin, or the angry press of his lips.

It was Bourlamaque who spoke next. "Père François tells me the medicinal herbs you planted in the garden are thriving, Amalie."

And so they passed the remainder of the meal in polite but forced conversation, Amalie regretting her temper if not the words themselves. Bourlamaque, Fouchet, and Durand spoke on topics they seemed to think might interest a woman—the uses of herbs, the new vestments Amalie had sewn for Père François, the weather—while Lieutenant Rillieux looked bored.

The last course had just been cleared away when she heard it.

The sharp retort of musket fire.

Then the front door flew open and a young sergeant dashed inside, a look of excitement on his face. He stopped when he saw Bourlamaque and saluted smartly. "It is MacKinnon's Rangers, monsieur! We have them!"

M organ knew it was a trap the moment the first powder keg failed to explode.

He'd waited until it was dark. Then with Connor and Joseph to guard the retreat, he'd crept along the riverbank with a small force of Rangers to fire upon the kegs and ignite them. But, though he knew for certain he'd hit his mark and the others theirs, not a single keg had gone up. Now the French were alerted to their presence, and with no explosions or fire to distract them, they would come after the Rangers with their full strength.

"Fall back!"

Even as he shouted the command, the French opened fire— but not only from the walls. At least twenty infantrymen stood on the deck of the ship moored behind them, muskets aimed at the pier below. 'Twas like shooting ducks on a pond.

Morgan and his men were trapped in a cross fire.

"To the river!" He drew his pistol, felt a ball whiz past his cheek, crouched down to make himself a smaller target, peering through the darkness to account for his men.

Killy. McHugh. Brendan. Forbes.

All running back to the riverbank.

Where was Dougie?

Then the forest behind them erupted with musket fire as the combined forces of the Rangers and the Muhheconneok—almost two hundred men—returned fire. They staggered their fire, giving the enemy no chance to breathe, sowing panic amongst the French, particularly those on the ship, who seemed to realize all at once that they were far outside the fort's walls.

That's the way, boys!

Morgan took cover behind a battered hogshead, aimed his

rifle at one of the soldiers on the ship, and fired, watching out of the corner of his eye as, one by one, his men reached the river-bank and dropped out of sight, Killy cursing all the way.

"Bastard sons of whores!"

But where was Dougie?

And then he saw.

Dougie lay on his back near the stack of kegs, reloading his rifle, a strip of white tied around his thigh. "Go on! Go!"

But Morgan wasn't about to leave without him. He'd led his men into this trap. He would bloody well get them out—all of them.

He glanced toward the riverbank, saw McHugh, Killy, Brendan, and Forbes nose their rifles over the top of the bank and take aim, ready to cover him. He hurled his rifle, his *claidheamh mòr,* and his tumpline pack to Killy and got ready to run.

And then it came—the Muhheconneok war cry. It rose out of the forest, primal and raw, terrifying the French, turning their attention away from the pier and giving Morgan the chance he needed.

Blood thrumming, he drew in a breath, dashed out from behind the hogshead, and ran a jagged path toward Dougie, barely feeling the ball that burnt a path across his forearm or the one that creased his hip.

"A fine time to get shot this is!"

But Dougie was ready for him, crouching on one knee, his injured leg stretched out beside him. "You're daft, MacKinnon!"

Morgan dropped down, took Dougie onto his back, and forced himself to his feet. "Och, you're heavy as an ox! And you stink!"

His gaze fixed on the riverbank a hundred feet away, Morgan ran, Dougie's added weight pounding through the straining muscles of his thighs to the soles of his moccasins, his heart slamming in his chest.

"You run like a lass!" Dougie shouted in his ear. "Can you no' go faster?"

But Morgan didn't have the breath to do more than curse. *"Mac-dìolain!"* Whoreson!

Sixty feet. Fifty. Forty.

A roar of cannon erupted behind him, the French firing their twelve-pounders at the forest just as they had last summer, trying to turn the shelter of the trees into a charnel pit. Jeers coming from the trees told him balls had fallen short of the mark—this time.

Thirty feet. Twenty. Ten.

Morgan sucked breath into his aching lungs, drove himself forward, hurling both of them over the edge. They tumbled, arse over elbow, down the embankment to the sand below. No sooner had they landed than McHugh and Forbes took Dougie between them and hurried him along the river toward the forest beyond.

Young Brendan clasped Morgan's forearm, helped him back to his feet, then hurried after McHugh and Forbes, already reloading.

Killy held out Morgan's rifle and his pack, a smile on his scarred Irish face. "You bloody daft Scot."

Another blast of cannon.

Morgan slipped the tumpline over his head, tucked his sword into place, grabbed his rifle, and then began to reload, shouting over the din. "Help McHugh and Forbes! I'll cover our backs in case those bastards on the ship try to follow!"

"Aye." Killy turned and was gone.

Morgan got into position, peeked over the edge of the riverbank, picked a target on the darkened deck of the ship, and fired. Reloading quickly, he kept up a rapid fire, glancing over to watch his men's progress until they disappeared amongst the trees. Then, feeling a rush of relief, he cast one last glance at the fort walls—and felt something strike him in the right shoulder.

Instantly, his right arm went numb, falling useless to his side. Something warm and wet trickled down his chest.

Blood.

He'd been shot.

It was then the pain struck, forcing the breath from his lungs, driving him to his knees.

He heard a shout of victory and looked up to see a French soldier high in the ship's rigging, musket raised over his head.

So this is how it ends.

The thought ran through Morgan's mind, detached from any fear.

But no' just yet.

Unable to load and fire his heavy rifle with one hand, he dropped it to the sand, withdrew his pistol, aimed, and fired, ending the soldier's celebration. But several other soldiers had climbed into the rigging to see what their comrade's cheering was about, and before Morgan could take cover, several fired.

A ball ripped through his right thigh, the shock of it like fire and ice.

And Morgan knew it was over.

He fell onto his side, forced himself onto his belly, and tried to crawl for cover, gritting his teeth against the pain.

"Morgan!"

He recognized Connor's voice and saw his brother emerge from the forest at a run, Killy, Forbes, and McHugh behind him.

"No, Connor! Stop!" From somewhere nearby Morgan heard the tromp of hundreds of boots and knew the gates of the fort had been thrown open. Were the French planning a counterattack? "I am lost already! Get the men out of here!"

Even in the dark, he could see the anguish and horror on his brother's face as Connor realized he would not be able to reach him in time to keep him from the swarming French.

His strength all but spent, Morgan met Connor's tormented gaze, his chest swelling with regret, grief, love. So long they'd been together, the four of them—Morgan, Iain, Connor, Joseph. And now . . .

Gathering all his breath, Morgan shouted. *"Beannachd leat!"*
Blessings go with you, brother!
And dinnae mourn me overlong. Tell little Iain—
But Morgan never finished the thought.

The last thing he heard before darkness claimed him was Connor's anguished cry.

Chapter 2

Amalie crawled out of bed early the next morning after a fitful sleep, dawn peeking through her window, the night's shadows still clinging to her mind. She poured water from a porcelain pitcher into its matching bowl and splashed her face, the water's chill helping to wash away her weariness and her lingering sense of dread. Although last night's fighting had ended quickly and the enemy had been driven away, war had followed her into her dreams, her slumber troubled by cannon fire, dying men, and that terrible, haunting cry.

It had risen out of the forest like the howl of demons, sending chills down her spine, making her blood run cold.

"It is the Mahican war cry," Bourlamaque had told her, seeing her fear. "The Abenaki have one very similar. Have you never heard it?"

"N-no, monsieur," she'd answered.

He'd looked down at her for a moment, seeming to consider her. "I forget that you've never actually lived amongst your mother's people."

Then he'd dismissed her, sending her to her room to await the outcome of the skirmish, while he'd gone with his officers.

Determined to put the night and its fears behind her, Amalie dried her face with a linen towel, then sat on her bed, loosed her braids, and began to work out the tangles from her hair. The *mère supérieure* had tried many times to get her to cut her locks, but Amalie had steadfastly refused—not her only rebellion. Unable to understand why God should care how long her hair was, she'd resisted even when she'd been warned that pride was a grave sin.

"A woman should be humble in all she does, Amalie," the *mère supérieure* had scolded. "Such willfulness endangers your soul."

Amalie had tried to explain that her long hair was but a way of knowing her mother, a way of being close to her. Though she could not remember her mother, her father had told her many times how her mother's dark tresses had hung to her knees.

"Like a river of black silk," he'd said.

But the *mère supérieure* had brushed this aside, saying it was far better for Amalie to know God than the woman who'd borne her. It had taken a letter from Amalie's father to decide the matter, though the *mère supérieure* had required her to wear her hair up lest its beauty stir envy in the hearts of the other girls.

Of course, the other girls hadn't envied Amalie at all, but had teased her about her darker skin and the strange color of her eyes—neither green nor brown but both. The few times she'd seen her Abenaki *cousines*—her female cousins—they'd done the same in reverse, calling her pale, laughing at her eyes, and teasing her about her hair, which was more brown than black and hung not straight and smooth like her mother's, but in tendrils.

Amalie did not resent their teasing, for she could see for herself that what they said was true. She *was* different. Her mother had been half Abenaki, Amalie but a quarter. Her features were neither French nor Indian. She was truly as her mother had named her—Child of Twilight.

"In her eyes, you were neither day nor night, sun nor stars, but a mingling of both," Papa had explained.

Sweet heaven, how she missed him!

Fighting a sudden pricking of tears, Amalie shifted her thoughts to the day ahead. If she hurried, she might be able to weed Bourlamaque's garden before the sun grew too warm. She braided her hair and tied it up with the blue silk ribbon her father had given her, then slipped into her stockings and petticoats. She would have liked to go without her stays, but Bourlamaque did not tolerate undress at his breakfast table. She left them loose instead, then pulled on her gray linen gown. She had just opened her bedroom door when shouting erupted from downstairs.

"It goes against my conscience as a surgeon and a Catholic! If you wished him to die, why did you bring him to me? Better to have let him perish where he lay!"

Amalie recognized the voice as that of the fort's surgeon, Monsieur Lambert.

"I do not wish him to die!" Bourlamaque spat out each word. "I wish him to live so that I can wrest from him all he knows! I cannot interrogate a dead man!"

"You do not mean only to interrogate him. That I could understand and condone. You mean to hand him over to the Abenaki, who will burn him alive!"

Chills skittered down Amalie's spine at the thought of anyone suffering such a fate, even an enemy.

"Have you forgotten the number of Frenchmen and Abenaki these men have slain or the Abenaki village they destroyed two winters past or the supply wagons they've pillaged, stealing medicines you needed to treat our men?"

Amalie felt her pulse leap.

They had captured one of MacKinnon's Rangers?

Captured and gravely wounded, it seemed.

And then she understood.

Monsieur de Bourlamaque wished the Ranger to live so that he might learn his secrets and give the Abenaki their promised chance at vengeance, but Monsieur Lambert clearly wanted no part of it, afflicted at the notion of saving a man's life only to hand him over to torture and death.

"I've forgotten nothing!" Monsieur Lambert's voice shook. "But I took an oath to heal men, not to harm them!"

"Then heal him!" Bourlamaque's shout made Amalie jump, his words booming through the little house. "What befalls him when he leaves your care is a military matter and none of your affair!"

For a moment there was silence.

Although she knew Monsieur de Bourlamaque was doing his duty, Amalie found herself feeling pity for Monsieur Lambert. On the one hand, healing this Ranger and turning him over to Bourlamaque would save French lives, appease an important

French ally, perhaps helping to win the war. On the other, saving the man's life so that he might suffer torment surely went against all a doctor was trained to do.

And what would you do, Amalie?

Would she have been able to tend the Ranger's wounds, ease his pain, and calm his fever, knowing she was sparing him for the cruelest of deaths?

She wanted to think that she would. The Rangers had killed her father, after all. They had destroyed her grandmother's village and sown terror in the forest. But the very thought of saving a man so that he might perish in flames made her stomach knot.

In truth, she did not know what she would do.

"Very well, monsieur, I shall do my best to save his life," Monsieur Lambert said at last. "But know this—I will treat him with the same diligence I would any officer. I will not deprive him of laudanum as Lieutenant Rillieux demands, nor will I suffer your soldiers to abuse him."

"I expected no less, *mon ami*. Leave young Rillieux to me. But how do we know this man is truly Morgan MacKinnon?"

"One of our partisans claims to have met him and recognized him, and when I spoke the name, he opened his eyes."

Not just a Ranger, but their leader!

And then Amalie understood why it was so important that he survive.

"If you need anything—"

"I should like Mademoiselle Chauvenet's help in tending him once I've removed the balls from his leg and shoulder. He is shackled and greatly weakened, so she will be in no danger. She speaks the English tongue and has a deft hand at healing, and I fear my young attendants harbor too great a hatred for these Rangers to care for him reliably."

"Consider it done."

Whatever else they said was lost beneath the din of Amalie's heartbeat as it thundered in her ears. One hand clasped over her mouth, she closed her door, and leaned against it, stunned.

Bourlamaque had just given her over to care for a man he had consigned to death.

And not just any man.

The leader of MacKinnon's Rangers himself.

* * *

Morgan drifted between agony and oblivion. He'd known when French soldiers carried him into the fort. He'd known when they'd realized who he was, shouting his name and cheering as if they'd taken a great prize. He'd known when they'd stripped him bare, shackled him, and called their surgeon to probe his wounds.

"Il a perdu beaucoup de sang. Ses blessures sont profondes. Il pourrait bien mourir."

He's lost a lot of blood. His wounds are deep. He might well die.

Morgan understood their words, and he welcomed death. He knew well what would happen to him should he survive. 'Twas far better to die now, his blood spilled upon the floor, than to perish in the fires of the Abenaki, his torment stretched over unending days.

Aye, he feared so terrible and painful a death. What man would not? But more than pain itself, he feared that the flames might prove fiercer than his courage, loosing his tongue, overthrowing his mind, breaking him so that he betrayed his brothers and the Rangers.

And that he could not do.

If there'd been any hope for escape, he'd have seized it and fought his way out like a man—or died trying. But shackled hand and foot and this close to death, he'd never get out of bed, let alone out of the fort.

Hadn't he always known this day would come? Aye, he had. But if a MacKinnon had to die, 'twas far better that it be him than Iain or Connor.

If only there were a priest . . .

He let himself drift, relinquishing his soul to God.

But the French were not going to let him go so easily. They forced laudanum down his throat and thrust a leather strap between his teeth. It was not out of mercy for him that they did these things. They were simply trying to heal his body so they could pry into his mind.

"Bite down," their surgeon said in heavily accented English.

Too weak from loss of blood to fight them and chained to the little bed, Morgan spat out the strap, his pain turning to rage. "Save your blade for another! I dinnae want your help!"

The surgeon looked down at him, his blue eyes troubled, Morgan's blood already on his hands. "That is not for you to decide, Major MacKinnon."

Rough hands forced the strap back into his mouth and held him down as the surgeon raised his knife.

The pain was staggering, far worse than Morgan had imagined. The shock of it drove the breath from his lungs, turned his stomach, made his entire body jerk. He felt his chains draw tight, iron biting into his ankles and wrists.

Holy Jesus God!

He clenched his teeth, squeezed his eyes shut, fought not to cry out as the surgeon cut into his chest, searching. A cold sweat broke out on his brow, the moment wearing on until he was aware of nothing but pain. He felt his body arch, as with one last excruciating tug the ball was pulled free.

Darkness dragged at the corners of his mind, drew him down. But it didn't last.

The surgeon cleaned the wound with brandy, the deep, fiery burn a new kind of torment. Then he stitched it, applied a stinking poultice, and wrapped Morgan's shoulder with linen strips.

By the time the surgeon had finished, Morgan felt strangely euphoric. Perhaps he'd gone daft. Or perhaps the laudanum was now at its full strength.

Then the surgeon moved to Morgan's right thigh, and the ordeal began anew.

"Il faudra peut-être amputer sa jambe."

Through a haze of pain, Morgan understood.

They were trying to decide whether to cut off his leg.

A bolt of fear surged from his gut, lodged in his chest.

Fàilte dhuit, a Mhuire, a tha làn de ghràsa . . .

Hail Mary, full of grace . . .

But even as his mind sought for the sacred words, pain swamped him and sent him hurtling into forgetfulness.

Amalie looked down at the unconscious prisoner and tried her best to *hate* him.

He and his men had killed Papa and hundreds more—nine

this past night alone. A dozen soldiers lay battered and bleeding just beyond this room because of them. They'd slain dozens of Abenaki men, leaving women, children, and elders to starve. They'd turned the forest around Lac Saint-Sacrement into a trail of death, evading every trap laid for them.

Until now.

"The secrets this MacKinnon holds might be the key to winning this damnable war," Bourlamaque had told her, looking more grave than she'd ever seen him. "This is your chance to avenge your father's death, Amalie, to serve France as he did."

Is that what she wanted—to exact vengeance?

If only she didn't know what lay ahead for Major MacKinnon. Saving his life so that he might be kept prisoner and questioned was one thing. Saving his life so that he could suffer the prolonged agonies of fire was quite another. She would not wish that on anyone.

It is not your choice, Amalie. It will not be your doing.

The thought helped to assuage her conscience, but it did not ease the ache in her belly.

She sat on a stool beside him and studied him, this warrior who had terrified so many.

He did not look like *chi bai,* but a man—a desperately wounded man. Yet, he was no ordinary man. He was perhaps the biggest, most striking man she'd ever seen, not only tall, but broad of shoulder and quite handsome—in a rugged, wild sort of way. His hair was long, dark as a raven's wing, and tangled from his thrashing, a plait at each temple. His skin was brown from the sun but smooth and unblemished. Long black lashes rested against high cheekbones, deep hollows making his cheeks seem even higher. His lips were unusually full, his jaw square and dark with several days' growth of beard.

They'd bound his ankles and wrists in iron shackles and chained them to the four legs of the little bed to hold him fast, still fearing his strength despite his wounds. And no wonder. His arms were easily three times the thickness of hers and muscular, his hands big enough to encircle a man's throat. She had no doubt that he was capable of killing with those hands, that he *had* killed with those hands.

She'd heard he'd been adopted by the Mahican, and she saw they'd made their mark upon him. Indigo-colored drawings had been etched into his skin from shoulder to wrist—geometric shapes, spirals, and a single bear claw on each shoulder. Leather cords beaded with wampum and strange amulets had been tied around his arms just above the bulge of his muscles, seeming to accentuate his raw strength. A leather cord with dark, wooden beads encircled his neck, disappearing beneath his blankets. Expecting to find some heathen symbol, she drew it forth—and gasped.

A little wooden cross.

It was not pagan adornment he wore, but a simple rosary of wood.

She'd forgotten he was Catholic.

The ache in her stomach grew.

She reached out, hesitated, then felt his forehead. His skin was hot with the beginnings of a fever. He stirred at her touch, groaned, his dark brows bent with pain, his suffering drawing forth compassion she did not wish to feel for him.

Brushing aside the unwelcome feeling, she reached for the little blue bottle of laudanum, uncorked it, and poured out a spoonful. Then, careful not to spill a drop of the precious potion, she eased the spoon between his lips and let the tincture trickle into his mouth. Instinctively, he swallowed. Then his eyes opened.

Amalie stiffened, unnerved that he should wake so suddenly.

He is shackled, silly girl! He cannot harm you!

His gaze met hers, then a look of confusion spread on his face. For a moment he simply stared at her through glassy blue eyes—not the bright blue of the sky on a summer day, but the deep, dark blue of midnight. Then he spoke, startling the silence, his voice deep and ragged. "I would think myself in hell but for the sight of you, lass."

Even had she had her English at the ready, she would not have known what to say, his words catching someplace deep inside her, making her pulse trip.

Then he shifted, raising one fettered wrist as if to reach for her.

She scooted backward, nearly toppling her stool in her haste to evade him.

But pain halted his motions even before his chains grew tight. He drew a shuddering breath through gritted teeth, his jaw clenched tight, his eyes squeezed shut.

"B-be still, or you will cause yourself to suffer needlessly."

She stood and reached toward the bedside table for the water pitcher and a tin cup, irritated with herself to find her hands shaking.

He is just a man, Amalie. You are childish to fear him.

But he was not just a man. He was a Ranger, perhaps the very Ranger who had sent Papa to his grave. It was only natural for her to feel afraid.

"My leg? Is it . . . gone?"

Another wave of pity washed through her.

"You have it still." Vexed with herself, she poured water into the tin cup, then returned to his side to find him watching her once more, a strange look in his blue eyes. "Drink."

She slid one hand beneath his head to raise it and held the cup to his lips.

He turned his head away, rivulets spilling down his jaw and over the thick muscles of his neck, pooling in the recess at the base of his throat. "Nay, lass! I cannae."

At first she thought he couldn't drink because of his fever or his injuries. Only when she'd placed his head back on the pillow and watched him turn his face away from her did she realize the truth. He meant to deny himself water.

He meant to let himself die.

Astonished, Amalie said the first thing that came to mind. "It is a mortal sin to cause your own death."

But is it not also a sin to save his life so that he can be burnt alive?

"Then I'd best go swiftly to hell and no' keep the devil waitin'."

With those shocking words, he closed his eyes and drifted into a restless sleep, leaving Amalie to fight the pricking of her conscience.

Chapter 3

Morgan gave himself over to his fever, willing it to ravage and consume him, eager to die and pass from this life with his secrets intact—the last thing he could do for his men, for his brothers. But dying wasn't as simple as he'd thought it would be.

The laudanum left him witless, unable to tell if he was dreaming or awake. More than once he'd turned his head away from the tin cup the beautiful French lass offered him, but he could not be certain she hadn't gotten him to drink in his sleep when his will was weakest. Ghosts of the past mingled with the present, memories with nightmares, English words with French. The woman's soft entreaties. Men's voices. His own fevered raving. And beneath it all a desperate, aching thirst.

Please, you must drink!

Nay, I willna. Be a good lass and fetch a priest.

You will report to me at Fort Edward by August twenty-first and serve me until death releases you or this war is ended. If you fail to appear or abandon your post, you will be shot for desertion and your brothers will be hanged for murder.

Dinnae do it, Iain! Curse him!

I am no' afraid to die. Let them hang us! We willna be the first Highlanders murdered by English lies, nor the last!

He will not drink, no matter what I try. He asked me to fetch a priest.

A priest? If he's going to die, then let it be without absolution. He deserves to burn in hell!

Surely you do not mean to deny him last rites, Lieutenant.

It is a mortal sin to cause your own death.

Then I'd best go swiftly to hell and no' keep the devil waitin'.

Perhaps we ought to interrogate him now, monsieur, see what we can extract from him.

Something struck Morgan, jarring him from his delirium.

"Parlez-vous français?" Dark eyes glared down at him from beneath a powdered wig. A French officer. "Do you speak French?"

Morgan didn't answer.

"What is your name?" The officer switched to accented English. "Speak!"

Morgan met the officer's gaze, pried his tongue from the roof of his mouth, and croaked out his reply. "Bonnie Prince Charlie."

A fist struck his face, the pain seeming far away. "You are Morgan MacKinnon, leader of MacKinnon's Rangers."

"If you kent my name, why'd you ask?"

"Where is your older brother? Why does he no longer lead?"

Iain. The officer was asking about Iain. Was he hoping to find Iain and bring him back in chains to suffer a fate similar to Morgan's? In Morgan's fevered state it suddenly seemed so.

An image of Iain as Morgan had last seen him came into Morgan's mind—his brother standing tall and proud, beautiful Annie beside him holding their wee son in her arms, as the men paid Iain one last honor, shouting his clan name in tribute.

MacKinnon! MacKinnon! MacKinnon!

Anger, clean and bright, cut through Morgan's confusion, fury that anyone should try to strike at Iain in his new life. *"Thalla gu Taigh na Galla!"* Go to hell!

Another blow, and Morgan tasted blood.

"Lieutenant Rillieux, you forget yourself! There will be no interrogations in my hospital!" The surgeon looked down at Morgan. "Besides, he is quite mad with fever, as you see. You will get nothing from him tonight."

The French officer stood, his angry face swimming out of

view. "Get him to drink, by saints! Force water down his throat if
you must! He must live!"

"His will is strong."

"Then force more laudanum on him! Weaken his will!"

And Morgan knew the hard truth.

The battle over how he was going to die had begun in earnest.

A malie dipped the cloth in the washbowl, squeezed the water
out, and pressed it to the prisoner's brow. He seemed to be
on fire, burning up from the inside, his skin ashen, his lips color-
less. He shivered, lost in a fitful sleep, murmuring in a language
she did not understand. So heavily drugged was he that she knew
he could not be in pain. Still, he seemed troubled, as if he were
fighting—fighting still to die.

For four days and nights she had tended him, watching him
struggle against Monsieur Lambert's best efforts to keep him
alive. Had it not been for the laudanum, he might well have gotten his way. It had taken four men to force that first big dose of
the drug down his throat, even injured as he was. But the medicine had overthrown his will, rendering him so helpless that it
took only gentle coaxing to get him to drink.

From sunrise till sunset each day, Amalie had bathed his
fevered skin, given him sips of water and willow-bark tea, and
changed his bandages, confused by the turmoil of her own emotions. Her confusion had grown each time he'd opened his eyes
and looked at her, speaking to her in a tongue she did not understand, his gaze seeming to hold so much sadness. She wanted to
hate him but couldn't, refused to pity him and yet did, tried to
escape feelings of guilt and was nevertheless smothered by them.

She'd sought Père François' counsel, confessing the conflict
she felt at the thought of saving a man's life so that he might be
tortured to death.

"It is never wrong to save a life, Amalie," he'd told her. "Like
you, I would rather no man be handed over to such a death, certainly not a Catholic. I have told Bourlamaque as much, but I
doubt he will listen. He concerns himself with little beyond
this war."

"I *hate* this war! I hate everything about it!" The words had
burst out of her, surprising her as much as they did Père François.

"And well you should." He'd patted her hand. "But go back to your duties, and do not be troubled by your role in this. You are blameless. For his part, Bourlamaque has agreed to let me hear the man's confession before he is given to the Abenaki, and I shall hold him to it."

And so she had walked back to the hospital, her guilt assuaged—for a time.

Amalie laid the cool cloth on the prisoner's forehead and pushed the blankets aside to change the bandage on his thigh, careful to bare no more than his limb. Although she'd cared for many a sick and injured soldier this past year, she couldn't remember being as aware of any soldier *as a man* as she was of this Ranger. She told herself it was simply the fact that he was a dreaded Ranger that set him apart in her mind, and yet she knew there was more to it than that.

He was the most intimidating man she had ever seen. It wasn't just his apparent physical strength, but also his animal wildness—his long hair with its braids, his sun-browned skin, the Mahican drawings on his arms that marked him as a warrior. Were all Rangers as big and fierce-seeming as this one? If so, she had no trouble understanding how they'd managed to inspire terror and legend along the frontier.

She removed the linen strips that bound his dressing in place, sliding her hand beneath his muscular thigh to pass the cloth through. Though his chest was healing, the wound in his thigh was much deeper and had festered badly. Monsieur Lambert had bled him twice to counter the fever and had made his customary poultice of rose oil, egg yolks, and turpentine to draw the sickness out of the wounds, but it was too soon to know whether these remedies would work.

Amalie set the linen strips aside and lifted the dressing, relieved to find that the wound looked no more savage than before. The surgeon's stitches were holding, and the redness had not spread. There were no streaks running up his thigh, nor had the surrounding flesh begun to swell. The Ranger might have to live with a limp, but it seemed as if Monsieur Lambert's decision not to amputate—

He won't live with a limp, Amalie, silly child! They're going to burn him!

Her stomach seemed to fall to the floor.

How could she have forgotten, even for an instant?

Of course, she hadn't forgotten, not truly. It was just the strangeness of the situation—caring for a man's hurts so that he might live to be killed—that was to blame. She was accustomed when caring for the sick to think of each small step toward healing as a little victory. Not this time.

And yet why shouldn't she consider each stride he made toward recovery a triumph? It meant she was doing her duty well, that she might play some small part in helping to end this war and bringing peace to New France. Although this Ranger might live only to die a terrible death, countless lives might yet be spared by the information Bourlamaque would take from him.

Seeking at least some comfort in that thought, she reached for the poultice and had just begun to dab it over the wound with a clean bit of linen when the door opened.

"Mademoiselle." Lieutenant Rillieux entered, gave her a crisp bow. "Bourlamaque sent me to inquire after the prisoner. How does he fare?"

Still upset with the lieutenant, she refused to glance up. "He is unchanged."

Lieutenant Rillieux stood for a moment, watching. "You are displeased with me."

"It is unbefitting a gentleman to deny a dying man last rites."

Lieutenant Rillieux came to stand behind her and placed an unwelcome hand upon her shoulder, his thumb caressing the bare skin at her nape. "You are young and a woman. I don't expect you to understand. Besides, he does not seem to be dying."

Why did he insist on touching her? She leaned forward, out of his grasp, and reached for more poultice, fighting to keep the anger from her voice. "He is quite feverish. It is still too soon to know whether he will live."

For a moment there was silence.

"Monsieur de Bourlamaque is most impressed with my conduct in this affair. He has written to Montcalm, praising me for MacKinnon's capture. I have reason to believe that I will find myself a captain by summer's end."

At this exciting news, Amalie glanced up and felt some of her anger abate at the look of satisfaction on Lieutenant Rillieux's face. She knew how much this meant to him. "Oh, Lieutenant! You must be so pleased."

"I knew you would be happy for me." He smiled. "It is an honor I have long sought and one I deserve, if I might be so bold. I accomplished something many believed could not be done—I captured one of the MacKinnon brothers. I shouldn't be surprised if dispatches bearing this news make their way to Paris and my name is read before *le Bien-Aimé*."

Amalie thought it unlikely that the king's ministers would trouble His Majesty with news from New France, but she didn't say so. She finished dabbing on the poultice and began to bind the prisoner's wound once more while Lieutenant Rillieux boasted at length about the night the Ranger was captured and how Bourlamaque never could have accomplished such a deed himself and how Bourlamaque knew this and even now treated him with a new regard, the stolen case of wine forgiven, if not forgotten.

"With this change in my fortunes, I feel emboldened to say that it is time you reconsidered my offer. It is no small honor to be the wife of a captain." And with that, his rambling ceased.

Amalie tied off the bandage, drew the blankets over the prisoner's leg, then stood, searching for words that would spare Lieutenant Rillieux's feelings but finding none. "You flatter me with your attentions, monsieur, but I cannot marry you. Even if I were wholly resolved not to return to the convent and take vows, I know you and I would not—"

"You speak with such conviction." Lieutenant Rillieux looked down at her as if she'd just said something absurd, his face a blend of insult and amusement. "But how can you be certain? You're a virgin and were raised in a convent. You know nothing of men or marriage."

She lifted her chin, met his gaze, no longer bothering to hide her anger. "I know my own mind, monsieur."

He stepped back from her, a mocking look in his eyes. "As much as I admired your father, he has done you a terrible disservice by encouraging such willfulness. If he had not insisted that Bourlamaque allow you freedom to choose your own path, you would already be my wife. You were not meant for the convent, Amalie."

With that, he turned and was gone.

Fort Edward
On the Hudson River
His Majesty's Colony of New York

Lord William Wentworth took in the news, caught off his guard
by the surge of distress that washed through him. He studied
the pieces on his chessboard without truly seeing them, struggling
to keep his face impassive. Beside him, Lieutenant Cooke found
the words to say what he, lacking his voice, could not.

"I am deeply grieved to hear of your loss, Captain. Major
MacKinnon was a skilled marksman and leader. I . . . I admired
him."

Given the undying animosity that lay between the Rangers
and His Majesty's Regulars, Cooke's confession was unusual, if
not unexpected. Most British Regulars viewed the Rangers as
nothing more than uncouth colonials, barbarians without the dis-
position necessary for the military arts. But the Rangers had
saved Cooke's life at Ticonderoga last summer, their skill clearly
having won his respect.

William cleared his throat. "Start at the beginning, Captain.
And go slowly this time."

Captain Connor MacKinnon, the youngest of the three Mac-
Kinnon brothers and the most unpredictable, closed his eyes,
drew a breath, and began again.

The Rangers, together with Captain Joseph's Stockbridge warriors, had watched from Rattlesnake Mountain as the French had
unloaded powder casks from a small ship. They'd waited until nightfall, then moved in under cover of darkness to blow up the casks
and burn the ship—only to find themselves ambushed. One of the
Rangers had been wounded, and unwilling to abandon him, Major
MacKinnon had braved French musket balls and borne the wounded
man out on his back, then stayed behind to cover their retreat.

"I was firing at the soldiers on the walls and didna see him get
hit. But I saw him fall. I ran out to fetch him, but the French had
opened their gates and . . ." The captain closed his eyes, a look of
anguish on his face. "He said he was already lost and ordered me
to retreat wi' the men. And, curse me, *I did*!"

"Your actions are commendable, Captain. You—"

"He was my brother, and I left him to *die*!" The captain

shouted the words in William's face, his eyes dark with rage, his jaw covered with thick stubble, his clothes stained with sweat and dirt from his buckskin breeches to the homespun of his blue checked shirt. "The French raised him over their heads and carried him inside the fort like a great bloody prize!"

Then, as if his outburst had cost him the last of his strength, the captain sank into the same chair he'd refused to accept not five minutes before, burying his face in his hands.

"Lieutenant, pour Captain MacKinnon a cognac."

The lieutenant's eyebrows shot up, almost disappearing beneath his wig. William had never offered any of the Rangers a drink from his private stores before. But Cooke was a disciplined officer and did as William had ordered without question.

It was surely a measure of Captain MacKinnon's misery that he accepted the glass and drank. Under normal circumstances, none of the MacKinnon brothers would have taken so much as a farthing from him. They hated him as they hated no one, except perhaps his uncle, the Duke of Cumberland—or his grandsire, their noble sovereign, King George.

William rose, turned, and faced the window, his hand slipping out of habit inside his pocket to feel the familiar outline of the cracked black king he'd saved as a memento of Lady Anne. She'd broken the marble chess piece in a fit of temper after he'd refused to release her husband, Iain MacKinnon, from His Majesty's service. He'd since had a new king made, but he'd kept this one—a token of the only woman ever to wound him.

"Major MacKinnon *is* a prize. If he was still alive when they captured him, I can only assume Bourlamaque asked his personal surgeons to tend him in the hopes that the major would survive to be interrogated."

For four years, the MacKinnon brothers had harried the French relentlessly, helping to turn the tide of the war. The French had been trying for most of that time to kill or capture them and had placed a bounty on their scalps that was roughly the equivalent of two thousand British pounds. But the brothers had evaded every trap set for them—until now.

"Interrogated?" Glass shattered. "You mean tortured! They'll do all they can to break him, and when they're done, they'll turn him, battered and bleedin', over to the Abenaki, who will *burn him alive!*"

William turned slowly to face the captain and found him on his feet again, shards of crystal scattered across the polished wooden floor. He ignored the mess. "*That* is the price of capture, Captain. Your brother knew it when he ordered you to leave him. But I'm afraid we must consider more than your brother lost. All of your supply caches, your hideouts and rendezvous points, your favorite paths, your passwords, the Rules—you must act now as if the French have knowledge of them all—"

The captain's voice sank to a menacing growl. "Morgan would *never* betray us or our secrets! Dinnae you dishonor him! You are no' fit to clean his boots!"

"I meant no disrespect, of course." William sat and reached for pen and parchment, finding something oddly reassuring in the captain's blatant hostility. "It is simply a fact that prolonged pain can loose even the most stalwart of tongues. But do not lose hope yet. If your brother is alive, it will take weeks for him to heal. I shall send a dispatch this very evening, offering Bourlamaque a prisoner exchange—the four French officers you captured last week for Major MacKinnon."

The captain frowned, as if perplexed. "You would do that for him?"

"Major MacKinnon is a highly trained officer. His life and the secrets he holds are of great worth to the Crown." There was more to it than that, but William refused to admit it, even to himself. "I would be foolish not to make every effort to recover him."

"The men and I leave in the morn to pay our respects to Iain. Captain Joseph and his men come wi' us."

"Are you asking me to grant you leave?" William opened his bottle of ink, dipped his quill, and tapped it on the brim.

"Nay, Your Holiness. I dinnae give a damn whether you say 'aye' or 'nay.'"

"Nevertheless, I grant it." The last thing William wanted near the fort was a hundred drunken Highlanders playing endless, wailing dirges on those godforsaken pipes. He looked up to meet the captain's gaze. "Report back within ten days. You're in command now, and I shall hold you responsible—unless you'd rather I call your eldest brother back into service."

The captain's eyes flew wide for a moment, then a look of utter loathing settled on his face. "Over my dead body."

"Very well, then." William put quill to paper and began to

write. "You should know that of the three of you, I found Morgan to be the most sensible."

"He'd be bloody fashed to hear that."

"You are dismissed, Captain." William scrawled words on the page until the door shut. But the moment the captain was gone, he set the quill in the bottle, rose, and crossed the room to pour himself a cognac. "We have suffered a great loss, Lieutenant."

"Aye, my lord. It is terrible."

William tossed back the cognac—something he would ordinarily never do—and wondered why he should feel so bereft.

Chapter 4

Amalie bathed the Ranger's face with a cold, wet cloth she'd dipped in water sprinkled with wild sage and juniper. It was a cure she'd learned from her grandmother's people. The wild sage would purify him, and the juniper would cleanse away the remnants of his sickness. His fever had broken early this morning. There was no doubt now: he would live.

His skin was no longer pale but flushed, his dark hair slick with sweat, little rivulets trickling down his temples, his neck, his chest, drenching the linens beneath him. He slept peacefully, his long lashes dark against his cheeks, his jaw shadowed by many days' growth of beard, his chest rising and falling with each deep, steady breath.

But his peaceful rest would not last long.

The laudanum would soon wear off, and whatever pain he still had would return. Monsieur Lambert, hoping to save their dwindling stores of the precious medicine, had given the Ranger his last spoonful a few hours past, vowing to force water down his throat should he refuse to drink again. But that was not the worst of it.

When she'd come down to breakfast, she'd overheard Lieutenant Rillieux and Monsieur de Bourlamaque discussing what to do with the Ranger next. As soon as he was able to stand, they would move him to the guardhouse—and his suffering would begin anew. And this time . . .

Amalie did not wish to think on it.

She dipped the cloth back in the scented water, squeezed it out, and nudged the linens down to his hips. She bathed first his arms, which were still stretched above his head, each wrist shackled to a bedpost. Then she wet the cloth again and bathed his shoulders, working her way over his chest and down his belly.

Although she knew it must be sinful, she couldn't keep her gaze from following her hands, his man's body so different from hers, the sight of him both disturbing and intriguing. His skin was soft, but the muscles beneath it were hard, the feel of him like iron sheathed in velvet. Although his nipples drew tight from the chill of the water as hers did when she was cold, his were dark like wine, flat and ringed by crisp, dark hair. Where her belly was soft and rounded, his had ribs of muscle—and a trail of dark curls that disappeared beneath the linens.

As if drawn by a will of its own, her hand left the cloth behind to press against those ridges, her fingers playing over his sweat-slick skin as she slid her hand slowly from his belly up to his chest, something tickling inside her at the feel of him. Her hand came to rest above his heartbeat, its rhythm steady against her palm.

"Your touch could bring the dead to life, lass."

Amalie gasped, jerked her hand back, and saw to her horror that the Ranger was watching her. Heat rushed into her face, made her cheeks burn, English words forsaking her tongue. *"M-mon Dieu! Pardonnez-moi, monsieur!"*

"Easy, lass. I didna mean to frighten you." He watched her through dark blue eyes, his gaze soft, a hint of amusement on his face, his speech accented by a soft lilt.

"Forgive me if I offend, monsieur."

Morgan's mouth was as dry as sawdust. His chest ached. His right leg throbbed. But at the moment he didn't care. He watched the play of emotions on the French lass's face—fear, shame, wariness—and found himself wanting to lessen her unease. "'Tis only nature's way for a maid to be curious about men. Besides, I wouldna be a Scotsman if I shrank from the touch of a bonnie lass . . . a beautiful woman."

Did she understand him?

The deepening flush in her cheeks told him she did.

And she *was* beautiful. Her eyes seemed to hold all the colors of the forest—greens and browns mixed together. He'd never seen any like them. They seemed to slant upward at the corners, or perhaps that was just the effect of her cheekbones, so high and delicate they were. Her nose was small and fine, her lips full and well shaped. Her skin was flawless, almost luminous. Her hair was the color of sable, dark and gleaming. It hung to the floor when she sat, tresses so long and lovely they made his hands ache to touch them.

She was French—that much he knew—but he'd bet his ration of rum she was also Indian. Her cheekbones, the slight slant of her eyes, the hue of her skin—like cream with just a hint of coffee—bespoke a mixed ancestry. And then there were the herbs she'd placed in the water. No simple French lass was likely to know about such things.

Was she Huron? Abenaki? Mi'kmaq?

What did it matter?

She's like to be the last lass that e'er you set eyes on, MacKinnon.

As Morgan had always loved the lasses, 'twas was a strange thought.

Roused by the blessed relief of a cool cloth against his skin and the fresh scents of sage and juniper, he'd come slowly back to awareness, thinking for a moment that he was a lad again, that he'd fallen sick and was in Joseph's mother's lodge in Stockbridge. Then he'd opened his eyes to find himself being perused by the same lovely French angel who'd visited him in his fevered dreams, and it had pleased him to know she was real.

He'd watched through half-closed eyes while she'd bathed his body, her gaze traveling over him with innocent curiosity. Then she'd laid her small, soft hand upon him, her timid touch burning a path over his skin, threatening to rouse him in an altogether different manner.

"The *mère supérieure* says I am far too curious." Her accent was soft and sweet.

"Who?"

"The mother superior." She hoped those were the right words. "From the convent where I was raised."

Aye, and *that* explained her bashfulness.

"Och, well, if you were raised in a convent amidst women-folk, 'tis even more reason for you to be curious about men, aye? No wrong has been done, lass. Dinnae trouble yourself. What is your name?"

She looked as if she did not want to answer. When she spoke, her voice was almost a whisper. "Amalie Chauvenet."

"'Tis a bonnie name. I'm thinkin' you already ken who I am."

She nodded gravely. "Morgan MacKinnon, the leader of MacKinnon's Rangers."

There was a hint of—was it anger?—in her voice when she spoke.

"How long has it been?"

She glanced at the window, at the ceiling, at her hands, which lay folded in her skirts—but she did not look at him. "Fifteen days since you were wounded."

Fifteen days!

No wonder he felt so bloody weak!

Connor, Joseph, and the men would have long since made their way back to Fort Edward. Surely, even Iain would have gotten word by now. Would his brothers believe him dead? Would they mourn him?

He pushed the questions from his mind.

"Might I have some water, Miss Chauvenet?"

She reached for the water pitcher, a surprised look on her face. "You no longer seek your own death?"

He shook his head. "I have lost that battle."

Her lovely face grew troubled. She poured water into a tin cup, then lifted his head and held the cup to his lips. Silken strands of hair slipped over her shoulder to fall against his chest, the scent of her like lavender. "Drink."

He asked her to refill the cup four times before his thirst was quenched, wondering as he drank at the distress he saw on her face. Had the sisters raised her to be so primsie that she still felt guilt for touching him? Perhaps she was afraid of him and did not wish to be here. "I thank you for your care of me, Miss Chauvenet."

The troubled look on her face became genuine anguish.

And he understood.

"You ken what awaits me, and it troubles you to be speakin' wi' a dead man."

She stood so quickly that her stool toppled over. Then she stared down at him with eyes that held the first sheen of tears. "I do not care what becomes of you, monsieur! Why should I? You and your Rangers killed my father!"

Then she turned and fled in a swish of skirts.

And as he watched her hurry to get away from him, Morgan knew that his sins had caught up with him at last.

Tears pricking her eyes, Amalie ran from the back room out the front door of the hospital, ignoring the surprised look on Monsieur Lambert's face, scarce hearing the questions he called after her.

"Mademoiselle? Qu'est-ce qu'il y a? Qu'est-ce qui ne va pas?"
What is it? What's wrong?

How dare he behave like this! How dare her enemy act as if he understood her! He was not a gentleman! How dare he behave as one!

She hurried across the grass, not sure where she was going until she found herself in the fort's cemetery. She threaded her way through the rows of small crosses until she came to the one that marked her father's grave. She knelt before it and let the tears come.

She didn't know what to think, what to feel. She wasn't even certain why she was upset and crying. Perhaps she was simply weary after so many long days of caring for the Ranger. Or perhaps caring for him reminded her of the terrible battle that had taken her father's life and the lives of so many others—the blast of the cannon, the cries of the wounded and dying, the stench of blood and gunpowder in the air.

If aught should befall me, Père François will take you to Montcalm or Bourlamaque. They will keep you safe.

Nothing will happen to you, Papa!

She ran her fingers over the carven letters of her father's name, the ache in her heart sharpened by memories. "I did as Monsieur de Bourlamaque asked, Papa. I helped keep the Ranger alive. Soon they will interrogate him."

You ken what awaits me, and it troubles you to be speakin' wi' a dead man.

How had he seen through her so clearly?

He'd spoken but a few words to her, and already she knew he was not the coarse and heartless man she'd expected him to be. She'd thought he'd up wake cursing Montcalm or pleading for release. Instead, he'd caught her touching him in a way no chaste young woman should, and he'd offered her understanding and reassurance, asking only for her name and water to drink, his manners faultless even when hers had failed.

I thank you for your care of me, Miss Chauvenet.

Politesse and understanding were not qualities one expected from a ruthless barbarian, a brutal enemy.

And that was the heart of it.

She'd watched over him, helped keep him alive to face a terrible death. He understood this, and yet he'd behaved not like an enemy, but like a gentleman. He'd sensed her guilt, and he'd forgiven her. For some reason, that made her feel worse, not better.

"Kwai, nadôgweskwa. Toni kd'ollowzin." Greetings, cousin. How are you?

Amalie recognized the voice. Hastily, she wiped the tears from her face with her apron, then stood and turned to face him. *"Kwai, Tomakwa, nagôgwisis. Kwai, Simo. N'wowlowzi, ta giya?"* Greetings, Tomas, my cousin. Greetings, Simon. I am well, and you?

The sons of her mother's sister walked toward her, Tomas in front, Simon behind him. Both were dressed in buckskin leggings and breechcloths, their long dark hair hanging free, their chests bare. Tomas wore a British officer's gorget as a trophy around his neck and a belt of wampum around his waist. Simon wore only a smile for adornment.

"So you remember the words I taught you. I am pleased." Tomas came to stand before her. He tucked a finger beneath her chin, examined her face, and frowned, his gaze dropping for a moment to her father's grave. "You have been weeping."

Knowing Tomas would not understand feelings she couldn't possibly explain, she let him assume her tears came solely from grief. "I miss him."

Beside Tomas, Simon watched her, his dark eyes warm with sympathy. *"Je suis désolé."* I'm sorry.

She reached out, gave Simon's hand a squeeze. "You have come to trade?"

Tomas glanced toward the hospital. "We have come to claim

that which Montcalm promised us—the Inglismôn, the MacKinnon. Does he still live?"

Suddenly Amalie felt light-headed. *"Oui."*

But the Ranger was no Englishman. He was a Catholic Scot. Not that her cousins would understand the difference.

"Kamodzi. Very good. We'll feed him to the flames and avenge both the village and your father." Then Tomas looked back at her and rested a big hand on her shoulder. "You should come with us, Amalie. Return to your mother's people. You can be the one to light the fires and thus end your grief."

At her cousin's words, an unwanted image of the Ranger, bound to a stake and burning, came into her mind. And Amalie felt her stomach turn.

W hen the door opened, Morgan hoped to see Miss Chauvenet. He would apologize, tell her how sorry he was that her father had been killed by a Ranger's rifle, and ask her forgiveness. His did not expect his words to matter to her, but they were all he could give her.

It was not she who entered but his captors. One of the officers he recognized from his fevered dreams—the bewigged lieutenant who had denied him last rites. The other he did not. But the grandeur of the second man's uniform left no doubt in Morgan's mind that this was none other than Brigadier le Chevalier François-Charles de Bourlamaque, Montcalm's man.

The brigadier was younger than he'd imagined—not long past forty. Like his lieutenant, he wore a fashionable powdered wig. He studied Morgan, a thoughtful frown on his face, then gave a little bow. "Major MacKinnon."

Morgan swallowed, his throat already parched. "Brigadier de Bourlamaque. Forgi'e me if I dinnae stand to greet you. I seem to be tied up."

"You have no idea how relieved I am that you survived, Major."

"Och, I've some notion of what I mean to you. After all, my brothers and I have had a high price on our heads these past years."

Bourlamaque did not smile. "For a time, it seemed certain you would perish and deprive me of the chance to make your acquaintance."

"Sure and it must be a grand day for you, then."

The lieutenant kicked Morgan's right leg, the pain making the breath rush from Morgan's lungs. "Do not be insolent!"

Bourlamaque cast his lieutenant a dark look, then met Morgan's gaze once more. "Indeed, it is a day for celebration. Today I have met a legend."

Then Bourlamaque turned to his lieutenant and spoke in French. *"Allez!"* Go!

For a moment the lieutenant looked vexed. Then, with a smart bow to Bourlamaque, he turned and was gone, closing the door behind him.

Bourlamaque turned to gaze out the window, his hands clasped behind his back. "I have already sent word to Fort Edward informing your commander of your unfortunate death. I see no cause for your men to risk their lives in a vain attempt to rescue you."

"You whoreson!" Heart thrumming, Morgan felt a hope he hadn't realized he'd had wither and die.

As long as his brothers believed he was alive, there'd been a chance that they would come for him.

But Bourlamaque was still speaking. "As I am sure you know, Major, you will not leave Fort Carillon alive. You and your brothers have cost France dearly in this war. Your men are the scourge of our frontier. It is not only France that demands your death, but also the Abenaki, whom you and your men wronged some winters past when you destroyed their village at Oganak, leaving women and children defenseless."

"At least we dinnae rape and kill women with babes in their bellies, as you and your allies have done. Do you ken what we found at Oganak? There were more than six hundred scalps hangin' from their lodge poles—the scalps of men, women, *and* children, scalps *you* paid—"

Bourlamaque cut him off. "A group of Abenaki men have just arrived to claim you. They will take you back to their village and burn you alive over a matter of days until you can remember nothing of this life but pain—not the color of the sky, nor the taste of wine, nor even your blessed mother's name. You will beg for death, plead for it, but it will be slow in coming."

Dread he'd been trying to ignore slowly uncoiled at the base of Morgan's spine and crept in shivers up his back. He was not impervious to fear, but he'd be buggered before he'd allow it to show. "You make it sound so pleasant."

Bourlamaque turned to face him, and beneath the rage on his face, Morgan saw something else—regret. "It won't be, Major, I assure you. And yet the lack of gallantry exercised by both sides in this war is appalling to me. Out of the respect I bear you as an adversary and officer for sparing the lives of women, children, and servants of the Church, I am prepared to offer you an arrangement."

Morgan said nothing, certain he knew what Bourlamaque's offer would be.

"Tell me all that I wish to know about the Rangers, about Fort Edward, about your commander, and I will see that you receive not only a swift, painless death, but last rites and a Catholic burial."

Morgan closed his eyes, the full horror of his plight laid out before him. Wentworth and his brothers believed him dead. Unless he somehow managed to escape on his own, he would be tortured and burnt alive. Whatever was left of his body would be hacked apart, his scalp hung on a lodge pole, a trophy to blow in the wind, his bones scattered in the forest for the animals. For there was no question of his being able to accept Bourlamaque's offer. He would sooner suffer a thousand unbearable deaths than betray his brother or his men.

He opened his eyes, met Bourlamaque's gaze. "I thank you for your generous proposal. Regretfully, I cannae accept. The darkest corners of hell are saved for betrayers. I would rather suffer the fiercest torment and die with my honor intact than face God as a traitor."

Bourlamaque studied him for a moment. "You have time to reconsider. My surgeon tells me you will not be strong enough to move to the guardhouse for at least a week. Should you change your mind in that time—"

"I willna, so you'd best get on wi' it."

"There is no cause to be rash, Major. Send for me if you wish to discuss my offer again." Then Bourlamaque gave a little bow, opened the door, and was gone, leaving Morgan with only his regrets and his fears.

Chapter 5

Amalie stepped carefully around mud puddles as she made the long walk to the hospital, so lost in her own thoughts that she scarcely noticed the rain-fresh scent of the morning breeze or the bright blue sky or the soldiers at morning muster. She had hoped to be free of this duty. She had hoped to be free of *him*. Now that he was out of danger, she'd hoped never to see the Ranger again. She'd asked Bourlamaque to let her return to her customary duties, but he'd refused to release her.

"Monsieur Lambert tells me Major MacKinnon asked about you yesterday evening. He believes MacKinnon has warmed to you. You might yet be of some use to us in the infirmary."

"But he is healing and no longer needs—"

"Continue to tend him, as you have done so well." Bourlamaque's tone allowed no argument. "Now that he is awake, be attentive. Listen to him, and then report back to me all that he says."

"You wish me to . . . to *spy* on him, monsieur?" The idea had seemed so absurd to Amalie that she could scarce speak it.

Bourlamaque had chuckled. "*Non,* sweet Amalie. It is not in your nature to deceive. I wish only for you to be exactly what you are—young and beautiful and innocent. He is a man who has seen much war, a man who knows he has come to his end. In his despair, he will seek solace in your gentleness. He will trust you and tell you things that he would never tell me. All you need do is inform me each day of all that was said. Can you do this?"

Ashamed of her own reluctance after all Bourlamaque and the men at Fort Carillon had done for her, she'd nodded. *"Oui."*

Oh, how she wished Bourlamaque had not asked this of her! How could she explain to him that caring for the Ranger had already left her feeling beset by blame? Must she now compound her guilt by spying upon him? For that's what it was no matter how delicately Bourlamaque had tried to paint it. She was to soothe his desperation with kindness in order to win his trust, then report all he told her to her guardian.

But why should the Ranger tell her anything? In her experience, most men deemed women unworthy of purposeful conversation, let alone confidences.

She opened the hospital door and stepped inside, giving her eyes a moment to adjust. A small fire burnt in the hearth, chasing away the early-morning damp. Two of Monsieur Lambert's young attendants bustled about, one cleaning chamber pots, the other gathering soiled linens for the laundresses. Six soldiers lay on their little beds, some sleeping, all but one of them still recovering from the Ranger attack.

And *this* was what she needed to remember. Major MacKinnon had commanded the Rangers who'd harmed these men. He'd attacked this fort, and not for the first time. He had French blood on his hands—perhaps even her father's blood.

One of the attendants turned toward her. *"Bonjour, mademoiselle."*

"Bonjour." She walked between the beds to the supply cupboard and took out two rolls of fresh linen, refusing to notice the beating of butterfly wings in her belly.

You have no reason to fear him, Amalie.

All she had to do was tend his simplest needs—food and drink—and listen considerately while he spoke. It was an uncomplicated task, not difficult at all. So why did she feel like running away?

She walked to the back room, found the door slightly ajar, and heard a man's voice coming from within.

"If you think this is painful, Major, wait until the Abenaki—"

Amalie pushed open the door to find Lieutenant Rillieux standing over the Ranger, the heel of his boot pressed cruelly against the wound in the Ranger's thigh. Jaw clenched in obvious pain, the Ranger glared at him with undisguised hatred, but didn't make a sound.

Aghast, she rushed in. *"Monsieur! Que faites-vous?"*

What are you doing?

Startled, the lieutenant jerked his leg away and turned toward her. A slow smile spread on his face. "I am just giving him the merest taste of what is to come, mademoiselle. It is better he be prepared, *non*?"

He spoke in English, his gaze shifting to the Ranger, who glared up at him, sweat beaded on his brow, a dark bruise spreading on his right cheek.

The Ranger's voice was a growl. "Do your worst, you *neach dìolain*!"

Outraged, Amalie answered Lieutenant Rillieux in French. "You go too far! Did you not understand Monsieur Lambert's orders that the prisoner was not to be abused?"

Lieutenant Rillieux took a step toward her, his smile gone. "You forget your place, mademoiselle. I do not answer to Monsieur Lambert, nor do I answer to you."

But Amalie refused to let him intimidate her, no matter that the look on his face frightened her. "In the hospital, Lieutenant, Monsieur Lambert's word is to be obeyed. It is cruel and cowardly to strike an injured—"

"You are in a fort in the midst of war, little Amalie, not in your convent." Lieutenant Rillieux sneered. "Here, military concerns prevail, not the frail sentiments of women."

Fisting a hand in her hair, he ducked down and pressed his lips hard against hers, the contact painful and frightening—and mercifully brief.

Amalie was so shocked that it did not occur to her to push away until after he'd released her and walked out the door. She drew a trembling hand to her mouth and tried to wipe his taste away.

Morgan watched the poor lass wipe the violence of that bastard's kiss off her lips and wished to God he had the strength to break iron. There'd be one less Frenchman walking the earth if he could. "Did he harm you, miss?"

She whirled about with a gasp, her fingers still pressed against her lips, her eyes wide. For a moment she simply stared at him, and Morgan found himself wondering if he'd slipped and spoken French to her.

Have a care, MacKinnon.

He'd understood every word of their conversation, of course, and it had only served to inflame his rage. The lass was an innocent, raised in a convent, and she'd been trying to protect him—only to suffer ridicule and ill use. Morgan would have liked to have kicked the bastard's teeth down his throat for touching her, then tossed him on his arse for insulting women. Morgan knew a great many women, and few of them were frail-minded. Had the planning of this war been in the hands of his Muhheconneok grannies, it would likely have been won by now. But he could not let on that he'd understood lest he lose the only advantage he had—listening in on their conversations.

At last Miss Chauvenet shook her head. "He merely startled me."

Morgan's blood still boiled. "No man has the right to treat you thus. You should report him to Bourlamaque."

Spots of pink appeared in her cheeks, and he realized she was ashamed that he had witnessed her humiliation. "Lieutenant Rillieux is a . . . good officer. I have wounded him. H-he wishes me to be his wife, but I . . . I have no interest in marriage."

And then Morgan had to ask. "Are you pledged to the Church?"

She bowed her head. "Were it not for this war, I should most likely have returned to the abbey at Trois Rivières by now."

At once Morgan felt both a sense of loss that so beautiful a woman should spend her grace on the Church and a strange surge of relief to know that no man would ever have her. "I am sorry."

She raised her head, met his gaze—then frowned. "Let me tend your face."

"Is it so bad, then?"

She did not answer but hurried to the bedside table, poured water from the pitcher into a wooden bowl, and dipped a clean cloth into it, a look of concern on her face. "He struck you. You are shackled and injured, and he struck you."

"Dinnae fret, lass. I wager I'll suffer worse ere I leave this place."

Abruptly, she stilled, the sodden cloth in her hands dripping water into the bowl. Then she seemed to catch herself. She squeezed the cloth out, but her motions were wooden, her face giving play to her distress.

So, the thought that he would be beaten upset her.

Morgan would remember that.

Without a word she pressed the cold cloth to his right cheek, the chill bringing relief from the sting of that whoreson's fist— Rillieux she had called him.

He watched her as she bathed his cheek, his gaze seeking out the details of her form. The dark and delicate sweep of her lashes. The soft curve of her cheek. The fullness of her lips. The slender column of her throat. The gentle swell of her breasts beneath the lace of her bodice. The silken length of her hair. And her scent— fresh linen, lavender, and woman.

She is promised to Christ, you lummox.

Aye, she was. And he to Satan.

'Twas then he remembered what he'd planned to say to her. He'd thought through the words all night, shaped them in his mind. 'Twas time to speak them. "'Tis sorry I am about your father, Miss Chauvenet. If I could call back the ball that stole his life, I would."

She met his gaze, a look on her young face that might have been astonishment—or anger. When she spoke, her voice quavered. "H-how can you speak to me of him?"

"There's naugh' I can say to ease your grief. I ken that. But I am deeply sorry that you should suffer, and I ask your forgiveness."

Unable to breathe, Amalie looked into the Ranger's blue eyes and saw only sincerity. It was the same earnestness she'd seen in the eyes of wounded soldiers who'd asked her to pray for them— the naked honesty of men who knew they were about to die and sought to make peace with the world.

As upset by the Ranger's unexpected apology as she was by Lieutenant Rillieux's loathsome kiss, she turned away, at a loss for words. She dipped the cloth back into the water, only vaguely aware of what she was doing.

How dare either of them! How dare Lieutenant Rillieux kiss her, knowing full well that she did not wish to marry him! And how dare the Ranger ask her forgiveness! He hadn't trodden upon her foot, after all. He and his men had slain her father, stealing the joy from her life, filling her nights with grief and loneliness.

"What kind of man are you, Major MacKinnon?"

"Just a man."

His humble answer shamed her. In God's eyes he was just a man, *oui,* but here on earth he was a British officer, a Ranger, a legend amongst both his people and hers. But now he was in her care, a wounded man and condemned to die. And he had asked as respectfully and gravely as any man might for her forgiveness.

How could she deny him and yet call herself Catholic?

Without forgiveness, Amalie, there can be no peace.

The *mère supérieure*'s stern voice echoed through her mind.

Amalie slowly turned to face him, the damp cloth in hand. He was watching her, his gaze gentle, a strange contrast to the fierceness of his appearance—bruised cheek, shackles, beard, warrior marks. "I . . . I loved him very much. He was my only real family. He was killed last summer in the first attack while I was here in the hospital helping the wounded. I thought for a time that he had survived, but—"

"Sweet Mary, you were *here* during the battle?" He stared at her, his blue eyes filled with what could only be dismay.

She swallowed the lump in her throat and nodded, looking down at her hands, trying not to remember that terrible day.

"Och, lass, 'tis sorry I am that you should have seen it. War is bloody and cruel. It makes monsters of men. 'Tis no place for a woman."

"It was awful."

"Aye, that it was."

Something in the tone of his voice made her look up, and she knew by the lines on his face that he had his own terrible memories. "You lost someone, too."

"Aye, many. Good men and true. They died for nothin', pawns in a war not of their makin'." The last words were spoken with a measure of bitterness.

She understood bitterness. "I have hated the Rangers since that day."

He grinned—a sad, lopsided grin. "And do you hate me?"

"I have *tried* to hate you, monsieur." She lifted her chin, fighting to ignore the way his smile touched her. "But I fear I have not succeeded as I should have liked."

He chuckled, a warm, deep sound. "Dinnae judge yourself too harshly. I'd wager there is little hatred in you, and 'tis hard to loathe an enemy you have helped to heal."

She looked into his eyes and wondered how he saw through her so clearly. "*Oui,* Major MacKinnon, I forgive you. May God rest my father's soul."

And a weight she hadn't known she was carrying lifted off her shoulders.

L ord William fingered the bloodstained bit of old plaid, then glanced down at the parchment once more, some part of him unable to believe the words he read. He'd watched the MacKinnon brothers cheat death so many times that he'd come to take their survival for granted. He'd fed the legend surrounding them, whispering a discreet word in the right social circles, quietly encouraging the papers to write about the brothers' exploits, exhibiting their skills to visiting commanders. When Lieutenant Cooke had questioned his actions, he'd explained that he hoped to help the British army drum up new Ranger recruits. Young colonials would admire the MacKinnon men and seek to be like them, he'd reasoned.

But in truth, the MacKinnon brothers were the finest fighting men he'd ever seen. Headstrong Highland Gaels, robust and well favored, they'd been exiled from Scotland as boys and had grown up on the frontier, living amongst the Mahican Indians, whom they counted as kin. They knew the land like few others, and there were no better marksmen in the world. William had seen them strike impossible marks, reloading on their backs when occasion demanded it, and firing with a speed that few men could match.

What a pity that something so small as a routine scouting mission should claim Morgan MacKinnon's life.

He heard a clamor outside his private study—shouts, curses, a string of Gaelic oaths—and had just tucked the plaid in his pocket when his doors were thrown wide and Iain MacKinnon strode in together with Captain MacKinnon and Captain Joseph, a red-faced Lieutenant Cooke struggling to keep pace behind them.

"My lord, the MacKinnon brothers are here," Lieutenant Cooke stammered.

"So I see. You are dismissed, Lieutenant—and close the doors behind you."

"Aye, my lord." Cooke gave a little bow and was gone.

"Your Immensity." Iain MacKinnon, the eldest of the three MacKinnon men, had never been one to waste time on pleasantries. "What word have you of Morgan? I would hear it now."

Had the MacKinnon brothers and their men not been so skilled at war and woodcraft, their treasonous insults and unceasing hatred of William and his royal grandfather might have earned them a berth on a prison barge. Most of the time, however, William found their disrespect a refreshing respite from the fawning and flattery that came with being the son of a royal princess. No one had dared call him a "wee German princeling" before he'd met the MacKinnon brothers. But there was no diversion in their behavior for him tonight.

He held out the parchment and watched as Iain read through it. The missive had arrived late this afternoon, borne by a French messenger carrying a flag of truce. It stated that, despite the care of Bourlamaque's personal surgeon, Major Morgan MacKinnon had died of his injuries and that his body had been claimed by the Abenaki.

The color drained from the eldest MacKinnon's face. "Och, Christ! Sweet Jesus, nay!"

Captain MacKinnon snatched the parchment from his brother's hand, his gaze searching over the page. Then he dropped the letter, sank into a chair, and buried his unshaven face in his hands. "Oh, Mary, Mother of God! Forgi'e me, Morgan!"

Captain Joseph glared at William through dark eyes, then bent down and spoke softly to Captain MacKinnon in his heathen tongue.

"So Morgan . . . My brother . . . is dead?" Iain MacKinnon met William's gaze, an expression of deep grief on his face.

"The message bears the signature of Bourlamaque himself. It arrived with this." William withdrew the strip of plaid from his pocket and handed it to his former major, who snatched it away from him, then clenched it in his fist. "My condolences for your loss."

"I should ne'er ha' left the Rangers," Iain said, almost as if speaking to himself, clutching the tattered and bloodied strip of wool. "I should ha' stayed wi' the men."

William watched their grief unfold, though with less anger than he'd imagined. He considered himself a student of human nature. He derived private joy from observing others, measuring people's sense against their passions, watching them struggle with their own natures and those of others. He found it quite diverting to use his insights into their foibles and flaws to predict and even manipulate their actions.

But although he had anticipated the brothers' grief, he could not say he understood it. He had never been particularly close with his siblings. As a superfluous third son, he'd had to compete with his two older brothers for their father's approval and their mother's attention from the moment of his birth. If he should perish in battle, he rather doubted they'd have two words to say about it. Neither of them had bidden him farewell when he'd set sail from London to New York, nor had he heard a word from them since.

Iain MacKinnon met his gaze once more. "'Twas more merciful a death than I feared he might suffer. At least he was spared flames."

Then Captain MacKinnon sprang out of the chair and pointed a condemning finger at William. "'Tis your fault, you heretic bastard. If no' for you, Morgan would ne'er have set foot near that accursed fort. You forced him to fight. You as good as killed him yourself, you bloody Sassenach!"

Anger at last.

"Whatever makes you say that, Captain?" William flicked the lace at his cuff, keeping his tone of voice dispassionate. "As I recall, Major MacKinnon volunteered to serve His Majesty."

Captain MacKinnon glared at him with undisguised hatred and might have struck him had his brother and Captain Joseph not restrained him. "Aye, he *volunteered*—but only after you entrapped Iain by threatenin' to see us hanged!"

It had been William's great fortune to observe the MacKinnon brothers in a street fight and to press them—through less than honest means that he did not regret—into service. And although they hated him for it, he cared not. Their successes in this war had added immeasurably to his own, earning him favor with his grandsire and helping to turn the tide of the conflict toward victory.

William allowed his voice to take on an angry edge. "Restrain yourself, Captain, lest you prove unworthy for command and force me to recall your eldest brother to his former post."

At those words, Connor immediately stilled, his sun-browned face blanching.

Then from the doorway came a woman's voice. "You wouldna dare!"

Lady Anne.

William's pulse tripped. Why had Cooke not informed William she was here?

Her chin high, she crossed the room to stand beside her husband, looking enraged and beautiful, tears on her lovely face, a sleeping baby in her arms. "My husband is no longer yours to command. I willna hear of it."

William bowed. "Lady Anne."

She no longer carried the title "lady," of course, having married a commoner, but William persisted in using it, his not-so-subtle way of refusing to recognize her marriage.

"Lord William." She returned the bow with a slight curtsy. "We have suffered a terrible blow this day. I ask that you forgi'e Connor his hasty words and let us tend to our grief."

"Very well." William studied her for a moment, then shifted his gaze to Captain MacKinnon. "Report to me tomorrow morning after muster, Captain. And unless you'd like to spend a week in the guardhouse, do so with your composure restored. You are dismissed."

William turned to look unseeing out the window, his hand once again creeping inside his pocket to feel the black king, his heart still beating erratically. Beautiful, unpredictable Lady Anne—daughter of the Earl of Rothesay, now the wife of a Catholic Scot, a Highland barbarian, a mere Ranger. She might have been William's mistress and lived a life of luxury.

He found himself tempted to call her husband back into service just for the privilege of seeing her about the fort each day. With Morgan MacKinnon dead, the Rangers would surely need the guidance and skill of their former commander, the man who'd led them for three years. Certainly, it would be in the best interests of the Crown to recall him.

And if Iain MacKinnon were to die in battle, leaving Lady Anne and her infant son alone? Would Lady Anne seek solace and protection in William's bed?

'Twas a tempting notion.

Chapter 6

Morgan looked toward the window, where darkness pressed against greased parchment, the long night weighing heavily upon him. He'd dreamt of battle—of gunfire and gore, the stench of blood and the sight of broken bodies, the crash of cannon and the cries of dying men. He'd woken from nightmares to find himself in this living hell, chained to this little bed, his wrists and ankles rubbed raw by his shackles, his joints and muscles aching from being kept in one position for so long.

Savor these wee pains while you can, laddie.

'Twould get no better from here. Once he was strong enough to stand, Bourlamaque would order him moved to the guardhouse. Then they would shackle him in a cage, and the interrogation would begin. Whatever was left of him after that would be given to the Abenaki to roast alive.

'Tis likely to hurt a bit more than being shot, aye?

The dread that slept in his belly was roused once more and crept into his chest. He closed his eyes, drew breath into his lungs, and forced it down. 'Twas surely part of Bourlamaque's strategy to leave him here, chained and helpless, where he could do nothing but think of the days to come and the torment they would bring. The bastard no doubt hoped that Morgan's fear would prey upon his courage and weaken his resolve. But the MacKinnons had never been cowards.

"Audentes fortuna iuvat."

Morgan whispered his clan's motto.

Fortune assists the daring.

He opened his eyes and stared into the darkness.

He would find a way out of this. He must.

Chained and as weak as he was, he could not hope to escape today nor even tomorrow. Even were he not shackled, he hadn't yet the strength to run or fight. Bourlamaque would expect him to attempt escape when they moved him to the guardhouse and would order him placed in heavy chains and set armed soldiers to escort him. Nay, there would be no chance to break away until he was outside the fort.

But once he was away, 'twas a fortnight's journey to the Abenaki village through leagues of dark forest, over raging rivers, through fen and bog. On that long journey, anything could happen. And 'twas there he must break away.

Morgan shifted, tried to ease the strain on his shoulders and ankles, iron biting into his bruised and blistered skin.

Had Bourlamaque's lying missive reached Wentworth? Did his brothers and the men now believe him dead? Would they blame themselves?

Aye, they would. Iain would curse himself for giving up his command and seeking a new life with Annie. Connor would hate himself, believing that he'd left Morgan to die when he ought to have saved him. Joseph would wonder why he hadn't foreseen Morgan's death in a dream. Even the men would blame themselves, Dougie most of all, for 'twas he whose life Morgan had stayed behind to save.

Och, the bletherin' idiots!

What they ought to do is get good and bloody drunk! They should play the pipes, curse the English in his name, and send him off to hell with a bit of mayhem, giving Wentworth a bad night's sleep. That would be a fitting farewell.

He looked back toward the window. 'Twould soon be dawn. The surgeon's lads would come before long to heap such indignities upon him as were necessary when a man was held like an animal and not allowed to care for himself. Lieutenant Rillieux would arrive to taunt him, as was his wont these past mornings. And then, if God were merciful, Miss Chauvenet would come.

She was his hope in this place, his candle in the darkness. He knew she was distressed by the fate that awaited him, knew she felt compassion for him. Hadn't she tried to protect him from Rillieux yesterday? Aye, she had. She'd stood up to the whoreson, dismay on her pretty face. Could Morgan play upon her sympathies, persuade her to unlock his fetters and help him escape?

You cannae bring her into this, lad. She is an innocent.

Aye, and he was condemned to die in flames if he did not escape this place. If there was any chance that she would aid him, he must seize that chance without hesitation or regret. Only a bloody fool would do otherwise.

And if Bourlamaque should blame her and hold her a traitor?

The thought jabbed at him, a splinter in his conscience.

Och, Satan's arse!

He did not wish harm to befall her on his account, but neither would he go like a lamb to the slaughter—or a pig to the spit.

Sweet Mary above, the lass was beautiful! The sight of her made it hard for him to breathe. She seemed to him like the first twilight of early spring when the trees were well budded out and the robins sat amongst the blossoms, singing down the sun. Perhaps it was a trick of his mortality that he responded thus to her—a man doomed to die drawn to the promise of a bonnie, sweet lass amidst the ugliness of his last days. Or perhaps she truly was the loveliest woman he'd ever seen.

Her outer beauty was more than matched by her gentleness and grace. Though it could not have been easy for her, she had accepted his apology and forgiven him. Then she'd quietly seen to his needs—giving him drinks of water, feeding him sips of broth, changing the dressings on his wounds. He'd tried to stay awake, tried to make conversation with her, but his long fever had drained his strength, left him in need of sleep. When he'd awoken, she'd been gone.

Footsteps.

It was growing light. The night had passed. A new day had come.

And only God knew what it would bring.

* * *

Amalie lifted the dressing from the Ranger's chest, aware as she worked that he was watching her. "It is healing well."

"I shall be fit as a fiddle in time for my execution." He spoke the words lightly, as if his own suffering and death meant little to him.

"Are you not afraid, Major?"

He chuckled. "Och, aye, I am, but there is naugh' to be gained by lettin' my fears rule me, lass. Bourlamaque may choose how and when I die, but it is up to me to decide how I face my death."

The raw courage in his words made something twist in her stomach. She had witnessed men's courage before, had watched young soldiers run toward the battle on legs that desperately wanted to run away, had held the hands of wounded men as the surgeon used his blade upon them, had watched as soldiers buried their friends then returned to their duties. But Major MacKinnon's unwavering strength went beyond anything she'd yet seen in this terrible war.

She lifted her gaze, met his. "I am sorry for what must come."

"It willna be your doin', lass. You bear none of the blame." Then his lips curved in a smile that softened the harsh appearance of his bruised and bearded face. "But let us no' speak of such things now. 'Tis a fine May morn, aye?"

She nodded, and remembering her task, reached for linen and salve to make a new dressing, her thoughts still bent upon Major MacKinnon. In faith, she'd thought of little else since yesterday. She'd tried to reconcile the fearsome tales about him to the humility he'd shown when he'd apologized for her father's death and to the protectiveness and decency he'd demonstrated when Lieutenant Rillieux had stolen that kiss from her.

No man has the right to treat you thus.

How could the man who'd destroyed her grandmother's village, leaving women and children to starve in the depths of winter, be the same man she saw before her?

"Are the stories they tell about you true, monsieur?" The words were out before she could stop them.

"Stories?" A dark eyebrow arched in question, amusement on his face.

She felt heat rush into her face. She looked down at her hands, fumbled with the dressing she was trying to make. "My cousins believe you and your brothers are not truly men, but spirits."

"Chi bai." He spoke the Abenaki word with ease. Where had he learned the language? "Aye, so I've heard. What do you think?"

And yet again he surprised her. Her father was the only man who'd ever asked her to share her thoughts or opinions. "If you were truly *chi bai,* you would not be here. You would turn into smoke and disappear on the breeze."

His chuckle warmed her. "That I would."

She spread salve over the red, pinched ridge of sewn flesh on his right breast where Monsieur Lambert had cut him to remove the musket ball. "They also say they've seen you and your brothers fly."

He laughed at this. "What they saw were snowshoe prints that led to the edge of a cliff and us at the foot of it. What they didna ken is that we'd come to the edge, then put our snowshoes on backward, doubled back and found a hidden way to the bottom."

The trick he described was so clever and yet so simple that Amalie couldn't help but smile. "You deceived them."

"Aye, and lived to fight another day." Then a strange look crossed his face. "'Tis the first time I've seen you smile."

Feeling strangely *embarrassée,* Amalie bent to her work once more, setting the salve aside, then pressing the dressing over the wound and reaching for a long strip of linen to bind it in place.

"Dinnae be fashed, lass." His voice was deep and soft, both soothing and disturbing. "I didna mean to discomfit you."

Careful not to look into his eyes, she slid her hand beneath him to pass the roll of linen through, but he was so broad in the shoulders that she had to lean across him to retrieve it. Just as she bent over him, he arched his back to let her hand pass beneath him, inadvertently pressing his chest against her bodice. And for a moment—one astonishing moment—she could feel the beating of his heart.

Awareness burnt like heat through the cloth of her gown to her skin, making her breath catch. Astounded by the unfamiliar sensation, she looked up, her gaze colliding with his, their faces only inches apart. And staring into his eyes, she knew he'd felt it, too.

"You've eyes the color of the forest."

His words and the sound of his voice called her back to herself. Feeling chagrined and more than a little confused, she passed the roll of linen beneath him three times in quick succession, then sat back, drawing breath into her lungs, her body warm as if it were summer, not spring. She tied off the bandage with fumbling fingers, her mind seeking a way to fill the awkward silence.

"I—I have also heard that you and your brothers once protected French women from ravishment by British soldiers and saved the life of a priest. Is this true?"

"Aye, lass. MacKinnon's Rangers dinnae take scalps, nor do we suffer any to harm servants of the Church or to make war upon women and children."

All of her confusion and embarrassment came together in a pique of temper. "Then why did you and your men leave the women and children of Oganak to starve and freeze to death?"

His brow bent in a frown, but the look in his eyes was more akin to sadness than anger. "Do you ken what we found at Oganak, Miss Chauvenet? More than six hundred scalps—some of women, aye, and wee children, too."

Amalie shook her head, sure he must be lying. "I do not believe you, monsieur. It is the British who pay Indians to collect such hideous trophies, not us!"

"Are you so certain? Do not I, myself, have a price on my scalp?"

"Yes, but that is diff—"

"Ask Bourlamaque if he's ever paid trade goods to warriors bearing English scalps. And ask him, too, about the other horrors visited upon frontier families by his soldiers. I have seen brutality that would chill your marrow, lass—women far gone wi' child lyin' ravished and slain upon the grass, babes dead at their mothers' breasts, children . . ." Clearly angry now, the Ranger stopped, drew a breath. "Nay, I willna speak of it, for I can see it distresses you. But ken this: the men of Oganak had preyed upon women and children for too long, and we Rangers put an end to it. But we were no' so cruel as they had been. We slew only grown men. We *spared* their women and children and the stripling lads, too."

"You left them without food or shelter." Why did he not understand? "To leave them helpless is no better than to have slain them with your own hands."

"We didna ken that winter should set in so hard. We paid for that sin many times over, stranded in deep snows for weeks on end wi' naugh' to eat but our belts and moccasins, our bellies grinding wi' hunger, our bodies weak and frozen. I watched men who were my friends starve to death on the terrible journey home. Nay, dinnae speak to me of Oganak, unless you can tell me how a man can take a helpless child into his arms and draw his blade."

Morgan watched Miss Chauvenet at her needlework and regretted having spoken so harshly to her. 'Twas clear that she'd been sheltered from the horrors of this war. There'd been no cause for him to thrust those horrors into her face. And yet it had galled him that she should think him the very devil without knowing the full truth.

Are you feelin' better now, laddie?

He could see she was vexed with him. She'd spoken nary a word since then, a troubled look on her face, her head bent over her embroidery, refusing to look up except to fetch him water or broth or one of the surgeon's lads when he had need. She sat, spine stiff, the light of the parchment window behind her, her dark hair spilling around her shoulders and tumbling almost to the floor in soft waves, her fingers nimble with needle and thread.

Morgan sought for something to say to her, to break the brittle silence that stretched between them. "How did you learn to speak English so well?"

Her spine grew straighter, and she did not look up. "Four of the sisters were English, exiled Catholics who'd made their way to the Americas and then to Trois Rivières. The *mère supérieure* felt we must learn their tongue, as they must learn ours."

"She sounds like a wise woman, this *mère supérieure*." He pretended to stumble over the words. "How did you come to be raised in a convent?"

"My mother died in childbed when I was two." And still she did not look up, but kept to her stitching. "My father sent me away to Trois Rivières."

"Such a young age to lose your mother. 'Tis sorry I am, lass."

Her hand stilled. "I do not remember her."

He took a chance and switched to the Abenaki tongue. *"Kigawes Wabanaki?"* Your mother was Abenaki?

Her head came up and she gaped at him as if in astonishment.
"Yes."

"Och, dinnae look so surprised, Miss Chauvenet. I kent when
first I saw you that you were of mixed birth. I can see it upon your
face. Besides, didna you yourself just tell me your cousins
thought I was *chi bai*? That means you must at least carry some
Abenaki blood in your veins, aye?"

"I've been told that the English believe Indians are . . . *des
sauvages*?" She seemed to search for the right English word, but
because he was pretending not to speak French, Morgan did not
help her find it. "Savage men? I've been told they hold all with
Indian blood in contempt."

"Some do, aye, and they're bloody fools for it. But as I think
you ken, lass, I am no' an Englishman."

"No, you are not." Her delicate brow bent in a frown, and she
seemed to hesitate. "I do not understand why a Catholic Scot
would fight against French Catholics on behalf of the German
Protestant who has slain so many of his kin. Have not the French
long been friends and allies to the Scottish? Even now France shel-
ters the true heir to Scotland's throne. Why do you kill for them?"

How many nights had Morgan lain awake trying to answer
that question for himself? "'Tis a long tale, lass, a tale you wouldna
believe if I—"

From the room beyond came shouts and the moans of a man
in pain, and the door was thrown open wide.

One of the surgeon's lads appeared. *"Mademoiselle, venez
vite! Un soldat s'est tiré dans le pied et on a besoin de votre
aide!" Mademoiselle come quickly! A soldier has shot himself in
the foot, and we need your help!*

And in a swish of skirts, she hurried away, leaving Morgan
with a mouthful of unspoken words.

A malie felt her stomach turn, tried to keep the disgust and
shock she felt from showing on her face. "So it is true?"

Bourlamaque gazed at her from across his writing table and
smiled indulgently. *"Oui, ma petite,* it is one of many terrible
truths of this war. The British pay for scalps, and so upon occasion must we. We prefer to take live prisoners and trade them for

the safe return of our own officers and partisans, but our allies have their own customs and traditions."

"Can we not prevail upon them to change, even as they accept our faith?"

He shook his head. "We need them, Amalie. We cannot now in the midst of war curb their hostility. Innocents are slain on both sides. It is the regrettable consequence of war."

"The consequence of war?" The words seemed so heartless, so terribly cold. "Forgive me, monsieur, but MacKinnon's Rangers do not take scalps. They do not slay women and children. Surely, our soldiers and allies can learn to do—"

"We will do what we must to prevail, Amalie." Bourlamaque gave a sigh, his patience with her clearly stretched. "Remember, we did not start this war. We merely fight to finish it. Did the prisoner have anything else to say?"

"*Oui, monsieur.* He guessed that my mother was Abenaki and said not all amongst the British loathe Indians or those with Indian blood. He reminded me that he is not English, and when I asked him why he fought for them, he said it was a long tale."

"Very well. If there is nothing else, you may go."

No man has the right to treat you thus. You should report him to Bourlamaque.

Knowing Bourlamaque was already vexed with her, Amalie hesitated. "I feel I must tell you, monsieur, that Lieutenant Rillieux . . . forced a kiss upon me yesterday in—"

"He confessed the misdeed to me this morning and seemed quite contrite." Bourlamaque stood, walked round the writing table, and took her hand, urging her to her feet, a sign that her time with him had come to an end. "You must understand that your refusal to consider his offer of marriage has left him frustrated. He is a man, Amalie, and men have certain needs. If only you would . . . Ah, but I can see from your face that you feel nothing for him. A pity. But stealing a kiss is not so great a transgression. In fact, many young women enjoy a stolen kiss now and again. Now, go and dress for dinner."

Enjoy? How could any woman enjoy that? Amalie certainly had not. If that's what it was like to kiss a man, then Sister Marie Louise had spoken truly when she'd warned Amalie that life with a husband was misery.

"*Bien, monsieur.*" Feeling as though she'd just been admonished, Amalie curtsied, then made her way upstairs to her room, where she sat at her dressing table and stared at her reflection in the looking glass.

How could she look the same when her whole world had just turned upside down?

Chapter 7

"Dinnae trouble yourself, lass." Morgan watched as Miss Chauvenet readied hot water, soap, clean linen, and salve on the table beside his bed. "What point is there in tryin' to make it better when we both ken I shall be dead soon?"

She didn't look at him, but sprinkled dried sage and cedar into the water, her dark hair tied back with a pink ribbon and hanging in thick waves down the back of her gray skirts. "It is my duty to care for your injuries, monsieur."

But Morgan could tell there was more to it than her sense of duty. She'd had an oddish way about her since she'd walked through the door an hour past. She seemed more troubled than before, and there were dark circles beneath her eyes as if she had not slept. And yet something in her manner toward him had softened.

She'd stepped through the door to his little prison, and her expression had turned to fury when she'd seen the fresh bruises on his face. She'd called for the surgeon's lads and had blistered their ears, admonishing them for failing to watch over him.

"Where is your honor that you allow a helpless man to be beaten?" she'd scolded in French. "Do you not have a duty before God to care for him? How would you feel if English officers treated wounded Frenchmen thus? The next time anyone tries to

inflict harm on Monsieur MacKinnon, you are to send for me or
for Monsieur Lambert at once!"

Rillieux's fist had hurt Morgan far less than hearing a pretty
fair maid call him "helpless." Still, some part of him had been
pleased to see her so fashed on his behalf.

After that, she'd bathed his cheek with a cool cloth. 'Twas
then she'd noticed that the skin of his ankles and wrists had blistered and bled where the shackles had chafed him. Now she was
dead set upon cleaning the wounds and binding them.

"Leave it be. I shall be in shackles for the rest of my days." *If I
dinnae escape.* "There is naugh' to be gained by your doin' this."

She sat beside him on her stool and met his gaze, a look of
deep sadness in her eyes. "I cannot change what is to come, monsieur, but I can ease your suffering today."

Her compassion—so pure and sincere—struck him silent. He
was searching for the words to thank her, when she drew something from her skirts.

A key.

It was the key to his shackles.

Blood rushed into Morgan's head, new strength filling his
limbs. If she would but unshackle even one wrist, he could wrest
the key from her, free himself, and break away from this place.
The surgeon and his lads offered no serious challenge. He could
subdue them, steal a French uniform, and try to reach one of the
gates before anyone was the wiser. Once he reached the forest . . .

If he reached the forest, he'd face a perilous journey of three
days and nights with no food or weapons, walking upon a
wounded leg he was not sure could bear his weight.

You've survived worse, MacKinnon. You can do it!

And if he failed? What could they possibly do to him that
would be worse than what they were already planning?

They could punish Miss Chauvenet.

Through the buzzing of his thoughts, he heard her speak.

"To clean your wounds I must remove the shackles one limb
at a time." She held up the key with a trembling hand. Was she
still afraid of him? "There will be nothing to stop you from hurting me or forcing me to free you. I'm certain you could kill me
with your bare hands if you chose. Therefore, I must ask for your
word as a Catholic that you will not try to escape."

So she would loose his bonds only to bind him with words.

Och, Satan's hairy arse!

Morgan drew a deep breath, fighting back frustration. "Even were these chains to fall away, lass, you'd have no cause to fear me. I've told you I willna harm you."

"Then I have your word?"

He hesitated, wondering how much of a sin it would be to break this promise if breaking it saved his life. "Aye, you have my word as a Catholic—and a MacKinnon."

She reached toward his right wrist, seemed to falter. "The surgeon does not know I have this key. If I am discovered . . ."

And then Morgan understood. She was just as afraid of being caught as she was of him. "Then dinnae do this. Return the key. I wouldna see you risk yourself on my account, lass."

But she did not heed him. She stuck the key in the lock, turned it. And his right wrist was free.

He tried to draw his arm down to his side—and found he could scarcely move it. Sharp pain shot through his shoulder, driving the breath from his lungs. "Och, Christ!"

And you were thinkin' of escapin', lad?

"Lie still." Gently she took his arm, lifted it, and rested it across her lap. "You've been bound like this for so long your shoulder is . . . How do you say? It is locked. Frozen."

But Morgan couldn't open his mouth to answer for fear he'd curse again, as much from pain as from fury with his own weakness. He breathed deeply, willing the knotted muscles and locked joint to loosen.

Wait, lad. There will come another chance, and you'll be stronger.

"I do not mean to hurt you." She dipped a cloth in the warm water and began to bathe the flayed skin of his wrist.

He gritted his teeth. "Dinnae fret, lass."

But as his shoulder began to loosen, Morgan was assailed by new feelings. The sting of soap. The scents of sage and cedar. The soft stroke of her fingers as she spread salve on his wrist, then bound it in a clean strip of linen.

"Try to move your arm now."

Morgan made a fist, bent his elbow, then rolled his shoulder, the motion tugging at the healing wound in his chest. " 'Tis much better now, lass. I thank you."

She smiled, a sight so sweet that his heart seemed to trip.

Without thinking, he raised his hand to her face, traced the soft curve of her cheek with his thumb, his fingers catching in the dark silk of her hair. But rather than pulling his hand away, he delved deeper into her tresses, sliding his fingers slowly down their length, drawing a handful to his nose, breathing deep, the scent of lavender filling his head, desire for her lancing unexpected and fierce through his gut.

She isna yours to touch, lad.

Nay, she was not. Even had their nations not been at war, even had she not been promised to the Church, she was an officer's daughter. She might as well have been a star—beyond his reach, untouchable.

Even so, Morgan wanted her.

Amalie could scarcely breathe, her cheek still burning where he'd touched her. She watched him inhale the scent of her hair, his eyes drifting shut, his brow knotting as if with pain. Then he opened his eyes and looked at her once more, the heat in his gaze calling to something inside her, making her belly flutter and her heart beat faster.

"Forgi'e me." He released her hair, a look of remorse on his face. "I have no right to touch you thus."

Her pulse still racing, Amalie reached for the heavy iron shackle. "I . . . I am sorry, monsieur, but I must—"

There came a sound at the door.

Amalie froze.

Then she heard Monsieur Lambert's voice, calling for someone to bring water.

"Do it. Be quick!" The Ranger stretched his arm over his head, offering her his wrist, when he just as easily might have grabbed her throat.

He was keeping his word. Hadn't she known he would?

Hurrying lest she be discovered, she fit the shackle around his wrist and clamped it shut, the lock sliding into place with a click. But the moment passed, and the surgeon did not enter, his voice fading as he walked on by.

Amalie released the breath she hadn't known she was holding. "Is that better?"

"Aye. My thanks. You've a healin' touch."

She stood, key in hand, and began to move all that she needed to the foot of the bed so that she could care for his ankles, determined to do all she could despite the risk to show him mercy before even mercy itself was taken from him.

She'd lain awake much of the night, the Ranger's words—and Bourlamaque's—running through her mind. She'd always believed France was the unassailable bastion of civilization, while the English were heretics, unrefined and prone to acts of cruelty. To hear Bourlamaque admit that French commanders also paid for scalps, that French soldiers and allies also slew women and children . . .

It was as if the ground had vanished from beneath her feet.

She'd gone to the chapel before first light to speak with Père François, hoping that he might be able to guide her, but he had simply reminded her that France was true to Rome and the pope, while the English were heretics who had turned away from the Church—as if religion alone, not actions, were the seat of a people's honor.

"Is it less of a sin against God for a man to kill women and children because he is Catholic?" she'd asked the priest. "Should not we who live by the true religion demonstrate our faith through Christian compassion? What kind of Christians are we if we behave as heretics behave?"

He had merely smiled and patted the back of her hand. "You and I might wish it so, but life is far more complicated than that."

When the sun had at last risen, it had seemed to shine on a changed world, one in which there were fewer true colors and many more shades of gray.

She wanted to apologize to the Ranger for the things she'd said yesterday. She'd all but accused him of lying when he'd been telling the truth. But how could she admit to him the disappointment she'd felt when Bourlamaque had admitted that his worst accusations were true?

She sat at the foot of the bed, pushed the blanket aside, and unlocked the iron that bound his ankle. "Try to bend your leg."

He wiggled his foot, then bent his knee, the blanket sliding down his thigh, exposing his leg to the hip. Breath hissed from between clenched teeth, and she knew it was his injured thigh that pained him. "Satan!"

She could not help but notice yet again how big and well made he was, his thigh as big around as both her legs together. "Your wound has grown stiff."

"Aye—och!" He squeezed his eyes shut and let go a few shuddering breaths as he straightened his leg and bent it a second and third time. By the time he'd stretched it out on the bed again, his face was pale, and there were beads of sweat on his forehead. "Dinnae expect to see me dancin' a jig anytime soon."

Amalie was not sure what he meant by *jig,* but she knew he would never dance again. She'd seen her cousins building a travois this afternoon and had realized at once what they purposed to do with it. When Bourlamaque was finished with the Ranger, her cousins would strap him to the travois, bind him by hand and foot, and drag him back to Oganak to feed the fires.

"If he is able to walk, it will keep him from escaping," Tomas had told her, sharing a smile with Simon. "And if he cannot walk, it will enable us to move him swiftly back to the village."

A desperate sadness swelling inside her, Amalie quickly tended the blistered, broken skin of Major MacKinnon's right ankle, then shackled him again and moved to his left, repeating the routine, listening for the sound of approaching footsteps.

The Ranger was right, of course. In a few days, any good she could do for him would be undone many times over. And yet, if she could make this moment more bearable for him, then at least she would have done *something.*

"Somethin' troubles you, lass. Aye, I can see it on your face."

Could she admit the truth to him? "I . . . I spoke with Bourlamaque."

"Did you tell him about Lieutenant Rillieux?"

"Lieutenant Rillieux had already confessed, and Bourlamaque told me that many women enjoy stolen kisses." Amalie still could not fathom that and wondered, not for the first time, whether she wasn't better suited to become a nun than a wife.

"That wasna a stolen kiss! The bastard hurt you!"

For some reason, the Ranger's angry protectiveness felt gratifying to Amalie. But it wasn't Bourlamaque's words about Lieutenant Rillieux that had kept her up all night. "I also spoke with him of the things you told me about Oganak."

Finally, she'd said it.

"Then you ken that I spoke truly."

She nodded. "He said he does not wish to buy scalps, but has no choice, as the British do it openly. We did not start this war, Monsieur MacKinnon. Our soldiers fight only to finish it."

"I dinnae think such fine reasons matter to the six hundred souls whose scalps were a-flutterin' in the wind at Oganak." He spoke the words gently, without a trace of anger or scorn or smugness.

But what he'd said struck her hard just the same, for it was the truth, and it showed her words for what they were—excuses.

"I have always believed that France is the light of the world, but now . . ." How could she explain it in his language when she struggled to understand it in her own? "You make me doubt all I once knew, monsieur."

"Nations are made of men, Miss Chauvenet, and war turns men into animals."

Some men became animals, it seemed. But clearly not all men.

"This war has not made you into an animal."

He raised a dark eyebrow. "You're certain of that, are you, lass?"

She closed the shackle around his wrist and locked it, slipping the key that he might have stolen from her into her apron pocket. "Yes, Monsieur MacKinnon, I am."

Morgan watched and listened while Amalie read aloud to him—something by a philosopher lad named Rousseau. Her eyes were downcast, her lashes dark on her cheeks, her hair spilling over one shoulder to the floor. The sight of her and the sweet sound of her voice were almost enough to make him forget that his days were running out. She could read well—better than well, given that she was reading French words but speaking English ones. Her mind was quick, her thoughts agile, her wit sharp.

And it only made him want her more.

She'd already read through the philosopher's notions of original man, explaining to him that Rousseau believed men were creatures of nature whom society and civilization made weak. Morgan thought he agreed, at least in part. He'd seen Indian villages that had once been strong destroyed by the trappings of civilization—rum that enslaved minds, muskets that made men lazy so that they forgot how to use bow and arrow, copper pots and kettles and steel knives that made people dependent on trade with Europeans.

But when it came to notions of love and desire, 'twas clear that Rousseau was a blethering idiot.

"'It is easy to see that the moral part of love is a contrived feeling, born of social habit and enhanced by women with much care and cunning in order to build their empire and put in power the sex which ought to obey. This feeling, being founded on notions of beauty and merit that a savage does not know, and on comparisons he cannot make, must not exist for him.'" She paused for a moment, and a blush stole over her cheeks. "'He follows only the character nature has given him and not tastes that he could never have acquired, so that every woman equally answers his purpose.'"

Morgan couldn't help but laugh, amused by her shyness and humored by the ridiculousness of Rousseau's thinking. "'Tis clear this Rousseau spends too much time wi' his books and no' enough time wi' women. Surely, the poor man has never been in love."

She lifted her gaze from the page, her cheeks still pink. "You do not agree?"

"Nay, lassie." He looked straight into her eyes. "I think even the most savage man can tell a beautiful woman when he sees her."

She drew a quick breath, looked away, then met his gaze again, her blush deepening to a glow. "You say war makes men into animals, but the *mère supérieure* would say the same of passion."

Morgan considered this for a moment, thinking of all he had done out of lust, his mind coming to rest on Iain and what he had endured out of love for Annie. "Aye, unbridled lust might turn a man into an animal if he allows it to rule him, but desire tempered by love can make him a saint."

And then he told her how Iain had found Annie alone in the forest, the sole survivor of a massacred homestead, about to be raped and slain by a group of French and Abenaki warriors, and how he'd violated his orders to save her life, enduring a hundred lashes as punishment. He told her how Iain had defied their commander to keep her near him, how he'd kidnapped a French priest in order to marry her though she was Protestant, and how he'd faced her depraved uncle in battle, almost losing his own life to save hers.

As he told Amalie his brother's story, he watched the play of emotions over her face—horror, surprise, distress, even longing.

"He must love her very much," she said when he had finished.

"Enough to die for her."

She watched him for a moment, those green-brown eyes of hers like a window to her heart. He knew what she was going to ask him before she spoke. "Have you ever loved a woman?"

Had he ever loved a woman? He'd *made love* with his fair share—dark-eyed Muhheconneok lasses in Stockbridge, fair-haired Dutch beauties in Albany, a plump alewife's daughter or two. But although he'd cherished them—and savored the pleasure he'd shared with them—he'd yet to feel the bond that had driven his brother to risk *everything*.

And suddenly his life seemed so empty.

But it was better this way, aye? 'Twas better never to have known that kind of love than to leave behind a bereaved wife to raise his bairns alone. This war had already made too many widows, too many fatherless children.

"Nay, lass."

"Then there is no woman to mourn you?" On her sweet face, he saw reflected the bleakness of what awaited him should he fail to escape—an agonizing death, an unmarked forest grave, only his brothers to remember him.

He grinned, tried to make light of it, needing to see her smile. "Och, I'm thinkin' there will be a tear or two shed in Stockbridge, and perhaps in Albany, too."

"I shall pray for you."

Her simple offering left a tightness in his chest, made it strangely hard for him to breathe. "You . . . would do that? You would spend prayers upon your enemy, upon a man who might have slain your father?"

"War killed my father, monsieur." Then she smiled, a fragile, sad smile. "Besides, I have forgiven you, have I not? *Oui,* I will pray for you."

He lifted his head, looked down toward the wooden cross that rested against his chest. "Then take this. Pray the words with it. It will give me strength to wear it and ken that you have touched it."

She set her book aside, walked to the bedside, then reached down and lifted the rosary over his head, her fingers closing around the wooden beads and the small wooden cross. "I shall pray with it tonight, monsieur, and return it in the morning."

Chapter 8

Amalie hurried through her morning toilette, washing her face, combing the tangles from her hair, and tying it back with a red ribbon her father had given her. Then she drew on her petticoats, fastened her stays, and slipped into her gown, choosing the blue one over the gray. She tucked the white stomacher into place, smoothing her hand over the lace ruffles and straightening the lace at her wrists, then glancing in the glass to be certain she was presentable. If only there were a way to hide the dark circles beneath her eyes . . .

She'd slept but little last night. She'd spent the night upon her knees praying the rosary just as she'd promised, holding the Ranger's simple wooden beads, his scent upon them, the leather cord that held them stained with his sweat. Then, unable to keep from weeping, she'd remained kneeling and had asked the Blessed Virgin for some miracle that would spare him torment. When at last she'd fallen asleep, her dreams had been troubled with visions of fire.

Why, oh, why did he fight for the British?

She could not deny it. Not only had she failed to hate him, she had come to admire him, even to feel . . . *affection* for him. A Ranger he might be, and fearsome in battle, but he was also a man who kept his word, a decent man, a man of deep morals and intelligence. He'd discussed Rousseau's writings with her as if her opinions mattered, listening to her thoughts and sharing his own. Though he could easily have stolen the key from her yesterday, he had not. And although she knew that he—how should she describe it?—felt some *attraction* to her as a woman, the look in his eyes hadn't frightened her the way men's regard usually did. Instead, it had left her feeling warm, almost breathless.

I think even the most savage man can tell a beautiful woman when he sees her.

She picked up his rosary, clutched it tight in her fingers, whispering a quick Hail Mary. Then she tucked it into her bodice lest anyone see it and went down to breakfast.

She was relieved to find Bourlamaque conversing with Lieutenant Rillieux and the other junior officers in his study, a breakfast of breads, cheeses, and cold meats from last night's supper left out for her. Though she cared for Bourlamaque and enjoyed his company, she was no longer so fond of Lieutenant Rillieux, her anger with him for striking Monsieur MacKinnon unabated. It was far better to break her fast alone than to endure his company.

She ate quickly, then left the house, hurrying across the parade grounds toward the hospital. The sun was well above the horizon now, the days growing longer as spring stretched toward summer. A slight breeze blew in from Lac Champlain, carrying the scent of wood smoke from the soldiers' cook fires. The crow of a rooster. A dog's bark. Men's hearty laughter.

She entered the hospital to find Monsieur Lambert's attendants playing at cards, only one soldier left in their charge—the one who'd shot himself in the foot. Three others had healed and been sent back to their posts yesterday. One had died, another little wooden cross planted in the ground.

The young men looked up as she entered, exchanged a meaningful glance, then went back to their game. They were no doubt upset with her for yesterday's scolding, but she had not been able to let their negligence go without censure.

"*Bonjour,*" she called to them, threading her way amongst the empty beds toward the back.

"*Bonjour, mademoiselle,*" they called in return, a bit sheepishly it seemed to her.

And then she saw.

The door to the back room was wide open—and the bed empty.

M organ leaned back against the rough, wooden planks, trying to take the weight off his injured leg, the iron collar
heavy against his shoulders. Standing upright was more difficult
than he'd imagined and yet he had little choice but to keep standing. Still, he supposed he was grateful to know that he *could*
stand and walk, even if it hurt like hell.

He'd known there would be trouble the moment the surgeon
discovered the bandages on his wrists and ankles. A frown had
come over the man's face and he'd poked his finger into the gap
between the bandages and the shackles as if trying to figure out
how someone could possibly have accomplished it.

"Who did this?" he asked in heavily accented English.

Unwilling to do or say anything that might expose Amalie to
harm, Morgan had stared at him as if in surprise. "It wasna you?"

"Of course it was not me!"

Knowing it was probably futile, Morgan had lied. "I was
sleepin', and when I awoke, 'twas already finished. I thought
you'd done it."

The surgeon studied him through eyes that held suspicion,
then left him to question the young lads who worked for him.
There'd been some shouting and then silence, and Morgan had
known it was only a matter of time before the surgeon uncovered
the truth. A short time later Lambert had returned with Lieutenant Rillieux, who, together with two soldiers, had unshackled
him, stripped off his bandages, and made him put on breeches.
Then they'd forced him to walk barefoot, shirtless and in shackles,
from the hospital to the guardhouse through a throng of French
soldiers, who'd shouted at him, cursed him, and spit at him as if he
were Satan himself.

And in their eyes surely he was.

He'd held his head high, pretending not to understand their
curses, pretending he felt no insult, no fear, no pain, his injured
leg barely able to hold him. The heavy irons forced his thigh to
work harder, rubbed against his raw and blistered skin. Then, just
as they'd neared the guardhouse, he'd seen them—perhaps a
dozen Abenaki warriors, broad smiles upon their faces.

"Kwai, nichemis! Paa-kuin-o-gwzian!" the tallest one had shouted. *Hello, brother! I am happy to see you!*

Morgan had met the man's gaze, said nothing.

Up your arse.

Now Morgan was imprisoned in a small cell, chained by a heavy iron collar to the wall, the chain a few links too short to permit him to lie down or even sit, his wrists and ankles still shackled. Rillieux had left him like this all night, no doubt trying to add to his miseries and sense of dread by forcing him to stand and depriving him of sleep.

He'd have been a liar if he'd said it'd had no effect upon him, for in the darkest hours of the morning, surrounded by shadows and silence, exhausted, his body aching, he'd found it all but impossible to escape his own thoughts.

Morgan had never doubted his courage. He'd faced wild animals, once saving a little Muhheconneok girl from the jaws of a cougar that had wandered into Stockbridge. He'd gotten into his share of collieshangies in the public houses of Albany and come out unscathed. He'd fought more battles than he could remember, facing down the enemies of Britain and of his Muhheconneok kin, charging headlong into the fray, and staining his *claidheamh mòr* red with blood. But against the enemy of prolonged pain he had not yet been tested.

Would he break? Would he beg and plead for mercy? In his desperation to end the agony, would he betray his brothers, his men, himself?

Nay, he would not. He *could* not. For as terrible as it might be, his pain meant life for Iain, Connor, Dougie, Killy, and the others, his silence the last gift he could give them.

Images flashed through his mind. Connor getting a musket ball cut out of his shoulder last spring. Iain taking a hundred strokes of the lash without making a sound, his back bloodied. Lovely Annie facing a murderous war party alone with nothing more than a stone in her wee hand. And Amalie, sweet Amalie, forgiving a man who might have killed her father, finding the strength to offer him mercy, defying her own people to treat him with dignity.

Their courage would be his courage.

Outside, the sun climbed past the horizon. It would not be long now. He closed his eyes, drew a breath, began to pray.

God in heaven, dinnae forsake me! Mary, Mother of God, pray for me!

Then, from outside, he heard men's voices.

He drew another deep breath, forced himself to stand upright on both legs, ignoring the pain, dismissing his fears. He was Morgan MacKinnon, brother to Iain and Connor MacKinnon, blood brother to the Muhheconneok, and grandson of Iain Og MacKinnon. He would not break.

Come, Rillieux, you son of a whore. Do your worst upon me.

"Lieutenant Rillieux said that no one was to attend the prisoner until he himself returned." The guard, a young soldier not much older than Amalie herself, stood at rigid attention, clearly afraid of Lieutenant Rillieux.

"Of course he did, and you have done your duty well." Amalie forced herself to smile, then leaned closer, as if imparting a great secret. "But my guardian, Monsieur le Chevalier de Bourlamaque, ordered me to visit the prisoner each day so that I might win his trust and perhaps steal secrets from him."

She was treading dangerously close to a lie, she knew, but what choice did she have? She could not rest until she'd returned the rosary to Monsieur MacKinnon. She had tried to make him more comfortable and in so doing had brought this upon him.

It was Monsieur Lambert who'd finally told her what had happened. He'd found the bandages and discerned that someone had unlocked the shackles. After realizing that it could only have been she, he and Lieutenant Rillieux had agreed that the Ranger was too dangerous to remain in the hospital, and Lieutenant Rillieux had moved him to the guardhouse with Bourlamaque's approval.

"Your compassion does you credit, Miss Chauvenet, but it was an incredibly foolish risk to take, even with the prisoner sleeping as he was," the surgeon had chided her. "I am grateful he truly was asleep and not just feigning. I cannot imagine what he might have done to you otherwise."

It had been on the tip of her tongue to tell him that the Ranger had not been asleep but had instead given his word, but then she'd realized that they must have questioned Monsieur MacKinnon and that he had lied to protect her, thinking perhaps that she would be punished if the truth were known.

"I—I am sorry, monsieur." She'd bowed her head as if in contrition, her mind racing for a way to return the rosary. "I meant
only to help."

"Of course. But your help, so graciously given, is no longer
needed," he'd said. "You have spent far too much time in this
dismal place. Return to your needlework. Forget this unfortunate
affair."

Amalie had been incensed. Return to her needlework? Did
they think so poorly of her as to believe she could be distracted
from Monsieur MacKinnon's plight by embroidery?

"Bien, monsieur."

But knowing that if she returned to the house she'd have to
face Bourlamaque, who would surely forbid her from seeing the
Ranger again, she'd come straight to the guardhouse instead and
had been relieved to learn that Lieutenant Rillieux was still occupied elsewhere.

The soldier on guard duty looked down at her, doubt upon his
face. "He asked you to *interrogate* the prisoner, mademoiselle?"

She smiled again, leaned closer. "Monsieur le Chevalier believes
the prisoner might find it harder to resist a woman's more subtle
ploys than a man's threats."

His gaze dropping to her bodice, the soldier nodded, as if he
understood that line of reasoning at least. "Very well. But if Lieutenant Rillieux blames—"

"He shall not blame you, monsieur." How could she sound so
calm when her heart was pounding? "I shall see to that."

Amalie followed the soldier inside, her eyes taking a moment
to adjust to the darkness. And when they did, she felt sick.

The Ranger stood in the tiny cell, chained by his neck, wrists,
and ankles, wearing only a pair of ill-fitting breeches, new and
old bruises upon his face, his long hair tangled, the fresh scar on
his chest exposed. The hollows in his cheeks seemed even more
pronounced over the dark growth of his beard, and there were
shadows beneath his eyes. *Mon Dieu,* had they left him standing
all night long?

He stared at her, clearly surprised to see her. "Miss Chauvenet?"

Amalie turned to the soldier. "Thank you, monsieur. You may
leave us."

The young man gave a sharp bow and was gone.

The Ranger took a step in her direction, his gait marred by a slight limp, his chains dragging through the straw. Standing upright, he seemed so much taller, so much more threatening than he had lying in bed. His body all muscle, he reminded her of a caged animal—fierce, dangerous, untamed. "You shouldna be here, lass."

"I am so sorry, monsieur." She walked over to his cell, grasped the cold iron bars. "In seeking to ease your suffering, I have hastened you to this moment."

He took another step toward her. "Dinnae fret. It isna your doin'. I pray they didna punish you."

She shook her head. "No. Not yet."

"Then leave me!" His voice took on an urgent tone. "Go afore they find you here. I wouldna see you risk yourself further for my sake."

"I came only to bring you this." She reached inside her bodice, drew his wooden rosary from between her breasts, then reached between the bars and held it out for him. "I could not rest until you wore it again."

For a moment he stared at her, a strange look in his eyes. Then he took another shuffling step, the chain that held him clanking. "You spoke the prayers wi' it?"

"Yes, monsieur, as I promised."

He reached out for it with his shackled hands, the naked gratitude on his face putting a hard lump in her throat. "I am most grateful. Thank you, lass."

But rather than taking the rosary from her, he closed his big hands over her smaller one, raised her hand to his lips, and kissed it, his gaze seeking and holding hers. It was the merest brush of his lips against her skin, and yet the heat of it quivered through her, scattering her thoughts, the intensity in his eyes making it impossible to breathe.

"M-monsieur?"

Morgan saw in Amalie's eyes that he'd startled her, but he saw something else there, as well—need. Aye, she felt the pull of it, just as he did. And yet, 'twould surely be the last time he'd see her. He had no right to do this to her, to rouse desires that could only trouble her. She was pledged to the Church, after all, an innocent who had showered him with compassion when she'd had every right to hate him. His debt to her should not be repaid like this.

Fighting to control himself, he took the beads, the smooth wood warm with the scent of her skin, and slipped the rosary over his head and beneath the iron collar. "There is no way to repay your kindness, no words to tell you how grateful I am for all you've done—most of all for your forgiveness."

"In the end I have done nothing." A bright sheen came into her eyes. Tears? For *him*? "Why must you fight for the British? Why could you not have chosen to fight for France instead?"

He'd tried to tell her the story once, but they'd been interrupted. Now there wasn't time. "I chose nothing, Amalie. It was forced upon me."

Her brow furrowed as if in confusion. "What do you mean?"

"There's no time for this. Leave this place afore Rillieux finds you here, and dinnae return. I wouldna have you see me after today." In truth, he wished she had not seen him as he was in that moment—filthy, stinking, weak, blood matted in three weeks' growth of beard, his warrior braids undone, his hair a tangled mess.

But she didn't seem to hear him. "The British *forced* you to fight for them?"

"Aye, my brothers and I were compelled to fight by that whoreson William Wentworth. He accused us of a murder we didna commit and gave us the choice of bein' hanged or takin' the king's shilling. I myself would have been glad to die, but I didna want to see my brothers dancin' at the end of a rope."

"How could he do such a thing?"

Because it was clear she would not leave until she knew the full story, Morgan quickly told her how Wentworth had seen them fight a street brawl, attempting to protect a whore from a man who'd tried to pay for her services with the edge of a blade. He told her how Wentworth had set men to follow them, then had them arrested the next morning. He told her how the *mac-dìolain* had made it clear that he would use his position as the grandson of Britain's king to make sure they died at the end of a noose— unless they agreed to serve him as Rangers.

You will report to me at Fort Edward by August twenty-first and serve me until death releases you or this war is ended. If you fail to appear or abandon your post, you will be shot for desertion and your brothers will be hanged for murder.

As he recalled the words that had damned them, it seemed to

Morgan as if it had happened only yesterday. And now it had brought him to this.

"There is no court in the colonies nor in Britain that would take the word of a Scot over that of their king's grandson," he explained. "Now go, lass!"

But a strange look had come over Amalie's face. "I must tell Bourlamaque."

"It willna matter to him. I have slain too many of his soldiers, and now my life is forfeit. You must go and let this trouble you no longer!"

But then the door was thrown open, and Rillieux walked in, fury on his face. He shouted angrily at Amalie in French, sparing only a quick, hate-filled glance for Morgan. "What are *you* doing here? You would defy my orders?"

Clearly afraid of him, she took a step back, but her chin went up. "I am not a soldier to be ordered about, Lieutenant Rillieux. I came to pray with—"

As if he'd forgotten Morgan was there, Rillieux grasped her arm, jerked her roughly to him, hissing at her from between clenched teeth. "For all your piety, you have not learned to obey as a woman should."

Her face the image of feminine outrage, Amalie tried to pull away from him. "Let go of me! You cannot treat me—"

Rillieux slipped a hand behind her neck and yanked her against him, cutting off her words with another violent kiss, his other hand grasping her bottom.

Before Morgan knew what he was about, he lunged forward, thrust one hand through the bars, and grabbed the bastard by the throat. "Let . . . her . . . go!"

Chapter 9

Amalie shrank back from Lieutenant Rillieux's hateful kiss, abruptly freed from his painful grip. Then time itself seemed to stop—and she saw.

Reaching with his body turned sideways, the chain that bound him drawn tight, Monsieur MacKinnon had the lieutenant by the throat, his eyes dark with rage, one big hand thrust between the bars and choking the life from Lieutenant Rillieux's body, even as the iron collar that encircled his neck cut off his own breath. Lieutenant Rillieux's face was red, his eyes seeming to bulge out of his head, his fingers scrabbling to break the Ranger's deadly grip, his mouth open and silent.

Stunned by the brutality of the kiss and the scene before her, Amalie struggled to find her tongue. "*Arrêtez!* Stop!"

Monsieur MacKinnon met her gaze and choked out one word. "*Go!*"

The Ranger's muscles shook with effort, most of all his injured leg, and Amalie realized he lacked the strength to sustain this for long. He wasn't trying to kill the lieutenant. He was trying to protect her.

Then the terrible truth came to her. If no one were here to stop him, Lieutenant Rillieux would beat the Ranger to within an inch of his life the moment the Ranger released him.

Bourlamaque!

She picked up her skirts and ran. Out the door and across the parade grounds she ran, heedless of soldiers' stares, not stopping until she reached Bourlamaque's study. Terrified of what might be happening back in the guardhouse, she opened the door and ran inside without knocking. "Monsieur! Please, you must come! Lieutenant Rillieux and the Ranger are going to kill each other!"

Bourlamaque stood beside his writing table, his finger pointing at something on a chart of New France, Lieutenant Fouchet and Lieutenant Durand beside him, the three of them staring at her with startled looks upon their faces.

Bourlamaque frowned. "Catch your breath, Amalie, and explain yourself."

So Amalie did, the story pouring out of her in a rush, tears stinging her eyes, fear making her tremble. She told Bourlamaque how she'd prayed with the Ranger's rosary last night and had tried to return it this morning only to find his bed empty. She told him how she'd gone to the guardhouse to return the rosary when Lieutenant Rillieux had found her and shouted at her, then grabbed her and forced another painful kiss upon her. She told him how the Ranger had grabbed Lieutenant Rillieux by the throat to stop him, choking the lieutenant while strangling upon his own chains.

"I fear Lieutenant Rillieux will kill him, monsieur! Please, you must stop them!"

Bourlamaque turned to his two young lieutenants. "Go to the guardhouse at once, and bring Lieutenant Rillieux to me. Do not harm MacKinnon."

Fouchet and Durand bowed—and were gone at a run.

Amalie met her guardian's gaze and saw that he was not pleased with her. She sank into a curtsy. "Forgive me, monsieur. I did not mean—"

He walked over to her, reached out his hand. "Rise, Amalie."

She stood, certain that he was about to censure her.

But instead, he grasped her chin and tilted her head to the side, his gaze dropping to her neck, a dark look spreading over her face. "Did Lieutenant Rillieux do this?"

Amalie raised a hand to her neck, suddenly aware of the sting of scratched skin. She touched the scratch, felt something wet, and withdrew her fingers to find her own blood on her fingertips. *"Oui."*

He motioned to a chair before his writing table. "Sit. Tell me once more what happened. And go slowly this time."

She repeated the story, filling in missing pieces—Lieutenant Rillieux's morning visits to the hospital to beat the Ranger, the humiliating cruelty of his first kiss, the way he'd touched her on her bottom this time, his fingers digging into her flesh. "I do not wish to be near him, monsieur. He . . . frightens me."

Bourlamaque sat behind his writing table, a look of weariness on his face. He rubbed a hand over his clean-shaven jaw. "Amalie, Amalie, whatever shall I do with you? You have done everything I've asked of you, and yet now because of you I must chastise one of my best and most promising officers."

Because of *her*?

The surge of temper she felt must have shown on her face, for in the next instant Bourlamaque spoke as if he'd read her thoughts.

"No, Amalie, I do not blame you for his actions. A stolen kiss is one thing, but this . . ." His gaze dropped to her neck. "He knows full well that to touch you in such a fashion is wicked. But he was right when he said that it was a mistake to have you tend MacKinnon. What you did yesterday—unshackling him while he was sleeping—was incredibly foolish. You are too soft-hearted, too inexperienced to be entrusted with the care of such a man. You are not to go near him again."

Amalie had known this was coming, but to hear Bourlamaque speak the words felt like a blow. She would not see the Ranger again. And soon, he would be dead.

Her throat grew tight. She swallowed. *"Bien, monsieur."*

He stood, a troubled look on his face. "You have had a most distressing day. I am sorry for that. I wish I knew how best to comfort you, but I am only a soldier. Please go to your room and rest. I shall have tea brought up and send Monsieur Lambert to have a look at you."

Amalie stood, gave a curtsy. *"Bien, monsieur. Merci."*

She had reached the door when she remembered.

How, oh, how could she have forgotten?

She turned to face her guardian once more. "Forgive me,

monsieur, but there is one other thing, something important the Ranger told me that you will want to hear."

Bourlamaque's brow bent in an impatient frown. "And what is that?"

"He and his brothers do not fight for Britain of their own choice. They were pressed into service by a British officer, who threatened to see them hanged as criminals if they refused."

Bourlamaque's frown deepened. "Men are pressed into service every day, Amalie. This is of no importance. Go to your—"

"But, monsieur, it *does* matter!" The words were out before she could stop them. "Could we not use this knowledge to win him to our side?"

Bourlamaque shook his head, looking truly vexed with her. "He will not betray his men, Amalie. I have already tried to bargain with him. I offered him a painless death and Catholic burial in exchange for answers to my questions, and he did not accept. Please go to your room, and stay—"

"You offered him only death." It seemed so obvious to Amalie. Why could Bourlamaque not see it? "What if you offered him life? What if you gave him sanctuary instead of death and invited him to fight beside you?"

"Sanctuary?" For a moment Bourlamaque stared at her as if she'd gone mad. Then his expression slowly changed from vexation to something like amazement. "Surely, it cannot be done. Orders have been given, promises made. And yet to have a MacKinnon fighting for France . . ."

From outside came the sound of men's voices—Fouchet, Durand, Rillieux.

"Go now, Amalie. Stay in your room and rest. Trouble yourself no more about these matters. I shall see to Lieutenant Rillieux."

Not wanting to see the lieutenant again. Amalie hurried out the door and up the stairs, shutting the door to her room behind her.

Would Bourlamaque consider what she'd said, or was it already too late?

Hungry enough to eat a bull moose complete with hooves and antlers, Morgan shifted in the straw, trying to ease the pain in his bruised ribs so that he could sleep, knowing he'd need all his strength come the morn. At least they'd removed the collar from about his neck, enabling him to sit and lie down. The surgeon, who'd been sent to examine him in the wake of the beating Rillieux had given him, had been horrified to see him constrained thus and had warned Bourlamaque's men that it wasn't safe.

"Should he lose consciousness in the night, he will hang, and then what good will he be to you?" he'd shouted in French.

In short order, the collar had been removed, the blood washed from Morgan's neck and face, and a breakfast of cold tea and stale bread set before him. Then he'd been left alone again. He'd expected the *mac-dìolain* to return to interrogate him, but it seemed that Rillieux's assault on Amalie had outweighed Bourlamaque's interest in him today.

As it bloody well should.

Rillieux had hurt her this time, his nails drawing blood where they'd scraped over her skin, his hand groping her bottom as if she were a tavern whore. Morgan had no doubt the bastard was capable of rape if given the chance. But it seemed Bourlamaque had taken the attack to heart this time. The lieutenants he'd sent to fetch Rillieux—the men who'd stayed Rillieux's fists and pulled him away from Morgan—had made it clear that Bourlamaque was angry with him. They'd seemed fashed with him themselves.

"You've gone and done it now," said one. "You'll be lucky if Bourlamaque doesn't castrate you."

"She's Major Chauvenet's daughter, Rillieux, not your little *putain*!"

Morgan felt that castration might not be a bad idea. He'd gladly have ripped the whoreson's cods off if he'd had the strength to do it. But, strangling in his chains and weak from his long fever, he'd been able to hold Rillieux only long enough for Amalie to get away. The thrashing that had followed had been more than worth it.

He reached up, closed his fingers around the little wooden rosary, rubbing his fingers over the cross, still touched that she'd gone to such lengths to return it to him. When they'd removed him from the hospital, he hadn't expected to see her again, certain that her guardian wouldn't permit her to go anywhere near the guardhouse. But she had come to him, risking Bourlamaque's wrath to fulfill her promise, his rosary hidden between her breasts.

Had he thanked her? He could scarce remember. His mind had been so filled with her that he hadn't been able to think. And then, when he ought to have drawn away, as filthy as he was, he'd kissed her hand. He'd meant no disrespect by it, but neither had it been a chaste kiss. There'd been far too much heat in his blood afterward—aye, and in hers, too, to judge by the look in her eyes.

She would remember him. Of that he was certain. Why it mattered to him he knew not, but as he lay here on the straw in the dark waiting for his torment to begin, matter it did.

Ignoring his hunger and the ache in his ribs, he closed his eyes and willed himself to sleep, still grasping the rosary in his fist. He'd just drifted off, when he heard men's voices. He sat up, then stood, wondering whether Rillieux had come back under cover of night to finish what he'd started this morning. Then the door opened—and three young soldiers entered bearing silver trays heaped with food, delicious scents mingling in the air, making his empty stomach rumble and his mouth water.

And behind them strode Bourlamaque.

M organ took a swallow of red wine, washing down the last of his supper. 'Twas a feast that had been laid out before him. Turtle soup, roasted duck, roasted venison. Buttered peas, baked beets, onions in brandy. Preserved fruits, cheeses, wheaten bread with butter. The meal had been served from silver platters and tureens set upon a small table that Bourlamaque's men had carried in. Though still in shackles, Morgan had been given a chair to sit upon. Bourlamaque had not eaten, but he had poured the wine, enjoying a glass or two himself.

At first, Morgan had believed he was being rewarded for protecting Amalie, and, indeed, Bourlamaque had thanked him. But then Bourlamaque had steered the conversation toward other matters, asking about the Clan MacKinnon's role in the Forty-Five and how his grandfather, Iain Og MacKinnon, had helped Bonnie Prince Charlie escape, only to suffer years on a British prison barge. They'd talked for a time about the German heretic who sat upon Britain's throne. Then Bourlamaque had wanted to know whether the story he'd heard from Amalie was true—

whether Wentworth had threatened to hang him and his brothers if they refused to fight for Britain. And so Morgan had repeated the tale, wondering if finally they hadn't come to the true reason for Bourlamaque's strange visit. The brigadier's gaze—and the expectant silence that now filled the tiny cell—told him they had.

It was Bourlamaque who broke that silence, speaking in his heavily accented English. "I find myself on unfamiliar ground when it comes to you, Major MacKinnon. You are an enemy of France, and yet, as we have just discussed, your clan has long been allied with France. Your noble grandsire served his prince with honor, and you and your men fight with honor. It is only the circumstance of this war—and the hateful actions of your commander—that lie between us."

Something in the tone of Bourlamaque's voice made Morgan's heart beat faster. Was the old man reconsidering his decision to allow Morgan to be tortured and given to the Abenaki? Perhaps he was considering trading Morgan as part of an exchange of prisoners. Or maybe he was thinking of sending Morgan to Hudson Bay to sit out the war in the hold of a rat-infested French prison hulk. Then again, he might simply hang Morgan and call it mercy.

Morgan met Bourlamaque's gaze. "So my brothers and I have often remarked."

Bourlamaque looked away and drew a slow breath through his thin nostrils, his brow furrowed and his lips pursed as if he were about to make a troubling decision.

Morgan's heart beat faster still.

"I cannot release you," Bourlamaque said at last. "You are far too dangerous an opponent to be traded back to the English. Montcalm would have my head."

You're going to rot in the belly of a ship, lad—worms in the biscuits, lice in your hair, rats at your feet. That's why he asked about Grandfather.

Bourlamaque went on. "Yet I find I cannot turn you over to the Abenaki for slaughter. And so I find myself seeking a third path."

Freezing damp in the winter. Sweltering heat in the summer. Fetid darkness. And you'll feel grateful, for 'tis better than flames.

Bourlamaque shifted his gaze back to Morgan. "I am prepared

to make you an offer—one that differs substantially from the last."

Morgan took another sip of wine, certain he knew what Bourlamaque would say. But Morgan would not betray the Rangers, even to spare his own life. He waited.

Bourlamaque leaned forward in his chair, fire coming into his eyes. "I am willing to grant you not only clemency, but sanctuary. Turn your back on the heretic who has enslaved you, and fight for France! No longer will you be a slave, but an honored officer whose pleasure it is to serve an anointed Catholic king."

Morgan stared at him, unable to speak, his head seeming to spin. He couldn't have been more astonished had Bourlamaque sprouted wings and flown about the room. It took a moment to sort through what the man had said.

Fight for France. Serve an anointed Catholic king.

"You want me to desert . . . and fight for *you*," Morgan stuttered like a fool, his mind still reeling.

Bourlamaque smiled. "How can it be desertion when you were forced so dishonorably to fight? Like the rest of his accursed family, this Wentworth has no sense of honor. It is his chains that bind you now, not mine."

Morgan weighed Bourlamaque's offer, wishing it had come four years ago when Wentworth had first ensnared him and his brothers. They'd have gone over to the French with nary a second thought. It had always galled them to fight on behalf of the German king. But to desert now? It was impossible.

"I am honored by your most generous offer, but I regret I cannae accept. I could never fire upon my brothers—or my men."

Bourlamaque smiled again. "But of course not! Nor would I require you to do such a thing. Though my men and I must continue to engage your brothers as long as they remain our enemies, I am prepared to offer clemency to any Catholic amongst your men, including your brothers, who surrenders to us. All you need do is train my soldiers to fight as you fight—and tell me all I wish to know about the Ranger Corps and Fort Edward."

There came the crux of it. Bourlamaque was making the same offer as before, only this time he was tempting Morgan with life as an officer in the French army instead of a less horrific death. He wanted Morgan to betray secrets not because he was tortured, but because he was *no longer the enemy.*

'Twas a bold proposal, and Morgan knew what lay behind it—
or, rather, who.

Amalie.

It was she who had carried the truth about why Morgan fought
for the British to Bourlamaque. It was she who had worked so
hard and so long to save his life. It was she who was so deeply
troubled by his impending death that she'd prayed for him. Perhaps this was the answer to her prayers.

But there was no question of his being able to accept. Though
Connor might be persuaded to join him, Iain and Joseph would
not. Iain was married to a Protestant who considered herself a
loyal British subject, and the Stockbridge were steadfastly loyal
to Britain. And then there were his men. Though they were Catholics, many had lost kin in this war and had come to hate the
French every bit as much as they hated the British. Most had
families who lived on British land beside British neighbors.
Should they desert, their farms would be confiscated, their families made outcasts and left to starve.

It was on the tip of Morgan's tongue to explain this and refuse,
when another possibility came to him—an intriguing, terrible,
dangerous possibility.

What if he were to accept Bourlamaque's offer—and use his
newfound freedom to spy on the French until he found a way to
escape? He could answer Bourlamaque's questions with half-
truths, offer him obsolete, useless information, teach his soldiers
to be better fighters without betraying Ranger secrets. Then,
when Morgan had earned Bourlamaque's trust, he could disappear while outside the walls, on a scout or shooting at marks.

And yet, every French soldier he trained would eventually
point his musket at the Rangers, at Joseph's warriors, and at the
British Regulars who'd fought beside them these past four years.
Amherst was planning to take Ticonderoga this summer. The
Regulars and Rangers of Fort Edward would journey northward,
surround the fort once more, and attempt to succeed where Abercrombie had failed last year. If any amongst them were slain
because Morgan had taught a Frenchman to shoot with better
aim, their blood would stain his hands.

And then there was the threat that Wentworth had made four
years ago—that if any one of the brothers deserted, the other two
would be hanged for murder. Even if Wentworth didn't follow

through with that threat, there was every chance he'd recall Iain to service, forcing him to leave Annie and little Iain Cameron alone.

Morgan shook his head, freedom calling to him, even as imaginary flames lapped at his skin. "If I desert, Wentworth will see my brothers hanged. 'Tis the threat that has always hung like a sword above our heads."

This time Bourlamaque laughed. "Wentworth believes you are dead."

Morgan had forgotten. *"Your letter."*

Bourlamaque nodded. "Say but the word, and these chains shall be removed. You shall be bathed and shaved and clad as the officer and nobleman you are and not as a mean prisoner."

Audentes fortuna iuvat.

Morgan drew a deep breath, feeling as if he stood on a precipice and was about to leap. "Aye, I will join you. I will teach your men to fight as I fight. I will share wi' you all I ken about Wentworth and his ways. But I willna fire upon my brothers or the Rangers."

"Agreed." Then Bourlamaque threw his head back and laughed.

And in the sound of that laughter, Morgan heard the echo of a single word.

Traitor.

Chapter 10

Amalie jabbed at her needlework, unable to concentrate. Still confined to her room, she hadn't seen Bourlamaque since yesterday morning and had no idea what had happened since then. Twice yesterday she'd heard shouting, men's voices raised in anger, but she hadn't dared to open her door to eavesdrop. Now this morning there seemed to be many comings and goings, footsteps treading up and down the hallway below. With nothing but needlework and her own imagination to keep her company, Amalie couldn't help but fear the worst.

She imagined the Ranger, badly beaten, left to stand in chains in his cell through another night. Or Lieutenant Rillieux, bruised and angry, denying he'd touched her, leading Bourlamaque to doubt her. Or Bourlamaque, constrained by circumstances, dismissing the idea of sanctuary and giving the order for the Ranger's interrogation to begin at once.

Surely, it cannot be done. Orders have been given, promises made. And yet to have a MacKinnon fighting for France . . .

She'd seen it on Bourlamaque's face, knew that he'd found at least some merit in her idea. But would his duty to Montcalm prevent him from acting? And how long did he intend to leave her confined like this? Was she being punished?

She set her needlework aside and rose from her chair, then

walked to the window and looked outside. The sky was overcast with the promise of rain, a breeze playing with the clean linens that the laundresses had hung out to dry. Soldiers bustled about, hard at work with their chores. In the distance, a group of Abenaki stood gathered about a cook fire, Tomas and Simon amongst them.

At the sight of them, her stomach sank. Bourlamaque would not be able to give the Ranger sanctuary. Monsieur MacKinnon and his brothers had long been promised to the Abenaki, and denying them their prisoner would surely lead to strife with an ally France could not afford to lose. Bourlamaque was a noble-man, a loyal officer, a servant of France. He would do his duty. He would turn the Ranger over to the Abenaki, and Monsieur MacKinnon would suffer the torments of hell ere he died.

Grief for him stole over her like a sickness, bringing tears to her eyes, images of him filling her mind. The Ranger chained to the bed and delirious with pain and fever. The Ranger holding a lock of her hair to his nose, inhaling her scent. The Ranger laughing over Monsieur Rousseau's writings.

Even the most savage man can tell a beautiful woman when he sees her.

Yesterday she'd seen just how savage he could be. Still weak and in chains, he'd found a way to protect her, moving so fast despite his shackles that he'd taken Lieutenant Rillieux com-pletely unawares. At his full strength and unfettered, he would make a terrifying adversary. But he was no mindless barbarian, and she found it strange to think she now felt more at ease with him than with Lieutenant Rillieux, who'd served as her father's right-hand man.

A knock came at the door.

Thérèse, the cook's daughter, had come from the cookhouse to take this morning's breakfast tray.

Amalie didn't turn to face the kitchen maid, but continued to gaze out the window. "You may take the tray. Tell Cook I was not hungry."

"Then perhaps you will have a hearty appetite for dinner," Bourlamaque's deep voice answered.

She whirled about and gave a little curtsy, painfully aware that she was wearing only her chemise, a blush burning its way into her cheeks. "Forgive me, monsieur. I mistook—"

He dismissed her apology with a wave of his hand. "Please,

Amalie, do not distress yourself. I can see you are still upset. In fact, that is why I have come. I wanted to let you know that I have confined Lieutenant Rillieux to quarters for the time being. If he touches you again in any way that is improper, he shall be flogged."

Amalie did not know what to say. "I . . . I thank you for your care of me, monsieur."

He reached out, took her chin between his fingers, and tilted her head to the side, his gaze dropping to the scratches on her neck. "We must arrange to transport you back to Trois Rivières at our first opportunity. I know you do not desire to return to the abbey, but Fort Carillon is no place for a beautiful young woman. I shall do my best to find you a husband once the war has ended—unless, of course, you decide to take vows."

"Bien, monsieur." She barely managed a whisper in response. She couldn't imagine living in the abbey again, every moment of her day controlled by others. And yet she knew she could not remain in the fort.

"Now dress for dinner. We have a guest."

"A guest?"

He smiled. "I think you will be pleased."

She did not feel like meeting anyone, but she did not say this. "What of the Ranger, monsieur? Might I ask—?"

But Bourlamaque had already gone.

For a moment Amalie stared at the closed door.

A guest?

She couldn't recall any visitors arriving at the fort. Then again, she'd been confined to her room since yesterday morning. Wondering who it might be, she combed her hair and braided a long white ribbon into it. Then she struggled into her stays and slipped on one of the sack gowns her father had ordered sewn for her last spring. Lavender with ivory lace, it was the last gift he had given to her.

Glancing in the looking glass only long enough to be certain that nothing was out of place, she walked out of her room and down the stairs, hoping to find a few minutes before or after the midday meal to speak privately with her guardian about Monsieur MacKinnon. Perhaps she could press him to consider her idea and help him find a way to appease her mother's people. Or perhaps she could speak with Père François and seek his help in this matter.

She walked down the hall to the dining room, thinking through what she would say to Bourlamaque, her gaze falling upon the back of a tall and well-dressed gentleman who stood beside her guardian, a glass of wine in his hand. He was much taller than Bourlamaque and broader of shoulder, seeming to fill the space, his long dark hair drawn back with a ribbon that matched the shade of his dark brown frock coat. Then he turned toward her, and Amalie felt her footsteps falter . . . and . . . stop.

It was Monsieur MacKinnon.

Clean-shaven, bathed, and dressed in lace and velvet, he was the most beautiful man she'd ever seen, his smooth face astonishingly handsome, the hollows in his cheeks seeming more pronounced, his cheekbones higher, his eyes piercingly blue. Standing upright, he seemed to tower over her.

Feeling light-headed, she took a step toward him. *"M-monsieur MacKinnon?"*

"Miss Chauvenet." Morgan willed himself to speak, his tongue near to tied, unable to take his gaze from her.

She looked as fresh as springtime, her dark hair hanging in a braid as thick as his fist beyond her hips, her eyes wide with surprise. Then her gaze moved over him, and he knew a moment of utter mortification.

She's thinkin' you look like a peacock, laddie.

With lace cuffs, silk stockings and drawers, and shoes with shiny brass buckles, he *did* look like a bloody peacock or, worse, like someone that whoreson Wentworth would invite to his supper table. The shoes were not so supple as the moccasins he was accustomed to wearing and pinched his toes. The lace seemed to get caught in everything, the silk sliding over his skin in a troubling way, as if he were wearing women's undergarments.

Bourlamaque had been true to his word. No sooner had Morgan agreed to join him than he was freed from his shackles and brought in secret back to the hospital, where the bed he'd been chained to for so many days was waiting for him, clean and much softer than any bed of straw. He'd slept like a dead man, then awoken to find breakfast and a hot bath laid out for him. It had been heaven to bathe again, to scrub fever and filth from his body, to wash and comb his hair, to shave the whiskers from his face. And yet every moment of comfort reminded him of the new and dangerous game he played.

Morgan had become a spy.

No sooner had he finished bathing than Bourlamaque's personal tailor had arrived to measure him and had announced that nothing in their store of uniforms would fit Morgan. In the end, Bourlamaque had decided it might offend the soldiers to put Morgan in a French uniform before he had proved his loyalty, and so he'd ordered his tailor to dress Morgan as a nobleman.

"He is the grandson of one of Scotland's most loyal chieftains," he'd told the confused tailor in French.

But no Highland laird would be caught dead in such frippery. Besides, Morgan had come of age on the frontier, not in his grandfather's halls on Skye. What he wouldn't give for a butter-soft pair of buckskin breeches, a shirt of homespun, and fur-lined moccasins. Thank God in heaven his brothers couldn't see him. They would laugh until their sides split.

But there was no hint of mockery in Amalie's eyes as she gazed up at him. Instead, relief and happiness were written upon her face as clearly as words on a page. And Morgan felt an almost irresistible urge to duck down and kiss her.

"I . . . I am pleased to see you looking so well, monsieur," she said after a moment, a faint blush staining her cheeks.

He bowed, took her hand, raised it to his lips. "If I look well, miss, 'tis only a testament to your skills as a healer and your guardian's generosity."

He heard Bourlamaque's low chuckle of approval, then Bourlamaque spoke in French. "Did I not say you would be pleased, Amalie?"

Amalie looked up at her guardian, gratitude in her eyes. *"Si, monsieur. Et je vous en remercie." Yes, and I am grateful to you.*

Morgan kept his face expressionless, knowing that to give himself away would spell catastrophe. No one must know that he spoke the French tongue—not if he was to survive this little game and escape. "Bourlamaque has explained to me that this was your doin'. I am deeply in your debt, lass. I owe you my life. If there is ough' I can do, you need but ask."

The blush in her cheeks deepened. "You are welcome, monsieur."

From behind him came the sound of the front door opening and men's voices speaking in hushed French.

"I cannot believe we are made to suffer through this! Dining with this barbarian after all he and his men have done to France? Disgraceful!"

"Bourlamaque has lost his mind to grant the bastard his freedom! The Abenaki are outraged. I heard they're talking of taking the Ranger by force."

Taking in this bit of information, Morgan watched Amalie's smile turn to a look of worry, her gaze shifting to Bourlamaque, who glanced nervously at Morgan, as if to see whether he'd understood and was offended.

Then Bourlamaque frowned, his gaze shifting to the men in the hallway beyond. "Amalie, would you please guide our guest to the table while I greet my officers."

But Morgan knew it wasn't a greeting they'd receive. And, indeed, while Amalie led him to the table, he could hear Bourlamaque's angrily whispered chastisement.

"*Oui,* he is a barbarian, but he is also the grandson of a Scottish lord allied with our king, a Catholic, and a skilled warrior! We stand to gain much from him. You *will* treat him with respect!"

"*Bien, monsieur,*" they answered almost in unison.

So they expected a barbarian, did they?

Morgan would hate to disappoint them.

"I've no doubt Cumberland and his men would have run my brother Iain through had my grandfather not offered himself up instead. He wasna given the chance to fight, but was instead stripped of his sword and taken to a British prison barge to rot. As his heir, my father was exiled from Scotland, his holdings on the Isle of Skye and all that we owned forfeit to the Crown."

"And that is how you came to be in America?" Amalie asked, watching as Monsieur MacKinnon struggled to keep peas upon his fork.

"Aye." He frowned as the peas rolled back onto his plate. Though some might have mocked him for his lack of sophistication, she found it charming. "I was a stripling lad of thirteen. Iain was fifteen, and Connor but twelve."

To his right, Lieutenant Fouchet and Lieutenant Durand were

no longer exchanging smirks, as they'd done when he'd picked up his bowl to sip his soup. They were as caught up in his story as she was.

"Then your father is rightful heir to the MacKinnon titles and lands?" Lieutenant Fouchet asked, not seeming to notice the Ranger's faux pas.

Monsieur MacKinnon resorted to jabbing at his peas with the tongs of his fork, clearly unaware that many would consider his manners vulgar. "My father died four winters past, my mother several years afore him. She never grew accustomed to this land. The frontier is hard on the lasses."

As he spoke those last words, his gaze brushed over Amalie.

"Such a sad tale!" As she watched, she saw him as the young man he must have been, left without parents on the frontier. She knew how it felt to be alone. "It must have been hard to lose so much so young—your home, your possessions, your family."

He met her gaze, and something tickled in her belly. "Aye, it was, but no worse than what other loyal Highland clans suffered."

"So that is how you came to be such a skilled frontiersman," Lieutenant Durand offered. "You were forced to survive on your own."

The Ranger shook his head, then set his fork aside and herded peas into his soupspoon with his thumb. "My brothers and I were adopted into the *Muchquauh*, the Bear Clan, of the Muhheconneok people. As Iain tells it, the old grannies got so tired of us eatin' their food that they decided to make us part of their clan so they could quit treatin' us like guests and send us out to fish and hunt. Our father taught us to wield a sword, but it was the Muhheconneok who taught us to survive."

He popped the spoonful of buttery peas in his mouth and chewed with relish.

"The Duke of Cumberland," Bourlamaque said, a thoughtful look on his face. "Is he not the son of King George?"

Monsieur MacKinnon nodded, a hard look on his handsome face. "Aye, he is, and a bastard if e'er there was one. Pardon my tongue, miss."

"Is Lord Wentworth not the grandson of King George?" Bourlamaque asked.

"Aye, he is. We call him 'the wee German princeling.'"

"Surely not to his face!" Lieutenant Fouchet gaped at the Ranger in disbelief.

"Och, aye, to his face—and worse besides." Monsieur Mac-Kinnon grinned as if such insubordination were nothing more than an amusement.

Fouchet and Durand laughed and raised their glasses in tribute.

But Bourlamaque pressed on, clearly driving toward a point. "Then Cumberland, who so wounded your family, is Wentworth's . . ."

"Uncle," Monsieur MacKinnon finished, sharing a knowing look with Bourlamaque and breaking off a piece of bread with his hands. "Aye."

And Amalie understood. Monsieur MacKinnon and his brothers had suffered all of these insults—the loss of their inheritance, their home, and their freedom—at the hand of the same English family.

"Does he not punish you when you speak disrespectfully to him?" She set her fork aside, too full to eat more.

Monsieur MacKinnon grinned. "He doesna dare. He kens only too well that our men are loyal to us, and no' to him. The Muhheconneok fight beside us and would leave Fort Edward at once should he anger them by harming one of us. Force us to fight he might, but he doesna hold all the power."

"And now he finds himself deprived of your service." Bourlamaque smiled and raised his glass. "*Vive la liberté*. To liberty."

The Ranger raised his glass, his lips curving in a breathtaking smile. "Liberty."

Bourlamaque turned toward Morgan, two crystal snifters of cognac in hand. He offered one to Morgan, then gestured to the chair that sat beside his writing table. "Please sit, Major."

Morgan accepted the glass, then strode over to an ornate chair like the ones he'd seen in Wentworth's study and sat, knowing that the time had come to hold up his part of the agreement. He swirled the glass beneath his nostrils, inhaled, then sipped. It wasn't good Scottish whiskey, but it would do.

He let his gaze travel over the room. A dozen or so leather-bound books sat on a shelf, gold letters on their spines. Another shelf held scrolled maps and charts. An elegant rapier hung on one wall. On the other hung a painting of a woman. Was she perhaps Bourlamaque's wife? Young, bewigged, wearing an elaborate pink gown, she smiled at the viewer, a small dog in her lap, her slender fingers caressing its white coat.

Bourlamaque sat at his writing table, a pensive look on his face. "Before I call my officers in to join us, I must first make myself very clear, Major. If you betray me, I will turn you over to the Abenaki and light the bonfires myself."

Morgan saw in his eyes that he meant what he said. "Och, well, I thought as much. But I owe Wentworth nothin'. So long as you keep your word, I keep mine."

He spoke partly truth—he and his brothers owed Wentworth nothing. Bourlamaque was by far the more honorable man and a Catholic at that. But Morgan's loyalty lay where it always had—with his brothers, with the Rangers.

Bourlamaque nodded, but his expression remained grave. "You must understand that, given your formidable skill as a warrior and the degree to which some of my men hate and fear you, I cannot let you roam freely about the fort. By letting you live, I am taking a great risk. Until I am certain you can be trusted and are in no danger, you will remain confined to my house—as my guest, of course."

So Morgan was to be his prisoner.

"Of course." Morgan met the older man's gaze, raised his glass, and sipped.

Bourlamaque shouted for his men to enter, then settled in his chair, as one by one his officers filed into the study. Tellingly, Rillieux was not amongst them, and Morgan couldn't help but feel some sense of satisfaction. The bastard deserved whatever punishment Bourlamaque had seen fit to bestow upon him.

Morgan met the gazes of the men who stood about him—Fouchet, Durand, and others whose names he had not yet learned. They watched him, a mix of awe, wariness, and curiosity in their eyes.

"Now, Major, tell us everything you know about Amherst's plans for this summer's campaign."

Chapter 11

Morgan paced his room, cursing this idleness, this isolation, and the injury that had so weakened his right leg. No matter how he tried, he couldn't walk without limping. The surgeon had offered to have oxter staffs made for him, but he had refused. If he hoped to make the journey back to Fort Edward, he needed to strengthen his limb, not coddle it. But how could he do that locked in this cage?

And a gilded cage it was. The bed was softer than any Morgan had slept in since his childhood days on Skye, the dressing table of polished wood, the wardrobe filled with foppish garments—silks, fine woolens, and enough velvet and lace for a bloody brothel. Aye, Bourlamaque had given him every promised comfort, except his freedom. For a week now, he'd been Bourlamaque's *guest,* confined to this room except for meals—and those long hours when Bourlamaque had questioned him.

The man had been relentless. With his officers watching, he'd pressed Morgan for every bit of information that might be of use to him. He'd started by asking about Amherst's designs to capture Fort Carillon, the plan of Fort Edward, and how many British troops Wentworth had at his command. He'd wanted to know how Amherst and Wentworth got on and which Indian nations they'd sought to befriend. Then he'd begun to interrogate Morgan in earnest, pounding him with questions about the Rangers.

Who chose the men? How did they train? Where were their supply caches? Who determined how to use the Rangers in battle? Which paths in the forest did they use most frequently? How did they manage to move so silently and invisibly through the forest? What were their most common signs and countersigns? What supplies did they carry with them? How did they learn to shoot with such deadly accuracy? Did all Rangers carry rifled muskets? How many men had been at Morgan's command?

There'd been no time to think, no time to construct careful lies, but Morgan had expected as much. Some of the questions he'd answered truthfully because the answers gave Bourlamaque no advantage. Others he'd answered with half-truths, giving up the locations of old supply caches, abandoned campsites, and trails that the Rangers had long since deserted. Still others he'd answered with lies.

The Rangers had been handpicked by Iain with Morgan's and Connor's help, chosen for their woodcraft and skill with a rifle. They trained at the fort, shooting at marks and practicing with swords or bayonets. They'd learned how to move silently from the Indians. Wentworth chose the Rangers' missions, while Morgan, like Iain before him, commanded them in the field. Signs and countersigns changed with each new dawn. The men learned to shoot well at a young age because they depended upon hunting to fill their bellies. Only officers carried muskets with rifled carbines. Under Morgan's command, the Rangers had numbered six score and four.

His lies they had believed. But Bourlamaque and his officers had thought him dishonest on that last point, though he'd told the truth. Fouchet, Durand, and the other officers had laughed out loud, while Bourlamaque had glared at him.

"Do not trifle with me, Major," he'd said, his face turning an angry scarlet.

Morgan hadn't been able to keep the grin off his face. "I find your doubt flatterin'. You're thinkin' there must have been a thousand of us, aye? In truth, there are precious few. We eat and sleep together, officers and men. Aye, and we train together, too, and call each other by our Christian names. We ken one another well and fight as one. We are more a band of brothers than a company of soldiers. *That* is what makes us Rangers."

He'd all but shouted those last words. And in that moment he'd missed his brothers and his men so much that the pain of it had struck him like a fist to the gut. But the emotion behind his words must have impressed Bourlamaque, for he'd moved on to other matters.

But what Morgan would never tell Bourlamaque was that each Ranger was trained to memorize and follow a set of eight-and-twenty rules—the Rules of Ranging. The Rules had been created to hide the men's numbers, to give them every advantage in battle, and to enable them to work together silently and under fire, as each man knew what the others would do. Though Wentworth knew the Rangers had a set of rules, not even he knew what they were.

Rangers never marched in noisy, cumbersome ranks like British Regulars, but single file and far enough apart that two could not be killed by a single shot. When they marched through marshes or over wet ground, they walked abreast to make their numbers harder to count. When pursued, they circled back to their own tracks, surrounding the enemy in ambush. In battle, they staggered their fire, reloading while those beside them fired, giving the enemy no chance to rest. If the enemy's numbers overwhelmed them, they dispersed, each man for himself, making his way to the next rendezvous point. They never crossed rivers at the usual fords or walked the forest on known paths. They never stopped until long after dark so that the enemy could not see where they made camp, and only half their force was permitted to sleep at once, the others remaining ready to fight lest they be attacked. They rose before dawn and scouted the forest ahead before moving on. They never returned the same way they'd come lest the enemy lie in wait for them. And they never, ever left their flank unguarded.

The Rules of Ranging enabled them to emerge, silent and swift, from the forest, and to vanish again. The Rules helped them fend off much larger forces without heavy losses. The Rules kept them alive.

Morgan would die to keep them secret.

Och, how he hated the game he was playing! He would much rather face the French in an honest fight, rifle and *claidheamh mòr* in hand, than to battle them with lies and wylie words. Still, this was better than perishing in flames.

He strode over to the small glass window, lifted the iron hook, and thrust it open, needing to feel fresh air on his face again. The sun was setting, rosy fingers stretched across the sky, the breeze warm with the scent of wood smoke, roasting meat, and springtime. Somewhere in the distance, French pipes played out a merry tune.

The happy wail made him think of Ranger Camp, where the men were surely settling down with their nightly ration of rum under these same stars. McHugh would be playing his pipes while Dougie tuned his fiddle and old Killy told stories. Joseph and his warriors would be sitting around a fire, telling their own stories. And Connor, left to lead them, would be walking amongst them, speaking with each man, offering him a few words of encouragement, as Morgan had done and Iain before him.

An ache swelled in Morgan's chest, then rose into his throat. Sweet Mary in heaven, how he missed them!

I will see you again, lads, if God is willing.

He drew in a deep breath, ignoring the sentry who had just snapped to alertness and stood in the shadows watching him. Did Bourlamaque truly believe him fool enough to try escaping out his own bloody window? Then from overhead came soft footfalls and the creak of floorboards.

Amalie.

Morgan had seen her only at meals under Bourlamaque's watchful eye, their conversations more guarded than they'd been in the infirmary. Still, Morgan couldn't keep his eyes off her, aware of her as he'd been of no other woman—her every word, every glance, every movement. She seemed to grow bonnier each day, the worry that had lined her face now gone. One smile from her, and he became a blethering idiot, her femininity pulling at him from across the table, heating his blood, making him think of her in ways he shouldn't.

Almost directly overhead, he heard the hook on her window clink against glass, then heard her voice as her window swung open.

"Un bain serait merveilleux, Thérèse. Merci!" A bath would be wonderful, Thérèse. Thank you!

It was as if Morgan had been struck on the head with a bolt of lightning. Whatever thoughts had been in his mind vanished. He stood still and listened as something heavy—no doubt the same copper washtub he'd bathed in this morning—was dragged across her floor. Then came the sound of heated water being poured into the tub, bucket by bucket, followed by the soft murmur of female voices and—was he imagining it?—the rustle of skirts and petticoats. Moments later, he heard the tinkle of water, and he knew she'd stepped into the tub.

He turned his back to the night, leaned against the sill, and closed his eyes, his mind filling with images of her—sensual, arousing, forbidden images. Amalie stepping into the bath, naked, her skin golden in the candlelight, her long hair spilling down her back. Amalie rubbing the soap over her glistening skin, her nipples taut from the gentle lapping of the water. Amalie rising from the tub, water trickling down her skin in rivulets. Amalie reaching for a towel, running it over her breasts and the thatch of dark curls between her thighs. Amalie bending to dry her legs, the twin mounds of her bottom ripe for his touch, the dark cleft of her sex revealed.

He was hard as stone now, his cock straining against his silk drawers, his cods tight and aching for release. He knew he should stop himself, knew he should banish these thoughts from his mind. She was promised to the Church, soon to become a bride of Christ.

You're a cad and a bastard, MacKinnon!

Aye, he was. But even as he tried to stop himself, new thoughts assailed him. Would her nipples be rosy pink, dusky like wine, or a soft fawn brown? Would they be small and supple or large and soft like rose petals? Would they taste—

A knock came at the door, which opened to reveal Bourlamaque.

Morgan stayed where he was, leaning against the windowsill, grateful that his waistcoat covered the bulge of his erection.

Bourlamaque glanced at the open window, then at Morgan, a grin on his face. "My scouting parties returned from the locations you described, Major. They found supply caches precisely where you'd said they would. Tonight, we shall celebrate! I have ordered a feast prepared and have invited all of my officers to attend. Those who have not already met you are most eager to do so."

So, Bourlamaque had followed up on the answers Morgan had

given him and was satisfied that Morgan had told the truth. Morgan's half-truths had worked. He had earned Bourlamaque's trust—at least to some degree.

"Please wear appropriate evening attire." Bourlamaque looked him up and down, no doubt noticing that he'd shed his coat. The old man was astonishingly strict about matters of dress. "Shall I send my valet to assist you?"

"'Tis most generous of you, but I can dress myself."

"Very well." Bourlamaque smiled. "Festivities begin in an hour."

A malie stared at the woman in the looking glass, unable to believe she was looking at her own reflection. "Are you certain?"

"If you wish to catch the Ranger's eye," Thérèse answered, a mischievous smile on her face, "you mustn't be afraid to show the beauty God has given you."

Amalie bit back a laugh, imagining what the *mère supérieure* would say to that.

The musicians were already playing, the sweet strains of violins and flute mingling with the deep rumble of men's voices.

She hadn't meant to take so long, but she hadn't been able to decide how to wear her hair or which gown to choose. In the end, she'd called upon Thérèse, whose nimble fingers had accomplished what Amalie's inexperienced ones could not, shaping her tresses into something elegant atop her head with slender braids that looped down along her nape and disappeared again. It was also Thérèse who had dabbed her lips with rouge and who'd insisted she wear her ivory silk sack gown—the gown her father had given to her for her seventeenth birthday and then promptly forbidden her to wear. Embroidered with tiny pink rosebuds, the gown was cut lower in the bodice than any other gown Amalie owned, leaving the swells of her breasts exposed.

Now, her pulse skipping, she gazed in the looking glass and found a stranger staring back at her. She looked nothing like the girl who'd spent her life inside the gray walls of the convent. Her cheeks were flushed, her lips rosy, her breasts high and round above her décolletage. But most different were her eyes. They gleamed with excitement, anticipation, hope.

Her world had felt so bleak since her father's death—empty, dark, lonely. How strange it was that Morgan MacKinnon—the man who might have killed her father—should be the one to make her feel alive again. Was it wrong for her to feel this way?

She couldn't deny that he fascinated her. His courageous tales of life on the frontier enchanted her. His lilting accent charmed her. The warmth in his eyes when he looked at her left her feeling dizzy.

She'd never met a man like him.

More than once, she'd lain awake at night, thinking of him. She'd remembered how he'd touched her, tracing his thumb across her cheek, his fingers catching in her hair. She'd remembered the feel of him, his body hard where hers was soft. She remembered how he'd risked himself to end Rillieux's hateful kiss, enduring a beating for her sake. And she'd wondered what it would feel like if *he* were to kiss her instead of Rillieux, the very thought stirring her blood, making her heart beat faster.

She thrust the improper thought aside, turned to the left, then to the right, the silk of her skirts swirling about her legs with a pleasing *swish*. "Thank you for your help, Thérèse. I could not have done this without you."

"It was my pleasure, mademoiselle." The kitchen maid smoothed Amalie's skirts, then gave her arm a reassuring squeeze. "He won't be able to keep his eyes off you. But I must get back to the kitchen, or Papa will have my hide. *Bonne chance!*"

Thérèse opened the door and, fingers adjusting the lace cap that covered her brown hair, hurried off and down the stairs.

With one last glance in the looking glass, Amalie followed, pausing to look down over the wooden railing. Below, the sitting room was brightly lit with dozens of candles, the front door open, fresh night air carrying the savory scents of roasted meats in from the cookhouse. Officers stood in a queue that snaked through the house and into the sitting room. They were dressed in clean, crisp uniforms, most wearing wigs, some wearing their natural hair. They'd been invited to meet Monsieur MacKinnon.

She took the railing in one hand, lifted her skirts with the other, then descended the stairs, barely aware of the officers' admiring glances, her gaze seeking one man.

She found him standing beside Bourlamaque, listening to the captain of the grenadiers. Taller than any man in the room,

Monsieur MacKinnon wore a matching coat and breeches of midnight-blue velvet, creamy lace at his throat and wrists, his waistcoat of cream silk with gold brocade and shiny brass buttons. His hair was drawn back, a black ribbon at his nape. Unlike many men, he did not need to wear padding to create the appearance of strong legs; his creamy silk stockings stretched like a second skin over the muscles of his calves.

How different he seemed from the man who'd lain, naked and feverish, upon that little bed in the hospital, more refined gentleman now than fearsome warrior. And yet a warrior he was. She knew what lay beneath the velvet and silk, remembered the look and feel of him—warrior marks, wampum armbands, soft skin over bands of hard muscle.

Feeling almost breathless with excitement, she approached him. He did not immediately see her, but listened while the captain spoke, a look of respectful interest on his handsome face, a glass of cognac in his left hand.

"My wife's *cousine,* she is married to a MacDonald. His family fled to France after the misfortunate defeat of your prince."

"There are many MacDonalds. Do you ken which branch of the MacDonald clan—Ranald, Glengarry, Keppoch, Glencoe?"

The captain shook his head, seeming overwhelmed by the rush of exotic names. "No, alas, Major, but my wife tells me that it is a good match—seven children in nine years. Both the French and the Scots are passionate people, are they not?"

It was then he saw her, his gaze sliding over her like a caress. "Aye, Captain, passionate."

"Ah, Amalie, there you are!" Bourlamaque reached out for her, switching into French. "How enchanting you look tonight! I've never seen that gown before. Something your father bought for you?"

"Oui." She barely heard a word her guardian said, her gaze fixed on Monsieur MacKinnon, who watched her, a hungry look in his eyes that made her heart beat faster. She held out her hand to him. "Major MacKinnon."

"Miss Chauvenet." He bowed, raised her hand to his lips, his gaze never leaving hers. "You are the flower of us all, lass."

Amalie felt herself blush, wondering how she might thank Thérèse. "You are too kind, monsieur."

Morgan was surprised to find that he could still speak. He'd caught sight of her, and his thoughts had scattered like leaves in a storm, his tongue forced to find words on its own. If he'd been any more conflummoxed, he wouldn't have been able to talk at all.

Sweet Mary, she was beautiful! Hair arranged gracefully on her head, little braids like lace at her nape. Full lips, red and ready for kissing. The creamy swells of her breasts, ripe for a man's touch—*his* touch. Her eyes bright with feminine happiness.

She said something. He answered. She laughed, the sound like music.

And just like that, the images that had filled his mind when he'd listened to her bathe came back to him—nipples tight against lapping water, wet skin in candlelight, damp curls between her thighs.

She's an innocent, you radgie bastard. Pledged to the Church, aye?

But Morgan had never seen a nun who looked like this. He wanted to take off his coat and drape it around her shoulders or send her up to her room to change into something more . . . nunnish. But he wasn't her guardian. Nor was he her husband, nor even her lover.

It isna your place to object, lad.

Before he could act, Bourlamaque brought the next man forward to meet him. Grenadiers. Fusiliers. Infantrymen. Scouts. Artillerymen. His head swam with their names, but try as he might, he could not keep his gaze from returning to Amalie, who stood beside her guardian, offering a smile and kind words to each man.

And then it was time for supper.

Roasted venison, stuffed partridge, suckling pig—the tables groaned under the weight of delicacies prepared by Bourlamaque's kitchen, wineglasses kept full throughout the evening. Careful not to drink too much lest it loosen his tongue and set him to speaking French, Morgan ate his fill, his heightened sense of awareness a result not of wine, but of the intoxicating lass who sat across from him at the head table to Bourlamaque's left.

She asked him to share his stories, and for her sake, he did. He told them of the time he and Connor had rigged the bateau bridge so that Lieutenant Cooke fell in the river, the time the Rangers had dressed as Indians and set upon Fort Edward to distract

Wentworth from pursuing Annie while Iain was away, the time they'd dropped cannonballs from the fort walls to soften the rock-hard biscuits the British had given them to eat.

As the meal drew to its end, the officers gathered around the head table, the better to hear him. Though they seemed entertained by these tales, it was not their response that mattered to Morgan, but hers—the magic of her laughter, the beauty of her smile, the wistful look in her eyes whenever he mentioned Iain and Annie.

Aye, the lass was a romantic.

"We dropped a dozen six-pounders from a height of twenty feet, but 'twas the hogshead that shattered," Morgan said, eliciting laughter from the men and making Amalie smile again.

Och, how he wanted to pull the pins from her hair, one by one, until her tresses fell past her hips, thick and heavy and soft as silk. How he longed to kiss those lips, to taste her. How he ached to strip away layers of silk and lace, to expose her loveliness to his view, to mold her breasts in his hands and hear her sigh as her nipples hardened against his palms.

He forced his gaze away from Amalie's sweet face, afraid he would betray his thoughts by gaping at her like a lovesick fool. "Wentworth couldna deny that bread unbroken by a cannonade wasna fit for mice or men to eat. He sent it back to Albany wi' the sutler and ordered us fed from his own stores."

Amalie laughed, the sound sweet and clear. The men chuckled.

Then one man's voice rose above the rest. "Your lord Wentworth tolerates much insubordination."

Amalie's smile vanished as Rillieux stepped forward and came to stand beside her chair. In full uniform, he wore a scowl on his face, bruises still visible at his throat.

Morgan rose to his feet. "Wentworth isna my laird."

Silence fell over the room, the blood draining from Amalie's face.

Bourlamaque stood. *"Joignez-vous à nous, Rillieux, mais il n'est pas question de nous faire partager votre mauvaise humeur! Je ne tolèrerai aucune discorde entre mes officiers."*

Join us, Rillieux, but do not think to spread your ill humor here. I will not tolerate dissension amongst my officers.

Then he turned to Morgan. "Gentlemen, I ask that you make your peace and embrace as brothers. You fight for the same king now and must respect one another. Do you understand, Major? Lieutenant?"

Morgan would be damned if he'd embrace the bastard. Instead, he nodded and held out his hand to Rillieux, affecting a look of contrition. "Aye, sir. And right you are. I'm certain Lieutenant Rillieux and I are content to let bygones be bygones."

Lieutenant Rillieux took his hand and shook, squeezing hard. "*Oui, monsieur.* I harbor no ill will toward Major MacKinnon."

Amalie gave an audible sigh of relief.

Bourlamaque raised his glass. "To victory!"

"To victory!" The cry repeated through the room.

"To victory." Morgan lifted his glass and drank, his gaze locking with Rillieux's and finding the hatred there undimmed.

The *neach dìolain* hadn't meant a word he'd said.

Of course, neither had Morgan.

Chapter 12

A malie stood outside the gates, watching as Monsieur Mac-Kinnon prepared to demonstrate his skill as a marksman. She'd been finishing her breakfast, disappointed to have found herself alone at the table, when Thérèse had rushed in from the cookhouse breathless with news.

"Come, Miss Chauvenet! Monsieur MacKinnon is going to shoot at marks! Everyone is watching," she'd said, an excited smile on her face.

Amalie had leapt up from the table and hurried outside. Apart from those on sentry duty, the entire fort had come to watch, soldiers standing at ease in their ranks, grumbling to one another, a mixture of curiosity and resentment on their faces. She thought she understood. A man they'd hated as an enemy had now been raised above them, chosen by Bourlamaque to teach them to be better fighters. Their pride would not let them see the good in this.

And yet she knew that once they'd come to know Monsieur MacKinnon, they would see, as she and Bourlamaque and now most of the officers had come to see—that he was not a monster, but a good man, and more valuable to France as an ally than as an offering to the Abenaki.

Last night had proved to her that hearts could be changed. By the end of the evening, even Lieutenant Rillieux admitted a grudging respect for Monsieur MacKinnon, putting aside his jealousy and resentment. If Lieutenant Rillieux could do so after all that had transpired between him and the Ranger, so could these soldiers.

"We shall put your celebrated marksmanship to the test," Bourlamaque said first in English and then again in French so that everyone could understand. "Your marks stand at three hundred paces. You have a minute to fire three shots."

It was a hard task Bourlamaque had set for him. Everyone knew that only the best marksmen could fire so rapidly, and Amalie found herself wondering whether her guardian was trying to ensure that Monsieur MacKinnon failed.

But Monsieur MacKinnon acted as if he hadn't a care in the world. He smiled, said something to Bourlamaque, his gaze on the paper mark. He had removed his coat and waistcoat and stood, his long hair tied back in a thong, wearing only his shirt and breeches—a state of undress Bourlamaque as a rule did not allow except amongst Indians.

Amalie strained to hear.

"Begin at my signal," Bourlamaque said, raising his pistol.

Then he fired.

Monsieur MacKinnon moved quickly, priming and loading his weapon with a dexterity born of experience. His first shot split the air, but the marks were too far away for Amalie to see whether he had struck his target. Already he was reloading, Amalie's heartbeat seeming to tick off the seconds. He raised his weapon, fired his second shot, his big hands moving over the weapon with ease, his gaze still on his mark. Then his third shot rang out, his rifle coming to rest at his side before Fouchet called the time.

"*Excellent!*" Bourlamaque smiled, motioning to two soldiers to fetch the mark and carry it back for him to judge.

The target showed three holes, all close together in the center. A murmur passed through the crowd, grudging praise mixed with spiteful curses.

"So the whoreson is passable with a flintlock," said a soldier standing nearby.

"Passable? You couldn't have done that on your best day," answered another.

Amalie released the breath she hadn't realized she was holding, feeling an undeniable swell of pride. Then, as if he'd known she was watching, Monsieur MacKinnon turned his head and met her gaze, his lips curving into a lopsided grin. She smiled back, her belly seeming to flip, her cheeks suddenly warm.

"Shall we try three hundred and fifty paces?" Bourlamaque asked him.

"If you wish." Monsieur MacKinnon cleaned the barrel of his rifle while the paces were measured out and the target was set in place, then nodded when he was ready.

Bourlamaque raised his pistol again, fired.

Three shots, three more holes in the center ring of the target.

More murmurs, some now admiring.

"Very well done, Major." Bourlamaque was quite clearly pleased. "It is rare to see such accuracy at that distance."

"Let's raise the stakes of this little game, shall we?" Monsieur MacKinnon grinned.

"What do you suggest?"

"I shall try for four shots."

"Four?" Bourlamaque chuckled. "No man can fire four shots in a minute."

"Would you care to stake a wager? If I fire four shots—and strike the target each time—then will you grant me a boon?"

Whispers passed through the crowd of soldiers like a breeze. Four shots? It could not be done. This MacKinnon was mad. He must be!

Even from a distance, Amalie could see Bourlamaque's eyes narrow. "What would you ask of me?"

"If I succeed, then I ask that Miss Chauvenet set about teachin' me your tongue. I cannae be livin' amongst you never understandin' a word of your speech."

Amalie felt all eyes upon her, including Bourlamaque's. Her guardian looked as if he were about to deny the Ranger's request, or perhaps to suggest someone else serve as his teacher. But that would not do. Pulse skipping, she called out, "I accept!"

For a moment there was silence.

Bourlamaque looked from her to Monsieur MacKinnon, then back to her again. "Very well. This I should like very much to see."

A look of concentration on his face, the Ranger cleaned the

barrel of his flintlock once more, adjusted his powder horn and bag of shot, then gave a nod.

Bourlamaque raised his pistol, fired.

This time, rather than priming the flintlock, the Ranger took a handful of lead balls from his bag—and tossed them into his mouth.

The soldiers howled with laughter at the strange sight, mocking him.

"Is that how his kind grow so tall—eating lead?"

"The fool! Does he truly think he's that much better than the rest of us?"

"If he fails, we shall throw him in the river to teach him a lesson in humility!"

But Monsieur MacKinnon did not seem distracted by their words, perhaps because he could not understand them. His hands moved with practiced familiarity over the rifle, priming it, then pouring powder down the barrel. Then he did something Amalie had never seen done before. He spat one of the balls into the barrel, raised the rifle—and fired. Before the retort of the shot had faded, he was reloading.

And Amalie understood. By holding the lead balls in his mouth, he saved himself the few seconds it took to pluck one from his pouch and ram it into the barrel. And those few seconds would make all the difference in battle.

Two shots.

Three.

Then time seemed to slow down, Amalie watching each sure motion of his hands as he reloaded a fourth time, spat the last ball down the barrel, and took aim, the fourth shot exploding a moment before Fouchet opened his mouth to call the time.

All around her, soldiers cheered, their whoops and shouts growing louder when the target was brought forth, showing four dark holes.

Monsieur MacKinnon had hit his mark each time.

He lowered the rifle to his side, then glanced at Bourlamaque, an amused look on his face rather than one of triumph. And Amalie realized he'd made the wager knowing he could do it. He'd done it before.

Warrior or gentleman? 'Twas clear Morgan MacKinnon was both.

She took a step forward, wanting to congratulate him, but a strong hand closed around her arm, and she was pulled away.

"*Kwai, nadôgweskwa.*"

"Tomas!" She looked up to find him glaring down at her, fury unmistakable on his face, Simon beside him. "What——?"

"I have long wondered whether the daughter of my mother's sister thinks of herself as French or Wabenaki. Now I know. She is neither French nor Indian, but instead has become the whore of the Inglismôn, this MacKinnon." He spat on the ground.

Too stunned to speak, Amalie gaped at him.

"He was ours, Amalie, promised to us by Montcalm. Now he dines with Bourlamaque, while we, who kept our promises to our French brothers, camp outside the walls and are sent away with useless blankets, kettles, and beads! *You* asked Bourlamaque to spare him. Why?"

But Amalie was angry now, too, fury freeing her tongue. "I am no man's whore! You've a filthy tongue, Tomas! And though I am French and Abenaki, I am also Catholic. Do you hear nothing the priests say? It is barbaric and cruel to burn a man alive! The people of Oganak must learn to forgive him, even as I have forgiven him."

Tomas and Simon stared at her as if she'd taken leave of her senses.

Then the rage on Tomas's face turned to disgust. "You have lived your life amongst them. You cannot understand. Blood can only be avenged with blood. We *will* have him, little Amalie, and nothing you or Bourlamaque can do will stop us."

With that, the two of them turned and walked away, leaving Amalie to stare after them.

Morgan looked for Amalie in the cheering crowd, but she was gone. Though disappointed, he didn't think much of it, his spirits high. What a benison it was to feel the sun warm upon his face, to have the wind in his hair, to hold the weight of his musket in his hands. Breathing in the air, he felt alive again—truly alive. And it was sweet, so sweet, that he'd forgotten the peril he still faced and the devil's bargain he'd made—until Bourlamaque took his musket from him again and locked it away with his other gear.

The man did not yet trust him.

Clever fellow.

He did not see Amalie again until the midday meal, and he knew the moment he saw her that something was amiss. She said nary a word as she ate, her gaze meeting his, something urgent and unspoken in her eyes. Not until after the meal when Bourlamaque called him into his study did he discover what it was.

"Amalie is quite concerned," Bourlamaque said, sitting at his writing table and looking none too blythe himself. "It seems the Abenaki are displeased with my decision to grant you clemency."

Morgan kept his voice measured. "They've been cheated of their blood vengeance, aye? I kent they wouldna accept it."

"Her cousins told her that they would permit nothing to stop them from taking you back to Oganak—not even me." Bourlamaque raised a bushy eyebrow as if he did not know what to make of such defiance.

Morgan wondered if this was the first time he'd found himself at odds with his Indian allies. "Surely, they wouldna chance your wrath. They rely upon you for rifles, blankets, and many other things besides."

"You needn't doubt whether I will keep my word," Bourlamaque continued, "but I cannot say for certain whether all of my men will honor my agreement with you. I watched their faces today. Most were in awe of you. But some hated you all the more for your skill with a firelock. Should any amongst them collude with the disgruntled Abenaki, it would not be so difficult a task to spirit one man beyond the walls."

"I will do whate'er I must to defend myself." Morgan met Bourlamaque's gaze, made certain the older man knew he meant what he said.

"I expected no less." Bourlamaque glanced down at his writing table, where a missive lay, Montcalm's flowery script at the bottom, his seal upon it. "I have ordered my officers to spread the word that you are an honorable man and a good Catholic in hopes that it will defuse some of the hatred."

He made no effort to cover the letter, no doubt believing that Morgan could not read it. But even with the letters upside down, Morgan was able at a glance to recognize his own name and read the words *prisonnier* and *notre avantage,* and *le tuer.*

Prisoner. Our advantage. To kill him.

He looked away lest Bourlamaque catch him. "I'm grateful for all you've done, but 'tis I who must win their trust. You and your officers cannae do that for me."

"There is more." Bourlamaque leaned back in his chair. "The Abenaki are blaming Amalie in part. Her cousins called her your whore, accosting her in a way that alarms me. I am not familiar with their customs. Should I fear for her safety as well?"

It was on the tip of Morgan's tongue to demand her cousins' names so that he might answer their vile words with the edge of his sword or his fists, but he knew Bourlamaque would never allow it. He swallowed his anger, kept his face impassive. "I am blood kin to the Muhheconneok—the Mahican—not the Abenaki. But from what I ken of their ways, they wouldna seek to harm a kinswoman unless they felt betrayed by her."

Morgan would make certain that never happened.

Bourlamaque released a breath, seemed more at ease. "I'll be grateful when she's safely back at the abbey. Her father, God rest his soul, should never have permitted her to stay here. I would never forgive myself if anything were to happen to her while she was in my care. I had hoped she'd agree to marry Lieutenant Rillieux, but . . ." He shrugged, his voice trailing off.

He'd wanted Amalie to marry that arrogant bastard? Was he daft?

That's what Morgan thought, but it's not what he said, seeking instead for something tactful. "Och, well, she is pledged to the Church, aye?"

Bourlamaque shook his head. "Amalie? No, Major. She has not yet decided whether to take vows or marry. Her father told me that she found life at the abbey stifling, and yet I have little choice but to send her back to Trois Rivières until the war is over. She cannot remain here."

"Nay, she cannae," Morgan agreed, trying to take in what he'd just heard.

So, the lass was not quite as bound to the Church as she'd led him to believe. Aye, that explained the gown she'd worn last evening. But had she meant to mislead him?

He thought back.

Are you pledged to the Church?

Were it not for this war, I should have returned to the abbey at Trois Rivières by now.

He'd asked the question, and she had answered without answering. She hadn't trusted him then, hadn't wished to answer his questions. Now he knew the truth.

Amalie was free to marry, if she chose—free to know a man's loving.

Dinnae be longin' after what you cannae ha', laddie, for if she takes any man into her bed, it willna be you.

Nay, it wouldn't be him. It couldn't be him. His life lay elsewhere, with his brothers and his men. As soon as he was able, he would escape and return to them. Then Amalie would realize she'd been right to mistrust him.

And she would hate him.

A malie slipped into her nightgown, then sat at her dressing table and began to brush the tangles from her hair. She knew she was silly to worry. Bourlamaque would not let her cousins spirit Monsieur MacKinnon away, nor was the Ranger a defenseless child to be carried off like a bundle of firewood. If Tomas were foolish enough to try to steal Monsieur MacKinnon from Fort Carillon, he would likely be the worse for it.

Amalie did not want that either. Though she did not know her cousins well, they were her only tie to her mother's kin, and she was fond of them, especially Simon, whose bright smiles had always made her feel at ease. And yet as much as she hoped to retain their affection, she would not tolerate Tomas's foul insults— nor would she look the other way while he plotted to kill Monsieur MacKinnon.

Bourlamaque had assured her that he would not permit any man—whether French or Abenaki—to scheme against the Ranger and had promised to warn Monsieur MacKinnon himself. Then he'd told her not to worry.

"Go and enjoy the day, Amalie. It saddens me to see you so distressed."

It *had* been a beautiful day, and she'd spent most of the afternoon tending Bourlamaque's garden, the sky bright and blue above her and filled with calls of birds—the plaintive cries of gulls soaring over the water, the lively *purty-purty-purty* of cardinals that flitted along the forest's edge, the watery warble of bluebirds building their nest in the chapel's eaves. The warm air had been rich with the scent of earth and sun and growing things, life renewing itself all around her.

Still, she hadn't been able to forget Tomas's words.

We will have him, and nothing you or Bourlamaque can do will stop us.

Monsieur MacKinnon had been closed up in Bourlamaque's study all evening. She'd settled in the sitting room with her embroidery, hoping to congratulate him on his marksmanship—and to warn him to be careful. But the hour had grown late. Her eyes strained from trying to make neat stitches by candlelight, she'd set her embroidery aside and retired to her room.

Outside her bedroom window, a breeze carried the promise of rain, the strains of pipes and fiddles in the distance. Tomas and Simon were out there somewhere. Were they plotting against Monsieur MacKinnon even now?

Just as the question crossed her mind, she heard a door open and close below stairs, followed by footsteps in the hallway.

She set her brush aside, grabbed her blue silk shawl, and opened her door, then tiptoed over to the stair railing and peeked over the edge.

Monsieur MacKinnon stood in the sitting room below, arms crossed over his chest, looking through the window into the night. Even in the candlelight she could see the brooding look on his handsome face. Mindful that she was wearing only her nightgown, she wrapped the shawl tighter around her and tiptoed down the stairs.

Chapter 13

Morgan looked out the window, his gaze focused on the darkness beyond. Night was when he missed them most—Iain, Annie, Connor, Joseph, and the men. The dark seemed to press in on him, doubts and troubles niggling at him, his home so far away. Would he live to see them again?

'Twould be all but impossible to escape from inside Fort Carillon. Every man amongst the French now knew his face, so he could not hope to steal a French uniform and simply stroll out of the gates. Nor could he leave the house by night, as both his window and the front doors were kept under watch. Bourlamaque did not yet trust him enough to send him into the forest with French troops to scout. Until he did, Morgan would have no chance to slip away.

'Twas time he set about learning all he could of the French, of Montcalm and his designs for the summer campaign. Tonight was the night. Tonight Morgan would wait till Bourlamaque was asleep and then—

He heard her soft footsteps, saw her at the bottom of the stairs, and forgot all else. She tiptoed toward him in her white linen nightgown, a blue shawl draped modestly about her shoulders, her long hair hanging past her hips, her feet bare. Though he tried, he couldn't keep his gaze from sliding over her, for although her shoulders were covered, her bosom was not. He could see the dusky outline of her nipples against the linen, her breasts firm and full—made for a man's hands. She gazed up at him with trust in her eyes, her face angelic in the candlelight.

'Tis a bloody good thing she cannae read your thoughts, aye, laddie?

He sucked in a breath, willed himself to look away from her, tried to speak. "'Tis late to be out of bed, lass."

Did she know what she did to him? Nay, surely not. She'd lived far too sheltered a life to understand that she could bind a man in knots and set him aflame.

"I . . . I wanted to speak with you." She sounded troubled.

"Is somethin' amiss?"

"I . . . wanted to congratulate you, monsieur. You are quite the marksman."

"You forsook your bed to tell me that?" He didn't believe it for an instant.

She lifted her chin, pink stealing into her cheeks. "Also, I need to know when you should like to begin your French lessons."

"I must speak wi' Bourlamaque, for my time isna my own. You ken that, aye?"

"Oui." She looked away, unable to meet his gaze.

For a moment there was silence.

Then, unable to keep himself from touching her, he tucked a finger beneath her chin and forced her to look up at him. Her eyes were wide and dark and shadowed by fear. "Dinnae tell me that you've stayed awake to speak words that could have been shared over breakfast. Why are you standin' here in your nightgown, lass?"

Monsieur MacKinnon stood so near to Amalie that she could smell him—the spice and salt of his skin, the hint of cognac on his breath, the whiff of pine soap in his hair. He seemed to press in on her, to fill her senses, to surround her until there was nothing else but him.

She drew a shaky breath. "I fear for you, monsieur."

"Bonnie, sweet Amalie." He chuckled, his use of her Christian name startling. "Twice now you have protected me. You saved my life, and for that I am eternally in your debt. But you shouldna be losin' sleep over idle threats. I'm no longer defenseless and shackled. I can protect myself, aye?"

She nodded, knowing that he was right and yet still unable to shake her sense of misgiving. "If my cousins try to take you, someone I care about will suffer—either you or them."

"Ah." He drew a breath, cupped her cheek in his palm, his gaze seeming to pierce her. "Hear me, Amalie. I will do whate'er I must to protect myself, but I willna kill them unless they gi' me no choice. Och, if only you were in the safety of the abbey. You could forget this place and its troubles."

She drew back. "How could I forget Fort Carillon? My father died and is buried here. If we cannot hold this bit of land, it will not be long before the British reach Trois Rivières. And then where would I go? Besides, I am not at all certain I wish to return to life at the abbey."

"Then you wish to marry?" His voice was deep and as smooth as midnight.

Overwhelmed by him, Amalie stammered. "I—I thought I did, until . . ."

"Until what?"

She felt heat rush into her cheeks and knew she was trapped, cornered by her own words. She had no choice but to explain. "Until Rillieux kissed me."

In a rush of words, she told him what Sister Marie Louise had said about the miseries of marriage, embarrassed to share something so private with him.

As she spoke, a smile began to spread over his face, until he stood, grinning down at her. "So you're thinkin' that Rillieux's kiss proves that the good sister spoke truly when she said that servin' a husband is a travail?"

"*Yes.*"

His eyes narrowed, his gaze upon her as if he were studying her, a grin tugging at his lips. "There's one wee kinch to your thinkin'. What Rillieux did to you—that wasna truly a kiss."

"It . . . It wasn't?" The look in his eyes made her belly flutter.

"Nay, it wasna." He reached out, wrapped an arm around her waist, and—*mon Dieu!*—she knew what he meant to do. "*This* is a kiss."

He ducked down and brushed her lips ever so lightly with his, turning his head from side to side, the touch feather soft, warm. The contact stilled her breath, made her pulse skip and her lips tingle, something sweet shivering through her.

"Och, lass, you could make a man go daft!" He moved as if to withdraw, and for a moment she feared the kiss was over. But he shifted his hold to draw her closer, one big hand sliding into her hair to cradle her head, his mouth claiming hers.

And she realized it had just begun.

This was a kiss? It felt like a fever, wisps of flame flaring to life in her belly and licking through her as his lips coaxed and caressed hers. His tongue traced the outline of her mouth, then shocked her by slipping inside, seeking *her* tongue, tasting her, stroking secret places, his fingers caressing her spine through the linen of her nightgown. Overwhelmed by new sensations, she heard herself whimper, felt her knees turn to water, and melted into the hard wall of his chest, her fingers clenched in his thick hair.

Morgan knew he should stop. He'd been a bloody fool to start this. He'd wanted to show her that she needn't fear men, had wanted to blot out any memory of Rillieux's brutality. Or that's what he'd told himself. In truth, he'd wanted to kiss her since the moment he'd learned she was not promised to the Church—and so he had.

Aye, he should stop. But the lass was so warm and willing in his arms, kissing him back with a passion he had not expected, a passion that roused his own, making him want far more than a single kiss. But he could not take what he wanted, not tonight, not tomorrow, not ever.

Slowly, he released her and took a step back, stroking her cheek with his knuckles, his body drawn tight as a bowstring, blood pounding through his veins, rushing to his groin. *"Amalie."*

Breathless and trembling, she looked up at him through wide eyes, her lips wet and swollen, her hands fisted in the cloth of his coat.

It took every bit of will he possessed not to pull her into his arms and begin again. "Tell me, lass. Was my kiss a travail?"

She touched her fingers to her lips. "No, monsieur. It was . . . *wonderful.*"

The swell of masculine pride he felt was cut short by the sound of a door opening—and men's voices.

"You must go, Amalie, but first promise me one thing."

"What it is?"

"Dinnae put yourself in harm's way for my sake. Denounce

me to your cousins. Forsay me. Curse me if you must, but dinnae risk yourself, aye?"

Her eyes grew wide. "I . . . I could not do that, monsieur!"

The men's voices grew louder, Bourlamaque's amongst them. Morgan knew it was only a matter of moments before Amalie was discovered. He couldn't imagine that the old man would be pleased to see his ward standing half naked, her lips slick and swollen from kissing, beside a man he did not truly trust.

"Aye, lass, you can. You must. Now go!"

She turned and fled toward the stairs on bare feet.

Morgan called after her in a loud whisper, "And, Amalie."

She glanced over her shoulder at him.

"When we're alone, call me Morgan."

"*Oui.* Morgan." She smiled, his name like music on her lips. And then she was gone.

U nable to sleep, Amalie stared into the darkness, her fingers tracing her lips as she recalled every astonishing, delightful, exciting moment of Monsieur MacKinnon's kiss. The strength of his arms around her. The soft caress of his lips. The shock of his tongue inside her mouth. The hardness of his body against hers. The feel of his fingers clutched in her hair.

She'd never felt the way he'd made her feel—feverish, her heart beating too quickly, her blood thick and warm. Had it been the same for him?

Och, lass, you could make a man go daft!

Oui, it had.

A frisson ran through her, a lance of heat.

"Morgan." She whispered his Christian name, savoring the feel of it on her tongue, then repeated it, trying to say it as he said it, with the quick, rolling *R.* "*Mor*gan. Morgan MacKinnon."

And she knew for certain she did not wish to return to the abbey.

E ven had he meant to sleep, Morgan would not have been able to, not with Amalie's taste still in his mouth, her scent on his skin. He stared into the darkness, turning in his bed, his blood too hot, his mind filled with her—the soft sound of her whimpers, the press of her soft body against his, the silky feel of her hair in his fingers.

'Tis your own doin', you witless idiot.

Aye, there was no denying that. But at least now she knew what a kiss truly was. She wouldn't make the mistake of fleeing to the abbey and taking vows because of what that *neach dìolain* Rillieux had done to her.

How selfless and noble of you to help her wi' that, MacKinnon. You're a real gentleman, a bloody saint! The patron saint of conflummixt virgins—that's you.

In truth, it would be far better for her if he'd never touched her. He'd seen the light in her eyes as she'd walked upstairs. She'd begun to have feelings for him, and the kiss had only made matters worse. Whether she knew it or not, she could not risk being too closely bound to him. There was too great a chance that her cousins and, aye, the French soldiers themselves would take their anger out on her. 'Twas one thing to have played a role in sparing his life. 'Twould be something else if the men of Fort Carillon came to think of her as his woman.

And yet Morgan hadn't been able to restrain himself tonight, the lure of her lush body, her ripe femininity, her naive innocence a greater temptation than he could withstand, the feel of her in his arms so right, so perfect.

Tormented by his own lust, he tossed and turned for what seemed like hours, until he gave in to the inevitable, loosed the fall of his breeches, grasped his aching cock, and stroked himself to release, his thoughts wrapped around Amalie—the sweetness of her mouth, the soft press of her breasts against his ribs, the thrust of her dusky nipples.

His hunger for her blunted but not satisfied, he lay awake until the silences of the night deepened and the fort seemed utterly still. Then, forcing Amalie from his mind, he rose and walked on bare feet silently to the door. He knew there was a guard outside his window and outside the front door. Was there also a guard outside his door, someone charged with making sure he stayed in his bed?

He pressed his ear against the door and listened, but he heard nothing—no creaking floorboards, no telltale breathing, no brush of clothing. Only silence.

He grasped the handle, opened the door a crack, and peeked into the hallway. It was dark and looked empty. He opened the door wider and waited, knowing he could not blunder. If he were caught, he would burn.

He walked out of the room, treading carefully down the hall-way lest he step on a creaky floorboard and give himself away. Bourlamaque slept across from Amalie upstairs, but like any old soldier, he most likely slept lightly, one ear always listening for the fight. It would take little to wake him.

Past the sitting room Morgan walked, careful not to bump the large carven console, where a single thick beeswax candle burnt away the hours of the night, its flame reflected in the console's silver looking glass. On he went through the dark, step by slow, silent step, past the dining room to the far corner, where he found the door to Bourlamaque's study closed, as he'd thought it would be.

And now came the test. Would Morgan be able to open the lock without waking Bourlamaque or leaving telltale scratches upon the brass knob, or would he find himself thwarted? He drew from the pocket of his breeches the tiny awl he'd secreted away when Bourlamaque had given him leave this morning to take from his tumpline pack whatever he needed to clean and prepare his rifle. As a rule, Morgan used the little tool to repair moccasins or snow-shoes. Tonight, he would use it for espionage.

He grasped the knob, raised the awl to the keyhole—and felt the knob turn.

It hadn't been locked.

Bourlamaque had either forgotten to lock it or, believing that Morgan did not understand French, hadn't seen the need.

Morgan stood and tucked the awl back into his pocket, then he slowly opened the door and walked inside.

"*Vaudreuil again complained that after taking Fort William Henry I did not continue southward and also capture Fort Edward.*" Montcalm's handwriting was cramped, small, confus-ing, and in the weak light of a single candle, at times almost inde-cipherable. "*I ended by telling him quietly that when I went to war I did the best I could and that when one is not pleased with one's lieutenants, one had better take the field in person.*"

Careful not to drip wax, Morgan glanced through the letters once more, thinking through what he'd read, knowing it was past time for him to return to his room. 'Twould be dawn soon, and he had learned enough for one night.

'Twas clear from Montcalm's letters that he and Bourlamaque felt deep affection for each other, writing as familiars and discussing personal matters as much as military ones. Both men missed France and the families they'd left behind. Montcalm sought a husband for his daughter and a wife for his son, and had frequent correspondence with his mother, who kept both men abreast of matters in Paris. Morgan had also learned that Montcalm cared not one whit for the foppish French governor, le Vicomte Rigaud de Vaudreuil, who seemed to belittle him at every turn, perhaps out of envy. And he'd learned of Montcalm and Bourlamaque's shared frustrations—not enough coin, not enough trained soldiers, and seeming indifference on the part of King Louis to the small part of this war that was being fought in America.

As he'd read through the letters, he felt like he'd come to know both men. Both were honorable to a fault, men of duty and principle, high-minded men who loved their king and their country and were willing to give their lives in its service. They were better men in every way than Wentworth, men Morgan would have been honored to serve.

Instead, he must deceive and betray them.

He had also learned military secrets this night. The bulk of the French force—almost fourteen thousand men—was being deployed to defend Québec, leaving only about three thousand Regular troops and one thousand Canadian partisans for Bourlamaque, who was charged with holding the line at Lake Champlain. Redoubts, breastworks, and other defensive works were being thrown up along the St. Lawrence in anticipation of an attack.

"I regret I cannot send more men, but we are now certain Amherst intends to send a fleet against us up the St. Lawrence from Louisbourg, and I cannot let Québec City fall," Montcalm had written in his most recent missive. *"We shall save this unhappy colony or perish."*

He had also warned Bourlamaque against trusting Morgan.

"I, too, find the native people's ways distressing, but do not forget, my dear B., that, although you now call him your guest, he is in truth still your prisoner. Although you may yet turn this

impulsive decision of yours to our advantage, he is a cunning adversary and not to be underestimated. Should he prove false, do not hesitate to kill him."

And well Morgan knew that Bourlamaque would not hesitate.

Taking great care, he put the letters back where he'd found them, laying the most recent missive on the writing table faceup as Bourlamaque had left it. Checking to be certain he hadn't disturbed anything, Morgan walked quietly from the study, closed the door behind him, and made his way silently back to his room, setting the candle in its place on the console as he passed.

When at last he stretched out on his bed, he wondered which would be the greater sin—betraying the deceiving bastard he'd promised under threat of death to obey or betraying the honest, honorable men who by woesome chance were his enemies.

Chapter 14

As Père François recited the sacred Latin words of the Mass, Amalie knelt, her head bowed, her rosary clasped between her folded hands, her mind far from prayer. Morgan sat behind her. As if through heightened senses, she could feel the heat of him, smell him, hear his deep voice through those of every other man in the chapel.

"*Dominus vobiscum,*" Père François intoned.

The Lord be with you.

"*Et cum spiritu tuo,*" Amalie answered in unison with the others, not because she was truly listening, but rather out of habit.

Was it her imagination or was Morgan avoiding her?

He was, of course, bound by his duty to Bourlamaque and the army. She understood that and was not so foolish or selfish to begrudge him the time he spent at his labors. In truth, she admired his dedication. But why at the end of the day, when his duty was done, did he have no kind word and not a moment for her?

These past four days he'd been hard-faced, stern, even brusque with her. He ignored her at meals, saying only as much to her as was necessary for the sake of politeness. Each night he'd retired to his room after having a brandy with Bourlamaque and the other officers, not even glancing her way as he bade the others good night. And when she'd approached him and Bourlamaque to ask them when his French lessons should begin, he'd cut her short.

"I'm certain the chevalier has other things he'd rather see me doin', Miss Chauvenet," he'd said, his tone measured, his blue eyes devoid of any affection.

Bourlamaque had chided her in French. "Do not badger the poor man, Amalie!"

Blinking back tears, she'd bowed her head. *"Pardonnez-moi, monsieur."*

Then she'd hurried away to her room, feeling utterly humiliated. Hadn't it been Morgan himself who'd asked to learn French? And what about the kiss? Four nights ago, there'd been nothing dour or hard-faced or stern about him when he'd kissed her senseless. He'd seemed just as moved as she had been.

When we're alone, call me Morgan.

She'd thought that meant he intended to be alone with her again, that he perhaps even intended to kiss her again. Instead, he didn't seem to want to be near her.

Then again, what did she know of men and kissing? Certainly, the *mère supérieure* had never discussed such things with her, nor had her father. Perhaps kisses meant little to men. Perhaps her inexperience had dulled his interest in her. Or perhaps he'd only meant to kiss her that one time, as a lesson of sorts.

What Rillieux did to you—that wasna truly a kiss. This is a kiss.

Amalie bowed her head, turned it slightly, and looked furtively back at him. Wearing his finest new attire, he knelt, head bowed, wooden rosary between his big hands, his brow furrowed as if he were deep in heartfelt prayer. Even here in the chapel when she ought to have been tending to her immortal soul, the sight of him stirred something in her blood. The fullness of his mouth, a mouth that had worked magic against hers. The dark slashes of his eyebrows, eyebrows that had furrowed with emotion when he'd kissed her. His big, well-shaped hands, hands that fisted in her hair, slid up her spine, held her tight.

Abruptly everyone around her stood, and she realized she'd been so distracted, she'd lost her place in the Mass.

For shame, Amalie!

She crossed herself, rose to her feet, and joined the procession toward the altar for Communion, wondering what was the matter with her.

But, in truth, she already knew.

Morgan.

His kiss had kindled something inside her, woken her to something new, made her feel things she'd never felt before. And now she felt like a candle that had been lit—and then left to burn in the darkness alone.

She must find a way to talk with him—just the two of them.

Morgan walked alongside Bourlamaque and Rillieux as they made their way across the sunny parade grounds from the chapel, Amalie on Bourlamaque's arm. Distracted by her presence and wondering what penance the priest would require if he knew that Morgan had sat through most of Mass with a raging cockstand, he only half listened as Bourlamaque described his new plans for placing the artillery along the northern ramparts.

Morgan had purposely seated himself away from Amalie in the chapel, but clearly not far enough away. He hadn't been able to keep himself from watching her as she prayed, her hair hidden beneath a modest veil of white lace, her head bowed to reveal the graceful nape of her neck, her rosary of silver and seed pearls clasped between her delicate hands. Even as he'd closed his eyes and prayed to God to curb his lust, he'd been able to hear her voice—as sweet and clear as birdsong.

The Almighty, it seemed, was leaving the matter of lust up to Morgan.

Not that Morgan hadn't tried. He'd done his best these past days to dampen her affection for him, paying her little heed, treating her coolly when he spoke to her at all, and refusing to be alone with her. It pained him to see the hurt upon her bonnie face and to know that he was the cause. But it was far better to reward her affection with indifference than to see her shamed on account of him, her skirts torn, her head shorn bare, her face bruised from hateful blows, as had happened in his village on Skye to a lass who'd gotten herself with child by a redcoat just after the defeat at Culloden.

It did not help matters that he slept under Bourlamaque's roof and therefore shared his table. Each meal had become a test of his mettle, his resolve to deny Amalie his regard. He'd have asked Bourlamaque to banish him to the officers' barracks, but then how could he do his nightly spying?

He'd returned to Bourlamaque's study twice more to peruse new dispatches from Montcalm, memorizing what he'd read. More artillery on their way to Québec City. Redoubts being built along the St. Lawrence. An outbreak of smallpox contained. How he'd get this news to his brothers and Wentworth Morgan knew not.

"If Amherst makes the same mistake as Abercrombie and attacks without artillery, I should like—"

"He won't." Morgan cut across Bourlamaque. "Amherst is a far better soldier than Nanny Crombie."

"What did you call him?" Bourlamaque asked.

"Nanny Crombie—on account of his forever switherin' between one plan and another, never kennin' his own mind."

"You Scots do find many ways to demonstrate insubordination toward your superior officers, don't you?" The conceited tone of Rillieux's voice left no doubt that he would never have done the same.

Morgan grinned. "Only when they deserve it."

Out of the corner of his eye, he saw Amalie hide a smile behind her fingers.

Bourlamaque chuckled. "Lieutenant, let us take what we now know of the Rangers' aim and range and cut back the forest to deny them cover. Add the timber to the abatis. It saved us once, and it might yet again."

At these words, Morgan's mind echoed with cannon fire, gunshots, and the cries of dying men. 'Twas there amongst the trees that Bourlamaque wished to fell where the Rangers had fought last summer. 'Twas there they'd lost so many men—good men and true. Cam, a close friend and one of the best, had died with French lead in his chest. Lemuel had been shot in the belly. Charlie Gordon had lost his head to a cannonball—and it had never been found.

"We shall start tomorrow, monsieur," Rillieux said in French, giving Bourlamaque a smart bow, the unmistakable glint of loathing in his eyes as his gaze met Morgan's. "Until dinner, then."

"One moment, Lieutenant," Bourlamaque called after him.

"Major, if you would be so kind as to see Amalie the rest of the way, I must speak with Lieutenant Rillieux."

Then Bourlamaque and Rillieux walked toward the officers' barracks, speaking together in quiet French.

For a moment Morgan tried to catch their words, then he felt her beside him. He looked down—and knew he was in trouble.

She gazed up at him, uncertainty and hurt in her eyes. "What have I done to displease you, Morgan?"

Taken at unawares, he feigned confusion. "Whatever do you mean, lass?"

"Of late when you speak to me, you seem distant, as if I have offended you. You behave as if I were a stranger." There was no guile in her words, only deep unhappiness. "I am happy to teach you to speak French, but you seem no longer to wish to learn our tongue."

It pricked Morgan's conscience to know he'd upset her like this. He searched for an explanation, one that would not hurt her further. "You've done naugh' to offend or displease me, lass. 'Tis sorry I am if I've led you to believe otherwise. But Bourlamaque has spared my life, and I must do all I can to prove myself worthy of his trust. My duty to him comes afore all else, lass."

"I'd say you've earned some time for yourself." Bourlamaque's voice came from behind him. "And you did win that wager. You may have the afternoon to begin your learning of French."

Amalie smiled, her face as bright as a spring day. *"Bien, monsieur."*

Morgan hid his annoyance at having been overheard and willed himself to smile. "That is most generous of you, sir."

"It is a pleasant afternoon." Bourlamaque gestured around him. "Walk about the fort, learn the French words for all that surrounds you. You may go anywhere you like as long as you do not stray outside the gates."

But time alone with Amalie was precisely what Morgan had been working so hard to avoid.

"Are you certain it is safe for Miss Chauvenet to be seen in my company? There are many amongst your men who still think of me as the enemy. I do not wish to repay your kindness and hers by besmirchin' her reputation."

Bourlamaque brushed his words aside. "I know my men, Major. There is not one amongst them who would harm her."

And Morgan found himself caught in a web of his own making.

"Il . . . fait . . . beau." The weather is lovely. Morgan spoke the words slowly with what he hoped was a convincing lack of skill.

'Twas the perfect spring day, the sky stretching clear and blue above them, wee birds singing for their mates, the trees green with new leaves. All around them, the world was abundant with new life, flaunting its fertility.

Morgan felt it from the soles of his feet to the top of his head, that feeling known amongst the Muhheconneok as the spring rising. As the sap rose in the trees, so a man's blood rose in his veins—aye, and a woman's, too. Some animal part of Morgan wanted nothing more than to draw Amalie with him into some secluded copse of trees and mate with her on a bed of wildflowers as his ancestors had done of old at Beltaine.

As innocent as a rose, she walked beside him, looking much like a spring flower herself in a gown of soft petal pink. Her sweet face lit up with a smile. *"Très bien, monsieur."*

He leaned down, lowered his voice. "It's Morgan, lass. Remember?"

She looked shyly away, but her smile did not fade. *"En français s'il vous plaît."*

"Je m'appelle Morgan."

"C'est bien." She met his gaze from beneath sooty lashes, the sunlight catching her hair, making it gleam like polished chestnut. "Morgan."

For more than an hour now they had strolled about the fort, Amalie teaching him the word for everything they saw. If he hadn't already known the language, his head would have been spinning.

Dog. *Le chien.*

Cannon and cannonball. *Le canon. Le boulet de canon.*

Ramparts. *Les remparts.* Gate. *La porte.*

Rifle. *Le fusil.* Gunpowder. *La poudre à canon.*

Sun. *Le soleil.*

Each time he spoke a word well, she rewarded him with one of her beautiful smiles, encouraging him as a mother might encourage a small child. And like the steady fraying of an overstretched rope, Morgan felt his resolve to keep his distance from her unraveling. She would hate him soon enough. Could he not savor just this moment?

"Say, *'Écosse,'*" she said, turning up a small path that followed a high fence toward Bourlamaque's residence. *"Écosse.* It means 'Scotland.'"

He repeated the word, and asked a question he'd always wanted to ask. "How did they get *Écosse* from 'Scotland'? They sound nothin' alike."

Then again why did the English call it "Scotland," while the Gaels knew the country as "Alba"?

"I do not know." She laughed, then pushed open a gate. "Come, *Monsieur l'Écossais.*"

"What did you just call me, lass?"

She laughed. "A Scotsman."

"Och, well then." Morgan followed her through the gate to the other side of the high fence and found himself standing in a little Garden of Eden.

To the south grew rows of strawberries, greens, and cabbages, next to radishes, onions, carrots, herbs, peas, and potatoes. In the center, bean plants slowly crept up poles next to a dozen rows of foot-high corn. On the edges grew what looked like blueberries, raspberries, and roses. At the north end, there stood a wee orchard, the small trees in full bloom, their pink and white blossoms buzzing with bees. Sitting amongst the trees was a little wooden bench.

"What is this place?"

"This is Bourlamaque's private garden, where food and flowers are grown for his table. After my father was killed, I began to come here to be alone."

And that's when Morgan saw.

They *were* alone. Utterly alone. The garden was surrounded by a high fence and stood at the far west end of the fort where even soldiers upstairs in their barracks could not see them.

Aye, 'tis a wee Garden of Eden—and you're the snake, MacKinnon.

He knew he shouldn't stay here with her, knew it was folly to be alone with her, but when she beckoned him to follow, he did, feeling that he was lost in a dream.

She led him along the edge of the rows, naming the fruits and vegetables in French—*fraises, pommes de terre, carottes, petits pois, maïs*—working her way toward the fruit trees in the back. Though he repeated the words as she spoke them, he was not aware of doing so, his mind fixed solely on her. The glint of sunlight in her hair. The soft swishing of her skirts. The gentle sway of her hips. The curve of her cheek. The radiant smoothness of her skin.

When they reached the fruit trees, she leaned forward, pressed her little nose against a cluster of apple blossoms and sniffed. Her eyes drifted shut, and she smiled. "Mmm."

"How do you say 'beautiful woman' in French?"

Amalie felt herself blush at his question, but could not bring herself to look at him, her gaze fixed on the pink apple blossoms. *"Belle femme."*

He reached out, brushed the hair back from her face, his touch leaving a trail of heat on her cheek, then repeated her words, his voice deep and gruff in a way that made her pulse quicken. *"Belle femme."*

As if on instinct, she stepped away from him and walked onward. What a silly girl she was! She'd brought him here because she'd known they would be alone and unseen. Yet now that she was here, she felt almost afraid to be near him. But it was not Morgan she feared, it was the way he made her feel—a mix of excitement and trepidation, like she'd once felt after sneaking to the top of the highest tower of the abbey to gaze at the wide world beyond.

She walked to the next tree, leaned near to its branches, and inhaled the sweet scent, knowing he would follow. "This is my favorite."

He closed the distance between them in two easy strides, leaned toward the blossoms, and sniffed. "Plum."

She looked up at him, astonished. "How did you know?"

He was always surprising her, this Ranger.

"I wasna always a soldier." He turned and glanced around at the neatly planted rows, a wistful look on his handsome face. "I was raised to fight, aye, but also to farm. As the second son, 'twas my duty to do all I could to serve Iain, who would have inherited our lands had we not lost them after Culloden. My father brought us out here, hacked a farm out of the wilderness. We had an orchard, too. 'Twas much bigger than this, and amongst the trees were a few plum trees my father had planted for my mother."

"What happened to the farm?"

"For a time, it lay fallow, and the forest reclaimed much of it. But when Iain was released from service, we Rangers didna wish him to face such toil alone, not wi' a wife and a wee bairn in his care. So we dallied on one of our missions and put our backs into rebuildin' the house and barns and clearin' the fields as a weddin' gift to them." Then he smiled a sad smile. "The last time I saw Iain, he stood in front of his new home wavin' farewell to us, his son in his arms, Annie beside him."

Amalie tried to think of words to say to comfort him, but he went on.

"I'd hoped one day when the war had ended to join him there, perhaps take a wife, raise children of my own. But now . . ."

There was no need for him to explain. Amalie understood.

If the war should end today, his brothers would live on lands held by the British, while he would be in the Canadas and unable to return because the British, upon learning that he had gone over to the French, would consider him a traitor. He might even be shot or hanged.

And for the first time, she saw the choice he'd been given—face a terrible death or a life bereft of the things he had once loved.

But at least he is alive!

Oui, he was alive—but he was also very alone.

If anyone understood how that felt, Amalie did. She'd felt alone at the abbey, Maman gone, Papa far away. And since Papa's death, she'd felt alone in the world, with no place she could truly call home. She reached out, touched a hand to his arm, felt the wampum armbands beneath his sleeve. "I am sorry, Morgan."

"'Tis too fair a day to speak of such things." He turned his face toward her, met her gaze, traced the curve of her cheek. Then he grinned, the sadness gone from his face. And she knew he'd closed the door to that part of himself. "So, tell me, Amalie, why did you bring me here? For I dinnae think you truly wished for me to sniff the blossoms."

Caught unprepared, Amalie stammered. "It's one of my favorite places, and it's very pretty."

His grin widened to a smile. "Nay, lass. You brought me here because you wanted me to kiss you again, aye?"

Heat rushed into her cheeks, and she looked away, unable to meet his gaze. How could he of all men see through her so easily? "I . . . I . . ."

His arm stole around her waist, and he drew her close, his body pressed hard against hers, the feel of him sending a tremor of anticipation through her. Then he cupped her cheek, forced her to look him in the eyes. "Say it, Amalie. Say it . . . in French."

Trembling, she did, the words leaving her in a whisper. *"Embrassez-moi, Morgan!"*

Chapter 15

At the first tentative brush of his lips against hers, Amalie heard herself whimper. For four long days, she'd wanted this, dreamt about it, and now it was happening. He was kissing her again. She melted against him, wrapped her arms around his neck, felt his embrace tighten, his arms so strong, his mouth a brand, hot and persistent.

This time when his tongue sought hers she was ready for it and yielded eagerly, parting her lips for him, welcoming his intrusion, heat flaring low in her belly as he took the kiss deeper and tasted her. She answered the caress of his tongue with a flick of her own, felt his body tense—and her own heartbeat quicken.

He raised his head for a moment and looked down at her, his blue eyes dark, his lips wet, his brow furrowed. He traced her upper lip with his thick thumb, his heart thudding against hers. *"Amalie, mo leannan!"*

She didn't know what his words meant, and she didn't care, because in the next instant he was kissing her again.

But this time it was different, his mouth reclaiming hers with a fierceness that almost frightened her. Instead of pulling away, she found herself clinging to him, returning the heat of his kiss with a passion of her own, her tongue curling with his, her teeth nipping his lips, her fingers buried in his hair. She could not breathe.

She could not think. She could do nothing but hold fast to him, needing him, needing his touch, needing his taste.

Somehow kissing him was even better than she remembered, more potent, more thrilling. She'd never felt anything like this—the reckless abandon of it, the singing in her blood, the uncontrolled pounding of her heart. And then his lips left her mouth and burnt a path across her cheek to the lobe of her ear. He drew it into his mouth and sucked, the startling sensation making her gasp.

Before she could recover, his fingers twined in her hair, and he forced her head back, baring the sensitive skin of her throat. His lips were sweet fire, unleashing a cascade of goose bumps, making her shiver with pleasure. When he nipped her just below the ear, something deep in her belly clenched.

"Morgan!"

Morgan heard the raw need in her voice, felt blood rush to his groin, and forgot everything except how much he wanted her. With a groan, he lifted her off her feet, carried her a few paces to the bench, then sat, drawing her across his lap, his lips never leaving her skin. He bit her again, soothed the bite with his tongue, and felt her arch in his arms, her head turning to the side on a whimper to bare more of her throat to him, her hair spilling over his arm to the ground below.

He nipped and licked his way down her throat and across her collarbone, stopping to nuzzle the hollow at the base of her throat, her pulse beating frantically beneath his lips, her body trembling, her fingers clenched in his hair. Her response was much more passionate than he'd imagined, her eagerness astonishing, setting him on fire. He cupped one soft breast through the cloth of her gown, flicked his thumb over her nipple, felt it harden.

Her body jerked, and she arched upward on a moan. *"Ô, mon Dieu!"*

And that's when it struck him.

He was dangerously close to tupping Amalie. In daylight. In a French fort where he was little more than a prisoner.

Och, Satan's arse!

He dragged his lips from her silky skin with a curse. "Amalie, lass, forgi'e me. I didna mean to go so far."

Her frustrated whimper told him that she thought perhaps he hadn't gone far enough, the sound of her need almost enough to make him cast all caution aside to kiss her again. Och, it would be so easy! She lay trembling in his arms, her skin flushed rosy pink, her lips wet and swollen, her breathing rapid. But he couldn't take the risk, for her sake if not his own.

Unable to trust himself, he lifted her, and stood, setting her on her feet before him. But he couldn't let go, not yet. And so he held her, the pounding of his heart slowly subsiding, the world returning bit by bit—the singing of birds, the heat of the sun on his face, the sound of soldiers at their chores.

Then he stepped back, brushed a strand of dark hair from her cheek. "We must go. Someone's bound to pay heed if we are missin' overlong."

She looked up at him, something like confusion on her face, her skin still flushed, her lips still swollen. "I do not wish to go."

Morgan bit back a groan, her sweet and simple confession more arousing than a whore's most blatant proposal. "Nor do I, if the truth be told, but I wouldna bring dishonor upon you, *mo ribhinn*."

He thrust his hands into his pockets and held them there lest his will fail him altogether, walking beside her to the gate in silence, his hunger for her a living, breathing thing inside him.

He drew a breath, cleared his throat. "So . . . what's the French word for 'garden'?"

She smoothed her skirts. *"Jardin."*

"Jardin," he repeated, opening the gate and leaving the garden behind.

He'd half expected to find Bourlamaque standing on the other side with a half-dozen fusiliers pointing muskets at his chest. Instead, there was no one, the path open and clear. In no hurry to return to Bourlamaque, Morgan turned toward the south and followed the path to the fort's back wall.

"What did you call me?"

Morgan had to think. What had he called her? *"Mo ribhinn?* It means somethin' akin to 'beautiful lady' or 'nymph.'"

She glanced shyly at him, a smile on her lips. "And before?"

"Mo leannan." He tried to think of how best to speak the phrase in English, not entirely certain he should tell her. "It means—"

Two men, young Abenaki men, stepped onto the path in front of them, blocking their progress.

"Kwai, nadôgweskwa." Greetings, my cousin. The taller of
the two fixed Amalie with an angry gaze, then spoke in English.
"You say you are not his whore, and yet we find you walking
alone with him—this Mac-Kin-non."

So these were Amalie's cousins.

The taller one shifted his gaze to Morgan—and drew his knife.

A malie saw Tomas pull his knife from its sheath, Simon
standing wide-eyed beside him. In the next instant, she
found herself thrust behind Morgan, his body shielding hers. But
it was not she who was in danger. Heart pounding, she tried to
step forward, but Morgan shot out an arm, blocking her path.

"Stay behind me, lass." His voice was calm, but she could feel
the tension in him, like a wildcat ready to spring, his gaze fixed
on Tomas.

Peeking out from behind Morgan's shoulder, she saw Tomas
run his thumb along the edge of his blade, as if testing its sharp-
ness. "Do you believe we would hurt our own cousin, Mac-
Kin-non?"

"Would you?" Morgan asked.

"No." Tomas met Amalie's gaze, and she saw his fury—and
his hurt. "She is but a silly girl who spent too much time with
priests and not enough time with her mother's people. But, you,
Mac-Kin-non, you I would gladly kill."

Simon's gaze darted to Tomas, and Amalie knew he was as
terrified as she.

But, to her astonishment, Morgan chuckled. "Put your knife
away, lad."

Afraid to her bones, Amalie fell back into French. *"Rangez
votre couteau! Il est des nôtres maintenant, Tomas!"* Put away
your knife! He is one of us now, Tomas!

"One of us?" Tomas glared at her, shouting back in English.
"How can you say that when the blood of our people stains his
hands? Our French fathers might make peace with him, but we
Abenaki will not!"

Then Morgan spoke. "For my part, I would bury the hatchet."

"I will bury the hatchet when it is red with your blood!"
Tomas lunged, blade flashing.

And before Amalie could scream, it was over.

Morgan stood behind Tomas, his arm locked around Tomas's throat in a choking hold, Tomas still clutching the knife in one hand, making vain and clumsy attempts to strike at a target that stood beyond his reach. Then, one arm still around the young man's neck, Morgan grasped his wrist and forced his arm to bend, compelling the hand holding the knife inch by inch upward toward Tomas's throat.

And Amalie knew her cousin was dead. "No, Morgan, please don't kill him!"

But Morgan did not seem to hear her. He forced Tomas's elbow to bend until the blade rested just beneath the youth's chin. Tomas shook with the effort to resist him, his face contorted and flushed red from the strain, a strangled wail coming from his throat.

"You want blood?" Morgan drew the knife across his own forearm, leaving a trail of bright red. "Now you have it!"

Then he released Tomas with a shove, the knife blade edged with crimson.

But it was Morgan's blood, not Tomas's, and with a rush of relief, Amalie realized that's what Morgan had meant to do all along.

Tomas staggered forward, his gaze shifting between the blood on his blade and Simon's shocked face, his eyes telling Amalie that he knew he'd been bested—and not only bested, but shamed by an enemy who had defeated him, spared his life, then given him the very blood he hadn't been strong enough to take.

Morgan turned his back on Tomas, a grim look on his face. "Come, lass. Let us leave them to soothe their injured pride in peace."

But it was not Tomas or Simon who was injured. Blood ran freely down Morgan's arm.

Amalie took his wrists, turned his arm over, relieved to see the cut wasn't deep. Still, it would need cleaning. "We must get you to the surgeon."

"'Tis little more than a scratch and isna worthy of . . ." His words died away as the clatter of marching troops drew near.

Lieutenant Rillieux appeared from around the corner accompanied by a dozen armed soldiers. His gaze passed over Amalie, traveling from Morgan and his bleeding arm to Simon, Tomas, and the knife. Then he pointed to Morgan. "Put him in irons!"

* * *

Morgan leaned back against the clapboard wall, his wrists and ankles in chains, the cut on his arm still trickling blood. He hoped the combination of humiliation and bloodied blade would take the edge off the young Abenaki's rage with him so that Amalie, at least, need no longer fear for him or for her cousins.

No, Morgan, please don't kill him!

She'd been terrified, but there'd been nothing Morgan could do for it, apart from persuading the hotheaded young warrior not to attack him again.

What a strange coincidence that Rillieux should happen upon them just as the little shangie had come to an end and that he should happen to have a dozen armed soldiers with him. Of course, it wasn't a coincidence at all. Rillieux had surely set it up, preying upon the Abenaki's understandable hatred of the Mac-Kinnon name, urging them to provoke a fight, hoping to discredit Morgan in Bourlamaque's eyes.

Had he known Morgan would win? If so, he must have been willing to sacrifice the two young Abenaki men, even knowing they were Amalie's cousins. Had he believed Morgan would be slain? Nay, or the whoreson would not have brought so many soldiers with him.

And Amalie, sweet Amalie, she had tried to protect him once again.

"But Monsieur MacKinnon has done nothing wrong," she'd protested in French as soldiers had locked Morgan's wrists in irons. "Tomas attacked him, and though Monsieur MacKinnon easily could have slain him, he did not. You cannot do this!"

But, of course, Rillieux had not been moved by her pleas.

Morgan had tried to reassure her. "Dinnae fret, lass. Bourlamaque will soon set all to rights."

She'd watched through wide eyes as Morgan had been led away, a look of mingled disbelief and fury on her bonnie face.

Morgan closed his eyes, inhaled, her scent still upon him. What was it about her that rattled him so? He'd always loved the lasses, aye, and savored the pleasures to be found in their company. But never had he lost his head like this.

He'd been so drunk with desire for her just now in the garden that he risked her safety and his own mission to get just the merest taste of her. Had her cousins or Rillieux, discovered them there . . .

And what is your mission, lad? Is it to be wooin' and kissin' a lovely métisse *lass?*

Sadly, nay. His mission was to escape, to return to Fort Edward with the secrets he'd stolen, to rejoin his brothers. His mission was to survive.

You'd best be rememberin' that, aye?

Morgan heard Bourlamaque's voice outside the guardhouse and stood, dragging his chains with him. It had taken less than ten minutes by Morgan's reckoning, and from the sound of things, the old man was in a rage.

"Next time, come to me before you shackle him, unless you'd like to find yourself in irons instead!"

Aye, Morgan was going to enjoy this.

The door creaked open, light falling across the rough-hewn boards and straw at Morgan's feet. Bourlamaque stepped inside, followed by an enraged-looking Rillieux.

Bourlamaque met Morgan's gaze, his face tight-lipped with fury. He pointed to Morgan. "Release him and apologize."

Rillieux hesitated, drawing a deep breath. Then he took the key off its hook on the wall. "I regret the misunderstanding, Monsieur Mac—"

"*Major* MacKinnon," Bourlamaque corrected him.

Morgan saw a muscle in Rillieux's jaw jump.

"I regret the misunderstanding, Major MacKinnon," Rillieux walked to the door of Morgan's cage, jammed the key into the lock, and opened it, then knelt down to free Morgan's ankles.

"I accept your apology." Morgan grinned. "With me doin' the bleedin' and blood on his knife, I can see why you thought I was to blame."

The hatred in Rillieux's eyes when he looked up at Morgan left no doubt that the *neach diolain* wanted him dead.

Amalie burnt. Even with her blankets kicked aside, she burnt. She closed her eyes, tried again to sleep, but couldn't, her body coursing with strange feelings, her mind filled with Morgan. Each time she moved, her nightgown rubbed against her nipples, sending frissons of heat into her belly, just as he had done when he'd cupped her breast and run his thumb over its crest. And where her thighs pressed together, she felt an unfamiliar ache.

Was this the lust that the sisters had so often warned against? She thought it must be. Oh, but it was as sweet as it was maddening. They hadn't told her that.

Thinking of Morgan seemed to be the only cure for it, and yet it was no cure at all, for the more she thought of him, the more she ached. Morgan carrying her to the bench. Morgan nipping her skin with his teeth. Morgan kissing the swell of her breast. And afterward, the way he'd held her, his heart beating every bit as hard as hers.

But that wasn't the whole of it, for there were qualities about him that touched her heart as well. His sense of honor, the way he'd held himself away from her, his fists clenched in his pockets as they left the garden. His protectiveness, the way he'd thrust her behind him when Tomas and Simon had appeared in their path. His strength, the way he'd overcome Tomas without hurting him, offering his own blood to stem the fighting.

Amalie had never met a man like him.

She got out of bed, walked to her window, and thrust open the panes, hoping the cool night air might soothe her heated skin. The stars shone brightly in the sky, the moon hanging over the forest, a thick mist blanketing the trees, crickets and frogs singing their lullabies. The night breeze carried the mingled scents of forest, lake, and soldiers' campfires. Somewhere in the distance an owl hooted, a lonely sound.

She leaned against the sill, breathed in the cool, fresh air, her mind drifting.

How do you say "beautiful woman" in French?

It had seemed such a magic moment, his gaze warm upon her like sunshine, blossoms all around them. Did he truly think her beautiful?

You brought me here because you wanted me to kiss you again, aye?

Yes, she had. Somehow he'd known the truth of it.

Say it, Amalie. Say it . . . in French!

Embrassez-moi, Morgan!

She pressed her fingers to her lips, felt them tingle at the memory.

Then she heard what sounded like a man snoring. Below, his back propped against the officers' barracks next door, was a sentry, sound asleep at his post. No doubt assigned to make certain Morgan did not escape, he was fortunate that—

Amalie gasped, froze.

Morgan sat directly below her in his open window, clad only in his drawers, one arm resting on his bent knee—and he was watching her.

He said not a word, but looked up at her, his eyes dark, his bare chest rising with each deep breath, his warrior marks and the cut on his forearm visible in the moonlight, the wampum on his armbands seeming to glitter. Even from this distance, she could tell that he burnt as she did, his maleness calling to her.

She wanted him to hold her, to kiss her again, and yet she could not go to him or even speak to him, not without risking discovery. Should Bourlamaque find the two of them together at night in this state of undress, Morgan would surely be punished, perhaps even flogged. Still, she wanted to touch him, needed to touch him.

Barely able to breathe, an idea forming in her mind, she reached behind her, pulled the ribbon from her braid, and began to unbind it, strand by strand, until her hair hung freely past her hips. Then she leaned down and let the heavy mass spill out over the windowsill.

She heard his quick intake of breath, saw the muscles of his bare belly jerk. He sat upright and reached with his left arm, stretching higher and higher, but still he could not reach her. Then in one smooth motion, he stood, his bare feet balanced on the sill, his face mere feet away, his gaze locked with hers. He gathered a thick handful of hair, pressed it to his face, and inhaled, his eyes drifting shut.

She had no idea how long they stood there like that, the two of them in the moonlight. She only knew that it ended far too soon.

"Sleep, Amalie," he whispered, releasing her locks.

And then he was gone.

Chapter 16

Morgan swung the ax, then jerked it free and swung again. He pushed himself, striking hard, welcoming the strain, pounding out his pent-up frustration and anger, each blow sending up a shower of woodchips. Sweat trickled down his temples, down his back, down his bare chest, summer sun hot against his skin, the air close and sweltrie. He heard timber crack, saw the tree begin to lean, and stepped out of the way as the young conifer crashed to the ground.

"He hacks down trees as if they were the enemy," a young soldier said in French from somewhere behind him.

"Perhaps he does not like trees," whispered another, sniggering.

"Vous êtes des idiots!" said a third. "It was here last year where he and his men fought Montcalm. The Rangers fired upon us from behind these very trees, but many of his men were killed by our cannonade. Perhaps that is why he seems angry."

More sniggering.

Morgan felt an urge to give the three lads a thrashing, but willed himself to ignore them. He wiped the sweat from his eyes, then he dropped the ax, picked up a saw, and began to cut off the thickest branch with deep strokes.

Truth be told, he didn't know why he felt so restless, so bloody cankersome. 'Twas as if his skin were stretched too tight, as if he were suffocating, as if something inside him were about to burst.

Perhaps it *was* this place. The trees echoed with memories of bloodshed and anguish, but he'd expected that. He'd volunteered for this work crew only because it gave him a chance to prove to Bourlamaque that he could be trusted outside the fort's walls. He needed to build the man's confidence in him, to lull Bourlamaque into letting down his guard so that Morgan could escape. He needed to leave this place before he grew too fond of the old man, before he became too comfortable in the role of traitor, before he taught Bourlamaque's soldiers something that would cost Ranger lives.

But that wasn't the whole of it. He'd been on edge since hearing yesterday that Connor and the men had attacked and looted a supply train on its way down from Fort Saint-Frédéric. They'd taken everything of worth and killed thirty-two French soldiers, four civilian wagoners and one lad of sixteen, leaving only two camp followers alive. The survivors described killings that had been deliberately brutal—wounded men finished by bayonets, soldiers cut down while pleading for mercy, the wagoners shot, dragged to the ground, and shot again.

It hardly sounded like the Rangers Morgan knew. But there was no doubt that it *had* been the Rangers. The women had reacted with horror when they'd seen Morgan, pointing to him and bursting into tears, while the lad had accused Morgan of doing most of the killing. It had taken the surgeon five minutes to calm their fears and explain that Morgan was not the man who'd attacked them. But if Morgan's resemblance to the leader of the attack hadn't been enough to prove it was the Rangers, Connor had sent a message to Bourlamaque.

"Tell Bourlamaque that Connor MacKinnon seeks his vengeance!" he'd shouted in the lad's face.

'Twas regrettable that he'd shouted the words in French.

Morgan had been forced on the spot to concoct a lie about Connor's long bout with a wasting fever as a boy and how a French doctor, a friend of their grandfather's, had cared for him, passing the long hours by teaching him a bit of French. As Morgan was not now in chains, he supposed Bourlamaque had believed the tale.

Morgan had lain awake last night, thinking of Connor and the French lives that had been needlessly lost. It made his chest ache to think of the guilt and grief Connor would one day feel for having killed so mercilessly. From the sound of it, he'd been blood-drunk, wild with rage, indifferent to pity. Though it was not Morgan's doing that his brothers thought him dead—that sin lay solely upon Bourlamaque's head—he might have been able to prevent this had he managed to escape.

Instead, he lived trapped in a web of lies, while Connor and the men risked death in reckless fighting, and French blood was spilled in a mistaken effort to avenge him.

But that's not the only reason you cannae sleep, is it, laddie?

Nay, for Satan, it was not.

Most nights he'd lain in his own sweat, his blood thrumming through his veins, his thoughts bent on Amalie. Since the night she'd let down her hair to him in the moonlight—*Mary, Mother of God, have mercy!*—he'd thought of little else but her. Even should he outlive Methuselah he would never forget that night or the sight of her, so bonnie, her hair tumbling thick into his hands, a cascade of perfumed silk.

They'd had four more French lessons since then—or should he call them kissing lessons? The little nymph was a fast learner, but then he'd spent more time schooling her in kissing in Bourlamaque's accursed garden than she had schooling him in French. Morgan had kissed her until he'd tasted her lips, her throat, the swells of her breasts in every way a man could, until she'd gone weak in his arms, until his control was near to snapping. And each time he'd told himself it wouldn't happen again.

You're a bloody liar, and well you ken it, laddie.

Aye, but she *made* a liar of him with her big eyes, her sweet smile and soft curves. She was all softness and sweetness, soft skin, soft lips, soft breasts—and when he kissed her, soft trembling sighs. Eve and her apple he might have resisted, but Amalie . . .

How could any lass as innocent as she tempt him so sorely?

He sawed through the last bit of wood, caught the thick branch with the tip of his boot, and kicked it to the side. Before the young French soldiers could tie a rope around it and drag it toward the abatis, he was already sawing on the next.

Innocent Amalie was, aye, but behind that angelic face, beneath the stays she kept so properly laced, beyond the little pearl rosary that hung from her skirts, was a woman as passionate as any who'd ever lived. Whether she knew it yet he could not say.

But he did. Och, aye, he did. And the knowledge burnt inside him until she was a sickness in his blood, his lust for her a form of madness. How Iain would mock him if he could see Morgan now. It was not so long ago that Iain had been witless with desire for Annie. And what had Morgan said to him then?

Och, for the love of God, Iain! If you want her so badly, then bed her or wed her! But dinnae keep me awake wi' your randy tossin' about!

A fine comeuppance this was!

Morgan knew Amalie was at an edge, too. He could see it in her eyes, feel it in the way she moved against him when he kissed her, hear it in her pleading whimpers. She had a virgin's body, aye, but now that body was afire with a woman's need. She wanted more from him than kisses, even if she did not know what that meant. How much did she know about men and women? Had Sister Marie-whasomever told her the particularities of the sex act or had she merely frightened Amalie half to death with her tales of a bungling husband and the sufferings of childbed?

'Tis no' your place to teach her, MacKinnon. That pleasure belongs to her husband. Dinnae be forgettin' that.

If he'd been like most men, he'd have wooed her onto her back and left her with a big belly afore summer's ending. But he wasn't like most men. Och, he loved the lassies right enough and had the needs of a man in full vigor. But he'd ne'er been the cruel sort who'd ease his lust with a woman with no thought of the cost to her. Amongst the Muhheconneok, lasses took lovers at will and bore their children without shame. But it was not so amongst the British or the French or even the Scots. Were he to bed Amalie, her shame would be twofold—the shame of losing her innocence and the even worse shame of losing it to a man who'd betrayed her.

An image of the lass from his village came to his mind—*poor lass*—her head shorn, her face wet with tears, her wee bairn clutched tight in her arms as the villagers threw eggs and slops at her. Morgan cared for Amalie far too much even to chance such a fate. She deserved the love and protection of a husband, but because of the war, Morgan could not even hope to take her to wife, despite whatever girlish dreams of marriage her mind was spinning.

And if you cannae wed her, laddie, you cannae bed her.

The sooner Bourlamaque sent her back to Trois Rivières the better. Morgan knew Bourlamaque had written a letter to the *mère supérieure,* knew, too, that Connor's attack on the supply

train postponed Bourlamaque's plans to send Amalie beyond the
fort's protective walls. And though Morgan had assured him the
Rangers would never harm her and had offered to accompany
her, Bourlamaque had been adamant that she remain for the time.

"Perhaps next time your brother's restraint will be even less in
evidence," he'd said, his jaw clenched, deep regret in his eyes.
"Even if they spared her life, I would not want her to see such
carnage. God in heaven!"

As God was his witness, neither did Morgan.

And so, for now, Amalie remained.

Morgan heard a shout and looked up to see soldiers, Rillieux
and Durand amongst them, tossing what looked like a white ball
back and forth. Not so disciplined as Wentworth's redcoats, were
they, these French laddies?

He cut through the branch and kicked it aside in time to see
Rillieux approach, the strange ball in his hands, Durand behind
him, a troubled look on his face.

"This must be one of yours," Rillieux said, tossing the ball to
Morgan.

Morgan dropped the saw, caught the ball—and felt the breath
leave his lungs.

'Twas no ball. 'Twas most of a man's skull, the bones bleached
white by the sun, the empty eye sockets staring into nothingness.
It had been picked clean of flesh, apart from a thatch of carrot-red
hair.

Red hair.

Charlie Gordon.

Rage pounding in his veins, Morgan looked up, met Rillieux's
amused gaze, and knew what it was to *want* to kill. "You filthy
son of a whore!"

A malie jabbed the rose stem into the vase, then withdrew it
again, cross that she could not get the arrangement to look
the way she wanted it to look. The mouth of the vase was too
wide, the stems too fragile. She had cut them herself, hoping to
set them on the table during dinner not only for their beauty but
also as a reminder to Morgan of their time in the garden. Only
yesterday, he'd plucked one for her and—

"Ouille!" She gasped, popped her finger in her mouth, and

tasted blood where a thorn had pricked her, feeling an absurd impulse to cry.

She hadn't slept well last night, and lack of rest had left her cross. So many nights she'd lain in bed, unable to sleep for thinking of Morgan, wanting . . . Wanting what?

If only she knew.

Never had she been so aware of a man, of his every word, every glance, every gesture. Never had she imagined that the simple press of lips, the swirl of a tongue against tongue, the feel of a man's hands upon her skin could leave her feeling so frantic, so needy, as if her very blood could feel hunger. Each time he kissed her was better than the last, every touch making her long for more. But there was more to her feelings for him than desire.

For the first time since her father's death, she didn't feel alone. When she was with Morgan, she felt wanted, needed, at home. He listened to her, laughed with her, talked with her as if her thoughts truly mattered to him. He kissed her with that same attentiveness, as if her pleasure were every bit as important to him as his own. He was protective of her, without ordering her about as Lieutenant Rillieux tried—

A commotion at the front door interrupted her thoughts— men's angry voices, the heavy stomp of feet. She hurried to the hallway in time to see Lieutenant Rillieux and Lieutenant Durand pass by on their way toward Bourlamaque's study, Rillieux holding a handkerchief to his bleeding nose, Durand looking uneasy and pale.

"Bourlamaque will have no choice but to act!" Lieutenant Rillieux's face was bruised and twisted with rage. "He cannot ignore an assault on one of his own officers—a *French* officer—and hold the respect of his soldiers."

And Amalie knew.

Morgan had hit him.

A knot of dread in her belly, she waited until Rillieux and Durand had been admitted to Bourlamaque's study, then tiptoed to the closed door and pressed her ear against it.

"I showed him the skull," Lieutenant Rillieux was saying, "and he became as a man deranged and struck me! You must at the very least confine him, if not flog—"

"Is that the truth of it?" Bourlamaque asked, a warning tone to his voice.

For a moment there was silence, and then someone cleared his throat. "Not altogether, monsieur."

That was Lieutenant Durand.

"Lieutenant Rillieux and some of the grenadiers made sport with the skull, tossing it back and forth between them. Then the lieutenant threw it to MacKinnon, saying, 'This must be one of yours.' MacKinnon seemed to recognize it. Then he called Lieutenant Rillieux a . . ." Durand cleared his throat again. "A son of a whore . . . and struck him, monsieur."

"You were outside the gates when this happened?" Bourlamaque sounded angry. "Where is Major MacKinnon now?"

Lieutenant Rillieux answered. "He walked off, carrying the skull with—"

"Where is he?" Bourlamaque's shout made Amalie jump.

"I believe he was heading toward the cemetery, monsieur," Durand answered.

Amalie did not wait to hear more, but picked up her skirts and ran.

She found Morgan in the cemetery, just as Lieutenant Durand had suspected. Wearing only boots and breeches, he knelt upon the earth in the far corner, digging a hole in the soil with his ax blade. Even from a distance she could see the anger on his face.

She approached him in silence, then stood and watched as he dug a shallow grave, his jaw clenched, sweat trickling down his temples, dirt sticking to the slick skin of his chest and belly. Beside him, something white lay on the earth.

The skull.

Its jawbone was missing. Two wide eye sockets gazed at the sky as if in surprise. A shock of orange-red hair clung to its scalp.

Whoever he'd been, he'd died the same day as her father.

Amalie shivered.

Morgan did not seem to notice her, but dug in silence until he'd hollowed out a small grave. Then he hurled the ax aside and gently picked up the skull. He seemed to hesitate to lay it in the earth, and Amalie understood.

She drew the lace fichu from her shoulders and held it out to him. He looked at it, then looked up at her, the anguish in his eyes enough to bring tears to hers. Then he took the lace shawl, wrapped it carefully around the skull, and nestled the skull in the soil.

Amalie heard footsteps and hushed voices and looked around her to find dozens of soldiers watching, their faces solemn. Then Père François pushed through the throng, his Bible clasped in his hand, Bourlamaque beside him.

They stopped at Morgan's side.

"His name was Charlie Gordon." Morgan's voice was tight with emotion. "He'd nay been wi' us long, but he was a good lad and true. He was only eighteen. A cannonball took his head. We ne'er found it."

Until today.

Amalie bent down, picked up a handful of earth, and sprinkled it in the grave. Bourlamaque did the same, followed by Lieutenant Durand and Monsieur Lambert. Then Morgan picked up a handful of soil, sprinkled it onto the lace, and crossed himself while Père François began to speak the words of the funeral Mass.

"Requiem æternam dona eis, Domine, et lux perpetua luceat eis. Te decet hymnus Deus, in Sion, et tibi reddetur votum in Ierusalem. Exaudi orationem meam; ad te omnis caro veniet . . ."

As Père François continued, Amalie watched Morgan, who remained kneeling, his eyes squeezed shut, his little wooden cross clenched in one fist, his breath coming in shudders, as if whatever he was feeling barely fit inside his mortal body.

She swallowed the hot lump in her throat, stepped closer to him, and laid her hand upon his bare shoulder.

She did not see Lieutenant Rillieux standing by himself to one side, one eye blackened, bloody kerchief in his fist, blood caked on his nostrils, gazing at her with a look of utter hatred on his face.

Morgan sat on the windowsill, watching the full moon glide across the sky, the night breeze cool against his skin, a strange emptiness inside his chest. Across from him in the shadows, the sentry snored soundly, the sound lost amidst the chirps and croaks of wee night beasties. Above him, Amalie's window was open, her room silent.

He'd been a fool to do what he'd done today, and yet, as God was his witness, he hadn't been able to stop himself. He'd held what was left of poor Charlie in his hands, had seen Rillieux's amused grin, and something inside him had snapped. He'd felt true satisfaction when his fist had struck Rillieux's face.

If he'd had his sword, that *mac-dìolain* would be dead.

Bourlamaque would decide what to do with him on the morrow. But whether he was flogged or locked in the guardhouse or made to carry water from the river all day, Morgan cared not. Nor would he begrudge Bourlamaque his punishment, for once again Bourlamaque had shown he was a good man. Rather than dragging Morgan away in chains, he'd brought the priest and waited until the prayers were spoken before he'd confined Morgan to quarters.

Morgan hated the fact that he must soon betray him.

The soldiers, too, had been respectful, standing in silence while the good father spoke the words of benediction, nary a snigger to be heard. Lieutenant Durand had even joined him in sprinkling dirt in the little grave. And Amalie . . .

God bless the lass! She'd come out of nowhere, stood beside him, given him the lace from her shoulders, as if she'd known what he was thinking, as if she, too, were offended by the indignity of a man's skull lying bare against the dirt. And then he'd felt her hand, small and soft, rest against him, a simple gesture, but one that had required courage. She'd shown every man in the fort that it did not matter to her that the man whose remains they were laying to rest had not been French. It had touched him deeply.

A feeling he did not wish to name stirred behind his breastbone.

He could not love her, for if he loved her, he could not leave her.

And yet leave her he must. He could not stay. To stay would make him a traitor in fact as well as in deed. It would make him the enemy of his own flesh and blood, an enemy to the men he'd sworn to lead, an enemy to Joseph and the warriors of Stockbridge who'd fought beside him.

And that he could not do.

"Morgan?"

Startled, Morgan jerked his gaze around.

And there, just inside the closed door, stood Amalie.

Chapter 17

Morgan stepped down from the sill and closed the windows lest someone see or hear her. "For the love of God, lass, what are you doin' here?"

He took a step toward her, about to tell her to get back to her own room, when she stepped into the moonlight. His mouth went dry.

She wore only her nightgown, her dark hair hanging almost to her knees, her little toes peeking out from beneath her lacy hem. The thin cloth did little to conceal her body, the pale light revealing shadowed hints of her nipples, the curve of her hips, the dark triangle of her sex.

She walked slowly toward him. "It is hot tonight. I . . . I cannot sleep."

Some part of him that had not gone witless watched the play of emotions on her face—uncertainty, shyness, hopefulness. Then her gaze skimmed over his bare arms and chest and belly, and he saw something else—longing.

And who put that longin' in her, laddie? 'Twas you wi' your kisses, aye? She was utterly untouched afore you came along.

She stood before him now, her soft scent filling his head, heating his blood. "I am sorry about your friend, about what Lieutenant

Rillieux did today. I worry for you, Morgan. I pray that Bourlamaque will not punish you too harshly."

'Twas the absurdity of her words that brought him back to himself. She'd sneaked into his room in the middle of the night to tell him she hoped he'd not be punished too harshly? "If Bourlamaque finds you here, lass, he'll cut off my cods."

For a moment she looked confused, then her eyes went wide and her gaze flickered to his groin. She looked away. "Bourlamaque was upset and drank too much brandy. I could hear him snore through the wall. He will not wake before morning."

Morgan fought the urge to touch her, crossed his arms over his chest. "You have no' answered my question, lass. Why are you here? And dinnae tell me it's summer's heat that brings you, for 'tis hot in my bed, too."

She looked away again, distress on her face. "I . . . I needed . . ."

"Needed what?" He knew the answer, but he wanted to hear it from her.

When she spoke, her words were but a whisper. "I needed to be . . . *near you*."

So vulnerable, so innocent. She stood before him brimming with unspent desire and didn't know what to do about it—leastways not well enough to ask for it.

His hand betrayed him, reached out, and tucked a silky strand of hair behind her ear, the simple touch not nearly enough to satisfy him. "Och, Amalie, you are so bonnie. You tempt a man to his soul. But you dinnae ken what you're wantin', do you?"

Her head snapped up, uncertainty replaced with a look of feminine defiance. And then she did something he did not expect. She rested her palms against his bare chest, stood on her toes— and kissed him.

Both shocked and aroused by her boldness, Morgan willed himself to remain passive, letting her shape the kiss, her lips hot against his, her tongue exploring his mouth with sweet strokes, the heat of it shooting straight to his groin. She was a fast learner, his Amalie, she was.

He knew he was a bloody fool to let this go on, and it *had* been on the tip of his tongue to tell her she must leave. But now his tongue had other ideas. Besides, how could he send her away when he wanted her so badly, when even his bones ached for her, when she was the only thing that felt right and true in the midst of the lies and deceptions that had become his life?

Aye, he knew he could not claim her, knew he could not take her. He was still a prisoner of the French, still an involuntary guest in Bourlamaque's home, still caught up in a dangerous game of spying and survival. He might not live another fortnight, let alone survive this accursed war. She deserved more than a man who would love her, perhaps get her with child, and then forsake her. But here she was, in his room, an angel come to him in the dark of night, kissing him with all the fire in her soul.

Yet weren't there many ways for a man to pleasure a woman? Aye, there were. He could make love to her with his hands, with his lips, with his tongue. He could ease her longing, show her the fullness of her own response—and leave her maidenhead intact. He could be the first man to give her pleasure.

On a surge of pure lust, he drew her hard against him, wrested control of the kiss from her, answering the caress of her tongue with the bold thrust of his own, the rightness of it singing through him. Aye, she could not be *his,* but for tonight—just for tonight— he could be *hers.*

Amalie felt something inside Morgan snap, strong arms holding her against the hard wall of his chest as he gave in to her kiss and began to kiss her back. But this was not a sweet kiss, not the sort of gentle kiss they'd shared in the garden. It was fierce, wild, almost violent, making her knees go weak and her heart trip.

She knew it had been wrong of her to come here. Chaste women did not sneak into men's sleeping chambers in the middle of the night. But she'd lain awake tonight as she had so many nights of late, consumed by thoughts of him, wanting the gnawing hunger inside her to go away, and she'd known only that she had to be with him. She'd feared he might send her away, feared he might see her as wanton and her actions as shameful. And at first he *had* seemed angry with her, but now . . .

Ô, mon Dieu, this is what she'd needed!

"Amalie, *mo luaidh.*" He whispered her name, whispered words she didn't know, his voice gruff, then he lifted her into his arms, carried her to his bed, and followed her down onto the sheets, settling his weight beside her. "Tell me, lass, what is it you want from me?"

She shivered, looked up at him, knowing he awaited some kind of answer from her but uncertain what it was. "Kiss me."

He ducked down, nipped her lower lip, soothed it with his tongue, then sucked it. "Is it just a kiss you're wantin', or is it more? What do you ken of men and women, lassie? What did they teach you at the abbey?"

Unsettled by his question and yet hungry for the feel of him, she slid her hands over the hard curves of his shoulders. "I . . . I know that it is a wife's duty to lie near her husband and to bear his children in pain."

"Duty? Pain?" He brushed his lips over hers, kissed the corners of her mouth, making her lips tingle. "Did they teach you nothin' else? Did they say nothin' of pleasure?"

Pleasure? None of the sisters had ever spoken of pleasure.

Feeling strangely exposed, she looked away, unable to bear his gaze. "Sister Marie Louise told me that men . . . that men . . ."

She could not talk of this! It was too private, and he was too much, surrounding her with his strength, his heat, his scent, his little kisses making it so hard to think.

He nipped her lips. "Tell me, lass."

She squeezed her eyes shut, heat rushing into her cheeks. "That men mount their wives . . . as a ram mounts a ewe—*Dieu, que c'est embarrassant!*—and that they find this pleasurable, while women do not."

"She told you that?" He chuckled, nuzzled the sensitive skin beneath her ear, nipped her earlobe.

A cascade of shivers spread through her. *"Oui."*

He swirled his tongue against the whorl of her ear. "And what if I told you that the poor sister was wrong? What if I told you that a woman can feel every bit as much pleasure from love play as a man?"

She gaped at him, astonished. "Can that be true?"

"Aye, 'tis the truth. Haven't you enjoyed my kisses, lass?" Not giving her time to answer, he kissed her, slow and deep, kissed her until they were both breathless, until she couldn't help but arch against him, naught between their naked skin but the thin cotton of her shift and his drawers. Then he raised his head and looked down at her through dark eyes. "I ken why you cannae sleep. I ken what you're feelin', for I feel it, too. If you let me, I can ease the longin' inside you, Amalie. I can give you pleasure and leave you still a virgin."

A bolt of heat shot through her, made her belly tighten, a thousand questions darting through her mind, distilling into one. "Will you get me with child?"

He shook his head, gave a little nudge with his hips, and she felt a hard ridge press against her thigh. "For me to get you wi' child, I would have to join my body—this part of me—with yours and spend my seed. And that I willna do, upon my word."

Everything he said was new to Amalie, and she hesitated, feeling as though she stood upon a precipice. Could it be as he said it was? She wanted to know, wanted to go with him wherever he could take her, wanted to let the joy she felt with him carry her where it would. And yet never in her life had anyone bid her to seek her own pleasure in anything. At the convent, and even with her father, her life had been about duty—a Catholic girl's duty, a daughter's duty, a Frenchwoman's duty.

Even as she let his suggestion tempt her, Morgan nudged his nose into her hair, his breath hot on her ear, one callused hand sliding up her bare arm, his touch making her skin tingle. "Let me free you from this need, Amalie."

But she had one last question. "Is this . . . a sin?"

"I'm certain the priests would say that it is. And yet holdin' you in my arms like this—all I ken is how *right* it feels."

Amalie drew in a breath at his words—words that spoke fully her own feelings—and knew her own mind. "*Oui,* Morgan. Show me."

She closed her eyes, waited, uncertain what he would do next, her body beginning to tremble. But all he did was slide his hand to her cheek and kiss her, a deep, openmouthed kiss, his lips hot, so hot, his tongue teasing out her secrets, making her forget her uncertainty and fear.

Without taking his mouth from hers, he slid his hand slowly down her throat, his fingers pausing to caress the indentation between her collarbones before tracing a line of heat between her breasts, the unfamiliar sensation making her tense.

"Easy, Amalie." The words brushed over her lips, a flutter of breath.

His hand flared across her rib cage, smoothed circles over her belly, stroked the curve of her hip, a strange awareness spreading wherever he touched her, as if his hands had the power to call her body to wakefulness. But that was nothing compared to the scorching trail his lips left on her skin as he kissed his way down her throat, following the path his fingers had just taken. By the time his lips reached the valley between her breasts, she could scarcely breathe, her heart leaping against her breastbone as if to greet him. And then his hand skimmed over her breast, his fingers catching her nipple through the cloth of her gown, and she heard herself moan.

He moaned, too, as if touching her like this gave him just as much pleasure as it gave her. Then his hand slid beneath the straps of her nightgown, pushing the cloth over her shoulders and down to her belly, leaving her breasts bare to his perusal. She watched his eyes darken and felt a shiver of excitement, her nipples drawing tight.

No man had ever seen this part of her.

"Och, Amalie, you're far lovelier than I e'er could have imagined." He cupped the full weight of one breast in his hand, his thumb drawing circles over its bare crest, sending hot shards skittering through her belly.

"Oh!" She reacted on instinct, arching, pressing more of herself into his callused palm, wanting more, needing more.

And he obliged her, molding her breasts, caressing her nipples, stretching them, plucking them, until she whimpered with frustration, her breasts swollen and heavy, the heat in her belly spreading between her thighs. But he wasn't finished.

With a groan, he lowered his head, drew one aching nipple into the heat of his mouth, and suckled her, the shock of it making her gasp. Each tug of his lips, each flick of his tongue, was a sweet torment, her breath coming in pants, the heat between her thighs now a throbbing ache. Then one hand reached down and drew up the cloth of her nightgown in fistfuls, his fingers caressing the skin of one thigh, urging her legs apart.

Amalie gasped, caught his wrist, and squeezed her thighs together. She hadn't imagined he would try to touch her there. *"Non!"*

"Shhh, *mo luaidh*." He nuzzled her ear. "Let me touch you where you burn the hottest. Let me bring you release."

She stared into his eyes, saw an intensity there that almost frightened her, and yet her body was on fire, her nipples still wet from his kisses, her belly tight, the ache between her thighs both precious and terrible. Slowly, she relaxed her legs, surrendering her will to his.

His gaze still locked with hers, he slid his hand down to the bend in her knee and lifted her leg, resting it over his hip, parting her, leaving her exposed. Then his hand closed over her sex, the heel of it grinding in deep, slow circles against her.

She drew in a shuddering breath, astonished at the staggering pleasure, his touch somehow appeasing that aching need—appeasing it or provoking it. Oh, what was he doing to her? "Morgan!"

"So beautiful," he said in a husky whisper. Then his mouth returned to her breast, his tongue teasing her nipples, sucking, licking, tasting, each motion of lips, tongue, and teeth sending spirals of pleasure through her belly.

Amalie was lost, her skin damp with perspiration, her body trembling. Something was happening inside her—an emptiness deep within her that yearned to be filled, a sweet ache that grew stronger with each touch, a need that became more desperate with each beat of her heart. She clenched her fingers in his long hair, her breath coming in ragged whimpers, her body taking on a rhythm of its own.

"Amalie, my angel." He sounded breathless, his voice strained.

But if she thought he'd run out of new ways to tempt and torment her, she was mistaken, for in the next instant she felt his finger slide between her slick folds, parting her, stroking some secret part of her. The delight of it stunned her, frightened her, and she couldn't help but cry out. "Ô, mon Dieu! You must stop!"

He chuckled, a deep warm sound, his mouth shifting to the side of her throat. "There's naugh' to fear, lass."

With her next breath, she found herself hovering on some sharp and shimmering edge. She bit her lip, held her breath, fought not to fall, but he was relentless. His finger slid over that secret spot again and again, slick and wet, forcing her closer to that unfamiliar brink. The fire inside her blazed bright white and blinding—and then it exploded.

Ecstasy seared through her, molten and exquisite, almost terrifying in its intensity. She arched in his arms and cried out, her cries captured by his deep, thrusting kiss, as bliss lifted her up into the night, carrying her beyond the moon and the stars to a glittering place near heaven, then leaving her to drift. Slowly, so slowly, the night took shape around her once more—the beating of two hearts, sheets soaked with sweat, the sounds of mingled breathing—and she found herself lying, astonished and trembling, in Morgan's arms.

Morgan watched Amalie sleep, a strange tightness in his chest. She lay curled against him like a kitten, so soft and sweet, her breathing deep and even, her face peaceful, her long hair tangled about them both. The musky scent of her arousal teased his nostrils, mixing with the smells of night. He knew he needed to wake her, but he couldn't bring himself to let her go just yet. Dawn was still a few hours away.

This could never happen again. Not only was it far too chancie, but Morgan wasn't certain he could survive it again. Never had his will been put to such a test as this. To touch her and taste her but not to take her—*Jesus, Mary, and Joseph!*—it was, he supposed, the price to be paid for daring to do what he'd done. A price he was glad to pay, even if his balls still ached and his cock throbbed.

It had been like watching a rose bloom, its rosy petals slowly spreading, revealing its beauty bit by bit, then opening at last to claim the sunlight. And she *had* opened to him, her unschooled response more arousing than Morgan could have imagined. When at last she'd reached her peak—och, never had he seen anything more bonnie.

Aye, the bastard who took her to wife would consider himself blessed, indeed, for in her he would find not only a sweet and generous spirit, but a quick mind, quiet strength, and true feminine passion.

But what if she, like the poor sister, weds some bawheid who uses her body for his own pleasure with nary a thought for hers? What then, laddie? Will it help her or hurt her to ken what she's missin'?

Anger snarled in his chest at the thought of any man touching her, let alone using her so mindlessly. He hoped she'd have the strength and courage to demand her due from any *neach dìolain* of a husband who treated her that way.

Morgan brushed a strand of hair off her cheek and felt the sharp edge of regret. God Almighty, how he wished he didn't have to leave her! If he but could, he'd ask Bourlamaque for permission to court her. Or he'd make love to her, confess all once her belly began to swell, and allow himself to be forced to the altar. Then he'd spend the rest of his life cherishing her.

But his duty lay along another path—not with the lass sleeping in his arms, but with his brothers, with Joseph and his Muhheconneok grannies, with the men who'd sworn to fight and die at his command. No matter what Morgan felt for Amalie—nay, he would not name it—he was a Ranger and bound not to this woman, but to war.

And if there were some way he could take her with him, return to Fort Edward with bonnie Amalie beside him?

You've gone daft, MacKinnon. She deserves better than you!

Aye, she did.

Here amongst the French, Morgan was a MacKinnon, grandson of a Highland laird, but at home amongst the British he was the grandson of a traitor, a man who, together with his brothers, still stood in taint of murder, a man who was bound to this war until its ending.

Then why do you wish to go home, laddie?

'Twas the voice of Satan, but it came from his own head.

Then temptation crept out of the corners of his mind where it had been lurking and showed itself fully before him—so alluring, so enticing—and he saw the life that lay within his grasp. An honored officer in Bourlamaque's retinue. A husband to precious Amalie. A father to six or seven dark-haired sons and daughters, all of them with eyes like their mother's.

He closed his eyes, held that vision in his mind, and felt something break inside his chest, pain forcing the breath from his lungs.

But he could no more betray his brothers or the Rangers than he could slay them. He opened his eyes, the vision slowly fading, leaving emptiness inside him.

He ducked down, pressed a kiss to Amalie's hair. Just a few more minutes. Just a few more. Then he would wake her, see her safely to her room, and begin to plot his escape. Ere sunrise a week hence, he would be gone.

Chapter 18

The day was young when Bourlamaque summoned Morgan to his study.

"Please sit, Major." He gestured toward an opulent armchair, a troubled look on his face, the fingers of his right hand pressed against his temple.

Aye, the old man was on the biting end of a bottle of brandy.

Morgan sat and waited in silence to hear his fate, his mind still filled with Amalie, her scent still upon his skin.

"The first matter we must discuss, Major, is your conduct yesterday." Bourlamaque settled himself behind his writing table. "I cannot tolerate fighting amongst my officers. It breeds dissension and distracts us from our efforts to win this war."

"I understand, sir." Morgan met his gaze without wavering and pressed on, needing to say it. " 'Tis grateful I am that you allowed poor Charlie a Catholic burial and that you stood there beside me. You are a far better man and more honorable than he whom I was forced to serve. I will accept whate'er discipline you decide is fittin' wi'out complaint."

Bourlamaque's stern countenance softened slightly. "We French do not flog our officers as the British do, except for the most extreme of offenses, and this does not warrant such a response. Those who witnessed the incident agree that you were provoked. And yet I cannot ignore the fact that you struck Lieutenant Rillieux, who, despite his faults, is a dedicated officer and widely respected."

Morgan looked down to keep himself from rolling his eyes. "Aye, sir."

"I have therefore decided that you shall spend the day digging a new privy for the officers down on the riverbank."

Dig a privy? That was to be his punishment?

Morgan had hoped for a good flogging. It would at least have taken his mind off Amalie and relieved some of the gnawing guilt he felt for deceiving so honorable and decent a man as Bourlamaque. Aye, a good flogging would have done it. "Aye, sir."

Bourlamaque watched him, as if expecting some kind of reaction. "Lest you think I deal with you unfairly, you should know that Lieutenant Rillieux is even now hard at work cleaning the stables."

Morgan fought back a grin, imagining the haughty bastard up to his knees in horse shite and filthy straw. "I dinnae question your fairness, sir."

Bourlamaque nodded, the matter clearly settled. "It has been three weeks since I made the decision to spare your life. Despite yesterday's unfortunate events, I have not been disappointed. Your actions demonstrate qualities I hope to find in my officers— skill, strength, compassion, restraint."

Every word made Morgan's growing sense of guilt more difficult to bear. "You are most gracious, sir."

"I have decided it is time to give you a rank and place in our army—and to return your possessions to you. Alas, I cannot grant you the rank of major, for it would insult my officers, and Montcalm has forbidden it."

So there was a new message from Montcalm. Morgan would make a point of finding and reading it tonight.

The old man was still speaking. "From this day forward, you shall be Capitaine MacKinnon, my adviser on all matters pertaining to the Rangers and Fort Edward. You shall instruct my soldiers in marksmanship and woodcraft." He leaned down and picked something heavy up off the floor, then tossed it to Morgan. "You may have use for these things."

Morgan's tumpline pack.

Taken aback, Morgan stared at it for a moment before unbinding it to see what gear still lay inside.

"I assure you it is all there."

And, apart from his sword and rifle, of course, it was. Pistol. Powder horn. Bag of shot. Tin cup and plate. Salt horn. Tin cook pot. Fork and spoon. Clasp knife. Pouch of parched corn. A bar of soap. Two old onions. A bit of salt pork. Tin flask of poisoned rum. Leather flask of drinkable rum. Ground ginger and sugar, each wrapped in parchment. Needle and thread for stitching wounds. Jar of salve to keep them from festering. Linen strips for binding them. Ax. Water skin. Hunting knife.

It seemed a lifetime ago that these things had belonged to him, and the sight of them made his chest feel strangely tight. He'd thought he'd have to make the journey back to Fort Edward without them. Now it would be so much easier.

He willed his face to remain impassive. "And my rifle and sword?"

Bourlamaque pointed toward the corner by the door, where Morgan could see both his musket and his *claidheamh mòr*. "You may retrieve them on your way out, Captain. For now, we have one last matter to discuss."

Morgan's pulse sped up a notch. With his weapons returned, he had all that he needed to escape. "Aye, sir."

For a moment Bourlamaque said nothing, as if he were choosing his words with care. When he at last spoke, the troubled look had returned to his face. "This concerns my ward, Miss Chauvenet."

Whatever Morgan had expected him to say next, it was not this.

Easy, lad. If he kent she'd spent the night in your bed, he'd be geldin' you wi' yon sword, no' returnin' it to you.

"Miss Chauvenet spoke with me last evening and asked me to permit you to court her. This is unconventional, I know, but then her father made it clear that she was to be allowed to pick her own match insofar as the man she chose was worthy and could provide for her. She has developed a *tendresse* for you, *capitaine*. Surely, you must have noticed this as well."

Morgan almost choked. "Och, well . . . aye, sir."

Aye, he had noticed. Perhaps it had been the way she'd come to his room in the night, begging to be kissed. Maybe it had been the way she'd cried his name as she'd come against his hand. Or mayhap it been the way she'd looked up at him when he'd woken her, her eyes filled with wonder, aye, and a woman's love.

He'd wanted to admonish her not to let herself love him, to tell her that he was not the man she believed him to be, to warn her that he was about to repay her compassion, trust, and affection with betrayal. But then she'd smiled, a sleepy smile, and his courage had forsaken him.

"Do you return her regard?"

Morgan thought of the girl from his village and fully intended to lie, but he found he could not—not when it came to Amalie. "Aye, sir, I do."

Bourlamaque seemed to consider this, then nodded. "Then I should tell you I still intend to send her back to the abbey—and soon. I fear her affection for you might incense Lieutenant Rillieux, and I've no wish for further hostility between the two of you. Besides, events are unfolding that ought to make it much safer for her to make that long journey. I caution you not to take advantage of her innocence in the meantime. She is young and very inexperienced. You may pay your respects to her discreetly until she leaves, provided you give me your word that you will not debauch her."

"Upon my honor, I willna harm or dishonor her." It was a promise Morgan was happy to give and one he intended to keep—last night's madness notwithstanding.

But what events were unfolding? Morgan needed to see that letter.

"You are the grandson of a Scottish laird, a brave fighter, and an honorable man. Should the war end, and you prove faithful to France, I would give my consent for you to marry Amalie."

And with those words, Bourlamaque unwittingly offered Morgan everything he could have wanted—the honor of his clan name, a chance to fight as a free man, and Amalie as his wife. Did the old man know he was exacting a terrible revenge? With a few words, Bourlamaque had resurrected the vision Morgan had turned away in the night—and with it a terrible temptation.

Why do you wish to go home, laddie?

The words hissed through his mind.

And this time Morgan had no answer.

Amalie awoke feeling languid and replete, missing Morgan beside her and yet surrounded by him, the salt and musk of his scent still upon her, his touch still warming her skin, his words still sounding in her mind.

You have no' answered my question, lass. Why are you here?
And dinnae tell me it's summer's heat that brings you, for 'tis hot
in my bed, too.

Unable to keep from smiling, she stretched, crawled out of
bed, and threw open her windows to let in the fresh morning air.
Then she started her morning toilette, brushing the many tangles
from her hair, washing her face, shedding her nightgown. But
rather than dressing, she found herself staring into her looking
glass at the likeness of her own naked body.

She didn't look any different than she had yesterday. She had
the same eyes, the same face, the same skin. And yet nothing was
the same at all.

She let her gaze slide over her reflection, her fingers tracing a
path over lips that had burnt from his kisses, along her throat
where his mouth had conjured shivers, to the valley between her
breasts where her heart had beat so hard.

Och, Amalie, you're far lovelier than I e'er could have
imagined.

He'd been looking at her breasts when he'd said that, his brow
furrowed with emotion, his eyes dark. Were they beautiful? She
cupped them as he had done, explored their velvety crests with her
fingers, and watched her nipples slowly pucker into tight little
buds, their tips exquisitely sensitive. The only thought she'd ever
given to her breasts was how best to hide them, first from the dis-
approving gazes of the nuns and then from the lustful stares of
men. She'd known only that they were meant for suckling babies.
She'd never known they could be a source of such pleasure.

She remembered what it had felt like to have his hot mouth
upon them, to feel his tongue tickle her, to feel his lips nip her—
and desire, fresh and new, began to build inside her. Slowly, so
slowly, she slid her hands down over her rib cage to the rounded
curve of her belly, wondering at the tension she felt there. Then
with one hand she reached farther still, her fingers sliding over
dark curls to cup her sex as he had done.

I ken why you cannae sleep. I ken what your feelin', for I feel
it, too. If you let me, I can ease the longin' inside you, Amalie.

Oh, but she was sensitive there! 'Twas a place she'd never
touched except to bathe and stem her monthly flux, for the sisters
had punished girls who'd touched themselves beneath their
skirts. But she was not at the abbey now. She delved deeper, then

drew her hand away and found her fingers rich with her own
musky scent and damp with a strange, slippery wetness, as if her
body had wept silky tears in its need for him.

It felt as if a great mystery had been opened to her—a world of
pleasure she'd never known existed—and yet there were so many
questions she'd wanted to ask him, still so much she needed to
know. If she'd experienced so much pleasure, why hadn't Sister
Marie Louise? Was it normal for a woman's desire to return so
quickly after release? Would it be just as pleasurable if he joined
his body to hers, or was that when it hurt?

For me to get you wi' child, I would have to join my body—
this part of me—with yours and spend my seed.

That part of him had seemed very large, so she could certainly see why it might be painful. And yet she couldn't deny that
the thought of being joined to Morgan roused some primal part
of her. When she'd been aroused by his touch, she'd ached inside
as if her body longed for him to fill her. Did all women feel that
way?

She would ask him about all of these things tonight.

Just the thought of seeing him again sent a warm rush of
excitement through her. She slid her hands back up her body,
hugged herself, and spun on her toes, filled with the urge to
laugh. But she was already late for breakfast. She finished dressing, then hurried downstairs, her thoughts turning to Morgan's
punishment.

"Bourlamaque has set him to digging a privy," Lieutenant
Durand told her as he waited for his morning audience. Then he
grinned. "Rillieux is mucking the stables."

She sighed with relief, grateful Morgan had been spared some
greater humiliation. And the morning seemed even brighter.

Amalie drifted through the day in a dream. She tended the
roses in the garden, visited the hospital, mended one of
Bourlamaque's waistcoats. But although she spent the hours in
much the usual way, nothing felt the same.

The world had changed.

It was as if her heart had little wings, as if her body were made
of gossamer, as if everything around her were bathed in golden
light. She felt almost giddy and more than a little rebellious,

keeping the beautiful and precious secret of last night inside her.
Had she ever known such a feeling of happiness?

She was in love. She knew it. She must be.

She loved Morgan MacKinnon.

She moved through her day thinking of nothing but him. The
way he'd looked at her, his gaze both fierce and tender. The way
he'd been with her through every breath, every shiver. The way his
big man's body had pressed against her, surrounded her, his large
callused hands—hands that had killed—so gentle, unleashing
feelings inside her she'd never known before.

So much of her life she'd felt invisible, a dark girl in a world of
pretty, sun-haired children. Apart from her father, no one had
ever cared to hear her thoughts, unless it was to admonish her for
the nature of them. But Morgan, dear Morgan, listened to her. He
listened to her and saw things in her that no one had ever seen.

Oui, she loved him. He might be a Ranger, a *chi bai,* or even
the man who'd fired the shot that had killed her father, but still
she loved him.

The realization took her breath away, left her floating. And yet
it also left her with a niggling worry. What if he did not love her?

She did not see him again till supper, when he came to the table
in a French captain's uniform looking so handsome she found
it hard to breathe. His long hair was still damp from his bath, his
Scottish warrior braids hanging past his broad shoulders, which
were now adorned with golden epaulets. The dark blue of his coat
made his blue eyes seem even bluer, the sun-bronzed skin of his
face a sharp contrast to the white of his waistcoat. And across his
chest where a French officer of noble birth might have worn a
blue or red sash, he wore one of Scottish plaid in red, green, blue,
and white.

"Miss Chauvenet." He bowed, pressed a light kiss against the
back of her hand, his touch making her skin tingle. "How bonnie
you are this even."

But his gaze showed nothing of his feelings. Gone were both
the fierceness and the tenderness, replaced by a kind of distant
courtesy, as if he were only now making her acquaintance. And
though she tried to make conversation with him during the meal,

his attention and good humor were given to Bourlamaque and the other officers.

"To Capitaine MacKinnon, who was a French ally in his heart all along!" Bourlamaque said, toasting Morgan with a glass of his favorite Bordeaux.

Even Lieutenant Rillieux joined in the chorus of cheers, raising his glass and drinking deeply, his dislike for Morgan apparently overcome at last.

It ought to have been the happiest of moments, and Amalie *was* happy, but rather than the intimacy she'd felt this morning when Morgan had kissed her awake and sent her to her own bed, she felt only emptiness stretching between them.

It wasn't until after the men had retired to Bourlamaque's study for their nightly brandy that she had the chance to speak with Morgan. She found him standing alone in the sitting room staring out the front window as she had the night when he'd first kissed her. Even from a distance, she could feel the tension seething beneath his skin.

She walked up behind him. "Morgan?"

At the sound of her voice, he stiffened. "Let me be, lass."

She might have done as he asked, but she felt so lost and confused, and she needed to understand. Almost afraid to hear his response, she summoned the courage to speak. "Please do not turn me away. If you do not care for me, if I've done something to earn your displeasure, please tell me."

He kept his back to her, his body rigid, and when at last he answered her, his voice seemed strangely flat. "There was a lass in my village on Skye who let herself be wooed and deceived by an English soldier. They met in secret until her belly grew big and round with his bairn. After the babe was born, she was dragged from her father's house into the streets, where the women struck her and cut off her hair. Men and women and children threw slops at her and berated her with shouts and curses, drivin' her from the village and into the wild. I was only a lad at the time, but recall the horror on her young face. I dinnae ken whether she and the bairn survived or whether they died of cold and hunger. No one spoke of her again."

"Why are you telling me this?"

"Though Bourlamaque has accepted me, not every man here

has. To them, I am still the enemy. I wouldna see such a terrible fate befall you, lass."

"But how could such a thing happen?" The very thought was laughable. "You are one of us now. Monsieur de Bourlamaque would not permit it!"

"We are in the midst of a war, Amalie. None of us can see where this will end. If it should become known that you and I . . ."

His words unsettled her even though she knew what he was describing could never happen. "No man here would dare to harm me, not with you and Monsieur de Bourlamaque to protect me. Besides, Monsieur de Bourlamaque has given his blessing for you—"

"Aye, he has granted me permission to court you, and in turn I have given him my word that I willna dishonor you. And yet if you come to me again in the night, I dinnae ken if I can keep that promise."

It was then she noticed that his fists were clenched.

She wanted to reassure him, wanted to know what she knew—that he was an honorable man and would never deliberately hurt her. "Last night, you—"

He turned to face her, his eyes filled with anguish. "Aye, last night I kept my word, but I am a man, Amalie. My blood is as red as any man's. The fire has been put out in you, but not in me. All day I've suffered in a hell of my own makin', wantin' what I cannae have. I've tried to work you out of my blood, tried to sweat you out, but the moment I set eyes upon you or hear your voice . . . I ken you dinnae understand what I'm sayin', but for pity's sake, lass, keep to your own bed. You and I—we cannae be."

Then he turned and strode toward Bourlamaque's study to join the other officers, leaving her alone and shattered.

"My brother is dead! He died savin' another man's life! He is no' a traitor!" Connor MacKinnon's voice roared through William's study, his skin flushed with rage, his nostrils flared, his face pressed to within inches of William's.

"You yourself have delivered the evidence against him. These were taken in your last raid." William handed Captain MacKinnon the dispatches he and his men had stolen and watched as the rage on MacKinnon's face turned first to disbelief and then to shock.

William had had much the same reaction. Witnesses had watched Morgan MacKinnon fall in battle, had watched as the French had carried his body off in triumph. Bourlamaque's letter, signed by his own hand, had claimed that MacKinnon was dead. And yet Montcalm's missives revealed a very different truth.

The words ran through William's mind, words he'd read a dozen times this morning and then again this evening, some part of him strangely reluctant to believe his own eyes.

"As far as our new friend MacKinnon is concerned, it seems you may have been wise to offer him sanctuary. His obedience thus far commends him to me. I will admit I should like to have watched him shoot. I have never seen a man fire four shots in a minute, or strike his marks with the consistency you described in your last letter. His instruction of our soldiers might prove quite useful in this regard. And yet, my dear friend, I caution you again not to trust him fully, as you cannot be certain he does not possess some hidden purpose of his own."

Though he'd led the Rangers for only a handful of months, Morgan MacKinnon had proved to be as dedicated a commander as his elder brother had been. William had trusted him to lead his men through the most calamitous circumstances with a clear mind. He trusted him to carry out his mission without fail. He trusted him to put military objectives ahead of personal ones. He'd trusted him and had never been disappointed—until now.

For it seemed that Morgan MacKinnon was not dead, as Bourlamaque had led them to believe, but had instead taken shelter with the enemy.

Deserter. Turncoat. Traitor.

These were words William could scarce associate with Morgan MacKinnon. The man's loyalty to his brothers was unquestionable, his sense of duty to his men unflagging, his notion of honor—flavored by a certain Gaelic tendency toward romantic idealism—unimpeachable. It seemed impossible that he should choose to betray his brothers by teaching the French skills that would enable them to confront and slay his own men.

And then again, why not? He wouldn't be the first man to break under torture, nor the first to save his own life by yielding secrets to the enemy. His forebears were Catholic Jacobites, long allied with the French. What was to keep him from going over to the French the moment they took him captive?

His brothers. His men.

William could not imagine him betraying them, and yet Montcalm's dispatches to Bourlamaque were very clear.

Captain MacKinnon threw the letters down on William's writing table. "Lies! 'Tis naugh' but lies!"

"Is it?" William strode to the window and looked out at the darkened parade grounds. "In the past month, how many caches have you lost to the French?"

"We've lost three, but that doesna mean—"

"And in the three years prior to that?"

For a moment there was silence, and William could feel Captain MacKinnon's seething rage. When the captain finally answered, he spoke through gritted teeth. "One."

"How many rendezvous points and camping sites have the enemy taken from you?"

"Four, but they were old and rarely used."

"Does it not strike you as a strange coincidence that the French have had such successes only since your brother was—"

"I willna listen to such slander! My brother could no more betray the Rangers than he could slay me wi' his bare hands!"

"Then how would you explain it?" William turned to face him, found fifteen stone of angry Highlander standing close behind him, fists clenched, eyes filled with undisguised hatred. "How would you explain the meaning of Montcalm's letters?"

"I cannae explain it!" The captain grabbed the letters off William's writing table, crumpled them in his fist, then threw them back onto the table. "I willna believe it wi'out seein' it wi' my own eyes!"

This was the response William had expected. "In that case, I have a mission for you. And, Captain, let us keep this to ourselves."

Chapter 19

Morgan moved silently down the darkened hallway toward Bourlamaque's study, his bloody sense of duty the only thing driving him forward. Och, how he hated this—the lies, the deception, the damnable slinking about. A man who trusted him, a man he'd be honored to serve in battle, lay asleep in his bed, while Morgan crept about his home like a midden rat, stealing secrets to give to that whoreson Wentworth.

He'd waited until the darkest hours of night to leave his room, fearing Amalie might come to his bed despite his plea that she keep to her own. He'd sensed her hurt and frustration and had been certain she would defy him, but she hadn't. And although his mind was glad she'd heeded him, his body was not.

All day long he'd worked in the hot sun, trying to get her out of his mind. He'd dug halfway to hell it seemed, shoveling dirt and sand until his back and shoulders had ached, and still he hadn't been able to free himself of his need for her. He'd been assailed by memories of her lying beside him, her beautiful breasts bared, her silky thighs spread for him, her body trembling with pleasure as she'd claimed her peak and come against his hand.

And then memories had turned to daydreams, and in the secrecy of his own lustful thoughts, he'd done far more than give her ease. He'd kissed his way down her creamy skin and buried his face between her thighs, drawing her sweet nectar down his throat until she'd begged him to end her torment. Then he'd forced her thighs far apart with his own, grasped her hips, and buried his cock inside her, thrusting into her like an animal, driving them both over the edge, spilling his seed inside her. But no sooner had one daydream ended than the next had begun, until he'd taken her in every way a man could take a woman.

A barbarian—'tis what you are, MacKinnon.

Aye, he was a barbarian. And yet it was in the midst of his daydreams, his head buzzing with lust, that he'd realized he'd already gone too far with her. She'd saved his life—twice—and he'd repaid her kindness by rousing desires inside her that he could not fulfill, not if he cared even the smallest whit for her.

And, aye, he did care. That's why he'd pushed her away, warning her as best he could without giving himself away *not* to trust him, *not* to be seen with him, *not* to love him. His rejection had hurt her, he knew, and it had taken every bit of strength he had to walk away from her. But it was better this way. Anything else would risk not only her innocence, but also her happiness, her life—and his mission.

And what is your bloody mission, laddie?

To get home alive.

Aye, to get home to his brothers alive.

No matter what he felt for Amalie, this war, a war that was not of their making, divided them. She was French, while he was bound to the British. And although he would have had no trouble turning his back on that heretic Wentworth, he could not desert his brothers or his men nor join any who sought to harm them.

Forcing his mind off Amalie and onto the matter at hand, he took the candle from its place on the console and carried it to Bourlamaque's study, which, as always, stood unlocked. He set the candle down on the old man's writing table, quickly found Montcalm's latest packet of dispatches, and began to read.

The letter opened with the usual news of family and friends before turning to matters of war. *"Alas, my friend, we have word that Wolfe intends to land his forces at Québec and lay siege to the city. I do not need to impress upon you the peril we shall face, nor the consequences to France should we not prevail. I fear that if we lose Québec, we lose New France. Therefore, do not engage the enemy at Carillon, but rather withdraw in good time to Fort Chambly and hold the north of Lake Champlain to keep Amherst from gaining Montréal."*

So that's what Bourlamaque had meant when he'd said it would soon be safer to return Amalie to the abbey. She would be safe because she'd be under the escort of more than five thousand seasoned French troops and Bourlamaque himself. By high summer, she'd be safely returned to Trois Rivières.

Morgan felt a sense of peace at that, knowing she'd be far from the frontier—and far away from him. For by the time Amherst moved his army against Ticonderoga, Morgan would long since have found his way back to Fort Edward or died in the attempt. He would not be going north with the French.

And then it struck him.

If Bourlamaque fled at Amherst's approach, Morgan would not have to raise his rifle against him or his men—Durand, Fouchet, even that bastard Rillieux.

Thanks be to God!

Morgan had already been dreading the day he would have to lead his men against Bourlamaque and the fort's other inhabitants. To kill the man who had spared his life . . .

But there was more. The French were losing this war, and Montcalm and Bourlamaque knew it. The tide had turned. It was only a matter of time before Britain claimed the victory and—

He heard a gasp, jerked his head around. And there in the doorway, her eyes wide with shock, her feet bare, her body sheathed only by her nightgown, stood Amalie.

"Wh-what are you doing?" Even as she asked the question, Amalie could see very well what Morgan was doing.

Wearing only his drawers, he sat at Bourlamaque's writing table reading private correspondence by the light of the hall candle. And yet how could he, for he did not speak French. Unless . . .

"Non!" The word was a plea. She could not believe it, did not want to believe it. And yet, the truth was there before her eyes.

The man she loved was a traitor.

Something shattered inside her chest, leaving her staggered, the pain of it almost unbearable. Blood rushed into her head, panic making her heart trip, her tongue stilled by shock, the drone of her pulse drowning out the silence.

"Go back to bed, Amalie." His voice was hard, his hands fast as he stowed the letters away, clearly familiar with the contents of Bourlamaque's writing table.

As if he'd done this many times before.

Candle in hand, he walked around the writing table toward her, his gaze hard upon her like that of some wild animal measuring its prey.

Her heart thudding against her ribs, she took a step backward into the hallway, then another and another, watching as if under some spell as he followed her, soundlessly shutting the door to Bourlamaque's study and setting the flickering candle back on the console, his expression inscrutable.

Then she turned—and ran.

But she'd taken only a step or two when he caught her, one strong arm capturing her beneath her breasts and drawing her hard against his chest, a big hand covering her mouth, trapping her scream. Lifted off her feet, she kicked and thrashed as he carried her down the hallway to his room and shut the door behind them.

But he did not release her. Instead, he held her tighter, pressing his lips to her ear, his voice an angry whisper. "Quit your strugglin' afore you harm yourself!"

But his words only inflamed her rage, and she fought harder, kicking, clawing, biting at the hand that covered her mouth. To think she had kissed him! To think she had let him touch her! To think she had *loved* him!

"Ouch, for Satan!"

She tasted blood—then found herself thrown roughly onto the bed and pinned beneath him, her arms stretched over her head, both of her wrists held captive in one of his big hands, the weight of his body holding her unmoving.

A stranger, the enemy once more, he glared down at her. "You should have kept to your own bed, lass. Now what shall I do wi' you?"

But the pain in her chest was such that she did not hear the warning in his voice. "Bourlamaque gave you sanctuary, and you betrayed him! You betrayed me!"

"Aye, I deceived Bourlamaque, and I'll regret it to the end of my days. But long afore I pledged my loyalty to him, I made another oath—to my brothers and my men. Would you have me break that vow and become a betrayer and slayer of my own kin? As you loved your father, so I love them!"

She heard his words, felt the conflict within him, but was too hurt, too outraged to care, hot tears pricking her eyes. "Then it was lies, all of it—your being forced to serve the British, your hatred for your commander, your admiration for Monsieur de Bourlamaque!"

"Nay, it was the truth, every word." His brow was furrowed, his breath hot on her face. "I would much rather serve Bourlamaque than that bastard Wentworth, but I cannae forsake my brothers or the Rangers. I told Bourlamaque this when I lay in chains, but he chose to forget. He allowed himself to be deceived."

"And what of your feelings for me?" The question was almost too painful to ask. "Have I let myself be deceived as well?"

She should have known from the way his eyes darkened what was coming, but when his mouth claimed hers, it took her by surprise.

It was a brutal kiss, rough and forceful, his lips pressing hard against hers, his tongue demanding entry, his body grinding over hers. She ought to have been furious, ought to have found his touch revolting, ought to have turned her head away, fought him, kicked. Instead, she felt a desperate surge of desire.

Never had she hated anyone as she hated him—*Traitor! Deceiver!*—and yet never had his kisses affected her so. Anger, carnal need, love—she could not tell where one emotion ended and the next began. She arched against him, returning his ferocity with her own, nipping his lips, biting down on his tongue, fighting to take control of the kiss from him. And yet even as she fought him, even as he freed her wrists, her body surrendered. Hands that should have struck him slid eagerly over the smooth skin and muscle of his chest, caressed the hard curve of his shoulders, fisted themselves in his thick hair—and she knew the battle was lost.

Morgan gave Amalie no quarter. Once again, she held his fate in her hands, a word from her enough to send him off to be roasted by the Abenaki. She had defied him, leaving her bed to seek his, uncovering his treason. But it was bed play she'd sought from him, and so, by God, she would have it!

He bared her breasts to his roving hands and hungry mouth, teasing and tasting her until she writhed from it. Then he drew up her nightgown in urgent fistfuls, forced her thighs apart, and began to press deep circles against her sex, his fingers delving

PAMELA CLARE

down to tease her virgin entrance. She was already wet, proof of her need for him gathering like dew on his fingertips, her musky scent bidding him to take her, her frantic whimpers driving him mad.

Never had Morgan forced himself on a woman, but his mother's Viking blood burnt in him now, ruthless and hot, urging him to claim Amalie without ceremony, to mark her in the most primal way a man could, to satisfy himself with her sweet body again and again.

With a growl that sounded more animal than human even to his own ears, he shifted his mouth from one velvety nipple to the other, suckling her without mercy, his hand unrelenting. Then, ignoring her startled gasp, he slid one finger inside her, testing her maidenhead, stretching her, stroking that part of her no man had touched—and she shattered.

He captured her cry with a kiss, took her breath into his lungs, his hand keeping up the rhythm until her pleasure was spent, her slick inner muscles clenching tightly around his finger, making him wish for all the world it was his cock inside her.

And that is how Bourlamaque found them—Morgan on top of Amalie, her breasts bared, her head thrown back in ecstasy as she found release.

"What in the name of the devil is happening here?" Bourlamaque's voice filled the room like thunder.

Amalie shrieked, struggling to cover herself.

Instinctively, Morgan shielded her from the old man's view, helping her to draw her nightgown over her shoulders. "Easy, lass. We'll soon sort this out."

But Morgan knew nothing could be further from the truth. Not only was Amalie facing Bourlamaque's wrath, but she was also carrying a terrible secret, which, if revealed, would lead Morgan to his death.

'Tis a fine predicament you find yourself in, aye, laddie?

"Have I not treated you with kindness befitting my own daughter? Have I not granted you every comfort? Have I not shown you every consideration?"

Acutely aware that he was clad only in his drawers—and still sporting a raging cockstand—Morgan watched, his teeth grinding, as Bourlamaque, wearing his dressing gown, berated Amalie in French. She trembled before the old man, the blanket Morgan had draped around her shoulders for modesty's sake clutched tight around her, but her chin was held high.

"Si, monsieur," she answered, her voice all but a whisper.

She had not yet said anything about what she'd seen, though Morgan knew the secret weighed heavily upon her. He could see it in the distress on her face, in the tense way she held herself, in her unshed tears.

"And you!" Bourlamaque switched into English and stepped over to Morgan, his face mottled with rage. "Did you not this very morning promise me that you would not dishonor her?"

Morgan met Bourlamaque's gaze. "She is a virgin still."

The old man gaped at him as if he'd said something daft. "Is that all 'dishonor' means to you—taking her virginity? What of chastity, Captain? What of purity?"

"Believe me, sir, when I say I didna intend for this to happen tonight. I meant no insult to—"

Amalie's words cut him off. "I . . . I came to him, monsieur. I came to him though he bade me not to tempt him."

Astonished, Morgan met her gaze and knew in that moment that she would not reveal his treachery to her guardian. Though he could not fathom her reasons for this, the realization filled him with bittersweet sadness—relief that he would not burn in the fires of the Abenaki and yet remorse that she who had been blameless until he arrived should now share in his guilt.

"Is this true?" Bourlamaque asked him.

Morgan hesitated, his instinct to shield her from shame. But the words had already been spoken. "Aye, sir."

Bourlamaque looked from Morgan to Amalie, his jaw set, a strange light in his eyes. "Amalie, you have at long last made your choice. You shall marry Capitaine MacKinnon as soon as it can be arranged. Do you understand? Both of you?"

Marry?

For a moment Morgan thought he'd misunderstood.

"M-marry him?" Wide-eyed, she gaped at her guardian, looking every bit as stamagastert as Morgan felt. Then her gaze fell to the floor. *"Oui, monsieur. Je comprends."*

"Aye, sir."

A fine predicament, indeed.

* * *

The wedding took place three days later, for that was how long it took Bourlamaque's tailor, who claimed he had not the skill to make women's garments, to finish stitching Amalie's wedding gown. Bourlamaque had spared no expense, the entire fort working together to prepare for the event, war-weary men eager for a ritual that celebrated life, not death.

Amalie wanted to be as happy as any bride should be, but her heart was full of misgiving, for the match she had made was far from the love match her parents had found together. Not only was her groom being brought unwilling to the altar, he was a spy for the British. Not that Morgan had given away any French secrets; he hadn't yet had the chance. But he had clearly deceived Bourlamaque in hopes of one day passing on all that he had learned to his commander. And that meant he hoped to escape.

Amalie feared she would not have a husband for long.

She could have denounced him to Bourlamaque, telling him what she'd witnessed, but she knew that if she did, Bourlamaque would clap Morgan in irons and order his death. God save her, but she loved Morgan too much, even despite what he'd done, to see him come to such an end. Racked with guilt, her loyalties torn, she'd shed an ocean of tears, hiding them from the others, wishing she'd kept to her room that night, wishing she hadn't seen.

She wanted to talk with Morgan, to demand an explanation, to hear what he would say. But Bourlamaque had kept them apart, setting Morgan to hard labor during the day and sleeping with the door to his room wide open at night.

And so she found herself on Bourlamaque's arm, wearing a beautiful gown of ivory silk, being led into a chapel full of officers toward Morgan, who stood at the altar in full dress uniform, the most handsome man she'd ever seen. Seeming every inch the proud husband-to-be, he took her hand from Bourlamaque and gave her a reassuring smile, his blue eyes filled with tenderness, his hand steady and warm. But as he promised to love, honor, and cherish her all the days of his life, his deep voice filling the tiny chapel, she heard other words.

Long afore I pledged my loyalty to Bourlamaque, I made another oath—to my brothers and my men.

And she prayed for a miracle.

Chapter 20

"Congratulations on the occasion of your marriage and your acceptance into our army, Capitaine MacKinnon!" The young adjutant—Morgan couldn't recall his name—spoke in heavily accented English and raised his brandy glass.

Morgan acknowledged the kind words with a bow of his head, raising his own glass. "Thank you, sir."

So it had gone all evening, a sea of men in uniform pressing in to congratulate him on his good fortune and to offer their most gracious blessings, some sincere, some peppered with poorly veiled resentment.

"Why should he, a foreigner, wed Major Chauvenet's daughter when it was his Rangers who killed the major?" he'd heard more than one soldier ask in whispered French. "Lieutenant Rillieux asked for her hand and was rebuffed straightaway!"

Rillieux had been notably absent from both the wedding and the dinner feast that had followed. This surprised Morgan not at all. Rillieux was a prideful man, not the sort to accept defeat with grace. He would not find it easy to watch the lass he'd lusted after marry a man he hated. Nay, Morgan was not fooled by Rillieux's smiles and friendly manner. The *mac-dìolain* hated him still, and no mistake. He was not the sort to forgive and forget.

"Félicitations!" said a sergeant, who apparently could not speak English, a broad smile on his freckled face.

"You are a fortunate man, Capitaine MacKinnon!" A young man, a *sous-lieutenant* from the look of his uniform, stepped forward. "For you have plucked our fairest flower!"

The adjutant leaned nearer, a conspiratorial look on his face. "Here at Fort Carillon, she was the only flower that had not been plucked, *n'est-ce pas?*"

Morgan chuckled along with them, trying not to grit his teeth, this blether about plucking flowers making him surly, given that the flower in question was Amalie. "Aye, I am a lucky man, and well I ken it."

God in heaven, she'd been a beautiful bride! The sight of her in her wedding gown had made his chest ache, stealing his breath, robbing him of his wit. Like an angel she'd come to him. The officers in the chapel had watched her walk up the aisle, wistful looks on their uggsome faces. Even the camp followers had turned out, standing off in the distance to catch a glimpse of something none of them would ever be—a virgin bride.

Morgan had seen the trepidation on Amalie's face as she'd approached him and had known her fear to be more than a maid's wedding jitters, the secret she kept wearing heavily upon her. Mindful not to shame her before the men, he'd done his best in that hour to be the man she deserved, showing her every courtesy a gentleman should show his lady on the day of their wedding, knowing he would soon hurt her unforgivably.

She had retired to his room—*their* room—almost an hour past, the young kitchen maid with her. He'd felt a wave of pity for her as she'd walked away, a look of worry on her bonnie face when there ought to have been only joy. A woman in a world of rough soldiers, she had no female kin to tend her and prepare her for her wedding night, as any new bride should.

Go to her.

The call came to him, drowning out men's conversation, their raucous laughter, the lilt of fiddle music. Headier than brandy, it tugged at his chest, his gut, his groin, a promise of pleasures, of Amalie's soft sighs and caresses, of her feminine sweetness.

Go to her.

But Morgan stood rooted to the spot, as he had since she'd left his side, for theirs would not be a true wedding night. He would not lie with her, could not lie with her. No matter that her sweet body was now his by right. He would not rob her of her maidenhood and risk getting her with child when he would be leaving her ere the sun's rising. Better to leave her maidenhead intact so that she could seek an annulment once he was gone, freeing herself to marry the man who was worthy of her love.

Aye, 'twas the only honorable thing Morgan could do.

And yet he did not trust himself to do it. He did not trust himself to be near her, not when weeks of wanting her, days of kissing her, and nights of pleasuring her had left him starving for her, the hunger inside him so raw that he felt he could devour her in one succulent bite. And so he stood, fixed to the floor of Bourlamaque's front room amidst lingering revelers.

'Tis quite the irony is it no', laddie? You're husband to a bonnie sweet lass who is everything a man could ever want in a wife, a lass who even now awaits you in your bed—and you cannae have her.

Aye, it was an irony at that.

Somewhere, Satan himself was laughing.

Go to her.

"So the groom sips brandy long after his bride has gone to bed." Rillieux stepped forward through the throng, impeccably dressed, every button on his uniform polished to a shine, a grin on his face. "If she were my wife, I'd long since have joined her."

There were shouts of agreement, laughter.

Morgan met Rillieux's gaze, smiled. "A man should ne'er rush a woman when it comes to passion."

Rillieux's grin broadened. "Or perhaps you fear you cannot rise to the occasion."

Laughter turned to guffaws as the humor became more ribald.

Morgan chuckled. "You Frenchmen fight wi' wee sabers, aye? We Highland Scots carry broadswords. They ne'er fail us."

More guffaws and a shout or two of protest.

Some of the amusement faded from Rillieux's face, his eyes betraying the hatred he'd been trying to mask. "We French are renowned the world over as lovers, while you *Scots*"—he spat the word—"are known for your dourness."

There was no laughter now, only silence.

"Is that so?" Morgan tossed back the last of his brandy, set the crystal snifter aside. "Then remember this—in a fort full of Frenchmen, the lass chose a Scot."

Then Morgan turned and strode toward his room—and his waiting bride.

W hen would he come to her?
      Amalie sat on the edge of Morgan's big bed, waiting, the sound of violins and men's laughter loud through the walls. Perhaps she shouldn't have sent Thérèse away so quickly. Perhaps she ought to have asked her to stay awhile.

It was harder to wait alone.

Thérèse had prepared Amalie's bath, scenting the water with rose petals and lavender sprigs. She'd brushed Amalie's hair until it gleamed. Then she'd helped Amalie slip into her new nightgown, a shimmering garment of white silk so light that it felt like a whisper against her skin.

"He won't be able to think of anything but you," Thérèse had said. "Oh, how I envy you! To be brought to my wedding bed by a man as handsome and virile as Capitaine MacKinnon! Did you see how he scarcely took his eyes off you all day? He's in love with you, mademoiselle."

Amalie had managed a smile for Thérèse's sake, but inside she'd wanted to weep. Though Morgan had doted on her throughout the day, showing her every kindness a husband could, she knew he'd only married her because Bourlamaque had commanded it. Oh, yes, he cared about her and even desired her. He'd shown her that in the way he spoke with her, in the way he protected her, in the way he'd kissed her and given her pleasure.

But he did not love her.

Worse, he was set upon betraying her king and country. And no matter how much she hoped this marriage would dissuade him from that path, she knew in her heart that he would soon leave her, risking his life to rejoin his brothers and the Rangers. Then he would take up arms against the very men who now drank his health.

I would much rather serve Bourlamaque than that bastard Wentworth, but I cannae forsake my brothers or the Rangers. As you loved your father, I love them!

More laughter.

Amalie stood and paced the floor, drawing a steadying breath, her heart beating too fast, her belly aflutter with butterflies, unanswered questions that had troubled her for three long days chasing one another in dizzy circles through her mind.

Why, if he loathed his British commander, would he steal secrets for him? How could he think to betray Bourlamaque when Bourlamaque had spared his life and treated him with honor? Why could he not persuade his brothers to shake off their British yoke and join him here under the banner of the fleur-de-lis? How could he possibly think to escape the fort without being caught or shot? And what if he returned to his Rangers only to be killed in battle? How would she be able to bear it?

Then again, why should she care? How could she still love him after all he'd done? He'd taken advantage of his reprieve from death—a reprieve she'd won for him—to spy against the very man who'd shown him mercy. He'd lied about not speaking French, letting her play the teacher while he feigned ignorance. And while he'd been busy deceiving them, his Rangers had slaughtered French soldiers by the score.

He was the enemy.

And yet he was no such thing.

There was goodness in him and honor as solid as stone. She had seen it when he'd protected her from Rillieux, when he'd knelt at prayer, when he'd buried the remains of his friend. His betrayal of Bourlamaque was an act of loyalty to his brothers, to the men who'd fought and died for him. Although it might make her grief easier to bear if she could find it in herself to be angry with him or even to hate him for what he'd done, how could she fault him for being loyal to his own flesh and blood?

She walked to the open window, threw wide the panes, and breathed in the warm night air, trying to calm the turmoil inside her. Of course, it was not just his betrayal or the awkward circumstances of their marriage that had set her emotions on edge. It was also the thought of what would happen in that big bed tonight.

Dear, kind Bourlamaque had called her aside and, red to the roots of his powdered wig, had assured her that she had nothing to fear about the marital act because Morgan would teach her all she needed to know. "Which he seems already well on his way to having done," he'd added, with a slight frown.

Then it had been Amalie's turn to blush.

Thérèse had been a bit more helpful, if less reassuring. "Maman told me it only hurts the first time."

As if knowing that would make Amalie any less fearful.

Behind her, men's voices grew suddenly louder, and light spilled into the room. Then, just as suddenly, it grew dark again, and the voices faced. And she knew.

He had come to her.

She kept her gaze on the stars, barely able to breathe, knowing that turning to face him meant also facing the answers to all her unasked questions.

"Amalie, lass?" His voice was deep as night.

She heard the rustle of fingers on buttons and knew he was removing his coat and waistcoat. His boots hit the floor with a dull thud. Then came the rasp of breeches sliding down long legs to the floor. And footsteps.

She felt the heat of his body behind her before he touched her, his hands cupping her shoulders, sliding down the length of her arms. Then he pressed his lips to the side of her throat and kissed her. Her eyes drifted shut.

"Your heart is beatin' like a wild bird's." His lips brushed over her skin as he spoke, his breath warm and scented with brandy. "What is it that's frightenin' you?"

She swallowed, tried to speak. "Tomorrow."

He drew her backward against his bare chest. "Dinnae trouble yourself about tomorrow. We must first face this night."

"Are you angry with me?"

He kissed her hair. *"C'est vous qui devriez être en colère contre moi, non?"* *It is you who should be angry with me, isn't that so?*

She stiffened, his fluent French final proof of his betrayal. But that's why he'd spoken in her tongue, she knew. He was laying his sins at her feet.

"Oui." Then she turned to face him, found that he was still wearing his drawers, his features half in candlelight and half in shadow. "Why, Morgan? Please tell me why? I thought you were happy here! I thought you were proud to serve amongst fellow Catholics, to fight for a Catholic king!"

"I belong wi' my brothers." There was sadness in his eyes—and regret. "But tell me—why have you no' revealed me to Bourlamaque?"

"I would not see you hanged or handed over to my cousins to be burnt."

For a moment, silence stretched between them, the sound of revelry floating on the evening breeze.

"Can you not persuade your brothers to join you here?" She knew she sounded like a petulant child, but she wanted to know, needed to understand.

He drew a breath, stroked a finger down her cheek. "Iain, the eldest, is husband to a noblewoman whose family has long been loyal to the British. They have a wee son—Iain Cameron. Connor, my younger brother, doesna remember much of Scotland. He's seen more cruelty at the hands of the French than the Sassenach. He would never forsake Iain or the men. Joseph and my Muhheconneok kin have been loyal to Britain from the earliest days and have enemies amongst France's Indian allies as well. They willna join the French, and I cannae take sides with those who would make war on the people I love."

Do you not love me?

The question was a silent cry, hopelessness yawning dark and deep in the pit of her stomach. "Then there is nothing I can say or do to convince you to stay?"

"Nay, lass." He pressed a kiss to her forehead and drew her into his strong arms. "This war divides us, Amalie. We didna start it, and, sadly, we cannae stop it. We didna ask for this, and yet we cannae change it by wishin' it were otherwise."

Tears blurred her vision at the truth in his words. "When will you go to them?"

"Soon."

"I'm afraid you will be caught or shot—"

"Shhh, lass." He held her tighter. "I cannae hold you in my arms and talk of war and sadness. Do you ken what I thought when you walked into the chapel this morn? I prayed, 'God in heaven, help me to find my tongue when 'tis time to speak my vows, for You've sent me one of Your angels, and her beauty strikes me senseless.' Ne'er has there been a more beautiful bride, Amalie."

She looked up at him and tried to smile. "And you looked very manly and handsome in your officer's uniform."

He cupped her face, his eyes dark with emotion. "Hear me when I say that I never meant to hurt you. If there were any way for me to stay wi' you, I would. You are all a man could hope for

in a wife, all a man could desire. Let me give what joy I can
tonight, and dinnae think upon tomorrow."

Tears spilling onto her cheeks, she stood on her toes and
pressed her lips to his, her answer a kiss.

Morgan held Amalie against his chest as she drifted to sleep,
stroking her hair, the musk and spice of her arousal mingling with the salt of his sweat. He forced himself to say what he
needed to say, for he could not ask her to remain faithful and
bound to him after he had abandoned her, no matter what he
might desire. "When I am gone, you can ask Bourlamaque to help
you seek an annulment. They cannae hold you to a marriage that
wasna consummated. Then you can marry whom you choose."

He did not see that his words brought fresh tears to her eyes.

For a time Morgan simply held her and watched her sleep,
delighting in the moment, memorizing her scent, every curve
of her soft body and feature of her sweet face. After tonight he
might never see her again. He would return to the Rangers and
the dangers of the battlefield, she to the quiet and safety of the
abbey, each awaiting the end of the war. And when enough blood
had been shed and the British had won—for Morgan was more
certain than ever they would—what then?

There would be peace along the frontier. Morgan would be
free at last to leave the killing behind and return to the MacKinnon farm to work the earth with his brothers. But to the victor
alone went the spoils. Amalie and all the French in the Canadas
would face British wrath. For the British had made it clear that
they meant not just to win the war, but to seize the land for their
feckless German king. Would they allow the French in Québec
and Montreal to remain, or would they force them off the land as
they had had the poor Acadians?

An image sprang unbidden to his mind of Amalie, alone and
fatherless, far from Bourlamaque, being torn from the safety of
the abbey's walls by leering British soldiers, Catholic haters, men
who would find it amusing to rape women sworn to chastity.

And in that moment Morgan made a vow.

If he survived to war's end, he would be there to protect her.

You're in love wi' her, laddie.

The thought hit him like a fist in the gut, and he knew it was true.

Had not some part of him loved her since he'd been in chains and had awoken to find her beside him? What a fine twist of fate that he, who had made love with many women without loving any of them, should lose himself to a wee French virgin, the daughter of the enemy, a woman he could not have. God's blood, he loved her, for leaving her felt like cutting off a part of himself. And yet he could not stay.

What harm would it cause to stay one more night? One more week? A fortnight?

But Morgan knew better. If he stayed tonight, and the next, and the next, there would dawn a day when he'd lose his will to leave her altogether.

Marshaling himself, he slid from the bed, dressed in dark breeches, a linen shirt, and moccasins, and gathered his gear, thinking through his plan. He would make his way through the shadows to the postern gate—they'd led him through it when he'd dug the latrine—and he'd subdue the two sentries on duty there, doing his best not to have to kill anyone. Then he'd cross the pier to the same riverbank where he'd been shot. From there, he'd be free, provided no one spotted him from the walls and sounded the alarm. Once he reached the enfolding shadows of the forest, they would not be able to track him.

He loaded his rifle and pistol, pulled on his tumpline pack, and slipped his sword through the strap—a Ranger again at last. Then he walked silently to the bed and looked down at her, pain and regret swelling in his chest until he feared he would not be able to breathe.

He'd given her all the love he could give tonight without taking her maidenhead, undressing her, carrying her to his bed, kissing away her tears, caressing her, bringing her to her peak with his hands again and again, until she lay, weak and utterly spent, in his arms. Then he'd held her through the watches of the night, wishing dawn would never come.

"*Tha móran ghràdh agam ort, dh'Amalaidh,*" he whispered. *My love lies upon you, Amalie.*

He lifted the rosary from around his neck and placed the wooden beads in her palm. Then he took the tartan sash from his

French uniform and draped it across the pillow beside her, branding her with Clan MacKinnon's colors. Would she know what that meant?

He bent down and pressed a kiss to her cheek, then strode quietly to the window. Outside, the sentry was in his usual place, asleep. The skies were clear, the moon riding high, the open night beckoning. But not as much as the lass who lay sleeping in the bed behind him. He turned away from the window, needing one last glance, his gaze raking her in. She looked so peaceful, lost in the forgetfulness of slumber.

The blow came from behind, pain exploding against his skull, shattering his thoughts.

A burst of bright white.

And then only darkness.

Chapter 21

Amalie opened her eyes, unable to say what had awoken her. "Morgan?"

She felt something in her hand.

His rosary.

And beside her on her pillow lay his plaid sash.

He is gone.

She clutched the two precious objects to her breast, her breath leaving her in a rush, tears stinging her eyes. She'd known he'd be leaving soon, but so soon?

And then it made sense—the intensity of his kisses, the way he'd spared no effort to pleasure her again and again, his refusal to remove his drawers or to let her touch him or to share himself with her fully. He'd been telling her farewell, knowing that he was leaving tonight.

Pain swelled in her chest, something inside her seeming to break.

And then she heard something—a groan?

It came from outside the window.

Her pulse tripping, she sat up only to remember that she was still naked. Slipping the rosary around her neck, she rose and hastily donned her nightgown, feeling the entire time that she was being watched. "M-Morgan?"

But there was no answer.

She walked toward the window, instinctively picking up his sash as she passed the bed, crumpling it in her hand, the weight of it in her fist making her feel somehow safer. Slowly she tiptoed across the room. "Morgan?"

Still no answer.

Chills chased down her spine.

She reached the window, looked outside—and felt her blood turn to ice.

In the shadows stood Tomas and Simon, holding an unconscious Morgan between them, tying a cloth over his mouth. On the ground behind them lay the sentry—not asleep, but dead, his mouth slack, his neck at a strange angle.

She drew a breath and might have screamed had she not just then felt something cold and sharp press against her throat.

"Don't make a sound!" Rillieux moved into view from where he'd been lurking beside the window. He grasped her about the waist, dragged her through over the sill, and clamped a cruel hand over her mouth. Then his gaze raked over her, lust and hatred blatant on his face. "Sorry to disrupt your wedding night, my sweet little *putain,* but from the sound of it, I'd say you've already had enough marital bliss. Besides, it seems the groom was in a hurry to leave your bed."

Had he been listening at the window? The thought turned Amalie's stomach. But she had bigger worries.

Rillieux yanked the sash from her hand and tied it painfully over her mouth, trapping her curses in her throat, silencing her. Then he turned to Tomas and Simon. "You'll have to take her north with you. We can't leave a witness."

Take her north? To Oganak?

Tomas and Simon looked at each other, and Tomas nodded to Rillieux.

Mon Dieu, non!

Cold horror uncoiled in her belly, snaking its way up her throat like bile. They were taking Morgan to Oganak, where they would torture him and burn him alive—and they were forcing her to come with them.

She met Tomas's gaze, pleading without words for his help, only to watch him look guiltily away. And then Rillieux twisted her right arm painfully behind her back and forced her to walk before him.

Wake up, Morgan! Wake up!

But he did not wake—and she need look no farther than the tomahawk hanging from Tomas's belt to see why.

God, please don't let him die!

Through the shadows they crept toward the postern gate, following Tomas and Simon, who struggled to carry Morgan's body between them, his gear on Tomas's back. Amalie shivered despite the summer heat, her bare feet stumbling painfully over sharp stones, her legs not long enough to match Rillieux's stride, forcing him to half drag and half carry her. And though Amalie prayed that someone would see them and raise the alarm, no one came.

How could Rillieux think to get away with this? Bourlamaque would send troops after them to bring them home. Rillieux would be hanged for kidnapping, Tomas and Simon beside him.

But how will he know you've been kidnapped?

The answer came swiftly, leaving Amalie sick and dizzy. Bourlamaque would not know they'd been kidnapped. The open window, Morgan's gear gone, the sentry slain—he'd think Morgan had fled and had taken her with him. If he did send troops, they would head south, not north, hoping to capture Morgan on his way to Fort Edward.

Abruptly, Rillieux jerked her to a stop, then called out. "Marquet! Renaud!"

The two sentries standing near the postern gate stepped out of the shadows.

"I see it worked," said one.

They were a part of this plot, too?

Though Bourlamaque has accepted me, not every man here has. To them, I am still the enemy. I wouldna see such a terrible fate befall you, lass.

Morgan's words came back to her.

One of the sentries stepped into their path, his gaze on Amalie. "You didn't say anything about taking her! Are you mad? She's Bourlamaque's ward! He'll kill you for this! You'd best take her back."

Oh, thank God! Thank God!

But Rillieux only laughed. "She's no longer Bourlamaque's

ward. She's MacKinnon's whore. If I leave her here, she'll tell Bourlamaque everything, and the two of you will find yourselves in the guardhouse beside me. Now let us pass before someone sees us."

Amalie struggled against Rillieux's hold on her, tried to cry out, but her words were nothing more than strangled whimpers, his fingers digging like claws into her arms.

Please help me! Please!

The sentry did not move. "Look at her. Poor little thing. She's terrified."

"She's afraid for the whoreson she married, not for herself. These two men are her cousins. I'm merely sending her north to live with them. She'll come to no harm at their hands. Now get out of my way, Renaud—and that's an order!"

Hesitantly, the sentry stepped aside. "I don't like this."

Rillieux thrust Amalie before him, Tomas and Simon following with Morgan.

And then they were outside the gates, hurrying across the pier to the riverbank, nothing between them and the dark wall of the forest but sand.

Mary, Mother of God, help us!

They hadn't gone deep into the forest when Amalie heard voices, and a dozen or so men stepped out of the shadows, their chests and faces painted with ash.

Abenaki.

Her mother's people.

Sick with dread and shivering with fear, she watched as they greeted Tomas and Simon, who dropped Morgan to the forest floor and stood about staring down at him, as if he were a great antlered buck they'd brought down. Then, with smiles on their faces, they began to recount their deeds at the fort—at least that's what Amalie thought they were talking about, her Abenaki so limited that she understood only a word here and there.

"Come," Rillieux whispered in her ear. "I should like to speak with you before you leave on your long journey."

He dragged her off into a stand of trees beyond earshot of the others. But once he got her there, it was clear he wanted to do far more than speak with her.

In a heartbeat, she found herself drawn back against him and held fast, one of his hands sliding over her breasts, squeezing them, pinching her nipples, the other thrusting up beneath her nightgown to grope between her thighs.

"Still wet." Then he shoved her to the ground. "Whore!"

She fell to her hands and knees, tried to scramble to her feet, but he landed on top of her, crushing her to the ground, that part of him hard and pressing against her hip.

"You ought to have chosen me, Amalie." His breath was sour, his whiskers burning her cheek. "Now I'll take what I want anyway."

One moment he was upon her, the next his weight was lifted, and she knew he was fumbling with his breeches.

Terror clawing at her belly, Amalie rolled onto her back and kicked blindly at him again and again, driving her feet into his shoulders and chest and stomach, making him grunt and curse. He would not have her without a fight!

She tore off the sash that had silenced her and managed to scream. "Morgan!"

But though she fought Rillieux, she could not overcome him.

"You little bitch!" He drew back his fist and struck her across the face, once, twice, a third time, the pain of it stunning her, darkness threatening to swallow her.

She felt him force her thighs apart, but could not summon the strength to stop him.

And then something strange happened.

In the bushes, she thought she saw Morgan. His gaze was fixed on Rillieux, hatred in his eyes, his face covered with sweat and war paint. Between his teeth, he held a hunting knife. She tried to reach for him. "Morgan?"

But she must have imagined him, for in the next instant, she heard Rillieux grunt, and it was Simon who loomed over her, not Morgan.

"Come, cousin." Simon lifted her to her feet, helping her to walk away from Rillieux, who lay on his back, moaning and clutching his head, his breeches down about his knees.

Barely able to stand, her head throbbing, her mind numb with shock, she let Simon lead her back to the clearing, where the other men stood gathered around something, chuckling and whispering.

Then one of the men moved aside, and she saw.

Still unconscious, Morgan lay with his arms and legs spread, tied by wrist and ankle to a travois. And through her pain and shock, Amalie understood.

If she did not manage somehow to unbind him and help him to escape, he would burn to death in the fires of her grandmother's village.

M organ's first thought was that he'd once again drunk too bloody much rum. His head throbbed. His throat was parched as sand. And when he opened his eyes, the world seemed to spin, the forest canopy swirling above him and, beyond that, a darkened sky.

Then he heard men's voices.

"We can stop beyond the next marsh, and let the girl rest."

"My cousin needs to grow stronger if she is to live amongst us."

They were speaking Abenaki. And although Morgan didn't recognize the first voice, he did recognize the second. It belonged to Tomas, Amalie's cousin.

"If she is your cousin, why do you lead her on a rope like a slave?"

"She is my mother's sister's daughter, but she is also *that* one's wife. If I release her, she will try to aid him."

A man laughed. "She might try, but she would not succeed. There are thirty-two of us. She is but one small woman."

Slowly, the meaning of the words began to penetrate the ache in Morgan's skull, a vague sense of alarm threading its way from his belly to his brain.

Amalie?

He opened his eyes and found himself a prisoner, tied to a travois, leather bonds digging into his wrists and ankles, his mouth gagged with a foul-tasting cloth. What he'd thought was spinning was but the passing of the trees overhead as the travois bounced and jerked across the forest floor, dragged by two warriors. Around him walked more than a score of Abenaki warriors, including Simon and Tomas.

And behind Tomas walked Amalie.

He led her like a dog, a leather cord tied around her throat. She wore only her bridal nightgown, the white silk now stained by grass and dirt, but still revealing more than it concealed.

Although he could not see her face, he could feel her fear and despair, and he knew from her stumbling that she was exhausted.

Rage, red and scalding, burnt up from his gut and chased the fog from his mind, bringing him fully awake, life surging into his lungs and limbs.

Then she stumbled and fell with a cry.

Tomas turned on her, glaring at her. "Get up!"

Then a tall warrior with long hair strode angrily over to her. But rather than striking Amalie, he shoved Tomas away and jerked the leather cord from his hand. "I told you she needed to stop and rest. What would your mother say to see you treat her sister's daughter so?"

With that, the tall warrior drew out his knife and cut the cord from around her neck. "Tanial, bring me that spare pair of moccasins from your pack. You can have my share of MacKinnon's spoils."

That share happened to be the flask of poisoned rum.

As Morgan watched, infuriated by his own helplessness, the tall warrior slipped moccasins onto Amalie's bare feet and gave her water from his own water skin, muttering reassurances to her in French, tenderness on his face. Part of Morgan wanted to knock the bastard on his ass, but the other part of him was grateful.

If anything should happen to him, she would need a strong man to watch over her, someone who could both protect her and care for her.

"Merci, monsieur," she said, her voice sounding so small and frightened.

Then a warrior near Morgan shouted to the others. "He's awake!"

They crowded around him, painted faces staring curiously down at him.

You think you've got me, aye, laddies? But 'tis a long road yet to Oganak.

"Let me give him food and water!" Amalie stood toe to toe with Tomas, her body shaking with anger, water from the river they'd just crossed gathered in a spare water skin.

Do not show your fear, Amalie. Remember what Atoan told you.

Atoan, the tallest of the Abenaki, had seemingly taken her under his protection, freeing her from the cord Tomas had bound round her neck, giving her moccasins, water, and food, stopping their progress so that she could rest, whispering guidance to her, even bearing her on his back at the river crossing.

"Abenaki women are strong, little one," he'd told her. "Act like you are not afraid, and it will go easier for you."

Now she tried to do just that. "Monsieur MacKinnon spared your life, Tomas, or have you forgotten how he freely gave you his blood when he could have taken yours?"

Tomas's eyes narrowed, his face flushing red with mortification, and for a moment she thought he would strike her.

"What is this?" Tanial asked. "What does she mean, Tomakwa? Tell us."

Not waiting for Tomas's permission, she jerked her arm from his grip and pushed past him, leaving him to answer thorny questions. She walked to the travois, relieved to see that Morgan was both awake and alert, the rage in his eyes when he saw her bruised face proof that the blow to his head had not dulled his mind.

She eased the gag from his mouth. "Drink."

He drank deeply, swallow after swallow, his gaze never leaving hers.

"I will cut you free," she whispered. "When the time is right, I will cut you free."

"Nay, lass!" he whispered furiously. " 'Tis too chancie! They might turn against you. Now tell me—who struck you?"

"Eat!" She fed him little bites of pemmican, unshed tears pricking her eyes as she remembered this morning's horror. "Rillieux tried to . . . tried to rape me. Simon stopped him."

A muscle clenched in Morgan's jaw, his gaze going hard. "Is he dead?"

"I do not think so."

"He will be." The cold malice in Morgan's voice left no doubt what would happen should he encounter Rillieux again as a free man. "But listen—the tin flask holds poisoned rum. Any who drink from it will perish. Dinnae touch it, lass, and dinnae permit

Atoan to drink it. He cares for you and will protect you well if I am killed and—"

She pressed her fingers to his lips, then poured water onto the cloth of the gag and made a show of wiping his face. *"Non!"* she whispered. "Do not speak of such things!"

"Hear me, Amalie! We are being followed. If augh' should happen—"

"What are you doing?" Tomas called in French from behind her.

She finished wiping Morgan's brow, then leaned down and pressed a kiss to his lips, just as Tomas dragged her away.

On they walked, through leagues of untouched forest, the air growing hot and sticky as they approached midday, mosquitoes whining for blood in the shadows, the air thick with the scents of damp earth, rot, and fear. And although Amalie watched for any telltale sign that they were being followed, she saw and heard nothing—no movement in the shadows, no snapping twigs, no sudden flight of birds from the treetops.

Perhaps the blow had struck Morgan more senseless than he appeared; perhaps he was seeing things, just as she had done this morning when Rillieux had struck her.

Onward she plodded, listening as Tomas, Tanial, and Atoan argued in whispered Abenaki, Simon slinking behind his brother and casting Amalie guilty looks.

Would he help her?

She made her way over to him. "I have not yet thanked you for what you did this morning. You saved me from—"

A terrible cry arose from the forest, a wild shrieking she'd heard only once before, a sound that sent chills down her spine and roused pure terror in her blood.

"Amalie, get down!" Morgan shouted from somewhere behind her.

She fell to the forest floor just as the world around her exploded with gunfire.

And then two men—one big and dark-haired, the other small and wearing a cap—charged out of the undergrowth straight for her.

She screamed, scrambled to her knees, her only thought that she must get to Morgan. But the two men cut her off, grabbing her, thrusting her between them, pulling her behind a tree, as if to shield her from the battle.

"Dougie, you big lummox!" the smaller of the two said, his badly scarred face twisting into a frown. "You've gone and frightened her!"

"Dinnae be afraid, lass." The big one smiled. "I'm Dougie, and the uggsome fellow is Killy. We're MacKinnon's Rangers— Morgan's men. We're here to keep you safe."

And in the midst of the gunfire and shouting, Amalie sent up a prayer of thanks to God, the Virgin, Jesus, and every blessed saint she could remember, tears of relief streaming down her face. Morgan was safe!

It was over in a few moments, gunfire giving way to the startled silence that always followed battle. A dozen or so Abenaki lay still on the ground, their blood already drawing flies. Morgan's only regret was that Tomas was amongst them. He hoped the lad's death wouldn't be too hard for Amalie to bear.

The survivors—including Simon and Atoan—stood bunched together, surrounded by Joseph's Muhheconneok warriors, while Amalie, under the careful watch of Dougie and Killy, was making her way slowly toward Morgan, the two men picking a path that protected her from the sight of dead and dying men.

Still strapped to the travois, Morgan saw Connor stride into the clearing, his face covered with war paint, rifle in hand, and thought his heart might explode from the joy of seeing his brother again. "'Tis about bloody time. I'd begun to think you were goin' to walk wi' us all the way to Oganak."

"You seemed to be enjoyin' yourself, whilin' away the hours wi' a bonnie sweet lass to dote upon you, feed you, and wipe your brow." Connor drew his hunting knife from its sheath, cut Morgan's bonds, and reached out his arm.

Morgan clasped his brother's forearm, let Connor draw him to his feet. Then he threw his arms around his younger brother and embraced him with his full strength, Connor returning the embrace in equal measure, neither of them able to speak.

Around them, a cheer arose, men's raw, throaty voices shouting in unison. "MacKinnon! MacKinnon! MacKinnon!"

With one last bone-crunching backslap, he and Connor parted, and Morgan saw for the first time the strain on his brother's face. He looked older, more careworn than Morgan remembered.

"I thought I'd lost you," Connor said, his voice unsteady.

"I'm no' quite so dead as it seemed."

And then Amalie was there beside them, her bruised cheeks wet with tears, her gaze fixed on Connor, a look of stunned surprise on her face. "It was you! I saw you!"

"What do you mean you saw him?" But no one was listening to Morgan.

Connor took Amalie's hand, raised it to his lips. "Aye, lass, 'twas me. I'm sorry for your sufferin' today. But if the Abenaki lad hadna stopped the bastard, I would have. He'd no' have had his way wi' you."

"Merci." Amalie smiled at him through her tears, and Morgan wondered how much she'd been forced to endure. "But how did you know—?"

"That you were under the protection of the Clan MacKinnon?" Connor turned Amalie's hand over, withdrew something from his shirt, and pressed the rumpled cloth of Morgan's tartan sash into her palm. "You called my brother's name as well, aye? And you reached for me. But even were you a stranger to us, I'd no' have let any man harm you. But this puts me in mind of somethin', brother. I've a wee giftie for you."

Then Connor gestured to McHugh, who turned and beckoned Brandon forward. In Brandon's hand was a rope, and at the end of the rope was . . .

"Rillieux, you son of evil!"

Chapter 22

"So Wentworth thinks me a traitor and deserter?" Morgan could scarce believe it, the irony of it making him laugh. "Och, for the love of Christ!"

"Aye, and Amherst, too. Wentworth sent us up here to see whether it was true." Connor popped a piece of roasted rabbit into his mouth and chewed. "Does he truly believe I'd tell him if it were? I'd just kill you wi' my own hands."

There were snorts and peals of laughter, the men pressing in around the small cook fire where Morgan, Connor, and Joseph sat with the officers, finishing their supper of roasted rabbit and ash cakes.

Sweet Mary, how Morgan had missed them!

Then Connor frowned, his face lined with regret. "If I'd have kent what was in those letters, I'd have burnt them ere we reached the fort. Instead, I handed them straight to Wentworth."

"Dinnae think on it." Morgan met his brother's gaze. "You couldna have kent or even suspected what the letters held."

"I thought you were dead." Connor's eyes filled with shadows. "God's blood, those were dark days."

Around him, the men nodded.

Morgan knew they were thinking of the brutal raid they'd made to avenge his death. Knowing not what to say, he said nothing.

Then Connor jabbed a finger in Morgan's face. "But dinnae you be insultin' us by askin' us whether we believe you. No' a one of us misdoubts you."

There were shouts of agreement.

"We're wi' you, Morgan!"

"Wentworth wouldna ken the truth if it bit him on the arse!"

Then Dougie elbowed his way to the fireside. "You risked your own fool neck to save mine, Morgan. If no' for you, I'd be dead or rottin' on a prison barge. I owe you my life, and I'll ne'er forget it. When I heard you might be alive, I . . ."

The big man's voice quavered, and his words died away.

Morgan felt an answering tightness in his chest. "'Tis glad I am to see you wi' two strong legs, Dougie."

"Sing it for him, Dougie!"

"Aye, sing it!"

"Sing him 'The Ballad of Morgan MacKinnon'!"

Morgan looked at Connor, then up at Dougie again. "'The Ballad of Morgan MacKinnon'? You wrote a song about me?"

Dougie looked chagrined. "Aye."

"A passin' fair tune it is." Connor grinned. "He sang it and played his fiddle at your wake."

Then Dougie started to sing, his words telling of the night strike on the pier at Ticonderoga and how Morgan had braved a hail of lead balls to carry a wounded friend to safety before dying a hero's death.

"'Tis far tae Ticonderoga,'tis far through forest and fen, but 'tis there you'll find Morgan MacKinnon, bidin' untae the end."

His voice cracking with emotion, Dougie sang the last notes, then cleared his throat. "It sounds better wi' my fiddle."

Morgan found it hard to speak. "I am honored more than I can say. Thank you, Dougie. But I recall it a bit differently. I told you that you stank, and you called me daft and told me I ran like a lass."

Dougie kicked at the dirt, regret on his face. "I didna mean it."

Morgan grinned. "I did."

The men howled with laughter, and Dougie turned red.

"I'd best be writin' a new endin', aye?" he said with a wide grin.

Morgan looked at the faces around him—smiling faces, both young and old, faces baked brown by the sun and scarred from battle. Some of them had been with him since the beginning through four weary years of war. Others had filled the empty places left by men who truly *had* laid down their lives in battle—men like Charlie Gordon, Lachlan Fraser, Jonny Harden, Robert Wallace, and dear Cam. Both living and dead, they were family. They were clan, bound not by the blood in their veins, but by the blood they'd lost and spilled together.

If Morgan asked them, these men would follow him into hell.

They'd traveled hard leagues today, eager to put as much distance between themselves and the site of this morning's skirmish as they could, lest someone be drawn by the sounds of gunfire and overtake them there. Morgan had left the Abenaki to care for their dead, taking only Simon and Atoan with him—as guests rather than prisoners. The two now sat with some of Joseph's men, eating dried venison and sharing stories, ancient hostilities set aside in the strangeness of the moment.

The only prisoner, Rillieux, stood gagged and tied to a nearby tree, his face sporting dark bruises where Morgan's fist had pounded him. Morgan hadn't wanted to distress Amalie further by killing the *mac-dìolain* in front of her, so he'd ordered Rillieux bound and brought along at the rear, where she would not have to see him.

The day's events had been hardest on her, he knew. They had not yet spoken of it—so many things lay unspoken between them—but the horror of her ordeal was written on her face. Still, she'd shown great courage. Her attempts to protect him while he'd lain bound to the travois had been witnessed by the Rangers as they'd stalked the Abenaki and had earned her the respect of every man amongst them.

That respect had grown when, despite her weariness, she'd done her best to keep up with them on the perilous southward march, until Morgan had taken her upon his back. Once they'd made camp, she'd barely stayed awake long enough to eat her supper, then had fallen into an exhausted sleep on the bed of pine boughs he'd made for her. She lay there still, covered by a thin woolen blanket in the shelter of a lean-to.

Morgan heard his men laugh and looked back to find them watching him with knowing grins on their faces. They'd caught him watching her again. He shrugged. "I cannae help it."

"That much is obvious." Joseph cut another strip of meat off the rabbit, the vermilion paint on his face dried and beginning to flake, his dark eyes gleaming with humor. "But if you can keep yourself from her for a bit longer, I would hear the story, all of it—how you survived, how you came to wear a French uniform, and how you were taken prisoner with only a delicate French flower to protect you."

There were shouts of agreement.

"Aye, out wi' it!"

"Let's hear it!"

And so Morgan went back to the beginning, to the night he'd been shot. He told them how he'd known he would be interrogated and given to the Abenaki and so had refused to drink, hoping to let the fever take him, only to have his will overthrown by laudanum. He told them how Bourlamaque had written the letter proclaiming him dead in order to prevent the Rangers from attempting a rescue. He told them how he'd come to himself after a fortnight of fever to find Amalie beside him, terrified of him and blaming the Rangers for the death of her father. He told them how she'd slowly forgiven him, nursing him back to health with rare compassion, pleading his cause to Bourlamaque and winning him a reprieve.

"God bless the lass!" Connor said, looking her way.

Then Morgan told them how Bourlamaque had offered him sanctuary in exchange for answers to his questions and how he'd played a deadly game of wits these past weeks, feigning ignorance of French, trading away the locations of old campsites and caches in order to buy time to plan his escape, skulking about under cover of night to read Bourlamaque's correspondence.

"But the truth is, I came to admire Bourlamaque and to hate myself." And as he spoke, it struck Morgan that he'd lost a friend. "Bourlamaque treated me with honor and dignity, and all the while I kent I would betray him. He is everything Wentworth will ne'er be—honorable, compassionate, a good Catholic."

He told them about poor Charlie Gordon's skull and how Bourlamaque had not only allowed him to bury the remains in the French cemetery, but had even joined in the prayers. "Truth be told, a part of me came to wish I served Bourlamaque, so good a man is he. But there are none so good and brave as you, and my place is here beside you."

There were nods, a chorus of shouts, and many a raised flask.

"For certain!"

"Aye, and that's a fact!"

Then the only sound was the crackling of the fire, the gentle gloaming giving way to the dark of night.

It was Connor who broke the silence. "But what of Amalie? For unless I'm mistakin', there's another MacKinnon about to take a wife."

"Amalie *is* my wife. We were wed by a priest yesterday morn."

Looks of stunned surprise were replaced by wide grins, shouted benisons, and hearty slaps on the back.

And for the first time since realizing his men were stalking the Abenaki, Morgan felt an emptiness in his chest. "I thank you, but 'tis not as it seems. Amalie is Bourlamaque's ward. He forced us to the altar, hoping to ensure my loyalty and give Amalie a husband who could care for her."

Connor gaped at him, clearly starting to grasp the fullness of their situation. "Bourlamaque's *ward*?"

Then Morgan told them the rest of the story—not the *whole* story, of course, for he'd be damned before he'd dishonor Amalie with careless talk before his men.

"I didna consummate the marriage, for I wanted her to be free to seek an annulment. I was just leavin' her side when Rillieux attacked. Bourlamaque will likely think I've taken Amalie and tried to escape to Fort Edward wi' her. He could well send troops to find her and bring the two of us back. I fear what might befall her should she return. I dinnae want to see her take the blame for my treachery."

Around him the men lapsed into silence, contemplating what might lie ahead of them, their grizzled faces golden in the firelight. Then Joseph gave a snort and began to chuckle.

Morgan, who could find nothing to laugh about in the moment, glared at his Muhheconneok brother. "What's so bloody funny?"

Joseph grinned at him, teeth flashing white in the dark. "And I thought Iain made a mess of things when *he* fell in love."

At this, the men burst into raucus, thigh-slapping laughter.

More than a wee bit fashed, Morgan stood. "I'm done wi' the lot of you! Connor, Joseph, we'll hold a warriors' council in an hour's time."

Connor stood. "Where are you goin'?"

Morgan met his gaze. "To feed Rillieux to my *claidheamh mòr.*"

I n the end, it was quickly done.

Morgan untied Rillieux and forced him at the point of his sword to walk deep into the forest, Connor and Joseph stubbornly following him. "I dinnae need your help."

"I saw what he did to her, what he tried to do," Connor said, shoving Rillieux before him. "She's my sister by marriage. 'Tis my right to watch him die."

They reached a clearing far out of earshot of the camp.

Morgan pressed the tip of his blade to Rillieux's throat, forcing the bastard to meet his gaze. "Lieutenant Rillieux, you are hereby sentenced to die for kidnappin', beatin', and tryin' to rape my wife. On your knees, and may God have mercy upon your black and rotten soul!"

"You cannot mean to kill me in cold blood, even a barbarian like yourself!" Rillieux backed away.

"'Tis no' murder to execute a treacherous enemy in wartime. Did you think I would free you, givin' you a chance to harm her again? Nay, I'm no' so foolish as that. Besides, Bourlamaque would order you hanged if he kent what you've done." Morgan laughed. "Be grateful this *barbarian* is more merciful than you are. You sent me away to be burnt alive, aye?"

"It's not too late to let him taste fire." Joseph circled Rillieux, grabbed him by his collar, and hissed into his ear, his unsheathed hunting knife pressing against Rillieux's groin. "Any man who hurts women does not deserve the life his mother suffered to bring him. Be grateful my Scottish brothers are here, for if it were only the two of us, you would learn how my people deal with men who rape."

"One cannot rape a whore!" Rillieux jerked away from Joseph, took a step backward and then another, clearly hoping to run.

Connor came up behind him, grabbed him by his coat, and shoved him forward. "Watch your tongue, or I'll cut it out ere you die!"

Rillieux stumbled, fell to his hands and knees.

Broadsword already raised, Morgan swung, beheading Rillieux with one clean stroke.

For a moment he stood there, rage still seething inside him at the thought of what Rillieux had done. Then he drew a deep breath, letting his anger bleed away.

"Perhaps one day, someone will come along an play wi' your skull."

Amalie slept through the night, a deep and dreamless sleep. She did not see Morgan emerge grim-faced from the forest and clean his sword. She did not hear him and his officers discussing the dangerous road that lay ahead of them. She was not aware of the Rangers who watched over her through the night, feeding wood to the fire to ward off the chill and the mosquitoes, tiptoeing on big feet, and cursing at one another to be quiet.

Only when Morgan at last lay down beside her did she stir, snuggling against his chest, instinctively seeking his familiar scent, the steady thrum of his heartbeat, the shelter of his embrace.

"Sleep, my angel."

It was Morgan's lips on her cheek that woke her.

She opened her eyes to find it still dark, Morgan sitting beside her, leaning over her, his hand stroking her hair. Men bustled to and fro in the firelight, moving quietly about their chores, the entire camp alive with activity.

"Sorry to disturb your sleep, lass, but we must break camp afore dawn."

She tried to sit up, wincing at the unexpected pain of sore muscles.

Morgan's brow bent in a worried frown. "Where do you hurt?"

"Everywhere, I think." Her legs, her arms, her belly, the soles of her feet, her cheek where Rillieux had struck her.

Morgan reached over, picked up a small tin pail by its handle, and set it down before her. "It isna much, but the hot water should make you feel a bit better. I'll see that you get a cup of willow-bark tea."

Then he stood and strode away.

Amalie looked inside the bucket and found a clean cloth of homespun floating in clear, hot water. She picked up the cloth, squeezed it, and began to bathe as best she could, only too aware that she was the only woman in an encampment of men. But the hot water felt heavenly against her face, and soon she found herself wrapping the blanket Morgan had given her last night around her shoulders and using it as a sort of shield so that she could wash more of her body without exposing herself.

Not that the men were watching her. They seemed not to know she was there, going about their duties without glancing her way. Most were big men like Morgan, tall and broad of shoulder, some with gray hair, some with red hair and freckles. Many wore leather breeches as Morgan had done. Others wore Indian leggings. All of them had moccasins upon their feet and weapons at their belts.

Morgan strode amongst them, greeting them, encouraging them, exuding the confidence of an officer, a warrior, a man born to lead other men. Their gazes followed him just as hers did, and she realized that they loved him, too, and had sorrowed long for him.

Now it would be her turn to sorrow. Today, he would return her to Fort Carillon, then he would leave her, disappearing into this forest to make the long journey to Fort Edward with his men. She would never see him again. Unless . . .

Rather than seeking an annulment, could she not wait till the end of the war for him? He could come for her and claim her as her husband as soon as peace was restored. They could build a home in some growing frontier town where no one would care that she was part Abenaki or that he had once been a fearsome Ranger.

But what if he does not wish to stay married, Amalie? What if he wants the annulment?

And then one fear forced those worries aside.

What if he doesn't survive the war?

The thought chased all other thoughts from her mind, and for a moment she felt she could not breathe. Soldiers died every day in this war, and now Morgan would be in the thick of it once more. But God could not be so cruel as to take both him and her father away from her. No, Morgan would survive. He *must*.

Finished with her ablutions, she set the cloth back inside the bucket, and then began to run her fingers through her desperately snarled hair, trying to untangle it.

"Pardon me, miss." The short man who'd helped protect her during the battle stood beside the lean-to, a tin cup in his hand. "Killy's the name, miss. Morgan told me you might be needin' a bit of willow-bark tea to soothe your aches."

"Thank you, Killy." She took the cup from his hands, found it hot to the touch. "I remember who you are."

"Of course you do!" He grinned, his scarred face transformed from fearsome to endearing, his blue eyes twinkling. "'Tis my Irish charm. As the only man amongst us with any manners, let me be the first to welcome you to our company and to thank you for savin' our Morgan. If there's augh' you need, come to Killy."

Killy's visit seemed to be some kind of signal, for one by one the men stopped to greet her, many of them bearing small tokens.

A man who said his name was McHugh brought a wooden bowl of steaming cornmeal porridge with bits of salt pork in it. "Thank you for all you did for Morgan. God be wi' you."

Dougie brought fresh blueberries he claimed to have picked himself. "Morgan was shot savin' my life, and you saved his. If there's augh' I can do for you, tell me, and I'll see it done."

A young Ranger named Brandon gave her a penknife. "A pleasant morn to you, miss. My thanks to you for aidin' Morgan."

"I'm Forbes, miss. This salve is good for wounds. Good day to you, miss."

"I'm called Robert Burns, miss." Robert Burns flushed to the roots of his red hair. "Och, they said you were bonnie, and you are. Here's a bit of sugar for your tea."

Amalie ate her porridge and blueberries, and on it went. Powdered ginger root. Beaded thongs for her hair. An apple. Some pemmican. A leather pouch of parched cornmeal.

These were MacKinnon's Rangers?

For so long, she had feared and hated them, as did all French subjects in the Canadas, the name alone enough to fill her heart with dread. But now she saw them as they were—skilled warriors, strong men, and strangely softhearted, their simple gifts and words of thanks touching her more deeply than they could know.

And then Amalie found two men looking down at her— Connor, who was so like Morgan in appearance that there could be no mistaking him, and a tall Indian man with long black hair in which was tied a single eagle father. They knelt down beside her.

"I see the men have been payin' their respects," Connor said, smiling at the small pile of possessions that sat before her. "As well they should. Thank you for savin' my brother's life and showin' him mercy. Should you e'er need them, my life and my sword are yours."

"*Kwai, nichemis,*" the Indian man said in Abenaki. *Greetings, little sister.* "I am Joseph Aupauteunk, war chief of the Stockbridge Mahican people and blood brother to the MacKinnons."

The Mahican had long been enemies of her grandmother's people, and yet such was the warmth in Joseph's brown eyes that Amalie felt no fear of him.

Bare-chested, his skin stained by vermilion, he smiled and held forth a comb carved of polished antler. "I thought you might need this."

Amalie could have kissed him. "*Merci!* Oh, thank you!"

"Only a Mahican would bring a comb to war." Connor rolled his eyes, then leaned in as if about to tell Amalie a great secret, lowering his voice to a whisper. "It helps them keep their feathers pretty."

And for the first time in what felt like an eternity, Amalie laughed.

From the distance she heard Morgan's voice. "Scouting party, fall out!"

She took the comb, began to work it through her tangles. "How long before we reach Fort Carillon?"

Connor and Joseph shared a glance, something passing unspoken between them.

Then Connor spoke. "You'd best ask Morgan."

Chapter 23

"Fort Edward?" Amalie gaped at Morgan as if he'd struck her, looking small and vulnerable, the woolen blanket clutched tightly around her shoulders, her cheek bearing the marks of Rillieux's cruelty. "But—!"

"Nay, lass, no' to the fort." He didn't want her within a league of Wentworth. "I'm takin' you to the MacKinnon farm—my home."

Around them, the Rangers were falling out, heading southward on the heels of the scouting party, Joseph's men already deployed on their flank. In the east, dawn was about to break anew. It was time for them to move on.

"But how will I get back to Fort Carillon? How will Bourlamaque know what has become of me? Surely he is beside himself. I must let him know what has happened!"

She doesna want to stay wi' you, laddie.

The realization left barrenness in its wake. He had hoped . . .

"Simon and Atoan will take whatever message you wish to send."

The two Abenaki men stood at a distance waiting to depart, each bearing gifts from Morgan and from Joseph's men, tokens of this truce between them. They had agreed to inform Bourlamaque of all that had transpired, seeking his pardon and good graces for themselves and bearing Morgan's own missive, a letter that Morgan had written to confess his perfidy.

"I am but tryin' to keep you safe." He cupped her cheek, needing to make her understand. "I wouldna have you bear the brunt of my transgressions."

What Rillieux had done—plotting with soldiers to kidnap her—proved that even Bourlamaque could not keep her safe should the sentiment at the fort turn against her. Besides, Morgan did not trust anyone but himself, his Rangers, or Joseph's men to deliver her safely through the long reaches of the forest. But the greater truth was that he wanted her beside him. Perhaps with time . . .

Do you think she'll wake up one morn and decide she doesna mind bein' wed to a man who fights for the British, a man who betrayed her trust? Aye, and pigs will soon fly, laddie.

Amalie's gaze sought Simon and Atoan out of the shadows, her eyes glittering with tears. "And what of Lieutenant Rillieux? Are you sending him—"

"Rillieux is dead."

She gasped, stared up at him wide-eyed, and seemed to sway on her feet, her face pale. "You . . . k-killed him?"

"Aye, I did, and I dinnae regret it. I couldna risk keepin' him alive—no' so deep in French territory and no' after what he tried to do to you. He was a danger to you, to me, and to my men."

She squeezed her eyes shut, tears spilling onto her bruised cheeks. When she opened her eyes again, some of the color had returned to her face. "Am I to have no say in where I go?"

And something inside Morgan snapped. "'Tis my right to make such decisions for you, Amalie. You're my *wife.*"

"Your wife?" Her voice quavered. "Are you not the man who, on our wedding night, refused to give himself to me and told me to seek an annulment?"

Then, wiping the tears from her face, she walked away.

Morgan watched her as she made her way to her cousin's side, feeling as if he'd said something wrong.

Killy passed him, shaking his head, tumpline pack on his back. "You've no manner of tact at all, MacKinnon."

A malie plodded along at Morgan's side, doing her best not to be a burden, feeling hot and sweaty and terribly close to tears. The woolen blanket—the only means she had of covering her nightgown and preserving her modesty—held in the heat and made her itch. Her sore leg muscles, not accustomed to such exertions, ached from strain. But it was her heart that ached the most.

'Tis my right to make such decisions for you, Amalie. You're my wife.

How could he treat her in so overbearing a manner? Yes, it was the right of a husband to decide such things, but when she'd vowed to love, honor, and obey him, she'd thought they would be living at Fort Carillon—if they were able to be together at all. She'd never imagined that he would take her beyond French borders without so much as asking for her thoughts.

Still, she would not resist or argue with him about it, for her father had taught her that a commander must have the respect of his troops. She would not undermine or shame Morgan before his men by acting like a shrew. They were not at the fort, but deep in the wild. Many lives depended upon him, including her own. Besides, he believed he was doing his best to protect her. And perhaps he was.

As she now knew, the danger was only too real.

She'd thought it could never happen, but it had. Soldiers under Monsieur de Bourlamaque's command—her own countrymen— had allowed her to be taken from the fort against her will simply because they hated Morgan. And they'd done it with the help of her cousins, her very flesh and blood.

What would have happened had Morgan done what she'd wanted him to do and taken her back to Fort Carillon? Bourlamaque would have welcomed her with the affection and concern of a father, locking the sentries who'd let Rillieux kidnap her in chains. But she would have faced her own reckoning with Bourlamaque, for she'd have had to confess that she'd known about Morgan's spying. Bourlamaque would have been enraged—and terribly saddened—to find she'd betrayed him. She'd have found herself back at the abbey in a matter of weeks, never to see Morgan again.

She didn't want that—any of it. But she wished she could have thanked Bourlamaque and bidden him farewell.

Her throat grew tight, tears blurring her vision. She blinked them back, unwilling to let anyone see that she was crying.

Now Tomas and Lieutenant Rillieux were dead. And with every footstep, the world she'd known and everything in it—the gowns her father had given her, his pipe, her rosary, her beloved books—fell farther behind her, naught ahead but a long and uncertain journey.

Where was he taking her?

The MacKinnon farm, he'd said, a note of pride in his voice. *My home.*

Had she ever had a home?

No, she hadn't, not since her mother had died.

But would Morgan's family welcome her, a woman with Indian blood? Or would she be the outsider now?

M organ saw the tears on Amalie's cheeks and felt an answering tug in his chest. He feared he was the cause of them. Nay, he was certain of it.

He'd been an arse this morn, wanting to be with her and more than a little hurt that she didn't seem to want the same thing. Rather than explaining his reasons for not sending her back to Fort Carillon, he'd pressed the issue of his husbandly rights, even though their union was not complete.

Are you not the man who, on our wedding night, refused to give yourself to me and told me to seek an annulment?

Aye, he was, and he regretted it.

But how could he have known what was about to happen? Events had not shaped themselves as he'd imagined—the better for him, the worse for her. He was now free, while she'd been forced from her home and dragged into the wild. Driven by the need to get her and his men out of French territory, he hadn't had time to talk with her about her ordeal, much less comfort her, as a true husband should.

He would have to remedy that, wouldn't he?

A malie had no idea how long they'd been walking or how far they'd come, each stretch of dark forest looking so much like the last that they might have been walking in circles for all she knew. She understood now why scouting parties sometimes lost their way only miles from the fort—and why some never returned. How Morgan and his men managed to keep from getting lost she did not know.

They walked single file to disguise their numbers, stretching in a long column, each man several paces behind the man before him, moving swiftly and silently, their rifles loaded and at the ready. Every so often they would stop, speaking to one another in a soundless language of glances and hand gestures, almost as if they could read one another's thoughts. Although Morgan had told her that Joseph and his men were protecting the high ground to their right, she hadn't once spotted anyone.

Ahead of them, the ground grew steep, fallen trees littering the sunlit hillside as if some great force—perhaps a mighty wind—had felled them all at once. Some were bare, their bark stripped away by the weather. Others were buried in moss and grasses, making them harder to spot until one trod upon them.

She reached for Morgan's hand to steady herself as she climbed over a wide log, but he lifted her instead, picking her up by her waist and setting her down lightly on the other side. But no matter how she tried to keep up, it became clear that she was holding the men back. Several paces in front of her, the entire column stopped, both before and after her, giving her time to catch up.

Breathing hard, her thighs burning, she glanced apologetically up at Morgan, certain he must feel vexed with her—only to have him wink, a smile on his face.

Reassured, she pressed on, determined not to complain.

They'd just reached the top of the hill, when a bird called out—and Morgan drew her hard against him, pressing her down to the ground beneath him, his hand over her mouth to silence her.

Her blood froze, her heart thudding hard against her ribs.

"Easy, lass," he whispered softly in her ear.

They lay there, as if lifeless upon the forest floor, for what seemed an eternity. And then she heard it—men's voices. They were speaking French.

She felt Morgan make some kind of gesture, but could see nothing, her body pinned beneath his. Were the Rangers about to attack?

Please God, no!

Frantically, she shook her head as much as Morgan's hold upon her would allow, begging him in the only way she could not to ambush and slay her countrymen.

He pressed his lips against her cheek, soft butterfly kisses as if
to calm her, and she knew he was telling her that his men would
not attack—not this time.

Limp with relief, Amalie watched as a company of perhaps
forty Canadian partisans strolled into view, a handful of uni-
formed French soldiers amongst them, unaware that death surrounded them, watching them from behind the trees. Amalie
recognized one of the Frenchmen from the fort—she'd treated
his wounds during the battle that had killed her father, and he'd
called her pretty. He spoke with the soldier beside him, the lot of
them joking about the ugliness of British camp followers.

And then she saw.

Guarding the French party's right flank was a group of painted
Huron, their gazes roaming over the forest where the Rangers hid.

Amalie's heart gave another violent knock.

Had they seen something?

One of them spoke quietly to an officer and seemed to point
straight at the line of hidden Rangers. The officer and his men
fell silent, their heads jerking to the left, their gazes searching the
trees, their rifles loaded and ready.

Not daring to breathe, her pulse roaring like thunder, Amalie
watched as, with excruciating slowness, the French troops and
Huron made their way toward the crest of the hill, over the top,
and down the other side, disappearing out of sight.

And still the Rangers did not move, the seconds seeming like
hours.

Then, as if by some signal she did not know, they slowly got to
their feet, Morgan helping her to rise, giving her hand a squeeze,
and drawing her after him.

She glanced back over her shoulder toward the crest of the hill
where the French troops had disappeared. They would never
know how close they'd come to dying.

"Why did you not attack them?" Amalie whispered a short
time later.

Morgan knew what she was asking. "I didna want to risk your
safety, and you've seen enough death, aye?"

She nodded.

* * *

"But I don't need to rest. I would not be a burden to you or have your men think me weak or lazy."

Morgan studied Amalie's flushed face and knew she was much more tired than she was letting on. The hilltop encounter with the French had terrified her, and since then she'd been driving herself hard, clearly eager to put as much of the journey behind her as possible. But, although he admired her spirit, he could not permit her to spend her strength when many leagues yet lay ahead of them.

"No man amongst us expects you to hold your own against grown men and trained Rangers, Amalie. You're a lass, and though you've got courage aplenty, you're no' accustomed to war or beatin' about the wild."

She marched stubbornly onward. "I have held you back enough as it is."

Morgan glanced over his shoulder to where Dougie walked behind him. "Dougie, you're lookin' a bit worn. Are you needin' to stop and, um, rest a bit?"

Dougie looked at him as if he'd lost his mind. "*Rest?* Are you daft?"

Morgan glared at him and gave a jerk of his head toward Amalie, who struggled on determinedly before him.

Dougie winked. "Och, aye, I am a bit weary."

In no time, word had gotten up and down the line that Amalie needed to rest but was being too stubborn to admit it. And suddenly Morgan was besieged with whispered pleas to stop, his men whining of sore feet, headaches, and aching backs.

Then Connor appeared at his side, looking fashed.

"What in God's name has come over the men? They're complainin' like old wom—" He caught himself before he finished the word, glanced at Amalie, then seemed to understand. "I think the men need to rest and bide a wee."

By the time they reached the sheltered place Joseph and his men had scouted out for them, Amalie was more than willing to stop. Morgan settled her on a blanket in the lee of a large boulder and saw to it that she drank deeply from his water skin and ate a handful of parched corn. No sooner had he looked away than she'd fallen sound asleep. Clearly, their morning march had taken more out of her than he'd realized.

He brushed a lock of hair off her cheek. "Connor, fetch Joseph. I'm thinkin' we need a new strategy."

"Morgan?" Amalie was lost in a dark sea of trees, Morgan nowhere to be seen.

Where had he gone? Why had he left her here?

She knew she had to find him, knew she would be lost out here forever if she did not. But though she looked behind every trunk and boulder, she could not find him.

"Morgan?" Fear clawed at her stomach, constricting her chest. "Morgan!"

And then it started—a whispering from behind the trees, as if men were crouched there watching her. It grew louder, and yet she could not understand what was being said. She whirled about, her breath coming in ragged gasps, but all she could see amongst the trees were shifting shadows.

"Morgan!" she cried.

Then one of the shadows took the form of a man. He walked slowly toward her.

But it wasn't Morgan.

She screamed.

"Amalie, wake up! Wake up, lass!"

"Rillieux!" She jolted upright, felt strong arms surround her.

It wasn't Rillieux holding her, but Morgan.

He drew her against him, held her tight. "Easy, *mo luaidh.* 'Twas but a bad dream. It's over now."

Trembling, she clung to him, her fingers fisting in the linen of his shirt, the taste of horror strong in her mouth, the dream still dragging at her.

It had seemed so *real.*

He held her, kissed her, stroked her hair, murmuring to her. "You're safe wi' me."

How long he held her, she couldn't say, but slowly the dream began to melt away.

Morgan felt Amalie's trembling subside, her fists still clenched in his shirt, her face buried against his chest. She'd awoken screaming that *neach dìolain*'s name, which meant she could only have been dreaming about one thing. "Do you want to tell me about your dream?"

He already knew what Connor had seen—Rillieux groping her breasts, feeling between her legs, throwing her to the ground, holding her down, striking her senseless. The description had made him almost inconsolable with rage.

She shivered. "I was lost in the forest, searching for you. I looked everywhere, but could not find you. I knew I would never find my way home without you."

Morgan listened, stroking her hair, waiting for her to finish in her own time.

"And the trees . . . They seemed to whisper. But then there were shadows, as if someone were behind the trees, watching me. And then *he* stepped out, and he walked toward me. *Ô, mon Dieu!*"

"He's dead, Amalie." Morgan held her tighter, kissed her hair. "I killed him wi' my sword. I watched life leave him. He cannae hurt you—no' now, no' ever again."

She looked up at him, unshed tears shimmering in her eyes, something akin to shame on her face. "He . . . watched us. He listened outside the window. On our wedding night. He heard . . . me. He called me a *whore*."

And Morgan wondered if he'd let Rillieux die too easy a death. That son of filth had tried to make Amalie feel shame because she'd enjoyed her husband's touch. He'd tried to destroy the joys of love for her, first with vile words, then with violence.

Morgan kept the rage from his voice. "He was jealous, Amalie. He wanted to hurt you, to steal that pleasure from you, to twist it into something shameful and dark. But the shame and the darkness were in him, not in you."

And then she told him everything, the story spilling from her, tears streaming down her cheeks. Her grief when she awoke to find him gone, his rosary and sash beside her. Hearing the strange noise outside the window. The horror of seeing him unconscious, at feeling Rillieux's blade against her throat. Her desperation as the sentries let Rillieux take the two of them beyond the gates. The hateful feel of Rillieux's hands upon her. His crude words and her attempt to fight him off. The pain of his blows. The strange sight of Morgan lurking in the bushes, a blade between his teeth. Simon's sudden appearance.

"I was so afraid!" She sniffed, wiped tears from her face. "I knew what they would do to you if I could not find some way to free you."

He drew her close again, wishing he could take this fear from her, wishing he could steal the memories from her mind. "It's over now, and, praise be to God, we're both still alive and unharmed."

But the afternoon was wearing on.

"It's time for us to leave this place, *a leannan*. There is a good campsite not too far from here, but we must leave soon to reach it by nightfall."

She drew a deep breath, nodded. "I am ready."

Then she glanced around at the empty clearing, a look of confusion on her face. "Where are your men?"

"Connor needed to complete his mission and couldna dally. He and the Rangers are making their way back to Fort Edward wi'out us."

Her gaze fell. "I held them back."

He lifted her chin, forced her to meet his gaze. "'Tis no' your fault, and I willna hear you blame yourself. This journey is hard on strong men. For a wee woman who's done nothin' more vigorous than tend gardens and kneel at prayer, 'tis a trial, indeed. I felt it best that you be able to travel more slowly."

There was more to it than that, of course. Connor and the men also hoped to lure any French force sent to retrieve Amalie into pursuing them instead of Morgan, as they did not want Amalie to be retaken or to witness any further killing.

"Then we are alone." There was fear in her voice, her gaze skimming the trees.

He chuckled. "Nay, sweet. Joseph's men are with us, watchin' o'er us—a hundred strong Mahican lads."

But Joseph had agreed they would watch over them from a discreet distance.

For Morgan had done much thinking while Amalie lay asleep, and by the time she'd awoken he'd made his decision. He'd kept himself from her long enough. They'd been married in the Church, and what God had joined he would not allow anyone to put asunder. He would not send her back to Bourlamaque.

It was time for him to woo—and claim—his wife.

Chapter 24

By the time they reached the campsite, the sun was low in the sky, and Amalie felt grubbier and hungrier than she could ever remember feeling, her belly grumbling loudly. Joseph was waiting for them, crouching near a cook fire and turning something over the flames, his back to them, the scent of roasting meat making Amalie's mouth water. Without looking over his shoulder, he spoke to Morgan, and Morgan answered, both of them using words Amalie didn't understand.

It had been a long day and hard. Though she missed Morgan's men—she'd grown fond of them and enjoyed their teasing banter—she'd been grateful for the slower pace. Morgan had helped her when she'd needed it, offering her his hand when the ground became steep or rocky, catching her when she stumbled, carrying her through deep marshes. And as she'd watched him pick a safe path for her, he'd seemed both alert to danger and utterly at ease in the wildness of the forest. And she'd realized that she was seeing him for the first time as he truly was—not just the gentleman and soldier she'd known at the fort, but Morgan MacKinnon, the Ranger of legend.

She glanced about and saw that they stood in the midst of a small clearing not far from a little river. The river, its banks verdant with ferns and blue forget-me-nots, tumbled down the rocky hillside in three small waterfalls before flowing off through the trees. All around them stood thick forest, primordial and dark, tall spruce and fir trees spiring toward the darkening sky. Her dream still in her mind, she shivered.

Chuckling with Joseph over some shared jest, Morgan grinned down at her, his arm sliding about her waist, two days' growth of stubble and long, unbound hair giving him a rakish appearance. "Joseph has been busy."

And, indeed, he had.

Not far from the fire stood a lean-to just like the one she'd slept in last night, but spread upon the pine boughs was a thick bearskin, its black fur gleaming. In the middle of the fur sat a small pile of what was unmistakably women's garments—a gown of dark blue, ivory petticoats, and a clean white chemise.

"Oh, merci!" She looked up at Joseph, who smiled. "Thank you, monsieur! Wherever did you find them?"

"Thank him." Joseph nodded toward Morgan, his dark eyes warm. "He's the one who gave up a good hunting knife. One of my men traded for them before we left Fort Edward hoping to surprise his wife."

Morgan dropped his tumpline pack on the ground near the lean-to, unbound it, and drew out a long knife in its leather sheath. Then he handed it to Joseph. "Tell Daniel I wish him luck both on the hunt and in battle. And thank you."

Joseph met Morgan's gaze. "My brother who was dead has returned. I would do anything for him and his woman."

His woman.

The words made something catch in Amalie's belly, and she wished it were true. But this marriage had been forced upon Morgan and was still incomplete. Clearly, he cared for her and desired her, but did he truly want her for his wife?

If there were any way for me to stay wi' you, I would. You are all a man could hope for in a wife, all a man could desire.

She remembered his words—and dared to hope.

Joseph ducked down, gave her a kiss on the cheek, then, with a nod to Morgan, he turned and strode into the forest.

"He is not staying with us?" she asked as he vanished from sight.

"He has to see to his men." Morgan sat before the fire, drawing her down beside him. "Sit and eat, lass. Joseph has a feast set out for us."

Compared to the parched cornmeal she'd nibbled at since breakfast, it *was* a feast—roasted turkey, field greens, and tart wild raspberries. But there were no plates, no silverware, no serviettes. How were they supposed to—

"Like this." Morgan grinned, shifting the wooden spit so that it no longer sat directly over the open flames. Then he took his penknife, cut off a strip of roasted breast meat, and held it to her lips.

Amalie opened her mouth, took the succulent meat onto her tongue, and almost moaned at the savory taste.

"Now you feed me."

Amalie rose to her knees, leaned in, and using the penknife Brandon had given her, cut off a slice of meat, then brought it to his lips. He took her wrist and held it as he nipped the meat from between her fingers. Then he licked the juices from her fingers one by one, his gaze locked with hers, his tongue hot and quick.

Memories of that tongue licking other parts of her sent blood rushing into her cheeks and made her insides feel quivery. It was only two nights ago when he'd tasted not just her fingers, but her throat and breasts as well, suckling her until she'd gone almost mad from the pleasure of it. Was he remembering the same thing?

Morgan watched her eyes darken and knew she still felt at least some desire for him. Despite Rillieux's cruelty, she did not seem to fear a man's touch as some women did in the aftermath of such violence. Still, Morgan would not rush her. When he at last made love to her, he wanted her to want it as much as he did, wanted her to enjoy it as much as he did, the grim pronouncements of sad, old nuns be damned.

He cut off another strip of breast. "For you."

Feasting with their fingers, they fed each other sliver upon sliver of rich, tasty meat, then turned to the greens and then, last of all, the berries, Morgan following each sweet bite with a kiss, until one appetite was satisfied—and another was roused.

But it wasn't time for that. Not yet.

First he must woo her beyond shyness, beyond fear.

"Come." Morgan stood, drew Amalie to her feet with one hand, grabbed his tumpline pack with the other. "It's time for your bath."

"My bath?" Her gaze flitted toward the creek.

"Aye, your bath." He took her hand and led her up the hillside, over the ramble of rocks toward the middle waterfall. It hid a secret he and his men had discovered two summers past on their way back from a scout—a secret they'd kept carefully guarded.

"Watch your step. The stone is quite slidey when it's wet."

He led her behind the waterfall along a wide ledge where the rushing waters of the freshet had through the ages gouged out a row of deep pools in the stone. Once the freshet had passed each June and the waters had receded, the pools, filled with fresh river water, offered tadpoles a place to hatch and grow into frogs—and weary Rangers a place to bathe and ease their aches.

And now their waters would soothe Amalie's hurts, washing away the day's grime and the memory of Rillieux's touch. She hadn't said anything, hadn't complained at all, but he knew she must feel it—the lingering taint of near rape.

He dropped his pack onto dry stone beside the pools. "What do you think?"

"It is . . . *enchanté*!" She glanced back and forth between the pools and the waterfall and smiled, a smile of pure joy. Then she stretched out her hand, the tips of her fingers piercing the silver curtain of falling water, her laughter like music.

"Aye, I thought so, too, the first time I saw it—a place of magic. The water in the pools is warm. Feel it."

She knelt down, trailed her fingers across the water's surface, a look of surprised wonder spreading across her face. "But how can this be?"

"During the day, the sun warms the stone, and the stone heats the water."

She smiled up at him. "Such a wondrous thing!"

Morgan knelt down beside her, dug in his pack for the soap and her comb, and set them down at the edge of the deepest pool. "Whenever we come this way, I reward the bravest amongst my men with the chance to wash away the grime of battle. But tonight, 'tis yours to enjoy in peace."

She stood, her smile gone, her gaze shifting to the forest.

He knew what haunted her. He stood, grasped the folds of the blanket she held about her shoulders, and drew her close, pressing a kiss to her forehead. "You're safe, Amalie. There's no one to spy upon you and naugh' that can harm you."

She gazed up at him, looking like a battered wood nymph, her cheek bruised, her green-brown eyes deep enough to drown a man. "And you—"

"I'll be nearby." He willed himself to step back from her, some part of him unable to believe he was doing this—leaving her here to bathe alone when he might have joined her. His mother's Viking blood burnt in him again, urging him to give in to his need, to rip the blanket from her shoulders and her nightgown with it, to draw her into the sun-warmed water with him and claim her at last. She *was* his, after all . . .

You're an animal, MacKinnon. The lass has been through hell.

"Call if you've need of me." He turned his back to her, willing himself to walk away from her, to give her this time alone.

He'd gone but a few steps when he heard the whisper of silk as she undressed and the tinkling of water as she slipped into the pool. Then came her sigh of undisguised pleasure, and his blood went hot at the thought of her sweet body bared to the water's warm caress. Yet somehow he found the strength to take another step and another.

Amalie watched him go, disappointment welling inside her. She'd thought for a moment that he intended them to bathe together. The idea hadn't frightened her; on the contrary, it had stirred her blood, made her pulse skip. Didn't he know how much she needed him, how much she wanted to know the secrets of his body as he knew the secrets of hers? Did he not understand that she longed to give herself to him?

"Morgan?" The sound of her own voice startled her.

He stopped, kept his back to her as if he could not face her. "Aye?"

"M-must you go?" Stunned by her own boldness, she sought for the right words. "Is . . . is it not customary for a wife to bathe her husband?"

She heard the breath leave his lungs in a gust, saw his hands clench into fists, and watched as he slowly turned toward her, afraid she'd gone too far and he now thought her brazen. But when his gaze met hers, she saw only desire.

"Are you sayin' you wish to share your bath?" His gaze dropped to her bare breasts, a muscle tightening in his jaw.

She swallowed, ignored the impulse to cover herself. "Y-yes."

He strode toward her with slow steps. "Are you certain? I've a man's need for you, Amalie. You ken what that means now, aye?"

She knew he was giving her a chance to change her mind, but she'd never wanted anything more than she wanted him. *"Oui."*

"Very well."

His gaze unwavering, he walked toward her, drawing his shirt over his head and letting it fall beside his pack, baring the glorious expanse of his chest with its dark curls and flat nipples. Stopping at the edge of the water, he next removed his weapons—a hunting knife and his pistol—and set them aside. Then his hands dropped to the fall of his breeches.

Amalie's instinct was to turn away, to avert her gaze. But wasn't this what she'd wanted—to know him as he knew her? Yes, it was. And so she willed herself to watch as he loosened the ties and pushed his breeches down his muscular thighs until he stood wearing nothing but his wampum armbands, at last revealing himself fully to her.

She felt her belly clench—and stared at what she'd never seen before.

To her eyes, he seemed huge. The shaft of his sex was thick and heavy, seeming to grow thicker and longer while she watched, until it stood against the muscles of his belly. Beneath, his stones hung, full and heavy and covered by coarse black curls. Standing there, his body bared to her gaze, he seemed breathtaking in his male beauty—carnal, primal, untamed.

With one easy motion, he slipped into the water, disappearing beneath its surface, only to rise out of the water before her like some kind of pagan forest god, his hair hanging in dark, wet ropes that clung to his shoulders and chest, water spilling in rivulets down his sun-browned skin with its scars and Indian markings, his body so much bigger and more powerful than hers. Though the water reached her ribs, it barely reached his hips, *that* part of him visible just below the surface of the water.

And suddenly she couldn't breathe, or perhaps she was breathing too fast, desire tangling with nervousness inside her, making her tremble. Without realizing what she was doing, she took a step backward.

"Nay, *a leannan*, there is no retreat—no' now." He slid one strong arm around her and drew her against him, his mouth closing over hers in a deep, searing kiss, one of his hands pressing something into her palm.

A small bar of soap.

He released her, stepped back, and held his arms out to his sides, offering his body to her, his blue eyes gone the color of midnight. "Do what you will wi' me, lass."

Morgan heard Amalie's hungry little moan, watched one emotion chase the next across her sweet face—surprise, hesitation, feminine desire—and felt his own hunger flare like kindling. God's blood, she took his breath away! Locks of dark, wet hair clung to her cheeks, her delicate shoulders, and her breasts, her nipples poking through the dark strands, rosy and tight, as if seeking his touch. Wanting to see more, needing to see more, he drew her long hair behind her back, exposing her breasts to his view.

Och, God in heaven, she was perfect! Water droplets clung to her creamy skin, beading on the pink velvet of her nipples, which tightened at the water's touch as if at a lover's, making him ache to taste her. But this was her time to know him.

Ruthlessly, Morgan clamped down on his lust, giving himself over to her, letting her shape the moment, willing himself to be patient for her sake. She rubbed the soap between her hands, set it down on the rim of the pool, then nibbled her lower lip, as if uncertain how one went about this task of bathing a husband.

'Twas likely not a skill they'd practiced at the abbey.

"Dinnae be shy." He smoothed a dark strand of hair off her cheek, sought for the words to reassure her. "There is no shame between a man and his wife."

She pressed her soap-slick hands against his belly and slid them in slow circles up his to chest, her light touch making the muscles of his abdomen contract, her fingers threading through his chest hair. Then she circled his nipples with her thumbs, his sharp intake of breath making her look up, her unspoken question clear to him.

"Och, your touch is like magic, lass."

Seeming emboldened, she explored his shoulders and his arms, squeezing his muscles as if to test his strength, tracing his scars and warrior marks, smoothing soap as she went. He watched her reaction—the quickening of her breath, her parted lips, the rapid beat of her pulse against her throat—and again his passion flared.

Then slowly, hesitantly, her hands moved down his sides to his hips and then finally beneath the water to his thighs. For a moment he thought she hadn't the courage to touch his cock.

Then the fingers of her right hand curled tentatively around him. And, och, it was heaven!

Amalie felt Morgan's body jerk and looked up to find his eyes closed and his jaw clenched. She yanked her hand away. "I—I hurt you."

He opened his eyes, chuckled. "Nay, *a leannan*. Quite the contrary."

Reassured she hadn't done anything wrong, she let herself explore the strangeness of his stones, cupping their weight in her hand, kneading what truly felt like stones inside—before returning to touch his sex. She closed her fingers around him, stroked the silken length. "You feel so hard and smooth at the same time. This is what goes . . . inside me?"

"Aye." His voice was a hoarse whisper, his eyes drifting shut. "Och, lass!"

Slowly she stroked him from root to engorged tip, watched his brow furrow, the muscles of his belly drawing tight. It pleased her to know she could affect him so, this big powerful man suddenly weak in her hands. She tightened her grip and felt a thrill when his head fell back on a groan.

And then before she knew what had happened, she was lifted off her feet, crushed in his embrace, his lips pressed hard against hers, the fingers of one big hand clenched in her hair, the other squeezing her bottom. He kissed her long and hard, ravishing her mouth with lips and teeth and tongue, stealing her breath. The soap-slick heat of his chest scorched her breasts, his chest hair tickling her nipples. Then, breathing hard, he ended the kiss, letting her slide down his slippery, hard body.

He reached to the side and took up the soap, one arm still around her. "And now, *wife,* I shall bathe you."

He turned her to face away from him, his fingers deftly working soap into her scalp in slow circles, lingering at her temples, behind her ears, at her nape. "Does that feel good?"

"Yes." Goose bumps shivered over her skin, the feel of his fingers in her hair more sensual that she would ever have imagined.

"Duck under."

Amalie took a deep breath and sank below the surface to rinse her hair.

When she came up again, she found his hands had not been idle. Slick with soap, they skimmed over her shoulders, down her arms, then moved over her belly and rib cage with agonizing slowness, her breasts growing heavy in anticipation of his touch.

She did not have to wait long, slippery palms cupping her, his thumbs flicking the already tight buds of her nipples, sending shards of heat to her belly, liquid fire pooling between her thighs. She sank backward into him, rested her head against his chest, instinctively arching to offer him more of herself. "Oh, Morgan!"

He made a sound like a moan and gave her what she wanted, his fingers teasing and tugging at her nipples, his lips and teeth kissing and nipping the sensitive skin beneath her ear, his sex pressing insistently against her lower back—a burning reminder of what was still to come. It felt so good, her body weak and shaking with the pleasure of it, the heat between her thighs now a demanding ache. She writhed in his arms, unable to hold still, her legs parting in a silent plea, the sound of a woman's desperate whimpers—*her* whimpers—mingling with the melody of the waterfall.

Then his right hand slid down her rib cage, over her belly, to touch her where she needed him most, his fingers parting her, stroking circles over her until she ached not only with arousal but with emptiness, longing to be filled. "Morgan! Help me, please!"

He nibbled her earlobe, sucked it, his voice gruff. "What do you need, lass? Tell me."

"*You . . .* I need you *. . . inside.*"

Never had Morgan been so close to losing control, her innocent sensuality shaking him apart, her whimpered plea leaving his restraint in tatters. He pressed his face against her wet hair, inhaled her sweet, fresh scent, and bit back a groan as he sought and found her slick entrance, sliding a finger past the taut barrier of her maidenhead to stroke the pulsing heat within. "Like this?"

She cried out, her fingernails digging into his forearms, her hips tilting to take him deeper, her inner muscles clenching around him. She was impossibly tight, hot, ready for him, her nectar slick on his fingers, the thought of what it would feel like to bury his cock inside her making him groan aloud, lust for her grinding hot and hard in his belly.

And then he could take no more.

He withdrew his finger from her, turned her to face him, stilling her with a kiss, his tongue thrusting into her mouth in imitation

of the union to come. Then he sat back on a rock ledge and drew
her down onto his lap, forcing her to straddle him, her legs spread
wide, her breasts soft against his chest. He'd meant her first time
to go slowly, meant to take her on the bearskin, but there was
naught to do for it now. He'd wanted her for so long . . .

Barely able to drag his lips from hers, he drew back, lifted her
chin, forced her to meet his gaze. Her palms resting on his shoulders, she looked at him through eyes smoky with desire, her
breathing fast and shallow.

"There's no turnin' back from here, Amalie, so if you're longin' to go back to Bourlamaque, you'd best fight your way free
from me and run. After this, I willna let you go. You'll be mine in
every way, and I yours, until our dyin' day."

Amalie felt a wild singing in her soul, her body longing to
make their marriage complete. She reached up to cup his stubble-
rough cheek, tears pricking her eyes, his gaze like fire. "*Oui,
Morgan*. Make me yours."

He said nothing but watched her with a raw hunger that made
her heart skip, his eyes as dark as night, his fingers grasping her
hips, lifting her, then guiding her downward.

And then she felt it—the thick tip of his sex nudging between
her folds, pressing against her entrance, stretching her—and her
insides clenched, either with pleasure or from fear, she wasn't
certain. For a moment time seemed to stand still, his gaze locked
with hers, his sex poised on the brink of her innocence, his body
rippling with tension. Then with one quick thrust, he breached
her.

The pain was white-hot and sharp—but not nearly as bad as
she'd expected. She gasped, felt herself pulse around him, and
knew from the way his muscles tensed that he'd felt it, too, the
intimacy of the moment shocking her to her soul—to know him
like this, to feel what he felt, to be one with him.

"Easy, *mo leannan*." He stroked her cheek, the tenderness of
his gesture at odds with the strain in his voice. "The pain will
soon pass. I willna hurt you again."

"It is not bad." She shifted her hips, moaning at the delicious
feeling inside. "Oh!"

And then with a groan he began to move, rocking his hips
upward, stretching her with slow, silky strokes, forcing more of
himself inside her until she felt him against her womb, his sex

filling her as she'd never been filled before, the pleasure of it staggering.

"Och, Jesus!" Never had Morgan felt more in control—nor so completely beyond it. Buried deep inside her honeyed heat, her body sheathing him so tightly, he was on the brink and yet he was nowhere near it. Letting her response guide him, he kept his thrusts steady and slow, not wanting to hurt her, certain that she must be raw where her flesh was so newly torn.

She was so tight. He'd never felt anything like it, her body resisting his intrusion, then closing around him like a silken fist. Maybe it was just knowing that she'd never been loved by another man, that she was his, body and soul. Or maybe it was that he loved her. Aye, he loved her, loved her so deeply that he thought his heart might shatter from it.

He watched her, watched the effect his loving had upon her. Gone was the lass who might have been a bride of Christ. Instead, he held *his* bride, a woman ripe with passion, her eyes half closed, her breasts and cheeks flushed, her lips parted, each breath unraveling on a moan that sounded like his name.

"Amalie, my angel." With one arm around her hips and the other wrapped behind her back, he drew her closer, arching her backward, forcing her breasts up out of the water. Then he ducked down to take first one puckered crest into his mouth and then the other, suckling her, teasing the rose-petal softness with his teeth and tongue, gratified at her soft, shuddering gasps, at the way her nails bit deeper into his shoulders, at the way she tightened around him.

He quickened his rhythm, drew her hard against him, raining kisses on her lips, her cheeks, her forehead, his need for her pounding in his chest like the thunder of a heartbeat, the first hint of bliss dragging at his groin. It had been so long since he'd had a woman. So long.

But he couldn't let go. Not yet.

He thrust deep and held himself inside her, then ground the thick root of his cock against her swollen sex. "Take it, Amalie! Come for me, *mo luaidh*!"

"*Ô, mon Dieu!*" She clung to him, her body trembling. And then her breath broke—and the tension inside her shattered, her body arching against him with a cry.

He caught her cry with a kiss, felt her body clench rhythmically around him—and the last thread of his control snapped.

Amalie couldn't believe what she was feeling, bliss shivering through her in ripples of molten gold, Morgan still moving within her, his thrusts prolonging her pleasure, her inner muscles tightening around him. And for the first time in her life she knew what it was to be complete, love for him swelling inside her, drawing tears to her eyes.

She heard herself call his name and felt his rhythm shift, his thrusts coming faster and harder, his strong arms around her, his body shaking with need. And even as he drove her toward a second stunning peak, it dawned on her just how much he'd been holding back, his own passion at last freed.

"Amalie, lass!" He called for her, desperation in his voice. "Oh, sweet Jesus!"

She clung to him, blinding pleasure claiming her again, sensations too good to be true washing through her in bright, shimmering currents, his deep, powerful strokes sending her flying. But this time he came with her.

She felt his body shudder, his face pressed against her throat as he groaned out the pleasure of it against her skin, spending himself deep inside her, their mingled cries lost in the music of the waterfall as the last rays of the setting sun turned the curtain of falling silver to blazing gold.

Chapter 25

Morgan combed Amalie's wet hair, careful not to pull the tangles. Her eyes were closed, her head tilted to one side, a contented smile on her lips, her skin golden in the firelight. Still naked, she'd tucked the blanket beneath her arms and wrapped it around herself in a gesture of feminine modesty that he'd found charming and sweet.

Amalie. Sweet Amalie. His *wife*.

Making love to her had been beyond anything he'd ever known. Aye, he'd tupped his fair share of lasses, enjoying the carnal pleasures they offered and giving back in full measure. But with Amalie, the bliss of it hadn't stopped with his body. When he'd at last spent himself, he'd felt an ecstasy that had shaken him to his soul, drawing the very life from him and giving it back again.

Never had he felt so bound to another person. It wasn't his vows that tied him to her, though they would have been enough. Nor was it the fact that he'd taken her maidenhead, though he would have honored such a claim from her as well, for he had taken something that he could never give back. Nor was it the fact that she might now carry his child, though certainly he'd have done his duty by her in that regard, too.

It was love that held him to her.

Now her happiness meant as much to him as his own, her safety and her life far more. He would no more have been able to abandon her than he could have abandoned himself. They were one, he and Amalie, in ways he never could have understood before this night. He'd thought he knew all there was to know about making love to a woman. He'd never understood that there was more, never understood what it truly meant for a man and woman to become one flesh. In that way, he'd been every bit as much a virgin as she.

'Twas a strange and humbling thought.

"Are you cold, *mo luaidh*?" He leaned down and kissed the curve of her shoulder, a feeling of tenderness in his chest that he'd never known before.

She gave a slow shake of her head. "No. The night is warm."

The sun had long since set, the sky bright with stars, the forest alive with sound as the day creatures sought their beds and the night creatures began to wake.

"Shall I braid it for you?" He ran the comb through her hair once more, her tresses at last free of tangles.

She looked over her shoulder at him. "Do you know how?"

"Who do you think does these, lass?" He lifted one of his damp warrior's plaits, unable to hide his amusement. "Connor perhaps? Killy? My Mahican grannies?"

She laughed, the sound of it sweet to his ears.

As he braided her hair for the night, he told her about her new home, about the strong and sturdy walls that would shelter her, about the trees that would be heavy with fruit come the harvest, about the rich earth, the fields and the forest, and all that they would yield for her. "You'll ne'er go cold and hungry, I promise you that. Nor will you want for a man's protection. Though I willna be able to stay wi' you at first except when Wentworth gives me leave, Iain will watch over you as if you were his sister."

Her brows drew together in a worried frown. "Are you certain I will be welcome?"

"Why ever would you no' be welcome?"

"Your brother's wife is loyal to Britain and a Protestant, is she not?"

"Aye, but Annie is no' the sort to judge a person by their kin or their faith. If she were, she'd have no choice but to hate her husband and her own wee son, aye?"

But his words did not wipe the worry from her face. "Do not the British frown upon those of us of mixed blood? My skin is dark—"

"Your skin is lighter than mine, lass." He finished binding the end of her braid with a beaded thong, then stretched out his arm alongside hers, his skin a dark sunbaked brown. "See? Besides, Iain is blood brother to the Mahican, just as I am. He and Annie harbor no hatred of Indian people, nor would they tolerate any who do. They are your family now, and they will love you. Did my men no' receive you wi' open hearts?"

She turned around to face him, the blanket still bound round her, a smile on her lips once again. "They were very dear."

Morgan couldn't help but chuckle. 'Twould make his men turn red with conflummixt delight to hear themselves described thus. Unable to keep himself from touching her, he ducked down and kissed her little nose. "Then you dinnae hate them?"

She glared up at him. "No, of course I do not hate them!"

In the distance, a wolf howled.

Morgan saw her stiffen, her gaze darting toward the darkness of the forest beyond the firelight. And it occurred to him that, although Amalie had Abenaki blood, she had never lived amongst them and knew no more about the forest or the animals in it than any other convent-raised French lass.

He drew her into his arms, kissed her cheek, wanting to shelter her. "There's naugh' to fear. 'Tis just a wee wolfie."

The wolf howled again, and this time the call was answered by another, this one much closer. And though he could tell she was trying to act as if she weren't afraid, he could not miss her little intake of breath or the way her body tensed at the sound.

Amalie did not want to seem foolish or cowardly, but the forest seemed to press in on them from all sides, the wild howling proof that more lurked amongst these trees than she cared to know. "Are you not at all afraid?"

"Nay." Morgan kissed her hair, his voice deep and without fear. "Joseph's men encircle us, keepin' watch. They'll warn us should any danger come our way. Besides, I dinnae fear the forest beasties. In these woods, death walks on two legs, no' four."

"But the wolf—"

It howled again, the plaintive sound sending chills along her spine. The second one, so much nearer, answered.

"The wolf is but tryin' to find his way home." Morgan nuzzled her throat, nipping the sensitive skin beneath her ear. "His mate hears his call, and she calls back, guidin' him to her side."

Amalie shivered, Morgan's lips tracing fire over her skin, warmth curling through her veins, confusing her fear, making it hard to think. "Why . . . why is the wolf lost?"

He reached to where she'd tucked the ends of the blanket between her breasts and tugged, baring her breasts to his caresses. And heat that had so recently been extinguished flared to life in her belly. "He's been on the hunt, hopin' to find a fat rabbit for her to feed upon, for she carries his cubs and has need of meat. But rangin' far and wide in the dark, he lost his way."

Unable to help herself, Amalie slid her hands over his chest, savoring the hard feel of his muscles and the rasp of his chest hair against her palms, the knowledge that he was hers heady like wine. "Did he find one—a fat rabbit?"

Morgan caught her nipples, tugged them, plucked them, making her gasp, the sensation shooting straight from her breasts to her belly. "Och, aye, he did, for he is a good hunter, strong and swift."

Breathless, Amalie slid her hands down his chest to his belly, hungry for the feel of him, touching him as rousing to her as being touched by him. Then her hand bumped against the hardened length of his sex. She took him carefully in her grasp, gratified by his deep groan. "What will he do . . . when he finds her?"

"He'll do this." Morgan got to his knees, drawing her up with him, pulling her against him, his mouth taking hers in a deep and scorching kiss.

Then he did something she never would have imagined.

Tearing the blanket aside, he moved behind her and forced her onto her hands and knees, his hands sliding in smooth circles over the exposed flesh of her bare derriere.

"Morgan, what—? Oh!"

He nipped her bared bottom, nibbling his way up her back till his mouth found her earlobe, his right hand reaching around to stroke between her thighs, his left teasing her breasts. "You're mine, Amalie. My wife. My mate. *Mine*."

She felt the heat in his words, and her heartbeat quickened, some feminine part of her delighting in his male possessiveness.

In the distance, the wolf howled, the sound growing nearer.

Morgan nibbled her earlobe, sucked it. "Och, Amalie, you're makin' me burn!"

But *she* was the one on fire. She found herself rocking against his hand, unable to hold still, her need for him already sharp. "Morgan, please!"

The wolf's mate answered.

Then Morgan forced her legs apart with his thighs, positioning himself behind her, the thick tip of his sex pushing against her, and she realized with a sense of shock that he meant to take her thus.

Like a ram mounts a ewe.

Slowly, he nudged inside her, stretching her, filling her, his breath hissing from between his teeth. "I dinnae wish to hurt you again, but . . . Och, lass!"

A wild howl.

A faithful reply.

But her soreness was quickly overcome by pleasure, the hard feel of him already flowering into bliss. His slow and steady thrusts seemed to strike her inside where she needed it most, his hand still stroking between her thighs, his lips hot against her back, his man's body seeming to surround hers.

"*Ô, mon Dieu!* Morgan." Needing more of him, she began to meet his thrusts with her own, backing against him, tilting her hips so that he drove into her more deeply, the ache inside her growing unbearable.

As if he knew what she needed, he quickened his pace, his breath coming hard and fast. "You feel so good, *a leannan,* so wet, so tight!"

Another howl.

Another answering call.

But lost in the wonder of this wild coupling, she barely heard them, Morgan's deep thrusts carrying her closer and closer to her peak. Her breath came in pants, release seeming to stay just beyond her reach, leaving her hanging . . . needing . . . wanting. She could not bear this torment—*oh, sweet heaven*!—but she did not want it to end. Faster he went and harder, murmuring to her in his Scottish tongue, his breath hot on her skin, his stones slapping against her with each forceful thrust.

And then the heat drew to a tight ball in her belly—and burst into a thousand shards of light. She cried out, overcome by the piercing sweetness, her fingers digging into the thick fur of the bearskin as her inner muscles clenched around Morgan, his deep groan mingling with her cries, as the stars rained down around them, leaving them both breathless and replete in the warm summer's night.

A malie awoke to find the sun newly risen, a bouquet of wildflowers lying on the bearskin beside her. She stretched, smiling to herself, her body still languid from Morgan's loving. He was no doubt off talking with Joseph as was their wont early in the morning each day. He would be back soon and hungry for breakfast.

She sat, picked up the bouquet, and held it to her nose, inhaling the delicate, sweet scent of lily of the valley and the heady fragrance of wild roses, the bouquet bound by strands of long grass. Yesterday, she'd awoken to find wild blueberries. The day before that, she'd found a tin plate heaped with sweet, golden honey still in the comb, the red welts on Morgan's arms proof of the price he'd paid to give her such a wonderful gift.

It had been six days now since that magical afternoon in the rock pools—six days so bright and filled with happiness that her life before seemed but shadows. *Oui,* she missed Bourlamaque and Père François and her books and belongings, but even these losses could not dim the joy she felt at being beside Morgan as his wife. Never had she felt safer, happier, or more cherished than she had these past six days, never more contented or at peace.

Each day Morgan had guided her safely through the forest, his skilled woodcraft a source of amazement for her, making her respect him all the more. And each night, he'd shown her something new about the ways of men and women, revealing the mysteries of their bodies, bringing her pleasure she hadn't thought possible nor even imagined, turning the forest from a place of darkness into their wedding bower. Then he'd held her through the night, his body warm and strong, the forest singing them both to sleep.

Amalie set the flowers carefully aside and dressed quickly, unable to keep from smiling despite herself. Last night he'd taught her to bring him release with her hands as he'd first done for her, and she'd seen for the first time the power of his body's response. Every muscle in his body had gone tense. Then, his eyes squeezed shut, he'd groaned out her name, his hips bucking, his big hands fisted in the fur, his sex jerking in her hand as seed shot from its swollen head in creamy ribbons of hot white to pool on his belly.

While he'd watched, an amused grin on his face, she'd explored his essence, rubbing it between her fingers, fascinated to think that it somehow held the power to beget a life inside her. "How long will it take you to get me with child?"

Beads of sweat on his temples and chest from having spent himself moments ago, he'd chuckled. "If I can have but a moment to catch my breath, lass, I shall redouble my efforts, since it seems you're so eager."

Then he'd taken her beneath him, bringing her to the edge with his kisses and his touch and, when she could bear it no longer, making love to her with deep, slow strokes, carrying her to her peak again and again, his gaze never leaving her face.

Now fully dressed, Amalie stood and coiled her braid to keep it from the flames when she made breakfast. She had just tucked the ends in place, when she looked up to find him striding toward her, his breeches riding low on his hips, the neck of his linen shirt open to reveal a dark wedge of hair, his handsome face dark with stubble. The sight of him was enough to make her blood thicken, her hunger for him seemingly insatiable. Did all women feel this way?

"A good morning to you, husband."

Morgan took in the sight of his bonnie wife and felt a surge of protectiveness. He needed to get her far away from this place, but he did not wish to frighten her. He willed himself to set aside his worries and smiled. "A good morn' to you, wife.

"Thank you for your kind gift." She picked up the bouquet, pressed the blossoms to her nose, and inhaled. "Mmm—they smell so sweet!"

He kissed her cheek, savoring her scent. "No' near as sweet as the bonnie lass who holds them. Did you have a pleasant sleep?"

Her nose still buried in the bouquet, she looked up at him, her eyes filled not with innocence, but a woman's knowing sensuality. "Lying beside you is always pleasant."

And for a moment Morgan couldn't breathe, the animal part of him wanting him to toss her on her back, lift her skirts, and have at her, his brain telling him there was not time for such pleasures—not with the Wyandot war party Joseph and his men had encountered last night.

Morgan had awoken in the wee hours, roused by the distant sound of gunfire, and had known that his Muhheconneok brother had encountered trouble. Careful not to wake Amalie, who slept so peacefully, he'd risen, dressed, and readied his weapons, but the forest had fallen silent again, leaving him to wonder who had prevailed.

Then one of Joseph's younger men, Isaiah, emerged from the forest to bring him word. "The sentries spotted a war party of twenty Wyandot encamped near William Henry. They had captives—two women and a boy. Joseph sent half our number to attack. It is done. The Wyandot are slain and the captives unharmed."

To hear Joseph tell the story, it had been a swift victory with no losses or severe injuries amongst his men. A dozen warriors had been sent to escort the terrified captives back to their farm and to help them bury their kin.

But although the battle was over and the enemy slain, trouble was not far behind them. For if Morgan had heard the gunfire, so had any other party encamped nearby. And there almost certainly had been others. For here, near the blood-soaked ruins of Fort William Henry, all paths converged—French seeking to waylay Rangers and redcoats on their way back to Fort Edward, Indians seeking to plunder frontier farmsteads, British hunting for French, enemy Indians . . . and deserters.

'Twas no place for a woman.

"I'm glad sharin' my bed pleases you." Morgan brushed his knuckles over her cheek, knowing that what he was about to say would frighten her, but seeing no way around it. "We have no time to break our fast this mornin'. There was a fight in the night. Joseph and his men attacked a war party of Wyandot and freed their captives. Anyone who heard that firefight will be drawn toward us. We must leave as soon as we are ready."

Her eyes went wide for the briefest of moments, then she raised her chin. "Tell me what I must do."

And sooner than he expected, they were packed up and ready to move, Joseph helping Morgan to hide any sign of their presence.

"This will be the most dangerous day of our journey," Morgan told her, slipping into his tumpline pack. "We must move swiftly and in silence. With any luck we'll reach the farm the day after tomorrow."

She met his gaze with grave eyes. "I shall do my best not to be a burden."

"Sweet Amalie." He tucked a finger beneath her chin, ran his thumb over her lower lip. "You are ne'er a burden."

They moved in silence, stopping only rarely to drink, to eat a handful of parched corn, or to refill their water skins. Amalie half expected a party of Huron or Abenaki to swoop down upon them at any moment, every copse of trees, every outcropping, every ravine a potential ambush. But she knew that Morgan was alert to the danger in ways she was not, her trust in him holding her fear at bay. He seemed to read the forest as she might one of her books. And there were Joseph and his men as well, tall, silent men who kept pace close beside them.

It was not as difficult for her to keep up as it had been that first harrowing day, her body having grown more accustomed to the rigors of the journey. As she moved through the trees she couldn't help but feel a sense of pride that she had made it this far through the wilderness on her own two feet. What would the *mère supérieure* think to see her now?

Twice they found proof of other parties, mostly likely French or British soldiers, as they had left signs that even Amalie could see. And once they stopped to yield to a sow bear, who was leading her three cubs through the forest in search of ripe berries.

"Elle est très grande!" Amalie whispered, staring in amazement at the bear, momentarily forgetting her English.

"Aye, she is a big one—and hail to have borne three strong cubs."

The cubs—two black like their mother, the third a light brown—ran after her, bawling for her as they struggled to keep up. She stopped, looked back, scented the air with her snout, as if she knew she and her cubs were being watched. Then she turned into the trees and was gone, her cubs trundling behind her.

It was late afternoon before they encountered soldiers.

Morgan drew Amalie down beside him, pressing a finger to

her lips to indicate silence. But when the soldiers came into view, they weren't French. They were British. Confused as to why Morgan should hide from them as if they were the enemy, she glanced up at him, but he only shook his head, his gaze warning her not to ask questions now.

Slowly the column of British soldiers passed heading westward, their red uniforms glaring amongst the trees, their faces lined with trepidation.

It was only later that Morgan explained. "They've orders from Amherst to shoot deserters on sight. I didna wish to test their aim."

"We wouldn't want you to be executed before your trial, would we?" Joseph jested, a broad grin on his face.

Deserter? Trial? Execution?

It was only then that Amalie realized that Morgan's actions at Fort Carillon might have made him a traitor at home.

Chapter 26

"I ken 'tis sweltrie, but leave your gown on." Morgan laid the bearskin over the pine boughs, their pallet complete. "Tonight we sleep in our clothes."

Amalie nodded, and Morgan knew from the grave look on her face that she understood. They might be south of William Henry, but they were still too near to let down their guard. They'd seen signs of a half-dozen different war parties today, too many to think themselves alone in these woods. They needed to be ready to flee with little warning—and that meant remaining clothed. No fire. No warm meal.

"Come and eat." His own stomach growling, Morgan sat on the bearskin, dug through his pack, and drew out the pemmican Joseph had given him along with the bit of honeycomb he'd wrapped in parchment. "This will help restore your strength."

Still silent, she sat beside him, devouring each piece of pemmican as he handed it to her, then eating the honey, comb and all, then licking her fingers clean. Like the rest of them, she'd had nothing but parched cornmeal today, apart from the parfleche filled with blueberries that Joseph had picked and given to her.

Morgan felt a sense of pride in how well she'd done. Although he'd forced her to go at a faster pace than the previous seven days, she'd kept up without complaint, heeding his warnings to stay quiet, never giving in to her fatigue or fear. She might be a wee woman and sheltered, but there was strength in her. He had seen it, aye, and Joseph had seen it, too, casting Morgan more than one approving glance.

And yet the day hadn't been easy for her. He could tell from the exhaustion on her face and the lingering shadows in her eyes. The wilderness was hard on women, offering no pardon for gentleness or innocence.

"You did well today," he said, wanting to put her at ease.

"I hope I did not hinder you." Her voice was strangely flat.

Then she lay down on the bearskin as if to sleep, her back turned toward him. He might have thought her exhausted had he not felt the tension in her. And then her breath caught, and he realized she was weeping.

"Amalie?" He stretched out behind her, his hand caressing the length of her hair before settling on the curve of her hip. "What is it, lass?"

For a moment she did not answer, sniffing back her tears. "How long have you known that Wentworth believes you a traitor?"

So that explained the distressed look in her eyes.

Curse Joseph's loose tongue!

"Connor told me the night we encamped wi' him and the men. You were asleep. I saw no cause to trouble you after that."

"I'm your wife, not a child!" There was anger in her voice now. "If you knew it was unsafe to return, why did you insist on traveling all this way to Fort Edward? We might have returned to Fort Carillon at once—"

"Carillon? I couldna go back there, lass. Surely you ken that."

"Bourlamaque would only have known that Rillieux had taken us against our will. He wouldn't have learned about your spying if you hadn't told him. We could have gone back together and—"

"It doesna matter whether he kent the truth or no', Amalie." Did she not understand? "I could ne'er have joined an army bent on killin' my brothers or my men. Do you think either of us would have been welcome once the soldiers at Carillon got word that I'd killed Rillieux? Nay, lass. Besides, I couldna live a lie. I couldna accept Bourlamaque's hospitality wi'out confessin' to him all that I'd done, and then I'd be on my way to Oganak again."

She rolled over and looked at him as if he were daft. "Bourlamaque would never have condemned you to burn. He cared too much for both of us to do such a thing."

Morgan leaned down until they were only inches apart. "He told me he'd light the fires himself if I betrayed him."

Her face went pale, her eyes wide. "H-he said that?"

"Aye, he did. He and Montcalm discussed killin' me in their letters even after I'd been granted sanctuary. Nay, 'tis safe for neither of us there, and I willna take chances where you're concerned. 'Tis best I stand like a man and defend my honor, aye? The matter will be easily resolved once I explain the truth of it. Until then, you'll be safe wi' Iain and Annie."

And still she did not seem at ease, and he thought he knew why.

"I ken today wasna easy for you." He brushed a strand of hair from her cheek, resisting the urge to kiss her. "You're tired, and you're about to enter a new world—a new home, a new family, a new life. I've taken you from all that you ken. But I promise you, Amalie, you'll ne'er be without a home again. Afore the sun sets tomorrow, you'll have a hot bath and a warm meal. You'll sleep in a real bed and have a strong roof over your head."

Amalie saw the concern in Morgan's eyes, but her worries tonight were less about the things she was about to gain, however unfamiliar they might be, and more about the things she might lose.

"I'm afraid for *you*, Morgan, not for myself. I'm afraid of what the British will do to you! I don't want to see you in chains again or watch them flog you or . . ." She couldn't say it. "I do not trust this man who commands you, this *Wentworth*. You did all you could to be loyal to him, and still he doubts you. He does not deserve your loyalty!"

"Nay, he doesna." Morgan traced his thumb along her lower lip, and she knew from the way his eyes darkened that he wanted to kiss her. "But I am far more valuable to him alive than dead, lass. Once he's heard the truth, all shall be as it was. And when I feel 'tis safe, I'll bring you to live wi' me on Ranger Island."

Amalie drew a deep breath, taking reassurance from his words. "Are you certain he will believe you?"

"Why should he not? Och, you worry overmuch, *a leannan*! It seems I must gi' you somethin' else to think about." Then

Morgan slowly pushed her skirts up her thighs, baring her to her waist, his hands hot against her skin, his gaze never leaving hers.

Her heart seemed to skip. "Here? With Joseph and his men so nearby?"

"Aye." He settled himself between her thighs. "Here. Now."

He nudged down his breeches to free himself, caught the bends of her knees with his shoulders, and forced her legs back, pressing her thighs wide apart, opening her fully to him. Then, holding himself above her, his gazed fixed on hers, he entered her with one slow thrust, their moans mingling with the night sounds of the forest.

There were no kisses, no gentle touches, only the carnal union of man and woman, his hard, deep thrusts blossoming into gold against her womb, bringing them both to a swift and shattering end.

"Tell me about Iain."

They walked at an easy pace, Morgan holding Amalie's hand, savoring the feel of her small fingers laced with his, the afternoon blessedly cool thanks to a sky full of rain clouds. Joseph and his men had bid them farewell an hour past and turned back to Fort Edward, leaving Morgan and Amalie just north of MacKinnon lands on a rutted wagon road that would lead them back to the farm.

Soon Morgan would be home.

He fancied he could smell it now—that warm, familiar scent of his family's hearth, of the soil that sustained them, of barn and byre. It seemed such a lifetime since last he'd been this way, though it had only been since April.

"Iain is a born leader, a good fighter, and a good husband and father." Morgan felt a tug in his chest at the thought of his older brother and wondered how Iain would react when he saw him alive. "He's a little more than a year older than I and a mite taller, though we look much the same."

"Did he truly take a hundred lashes for Annie's sake?"

"Aye, he did, and she watched, though I think she'd have fallen to the ground in a heap of skirts had I not held her. 'Twas no' easy for her to see him suffer so."

"I cannot imagine it."

Afraid he'd set her to worrying again, Morgan sought to distract her. "Were there no girls at the convent who were as sisters to you, friends who felt like kin?"

"No, though Sister Marie Louise—"

"The one who filled your head with tales of terror about husbands?"

Amalie smiled, pink stealing into her cheeks. "She was a friend to me. But the *mère supérieure* found me prideful, and most of the sisters with her. The other girls teased me because of my dark hair and skin, though Papa said it was only jealousy."

"Aye, for certain it was." Morgan felt a pang in his chest for the little girl who'd grown up without the love of her mother amongst women who might have cared for her immortal soul, but couldn't find it in themselves to cherish *her.* "The abbey cannae have felt like home to you amidst such unkindness."

"There has never been a place I could call my home." She spoke the words simply and without pity.

And Morgan realized 'twas but the unadorned truth. Amalie could not remember living at her mother's knee because her mother had died when she was so little, and since then, apart from the short time before her father's death, she'd lived amongst strangers and behind high walls—the sheltering walls of the abbey or the ramparts of Fort Carillon.

He stopped, tucked a finger beneath her chin, tilted her gaze to his. "I promise you you'll ne're be alone again, Amalie, nor will you want for a home. My home is yours now. My family is your family."

Tears glittered in her eyes, and she smiled.

Amalie kept up with Morgan, listening to him tell stories of his childhood, a nervous trill in her belly. They must be getting close now. She could tell by the way his stride grew longer, his steps faster, as if home were calling to him, drawing him in. She thought she understood some of the eagerness he must feel, for there'd been a time when he'd been certain he'd never see his home again.

"Iain and Joseph returned at dawn, alive but battered, and the entire village welcomed them as men. One minute I was puffed up wi' pride that they had earned their warrior marks, then next all but daft wi' envy that I was still but a lad in their eyes." He chuckled at the memory. "I struck Iain ere the day was out."

She stared up at him, unable to keep from smiling. "You did not!"

"Och, aye, I did. I gave him a black eye."

"And what did he do?"

Morgan grinned. "He took the blow, then frowned down at me and told me that he wouldna strike back, for he was now a warrior and warriors did not hurt children. His words hurt far worse than his fist would have done."

Then Morgan stopped her and pointed. "There it is."

Just round the bend stood a large wooden farmhouse and two great barns. Long fields stood before it, heavy with crops, their rows straight and clean. An orchard of small, neat trees stood behind it. There were horses in the paddock, cows in the pasture, and chickens pecking at the dirt.

"It's lovely!"

And it was. A more perfect farmstead she could not imagine. *Home.*

The word slid easily into her mind—and stayed.

He ducked down and kissed her nose. "Come."

His hand grasping hers, strong and sure, he drew her forward. Then he shouted, his voice deep and loud. "Hallo in the house!"

A moment later, a man stepped out of the barn, rifle in hand. He took one look at Morgan—then stopped still. There was no mistaking his resemblance to Morgan and Connor—or the look of utter shock on his face, the rifle clattering to the ground, forgotten. He crossed himself, took one step and then another, his gaze fixed on Morgan. "*Mary, Mother of God!* It *is* you! But how . . . ?"

And then the brothers met in a bone-cracking embrace.

Amalie's throat grew tight, tears spilling down her cheeks, her heart swelling for joy for Morgan, who had thought never to see his brother or his home again, and for Iain, who had believed Morgan lost.

Then Iain stepped back, fierce emotion still burning on his face. "Saints be praised! Welcome home, brother! Och, but you've much to explain!"

"Aye, but first, I'd like you to meet my wife, Amalie Chauvenet MacKinnon." Morgan wrapped his arm reassuringly around her waist. "'Tis on account of her kindness and compassion that I'm alive."

Iain gazed at Amalie in seeming amazement, then clasped her hands in his, ducked down, and kissed her cheek. "Welcome home, sister. If there's augh' I can do for you, you need but ask. I must hear more of this—"

Before he could finish, the farmhouse door opened, and the most beautiful woman Amalie had ever seen stepped outside, a dark-haired baby in her arms. With long tresses the color of sunshine, she gave a little cry, then swayed on her feet and sank to her knees in a swirl of blue skirts.

"I think you'd best see to Annie, brother." Happiness shone on Morgan's handsome face. "She appears all of a dither."

Then, laughing, he turned to Amalie, scooped her into his arms, and carried her past an astonished and teary-eyed Annie across the threshold and into her new home.

Amalie soon found herself sitting at a well-built wooden table eating a bowl of Annie's delicious rabbit stew while Morgan told Iain and Annie the tale of his time at Carillon, from the moment he'd been shot to the moment he'd bid Connor and the Rangers farewell. Annie, the baby at her breast, was moved to tears several times, understandably still shaken by Morgan's sudden return from the grave, while Iain reminded Amalie of Morgan, his jaw going tight just as Morgan's did when he was angry, his blue eyes betraying the fierceness of his feelings.

When Morgan finished, there was a moment of silence.

Then Iain reached over and gave Amalie's hand a firm squeeze, his voice rough with emotion, his gaze filled with warmth. "There are no words to thank you for all you've done. You saved my brother's life more than once. 'Tis glad I am he's married you and made you part of our family, for now I shall have the chance to repay a small portion of your kindness. What is ours is yours, Amalie."

Amalie fought to speak past the lump in her throat. "Thank you."

Then Iain turned to Morgan. "So Connor kent you were alive and he didna tell me? He's goin' to catch the sharp edge of my tongue, so he is."

* * *

They spent much of the afternoon answering Iain and Annie's questions, Morgan showing his scars, the men jesting with each other in the familiar way of brothers, their robust laughter making the baby laugh, too, his smile revealing four tiny teeth. But as the shadows began to lengthen toward evening, Annie rose from the table, insisting she had much to do before suppertime. Morgan and Iain, now speaking in their Scottish tongue, went out to the barn to tend the livestock, leaving Amalie alone with her new sister-by-marriage.

To Amalie's great relief, she felt at ease with Annie, no matter that Annie was of noble birth and a Protestant. Annie showed her to the room she and Morgan would share—a large room with its own hearth, two glass windows, a broad bed, a table, and even a tall looking glass. Together, they swept the floor, wiped the dust from the looking glass, made the bed, and set fresh beeswax candles on the bedside table, taking turns holding the baby and sharing stories of how they'd met their husbands.

Then Annie left Amalie with little Iain, only to return with an armload of garments, which she laid across the bed—bright gowns in cotton and linen, starched petticoats, several clean chemises, a lacy nightgown, and cotton drawers.

"These ought to fit you, though we might need to take up the hems." Annie took the baby, who'd begun to fuss, and put him to her breast. "You're welcome to use them for as long as you have need."

"You're most generous."

Annie gave a sad smile, dismissing Amalie's thanks with a shake of her head.

"For as long as I live, I'll never forget the mornin' we got word that Morgan was dead and his body given to the Abenaki." Annie stroked her baby's dark hair, her gaze fixed on some faraway place. "Iain could scarce speak, both he and Connor blamin' themselves, beset with grief. I wanted to comfort them, but I was heartbroken as well. 'Twas Morgan who held me when Iain was flogged. 'Twas he who bought my weddin' gown. 'Twas he who sheltered me when Iain faced my accursed uncle in battle. I didna want to believe he was gone."

Then her gaze met Amalie's, her green eyes bright with tears.

"I've seen my husband newly back from battle, his eyes haunted by the men he'd lost. I've seen him wake in the night, his dreams full of death. But I've ne'er seen him as shattered as he was that mornin', thinkin' Morgan dead, his body desecrated. And Connor—God in heaven!—I thought he would be killed before summer's end, so reckless was he in his grief! There has been precious little joy in our lives since the day we heard Morgan had died. But you saved his life and brought him back to us—and no' without risk to yourself. 'Tis you who are generous, Amalie, my dear."

"And it does not matter to you that I am—"

"French and Abenaki?" Annie laughed. "Not one whit. Now, if my sweet wee lad has filled his belly, we shall get supper on the table."

And a little knot of tension Amalie had been carrying in her belly melted away.

"I dinnae like it, Morgan. If it were only Wentworth, all would quickly be put to rights, but Amherst is a hard, arrogant man. Should he decide you're a traitor, he willna let truth stand in his way. You must be cautious."

"Aye, I will be." Morgan sat on the porch, sharing a flask of rum with Iain, supper long since cleared away, the sky now dark. "I leave in the morn'."

"Does Amalie ken you're goin' so soon?"

"We've no' spoken of it yet. She kens I'm no' takin' her wi' me. I dinnae want Wentworth anywhere near her."

"Aye, that much is certain." Iain took the flask back from Morgan, drank deeply. "She's lovely, Morgan, beautiful and innocent. Wentworth would stalk her like prey."

"Aye." Morgan knew it was true. He remembered how Wentworth had tried to manipulate Annie into his bed, ruthless in his attempts to possess her. "Amalie has ne'er had a place she could call home. She's lived most of her life amongst strangers—in the convent, at the fort. No matter what happens to me, watch over her."

"You needn't ask. You ken I will—wi' my life."

"My love lies upon her."

Iain grinned. "And hers upon you. I can see it. Now go to her."

Morgan stood, clapping Iain on the shoulder. "Have a pleasant sleep, brother."

"You, as well. And Morgan—welcome home."

Amalie had just finished drying off from her bath when she heard the bedroom door open and close and turned to find Morgan.

"Nay," he said when she reached for her nightgown, his gaze sliding over her like a caress. "Stay as you are."

Slowly, he unbuttoned his shirt, then let it fall to the floor. Next, he set aside his weapons, moving slowly as if to give her time to watch him, the candlelight seeming to accentuate his muscles and the smoothness of his skin. Then he loosed the fall of his breeches, pushing them only down far enough to reveal his already rigid sex, before turning his back to her and baring the smooth mounds of his buttocks. When at last he shoved his breeches down his thighs, he stood sideways so that she could glimpse both his sex and his derriere at the same time.

And she knew.

He was trying to rouse her with the sight of his body.

And it was working.

There was scarce room for breath in her lungs, her pulse tripping, her nipples drawing tight as if he'd already touched them, liquid heat pooling in her belly. Oh, but he was a beautiful man, and she thrilled to think that he was hers.

He strode slowly over to the washtub, naked and feral, his face dark with many days' growth of beard, his muscular arms adorned by armbands and warrior marks, his hair hanging long down his chest and back. Then he spoke, his voice deep. "Is it not customary for a wife to bathe her husband?"

Amalie's belly clenched, and she knew he was deliberately echoing the words she'd spoken that magical evening at the rock pools. She sought for her voice. *"Yes."*

He stepped into the water, sat. "Then come, wife, and tend me."

Heart thrumming with excitement, she knelt beside the tub, first shaving his face, then washing his body, using what he'd taught her to please him. But even as she took his hard length in hand, he played with her, catching her nipples between his fingers, caressing her naked bottom, sliding his hand between her thighs.

By the time his bath was finished and he stepped from the tub, she was burning for him, desperate to have him inside her. He carried her to the bed and stretched out above her, his mouth scorching a path from her mouth to her breasts. Then he seemed to catch sight of something out of the corner of his eye—and he went still.

With a grin, he stood, walked over to the looking glass, and carried it close to the bed, angling it so that Amalie suddenly saw herself. She lay naked, her lips and breasts swollen from his kisses, her hair fanning across the sheets, her legs slightly spread, *that* part of her—something she'd never seen—revealed only slightly.

"Do you see how bonnie you are?" Morgan met her gaze in the looking glass, his hand reaching between her thighs. "Now watch as I pleasure you."

Chapter 27

Amalie expected Morgan to stretch himself out above her again, but instead he grasped her ankles and drew her toward him, bending her knees and spreading her legs wide, his gaze fixed on her most private flesh. Then he did something she could not have imagined. He knelt down and kissed her—*that* part of her.

She cried out in shock, her cry becoming a moan as his mouth closed over her and he began to suckle. *"Ô, mon Dieu!"*

Amalie couldn't believe what she was feeling, the pleasure so fierce as Morgan tormented her with his lips and tongue, licking, nipping, and sucking her most tender places. She clenched her fingers in his hair, her hips thrusting upward of their own accord, her thighs spreading wider.

"Open your eyes, *a leannan!*"

And then she remembered.

The looking glass.

She opened her eyes and felt the breath leave her lungs.

There in the silver depths of the glass, she saw a woman lost in carnal pleasure, her body writhing with arousal, her breasts flushed and full, her thighs far apart, her lover's head nestled between them. It was the most shocking thing she'd ever seen, arousing beyond belief, all the more so because the woman was *she*.

And then Morgan slid two fingers deep inside her—and her pleasure peaked, bliss washing through her in relentless, shimmering waves.

Morgan heard Amalie cry out, felt her inner muscles clench around his fingers, the nectar of her arousal sweet on his lips, on his tongue, in his throat, her scent filling his head. He kept up the rhythm until her peak had passed, then kissed his way up her body to her mouth, giving her a moment to catch her breath.

But he wasn't finished with her.

"Oh, Morgan!" she said at last. "I did not know."

There were many things she did not know.

"There's one more thing I'll be showin' you tonight."

"Wh-what is that?"

"You."

She gave a little gasp, her eyes going wide. "But, Morgan . . ."

Refusing to be dissuaded by her shyness, Morgan sat facing the looking glass and drew her onto his lap, forcing her to straddle his legs, revealing her hidden beauty to the looking glass. "I want you to see your own beauty, to see what I see."

Lust grinding in his gut, he parted her with his fingers, separating her thick outer lips from the delicate inner ones, stroking her, opening her. She was slick from his kisses and her own juices, her sex rosy in the candlelight. "You're like a flower with a little bud at the center. *Beautiful.*"

She stared into the glass, her gaze fixed on her own sex, her eyes dark with arousal.

"Now watch." Morgan clasped her hips and adjusted her so that her entrance rested just above the aching head of his cock. Then, grasping himself with one hand and parting her with the other, he nudged himself inside her.

Her eyes went wide, her breath unraveling on a moan as first the head of his cock and then the shaft disappeared slowly inside her. "Oh, Morgan! It's so . . . I never . . . *Oh!*"

Holding her hips in place with one hand, teasing her nipples with the other, he thrust upward, the sight of Amalie watching his cock slide in and out of her tight heat driving him perilously close to the edge, his stones already drawing tight. Harder and harder he thrust, needing her, needing to be deep inside her, needing to join himself to her so completely that they could never truly be parted. "Och, Christ, Amalie."

She was the most beautiful thing he'd ever seen, her breath coming in pants, her gaze fixed on the looking glass, on the place where their bodies merged, her hair spilling around them in a curtain of dark silk. Then her breath caught and broke, her body arching, her head falling back against his shoulder, a cry leaving her lips as delight claimed her once again.

And then Morgan could hold back no longer, the next thrust carrying him over that same sweet edge as, with a groan, he spilled his seed deep inside her.

"Iain and Annie are already quite fond of you." Morgan's voice was a deep rumble in Amalie's ear, her head resting on his chest, his fingers caressing her spine as passion slowly cooled into sleep.

She snuggled more deeply into his embrace, wishing they could stay this way forever. "And I them."

"I leave for Fort Edward in the morn'."

"I know."

Morgan watched the sutler ride past in his wagon on his way to Albany to purchase supplies, escorted by a score or more of redcoats. Though Morgan was fond of the sutler, he was uncertain what kind of welcome the soldiers would give him, and thinking it best to keep his presence secret until he was well within the fort's walls, he remained concealed behind the trees.

He'd left just after breakfast two days' past, finding it even more difficult to say farewell to Amalie than he'd imagined, something twisting in his gut at the sight of her tears. "I'll come back as soon as I can. I dinnae ken when that will be."

In the doorway behind her, Iain and Annie watched, and Morgan had known they would offer her what comfort they could once he had gone.

"H-how will I know whether you're safe?"

"If augh' should go amiss, Connor will send word." He kissed the salty tears from her cheeks. "You worry overmuch, lass. All will be well in the end."

She'd nodded, but he could tell she wasn't convinced. "I miss you already."

"And I you, *a leannan.*" He'd held her against him and kissed her long and hard. Then, giving her hand one last squeeze, he'd turned and walked away, pain flaring sudden and sharp in his chest.

But he'd not gone far when he heard her call after him. "Morgan, wait!"

He'd turned to find her running toward him, her skirts lifted off the ground, her dark hair streaming behind her. "Amalie, lass, what is it?"

She'd leapt into his arms and kissed him with a fierceness that had taken him by surprise, her arms thrown round his neck, holding him fast. Then she'd met his gaze through eyes brimming with fresh tears. "I love you, Morgan MacKinnon!"

The breath had left his lungs in a rush, the pain behind his breastbone seeming to split his chest wide open. He'd drawn her close, kissed her hair, wanting never to let go. "And I love you, lass."

It had felt better than he'd imagined to hear those words from her and to speak them himself. And he realized he'd wanted to speak them for a long, long time—perhaps since the first time he'd kissed her.

Now it seemed like weeks since he'd last seen her, and yet it had been only a couple of days. Traveling alone, he'd made swift progress and would soon be within sight of Fort Edward. The sutler rolled slowly by, disappearing down the road, the clatter of hooves and boots and steel fading into silence.

Rifle in hand, Morgan rose and moved quickly and quietly through the trees, mindful of the fort's sentries. Then the forest fell back and the Hudson spread out before him. To the south, in the middle of the river, stood Ranger Island, large enough to house six score of Rangers and a hundred Muhheconneok, together with gardens for growing food and parade grounds for morning muster. For the past four years, it had been his home.

On the eastern bank, connected to the island only by a bridge made of bateaux that had been lashed together and covered by planking, stood Fort Edward, its ramparts guarded by redcoats, the Union Flag fluttering in the breeze.

You ne'er thought you'd be glad to see this place, did you, lad?

Nay, he hadn't.

He took cover amongst the trees and whistled out for his men, the call that only a Ranger would recognize. Then he settled in to wait.

"The redoubts and smaller entrenchments will go here, here, and here with enough men to hold off an attack should the enemy try to come at us from behind. A force of no more than a thousand men should suffice. If supplies arrive as scheduled, we shall depart for Fort George in one week's time."

William listened as Amherst, who had arrived with his troops eight days ago, once again discussed the entrenchments he planned for the ruins of Fort William Henry. Determined to avoid the mistakes of both Munro, who'd found himself suddenly surrounded at William Henry, and that imbecile Abercrombie, who'd given away a sure victory, Amherst was leaving nothing to chance. He was a skilled strategist and ruthlessly ambitious—qualities William both understood and admired and which had helped Amherst earn the favor of William Pitt, His Majesty's irritating secretary of state.

And if his ambition on occasion ran to cruelty?

Though William admired him, he did not trust him.

"Indeed, sir, a thousand men ought to be sufficient." William gazed down at the map upon the familiar landscape between Fort Edward and Ticonderoga.

"We must also find a way to curb these desertions. Already this month, we've lost forty-three provincials and—"

Beyond the closed doors of William's study, there came a ruckus—raised voices. Then the doors were opened and Lieutenant Cooke hurried inside, wide-eyed, a stunned expression on his face. The reason for his astonishment stood directly behind him.

Major MacKinnon.

He filled the doorway, tumpline pack on his back, Captain MacKinnon and several Rangers forming an armed escort behind him.

"Why, Lieutenant, you look as though you've seen a ghost."

Unlike poor Cooke, William was not surprised by the major's sudden appearance. He'd been expecting him ever since Captain MacKinnon had reported rescuing him from a band of Abenaki.

When William had asked the captain why his brother had not returned with him, he'd said the major could not keep pace because of his injuries and was making his way as best he could, accompanied by Captain Joseph and his men. William had found himself hoping that the major would have some explanation for his survival—and for Montcalm's damning letter. Then, two days ago, Bourlamaque's missive had arrived, and William had realized there was more to this story than he yet knew.

"You are dismissed, Lieutenant. Please escort Captain Mac-Kinnon and the other Rangers back to Ranger Island and order them to remain there." He waited for the doors to close before he spoke again. "Major, you look remarkably well—for a dead man."

Then Amherst stepped forward. "Is this your traitor—your Major MacKinnon?"

William straightened the lace at his cuffs. "This is Major MacKinnon, yes. Whether he's a traitor remains to be seen."

The major strode forward, his gait marred by only the slightest limp, his countenance remarkably calm given the gravity of his situation. "'Twas perhaps too much to hope for a hero's welcome, but I'll no' be called a deserter nor a traitor by any man. Major MacKinnon reportin' for duty, sir. I bring word of Montcalm's secret plans for Ticonderoga."

"You instructed their soldiers in marksmanship?" Amherst asked the question again, this time in a tone of voice most men reserved for bairns.

A tall man with a strong jaw and prominent nose, he might well have been the only man Morgan despised more than Wentworth. For five long hours he had interrogated Morgan, insisting that Morgan be stripped of his gear and weapons and that guards be stationed outside the door. 'Twas clear he'd found Morgan guilty before Morgan had spoken a single word.

Morgan fought to keep his temper in check. "Aye, sir."

Wentworth sat in silence as he had for most of the interrogation, listening, his fingertips pressed together, his gaze focused on his infernal chessboard.

"You instructed French soldiers in marksmanship, knowing that these same soldiers would soon take aim at British troops and even your own men?"

"Aye, sir, but I wasna a very skilled teacher. They learnt little to their benefit from me, precisely because I didna wish to cost even a single British life."

"And the information you gave the enemy—the sites of your caches, your campsites and rendezvous points, your trails in the forest . . ." Hands clasped behind his back, Amherst rocked back and forth on his heels. "Did it not occur to you that your own men—*men loyal to you*—might die as a result of your loose tongue, or were you content to trade their lives for your own?"

Morgan found himself on his feet, his fists clenched. "I value their lives more than my own, which is how I came to be shot in the first place, *sir.* I gave Bourlamaque only information that wouldna be of use to him. I ken my men, sir, and no' a one of them is fool enough to blunder into a campsite or up to a cache wi'out first kennin' 'tis safe."

Amherst's lips curled in apparent disgust. "You cannot be certain of that, Major."

"Aye, I bloody well can. We Rangers have . . ." He stopped short of saying "Rules." "We have our own way of fightin', our own way of movin' through the forest. I ken what my men will do afore they do it. 'Tis how we stay alive and *how we win.*"

Amherst looked taken aback. "Is that so?"

Then Wentworth spoke. "The Rules of Ranging, sir."

Morgan sat with a groan, wishing he could make Wentworth swallow his words.

"Rules of Ranging?" Amherst repeated stupidly. "Why am I, His Majesty's major general, not familiar with these rules?"

"Because they are secret." Morgan glared at Wentworth. "No one who's no' a Ranger is permitted to ken them."

"Even I, His Majesty's *grandson,* do not know them, sir. Few are aware they exist. The Rangers protect them with their lives." Wentworth met Morgan's gaze with cold gray eyes. "Am I correct in assuming that your Rules remain secret?"

"Aye, sir. Bourlamaque kens nothin' of them."

Wentworth nodded, his dark eyebrows arching upward. "So you pretended to accept Bourlamaque's offer of sanctuary in hopes of one day escaping with information of value to His Majesty."

"Aye, sir." Morgan felt certain Wentworth believed him. "And, saints be praised, I did—though my escape came in a fashion I'd no' expected."

"Tell us once more why you did not accompany Captain Mac-Kinnon and the men back to Fort Edward?" Amherst asked. "They arrived six days ahead of you."

Morgan answered the question yet again. "I'd been struck on the head, and my leg is no' as strong as it once was. I didna wish to hinder them. I made the journey wi' Joseph and his men, stoppin' at the farm to let my brother and his wife ken that I yet live, then makin' my way here."

"Is that where you left her?"

Wentworth's unexpected question hit Morgan between the eyes. He fought to keep his face impassive, leaning back in his chair as if he hadn't a care in the world, crossing his arms over his chest. "I dinnae understand your question, sir."

Wentworth stood, walked to his window, looked outside. "Is that where you left Amalie Chauvenet? The Chevalier de Bourlamaque's ward. The young woman you brought back with you from Ticonderoga."

How in the bloody hell did he know about her?

Even as the thought raced through Morgan's mind, he understood.

Bourlamaque.

But Morgan was spared the need to answer Wentworth's question by Amherst, who crossed the room to Wentworth's writing table, took up a piece of parchment, and began to read aloud, his nasal baritone filling the room.

" 'My Dear Brigadier General Lord William Wentworth, and et cetera, et cetera, I write to inquire as to the welfare of my ward, Amalie Chauvenet, daughter of the late Major Antoine Chauvenet. She was forcibly taken from Fort Carillon some days past. You will find her with Major Morgan MacKinnon, who survived his injuries after all. I should like her given all respect due her station and am willing to offer recompense for her safe return. Yours, and et cetera et cetera, le Chevalier de Bourlamaque.' "

Morgan could feel Bourlamaque's wrath in each and every word, could feel his sense of betrayal, his injured pride. Bourlamaque was so angry with Morgan that he was willing to expose Amalie to the wrath of his men, rather than allow Morgan to keep her as his wife. And he'd dangled the perfect bait before Amherst and Wentworth's noses—a prisoner exchange.

Amherst looked up from the parchment, his gaze challenging

Morgan to gainsay the letter in his hand. "What say you to that, Major?"

Knowing there was no use in trying to hide the truth, Morgan stood. "Amalie Chauvenet is my wife, given into my hand by Bourlamaque himself and wed to me by his own priest in his own chapel at his command. He seeks her back out of anger that I betrayed him, but she's no' longer his to protect. I willna yield her nor leave her subject to any man's will *but my own*."

"Catholic unions are not recognized by the Crown, as you know, Major." Wentworth turned to face him. "If returning this young woman to her ward can free British officers from imprisonment on a French barge, it becomes your patriotic duty to cooperate."

It was all Morgan could do to keep his fists at his side. "I'll be dead afore I'll let you lay hands upon her."

"Aye," Amherst said with a smirk, "you might well be."

"We shall try him and hang him before I depart for Fort George." Amherst took a sip of his cognac.

"Certainly we shall try him." Wentworth poured himself a glass and set the bottle aside, weary of Amherst's company. "Whether he is to be hanged rather depends on the verdict, does it not? He does offer plausible explanations for all that he's done."

In fact, the major's explanations had done much to satisfy William that he was innocent of treason. The information he'd stolen from Bourlamaque's correspondence had been most revealing and, in the right hands, might speed a British victory. Truth be told, William felt more than a little pride that one of his officers had managed to play such a dangerous game—and survive. Unfortunately, it had become clear to him that Amherst's dislike for colonials, and for Catholics, had quite prejudiced him in this case.

"If we choose the right officers for the jury, we ought to be assured of the outcome. Watching MacKinnon dance at the end of a rope would do much to quell further desertions amongst these colonials."

William sipped his cognac, choosing his next words carefully. Though he himself was of noble birth and grandson to the king, Amherst was Pitt's favorite, and Pitt was fully in command of the war effort in the colonies. William could not afford to antagonize him. "It is my understanding that British justice seeks to avoid hanging innocent men."

Amherst gave an impatient flick of his wrist. "We must make an example of someone. I do prefer hanging over a firing squad, as hanging generates more suffering and therefore more terror amongst those who watch."

"By all means, set an example, but let us first find someone guilty."

But William's words seemed to fall on deaf ears.

"We shall have to force Miss Chauvenet's whereabouts from him before he is hanged, of course." Amherst sat in the chair William usually kept for himself. "Let us question him again in the morning, and if he still refuses to give up her whereabouts, I shall order him flogged."

"I doubt flogging will be necessary." William took another sip, let the amber liquid burn its way into his stomach. "I'm fairly certain I know where she is."

"Then send for her at once."

"With due respect, sir, I should like to go and get her myself." It was as good a reason as William had ever had to see Lady Anne.

Morgan sat back against the wall of his cage, the heat stifling, his wrists and ankles once again in shackles. Sweat trickled down his chest, anger churning in his gut, sleep impossible. He'd never have imagined that this would go so far. He'd thought he'd answer Wentworth's questions and be done with it. He hadn't been prepared for Amherst's determination to see him hang—or for Bourlamaque's letter.

After being interrogated, he'd been placed in chains and brought here with nary a crust of bread or a blanket or even fresh straw. Then Wentworth had arrived with Dr. Blake, ordering the guards to unshackle Morgan and strip him naked so that Dr. Blake could examine him.

"Indeed, he was quite gravely wounded, my lord," Dr. Blake had said, looking closely at the scars on Morgan's chest and thigh. "Either wound in itself could easily have killed a man. If the wounds had festered, as I believe the one in his thigh did, he would have been at death's door. One can see from the scars on his wrists and ankles that he was kept in chains for quite some time."

Morgan had met Wentworth's gaze, not bothering to hide his contempt. "Are you satisfied now?"

Wentworth had tossed him an apple, turned his back, and escorted Dr. Blake from the guardhouse.

But it wasn't the indignity of being inspected like an animal that kept Morgan awake, nor even the prospect of being hanged. Instead it was Amherst and Wentworth's plans for Amalie. They intended to find her, and when they did, they would question her, imprison her, and send her under military escort back to Fort Carillon, ignoring the bonds of marriage and using her like one of Wentworth's pawns. If only Morgan could get word to Iain and warn him . . .

Chapter 28

Amalie watched in dismay as the johnnycake she'd been trying to flip fell into pieces, golden batter spreading across the
bottom of the pan that Annie called a "skillet." She gave an exas-
perated sigh and tried to do better with the next one, only to
watch it do the same thing. If she'd been at the convent, someone
would have scolded her, and a part of Amalie grew tense, waiting
for the rebuke that would follow.

But Annie merely glanced into the skillet and smiled. "Dinnae
be disheartened. 'Twas the same for me when I was first learnin'
to cook. I'd never made a meal or milked a cow or plucked a
chicken afore I came here. A year from now, 'twill seem as if
you've made johnnycakes all your life."

Was this what it was like to have family—this easy forgiveness, this gentle friendship that asked nothing but gave so freely?

The tension ebbed away, and Amalie allowed herself to laugh.
"I hope so."

She'd tried her best to make herself useful in her new home,
only to find that life in a convent hadn't prepared her for the hard
work of living on the frontier. She did not mind working hard and
enjoyed feeling that she was helping Morgan's family—*her* family. But at times she wondered if she wasn't more of a burden than

a help. And yet Annie and Iain had been most patient, encouraging her, supporting her, making her feel cherished and safe—making her feel that she belonged.

Annie had learned how to do this, and so would she.

She set the skillet back amongst the coals, careful to keep her hems out of the fire. "Do you miss your life in Scotland?"

Holding the baby in one arm, Annie set the crock of butter on the table, a small bowl of salt beside it. "If you're askin' whether I miss Scotland, aye, I do. I miss the heather and the mist and the scent of the sea. But I'd no' trade my life wi' Iain for the cosseted and empty life I once lived. And now wi' you here, 'tis like havin' a sister."

Amalie met Annie's gaze, saw the sincerity in her eyes, and couldn't help but smile, warmth filling her breast, chasing away her fears. "*Oui,* so it is."

As they finished cooking breakfast together—eggs, salted pork, and rather wretched johnnycakes with butter and molasses—the two of them talked with an easiness Amalie had never known with another woman, not even Sister Marie Louise.

And yet even as they spoke, her fears began to return, creeping like shadows from the dark corners of her mind. What if Morgan had been attacked on his way to the fort? What if his commander—that dreadful Wentworth—didn't believe him? What if Wentworth flogged him as he'd done Iain?

Amalie had seen the scars on Iain's back and had cringed to imagine how much pain he had endured. She could not bear to think of Morgan suffering such torment, alone and in chains once more. Oh, how she missed him! She missed his smile, the light in his blue eyes, the sound of his voice. She missed the manly scent of him, the strong feel of his arms around her, the sound of his heartbeat beneath her ear as she slept. She missed his touch, the heat of his kiss, the warmth of waking to feel him beside her.

It was hard to be so far from him, harder still not to know when she would see him again. And if the days were long, the nights were even longer, the hours stretching on, the bed cool and empty beside her, the night filled with—

"—breakfast is ready?"

Amalie realized she'd gotten lost in her own thoughts and that Annie had just asked her to do something. "I—I'm sorry, Annie. I was just thinking of Morgan . . ."

The sympathetic smile on Annie's face told Amalie that she understood and took no offense. "You miss him."

"Yes. And I'm afraid for him. It is so hard to wait."

Annie shifted the baby to her other hip. "Aye, it is. Every time Iain was sent on a mission, I found myself countin' the hours, prayin' he'd be safe, prayin' he'd come home again. 'Tis no' easy bein' the wife of a soldier."

And Amalie realized Annie had been through this many more times than she. She took her hand, gave it a squeeze. "You must have been so happy when Wentworth released him."

"Aye—and surprised. And yet I live each day afraid that Wentworth will call Iain back into service." Then Annie seemed to catch herself. "Listen to me complainin' of my fears when Morgan—aye, and Connor, too—still risk their lives in battle. How selfish you must think me."

"But no!" Amalie tried to reassure her. "It gives Morgan peace to know that Iain is out of the war and living here on the farm with you. He spoke of it to me. He spoke of his brothers often, and I—"

Then the door opened, and Iain stepped in, rifle in hand, the grim look on his face making Amalie's stomach drop. "There's a pillar of smoke against the sky to the north no' far from Murphy's place. 'Tis likely just a haycock caught fire in the sun, but I want to make certain it doesna spread. The two of you stay inside till I return, aye?"

He kissed Annie, gave Amalie a wink, and was gone.

William hid with his men amongst the trees down the road from the MacKinnon farm, watching from a distance as his former major set off to investigate the fire they'd set. As much as William enjoyed testing his wits against Iain MacKinnon, today's confrontation was likely to turn to violence unless handled with care. MacKinnon would protect his brother's wife as he did his own—with his rifle if necessary. And although William found the idea of a widowed Lady Anne appealing, he had to admit a grudging respect for MacKinnon.

The big Scot disappeared amongst the trees, and William knew the moment had arrived. He turned to his men, a group of eager officers, each picked for his absolute loyalty and skill.

"Search the house, the barns, the privy, the fields, and the surrounding forest, but do nothing to harm Lady Anne or her child. When you find Miss Chauvenet, bring her to me unharmed. We haven't much time, so be quick about it."

William rode at the head of the column, reluctantly impressed by the farmstead that came into view. He'd been expecting a hovel with a small, weedy garden, not a large farmhouse and barns and well-tended fields. It appeared that the land yielded as readily to Iain MacKinnon as Lady Anne had done.

William had left Fort Edward as soon as he'd been able, riding until dark, then rising early again, hoping to ensure himself the element of surprise. Because Amherst had restricted the Rangers to their island, it was unlikely that they'd learned of his plans for Miss Chauvenet. But they would most certainly try to send someone to tell Iain MacKinnon of his brother's imprisonment, which would put him on his guard.

As they drew near, the farmhouse door opened a crack—and quickly shut. And he knew that Lady Anne had seen them.

"Mercy! 'Tis Lord William! Quickly, Amalie, we must hide you!"

Amalie stood, her breakfast forgotten, her heart thrumming as Annie barred the door and drew in the string. "Wh-where should I go?"

"This way!" A look of determination on her face, Annie led her into the back bedroom, laid little Iain in his cradle, then tried to push the heavy bedstead. "Help me move it! There's a chamber hidden beneath the floor. You can bide here until Iain returns."

Pushing with all their might, they moved the foot of the bedstead aside far enough to reveal most of the wooden floor beneath. Then Annie knelt down, stuck her finger into a knothole, and withdrew a bit of rope. With a tug, the floor came open to reveal gaping darkness beneath, the thick scent of damp earth drifting up from below.

"Hurry! There's a ladder on the side!"

Little Iain began to wail.

Amalie had just climbed over the edge, her feet on the first rung, when it came to her. "But what about you and the baby? What if Wentworth has come for you?"

Annie shook her head. "He wouldna dare harm us. 'Tis likely he's come for Iain, but if he sees you . . ."

Amalie's heart tripped. "What would he do?"

"God only knows."

From outside came the stamp of horses' hooves, men's voices, and the clatter of steel swords in sheaths.

Annie glanced over her shoulder, then met Amalie's gaze, her green eyes filled with urgency. "Stay hidden, and dinnae fret about me! Iain will return soon. Now go!"

Amalie climbed down the ladder as Annie closed the trapdoor over her head, engulfing her in darkness. From above came the scrape of wood against wood as Annie struggled alone to push the bedstead into place. Barely able to breathe, Amalie waited.

William heard a baby's crying, heard the heavy wooden bar lift, and watched as the door slowly opened, Lady Anne looking up at him in feigned surprise. She never had been skilled at lies or deception.

"Lady Anne." He gave a little bow, unable to deny the surge of excitement he felt whenever he saw her.

"Lord William!" She glanced outside at the thirty men he'd brought with him, her cheeks pink from exertion, her long golden hair bound at her nape with a single pink ribbon. "Is augh' amiss? Are Morgan and Connor—"

"Captain MacKinnon is well. Major MacKinnon is locked in the guardhouse and facing charges of treason. It is for his sake I've come. I'm here to take Miss Chauvenet back to Fort Edward. She may be the only one who can prove the major's innocence and spare him the noose."

It was the truth, though certainly not the whole truth, as he also hoped to use Miss Chauvenet to win freedom for two very important British officers.

Lady Anne's eyes went wide, and she seemed to hesitate. "She's wi' Iain."

"Forgive me, my lady, but I do not believe you." William stepped forward, nudged the toe of his boot inside the door. Then he turned to his men. "Be quick. Leave nothing unturned."

She blocked the doorway. "Iain is no' far from here. You must wait—!"

"I've not the time for that, I'm afraid." William forced the door open, careful not to hurt her, then drew her aside as his men filed past, enjoying the feel of her in his arms.

She tried to pull free of his grasp, anger on her lovely face, apparently unwilling to be held thus by him. "Would you deny my son his mother?"

From the back room, the baby wailed.

"Of course not, my lady." William released her, watched her walk away, feeling oddly chastised. While soldiers stomped up and down the stairs, he glanced about and found himself in a small but tidy room that served as the farm's kitchen as well as its sitting room, a rocking chair in one corner, a hand-carved table and chairs at its center, breakfast growing cold upon the table— three tin plates, three forks, three cups.

Aye, Miss Chauvenet was here.

Lieutenant Cooke stepped through the doorway. "We've searched the entire house, my lord. They found a woman's gowns and another bedstead upstairs. They also found a hidden chamber beneath the barn floor, but it was empty. If she's here, she's very well concealed."

William nodded, wondering whether perhaps the mademoiselle had fled out the back in pursuit of MacKinnon. "Search the house again and set a watch on the forest to alert us in case MacKinnon returns prematurely."

"Aye, my lord."

As Cooke disappeared to carry out his orders, William walked toward the back of the house, where he heard Lady Anne crooning to her child in Gaelic. He found her sitting on the edge of a large bed, the baby feeding hungrily at her breast, its little fists pressing against her creamy flesh, the sight both stirring and discomfiting. And then it dawned on him as he watched that this was the bed she shared with MacKinnon—an unpleasant realization. He glanced away.

Two soldiers entered the room and began to search, opening the wardrobe, checking inside Lady Anne's trunks, looking beneath the bed.

She looked up at him, shifting uncomfortably, as if being seen by him and his soldiers with her gown opened distressed her. "Can I no' be left in peace?"

He was about to order the soldiers to wait outside the door

when he saw them—scratches on the wooden floor. The bed had been moved and not quite set back in place. And he knew.

"I'm afraid I'm going to have to ask you to take your son to another room, my lady." He turned to his men. "Beneath the bed you'll find a hidden chamber like that in the barn. Unless I miss my guess, that's where we'll find Miss Chauvenet."

Lady Anne's head snapped back as if he'd struck her, those beautiful eyes filled with pleading. "Nay, my lord! Please, you must no' do this!"

Two soldiers strode toward the bed.

"Pardon us, my lady."

She drew her son from her breast, closed her gown with shaking fingers, then stood, holding her baby tight. "Iain willna permit this! When he returns to find—"

"When he returns, my lady, we shall be long gone."

"You!" Realization spread across her face—and with it rage. *"You* set the fire!"

"It seemed to me the better course to take Miss Chauvenet while Master MacKinnon was occupied elsewhere than to provoke an exchange of musket fire in which some of my men would be killed and he would surely perish."

But then his soldiers began to move the bed, and her attention turned to them. Before William could stop her, she'd moved to stand upon the newly exposed space of floor, presumably on top of the trapdoor that led to the hidden chamber.

"I willna let you take her!" Fear and defiance on her face, she stood with her baby clutched in one arm, a penknife in her other hand. "She is Morgan's wife, no' one of your pawns! She belongs here wi' us!"

One of William's men laughed. The other stared dumbfounded. Neither moved toward her, clearly uncertain what to do in this situation.

William stepped forward and caught Lady Anne's wrist with one hand, drawing her against him, holding her motionless, looking into her eyes. "Do not be foolish, my lady. You know you cannot fight us and win—one woman against thirty soldiers. Do you wish to see Major MacKinnon dangling from a noose? Now *let go of the knife."*

For a moment she resisted. Then, tears filling her eyes, she did as he'd demanded, the fight leaving her body, the little blade falling to the floor.

He pulled her aside, and his men moved in, quickly discovering a hidden lead of rope and opening the hatch. They leaned down, looked inside, and smiled, clearly enchanted by the prey they'd cornered. As one, they lay on their bellies and reached down, eager to help her.

"There's no need to be afraid, miss. We're not going to hurt you."

"Give us your hands. We'll help you up."

And then she came into view.

The first thing he noticed were her eyes—large and framed with dark lashes, they were the strangest color he'd ever seen, both green and brown. Her face was impossibly delicate, her cheekbones high, her lips lush and full. Her hair hung in dark tendrils well past her hips, its dark hue and the coffee tint of her skin revealing a mixed heritage. Though clearly afraid, she did not cower, but sought first Lady Anne's gaze, then watched him warily, like a cornered fawn.

For a moment William found himself strangely at a loss for words, his thoughts taking a decidedly carnal turn. And he understood why Major MacKinnon had sought to hide her from him. He released Lady Anne and stepped forward to claim his prize. "Mademoiselle Chauvenet, I am Brigadier General William Wentworth of—"

The blow took him utterly by surprise, her palm striking his face hard enough to turn his head, the pain sharp.

She glared up at him, her eyes filled with feminine fury. "*That* is for the sorrow you have caused my husband and his family!"

"Ah." William's cheek tingled. "I see introductions are unnecessary. What you might not know, mademoiselle, is that Major MacKinnon sits in chains awaiting court-martial for desertion and treason. 'Tis my hope that you have some testimony to offer that might save his life. Let us ride, for we've a long journey."

They reached the fort late afternoon the next day, Amalie stiff and aching from so many hours in the saddle. An imposing sight, Fort Edward was much larger than Fort Carillon. It stood on the banks of a mighty river, encircled by two sets of walls, its ramparts high and forbidding. Her only comfort as they rode through the gates was the sight of Connor, Dougie, and Killy, who spied her from their island and raised their hands in greeting, their faces grave. Exhausted and more than a little afraid, she returned their greeting, a hard lump in her throat as Wentworth guided his horse through the outer gates and they vanished from view.

Amalie could scarcely believe any of this was real. One moment she'd been setting breakfast on the table with Annie; the next Wentworth had arrived with thirty men to take her away. He'd refused to wait for her to gather clothes or other belongings, clearly hoping to ride away with her before Iain returned.

"Dinnae fear, Amalie." Annie had hugged her fiercely, whispering in her ear. "Iain willna abide this! We'll no' be far behind you!"

Wentworth had traveled fast, refusing to let Amalie sit a horse alone, keeping her before him in his saddle. "Your safety is of greater importance to me than you know. I'll not risk your falling or being separated from us in an attack," he'd told her.

She'd tried not to lean back against him, furious with him for the way he'd tricked Iain and frightened Annie and unwilling to suffer his touch any more than was necessary. But the journey had been long, and more than once she'd fallen asleep, only to wake and find herself lying against his chest.

Although she'd asked about Morgan, desperate to know that he was unharmed, Wentworth had said little, merely repeating what he'd already told her, leaving her with nothing but her fears as the leagues passed slowly beneath the horse's hooves.

"Welcome back, my lord." A young redcoat met the horse outside of a building that much resembled Bourlamaque's quarters.

"Thank you, Sergeant." Wentworth dismounted, not a hair in his white wig out of place, his uniform impeccable despite the long ride. Then he turned to help Amalie.

Ignoring his offer, she grasped the pommel and slid to the ground, fighting a moan as her aching legs took her weight.

"There's no need to behave so rashly, Miss Chauvenet. It will accomplish nothing if you fall or turn an ankle."

Ignoring his words, she smoothed her skirts. "When may I see my husband?"

"See whom? Major MacKinnon?" Wentworth's gray eyes were unreadable. "Not for some time, I'm certain. You would not wish to destroy the value of your testimony by speaking with him before the court-martial, would you?"

Amalie hadn't thought of that. She followed him through the front door into a lavishly appointed residence every bit as sophisticated as Bourlamaque's, up a stairway to a little room in the corner, the sight of the bed making her realize how weary she truly was.

"I shall have water sent up for a bath along with some refreshments. Someone will come for you within an hour so that we might begin."

"Begin what?"

He smiled. "Why, your interrogation, of course. Major General Amherst is most eager to speak with you."

Then he closed the door, shutting her in. And as the key turned in the lock, she understood. She was his prisoner.

Chapter 29

"I bet ye thought I was bringin' ye a nice juicy bit of venison."
The redcoat gave a chuckle, handing stale biscuits and water through the iron bars to Morgan. "Or a bit of boiled beef. Or maybe a spot of soup and a nice bottle of rum."

Ignoring his gaoler's attempt to provoke him, Morgan checked the biscuits for weevils, then bit into one, his stomach growling, his fetters clanking as he walked back to the corner and sat in the straw. For four days, he'd had scant more to eat than stale bread and water—no rum, no cheese, no meat. But hunger and thirst were the least of what vexed him.

'Twas the isolation—the not knowing—that gnawed at him.

Each morning Morgan had demanded to speak with Wentworth, and each morning he'd been told Wentworth would not see him. When he'd asked to speak with Connor, he'd been told that both the Rangers and the Muhheconneok had been forbidden from entering the fort at Amherst's command for fear they would try to help Morgan escape. If only he knew that Amalie was safe . . .

Och, for Satan, he *hated* feeling helpless! Amalie was in danger, and he could do naught about it but wait and pray. Wentworth had left no doubt that he planned to find Amalie if he could and trade her back to the French. Chained like an animal in a cage, Morgan could not stop him. The *mac-dìolain* cared nothing for the sanctity of marriage and was not above using women if it suited his purposes.

Catholic unions are not recognized by the Crown, as you know, Major.

If Wentworth went after Amalie, if he touched her, if he sent her back to Fort Carillon . . . Only God and his saints knew what kind of welcome awaited her there.

The biscuit turned to clay in Morgan's mouth. He swallowed, aware that the redcoat guard was still watching him, a gloating grin on his face. "You've somethin' to say to me, laddie?"

Morgan already knew Amherst was investigating him, his lieutenant asking questions around the fort. The guards had told him that. He knew that many thought him guilty and predicted he'd hang. The guards had told him that, too, seeming greatly amused by the notion. But soldiers tittled like old women when it came to such things. Their words meant naught.

"I've seen her—yer French chippy."

The words struck Morgan like a fist to the gut. He came slowly to his feet, dragging his chains with him, his rage flaring like tinder. "What is it you're sayin', old man? And have a care—she's my *wife!*"

The bastard chuckled. "My cousin was with 'is lordship when they went to fetch 'er. They played a right clever trick on your brother, they did. Set fire to an 'aystack, drew 'im away from the 'ouse, then went in and took 'er. Pretty little thing. I'll wager she makes good bed sport, eh?"

Morgan found himself pressed against the bars, his fists clenched around cold, unforgiving iron, his heart a hammer in his chest. "Watch your vile tongue if you wish to be keepin' it! *When?* When did this happen?"

Wide-eyed, the guard took a hurried step backward, the grin gone from his uggsome face. "They arrived back at the fort yesterday."

Yesterday?

Och, Christ!

"You tell Wentworth that if any harm comes to her, he'll answer to Clan MacKinnon and the Mahican of Stockbridge. She is under our protection!"

"And what can you do to 'is lordship from behind those bars?" The whoreson licked his lips, laughed, and walked away.

"Wentworth, you bastard!" Morgan shouted, his hands clenched so hard around the bars that iron bit into his hands.

But the door had already closed, and there was no one to hear.

"*Je vous salue, Marie, pleine de grâce . . .*" Hail Mary, full of grace . . .

Amalie ignored her hunger, ignored her thirst, ignored the aching in her knees and lower back, her fingers finding their way over the wooden beads of Morgan's rosary, her mind struggling to hold on to the words of her prayer against the noise in the hallway beyond her door.

"Miss Chauvenet, you must be reasonable!" Lieutenant Cooke called to her. "You cannot help Major MacKinnon by refusing to eat!"

But she would *not* be reasonable. She would not sit down to dine with the men who had taken her from her new home, the men who kept her husband in chains, the men who intended to send her away against her will and break the bonds of her marriage. Nor would she pretend that she was anything but their prisoner.

They had questioned her for endless hours yesterday, asking her the same things again and again, until she'd been so weary she'd scarce been able to keep her eyes open. Although they'd treated her as if she were a guest, inquiring after her welfare, offering her food and wine, she'd known their kindness and concern to be false, a way of trying to win her trust. Still, believing Morgan might be released once they'd heard what she had to say, she'd done all they'd asked of her, telling them how she'd found Morgan in Monsieur de Bourlamaque's study reading Bourlamaque's private correspondence and how he'd admitted to spying.

Yet, even after they'd heard this, Amherst had refused to release Morgan, insisting he face trial. It was as if her words had meant nothing. And her fear had grown.

During supper, she'd asked again to see him, but they'd refused, denying even her requests to send him the food from her plate.

"We have agreed with your guardian that you shall not see Major MacKinnon again," Amherst had told her. "The chevalier is most anxious to see you again."

"Monsieur de Bourlamaque?" And in one horrifying moment she'd realized that they intended to send her back to Fort Carillon. "He is no longer my guardian. It was he who gave me in marriage to Major MacKinnon! He cannot claim—"

"British law does not recognize Catholic unions, Miss Chauvenet," Wentworth had told her. "If the chevalier wishes us to return you to him, then we shall—in exchange for British officers, of course."

"You are despicable!" Unable to bear their company one moment longer, she'd stood, thrown her napkin onto the table, and fled toward the door.

"You've not been given leave to go!" Amherst's voice boomed after her.

She'd whirled on her heels. "I did not *ask* for your leave!"

Then she'd fled upstairs to her chamber.

Since then, she'd refused to leave her room, refused to eat, refused to speak with them. Though she was locked in, she'd blocked the door with a chair so that they could not open the door either. And she'd done the only thing she could do—pray.

"Sainte Marie, Mère de Dieu, priez pour nous pauvres pécheurs, maintenant, et à l'heure de notre mort." Holy Mary, Mother of God, pray for us sinners now and in the hour of our death.

The knocking came again.

"I say, Miss Chauvenet, surely you cannot think to bar the door and stay locked inside the room forever! If you do not open it, we shall be forced to break it down!"

She did not plan on staying in this gilded cage forever, for tomorrow Morgan would face his court-martial, and she would be called upon to speak. Only then would she open the door. But she would not eat again until Morgan was free.

"Je vous salue, Marie, pleine de grâce, le Seigneur est avec vous . . .".

And then Lieutenant Cooke spoke again, but not to Amalie.

"I'm afraid I have orders not to allow anyone—"

A woman's voice answered. "I ken this is no' your doin', Lieutenant Cooke. Please be merciful and permit me to speak wi' Mistress MacKinnon."

Annie!

Amalie stood and ran to the door, but she did not move the chair. "Annie!"

"I'm here, Amalie." Annie's voice came from the other side, strong and clear, the welcome sound of it putting a lump in Amalie's throat. "Are you well? Has anyone laid hands upon you or mistreated you?"

"No! I am well, but I fear for Morgan!"

"As do we all," Annie answered. "Dinnae despair. We've no' forsaken you! They willna let Iain into the fort, nor Connor, nor any of the Rangers either. Joseph has withdrawn to Stockbridge with his men in protest. But we've no' forgotten you!"

"Nor I you!" Amalie fought the tears that threatened her. "They're sending me back to Fort Carillon, but it is against my will!"

She heard the heavy stomp of boots and the sound of men's voices, and she realized that Annie had somehow passed the guards and defied Amherst and Wentworth to speak with her. Now soldiers were coming.

"I must go now. Is there augh' you need?"

"Tell Morgan I love him!"

"If I can, I will!"

And then Annie was gone, leaving Amalie to her tears and her prayers but with this ray of hope—Morgan's family had not forgotten her.

She was not alone.

Wentworth walked out his front door and off into the shadows, barely aware of the two sentries who snapped to attention at his sudden appearance. Though it was well past midnight, he knew his man would still be waiting. In all the years William had employed him, he'd never let William down.

The evening had been spent making final preparations for the army's march north to Ticonderoga, William waiting until Amherst had started upon his nightly cognac to bring up the subject of Major MacKinnon. He'd warned Amherst of the consequences should MacKinnon be hanged unjustly—the loss of the Mahican as allies, an uprising amongst the Rangers, resentment along the frontier, where the brothers were revered as heroes. But Amherst hadn't listened. And then William had understood.

He ought to have seen it sooner. He ought to have realized.

Amherst's determination to see Major MacKinnon hang had nothing to do with the major's guilt or innocence and everything to do with William. As His Majesty's grandson, William represented the adversary of Amherst's powerful patron—William Pitt. That alone was likely sufficient cause for Amherst to view William as a rival and do whatever he could to limit William's advancement. But Amherst was of common birth, and his overweening pride would ill tolerate a nobleman—least of all a man of royal blood—achieving renown in this war.

If Amherst could win a guilty verdict against one of William's most lauded and trusted men, he could darken London's perception of William and perhaps prevent William from being placed equal to him—or raised above him.

But William would not allow his reputation to be undermined by political scheming, nor would he repay Major MacKinnon's loyalty, however reluctantly given, with an ignominious death. And if he'd once threatened the MacKinnon brothers with hanging in order to manipulate them for his own political gain?

William had never claimed not to be a hypocrite, just a superior strategist.

As for Miss Chauvenet, that was another matter that greatly occupied his thought. He could not pass by the chance to win freedom for two loyal British officers, and yet he could not deny that he did not wish to see her go. Maybe it was her innocence that aroused this unlikely sentiment, not a deceitful bone in her lovely body. Or perhaps it was her utter devotion to Major MacKinnon, as demonstrated by her refusal to eat. Or perhaps it was simply her beauty.

If Lady Anne were like the sunshine, then Miss Chauvenet was the dusk—exotic, sensual, alluring. More than once, William had allowed himself to imagine what it would be like to bed her, her young body beneath him, her long dark hair spread across his bed. Her spirit and her unpredictable nature only made her more desirable.

He could not think of the last woman who'd dared to strike him.

But, alas, she was Bourlamaque's ward—or Major MacKinnon's wife, depending on whether one chose to act on the law. Either way, 'twas not worth the risks involved to attempt to seduce her.

William strode toward the officers' latrines, watching as a

form detached itself from the shadows, strode to the last latrine just ahead of him, and went inside. 'Twas frustrating to meet like this, but with Amherst ever under foot he had little choice.

"What have you learned?" William whispered, pretending to wait his turn.

"'Tis as you suspected, my lord. The officers are all men who owe their rank to Amherst and are known for their loyalty. I found little to aid your purpose. One has some moderate debts. Three have mistresses. One has a daughter who's hiding her *condition* at a country house outside Boston. One has a Jacobite grandfather."

"The very flower of British virtue, it would seem." This was not what William had hoped to hear. Men without scandalous secrets were difficult to manipulate. Though debts, pregnant daughters, and unsavory ancestors might cause these men embarrassment, such things weren't enough to bring them to their knees and change a verdict.

"So it would seem, my lord."

"Very well." William glanced about to be certain they were still alone. "I've a letter for Governor DeLancey to be delivered by you into his hands. Make all haste for Albany, and if you find him not in residence, seek him out by any means. Do not rest until he has received this missive. Bring his response to me at once!"

"Aye, my lord. I leave at once."

The latrine door opened, and his man stepped out, taking the letter—and a bag of coins—as he passed. And then he was gone.

"Then you admit to training the enemy in musketry, to giving up the location of the caches, campsites, and trails, to sharing what you knew of Major General Amherst's plans for this summer's campaign against Ticonderoga?"

Morgan fought to control his temper, furious to hear his words twisted thus. So it had been for the past hour, every answer he'd given bent and distorted to make him seem guilty. Connor's words had been twisted, too, his description of rescuing Morgan turned against Morgan simply because Morgan had been wearing a French uniform and hadn't left Fort Carillon of his own free will.

The grim look on Iain's face and the worry on Annie's told him what he already understood: the bastards wanted him to hang.

Och, he'd have been better off to stay with Bourlamaque! And yet he'd never have been able to live with himself for betraying his brothers and his men if he had.

Now you can take your clear conscience to the grave, aye, laddie?

"Aye, sir, I did, but it wasna what you—"

"Is it true that you went to Catholic rites whilst at Ticonderoga and took Communion at the hands of a French priest?" The officer—a colonel named Hamilton whose gray wig was too large for his fat head and kept leaning to the left—made a sloppy sign of the cross as if to mock the Catholic faith.

"Aye, sir, for I am Catholic. 'Tis no secret."

"Is it also true that the Chevalier de Bourlamaque supervised the Catholic wedding of his ward, Amalie Chauvenet, to you while you were his prisoner?"

"Aye, sir."

"So Bourlamaque gave his beloved ward to you—a dreaded enemy—to be your wife. Can you explain to the court why any man would marry a young woman under his protection to the enemy? Did Bourlamaque dislike his ward and wish to be rid of her?"

The men on the jury chuckled.

Morgan answered with the truth. "I deceived him into trustin' me, and he was bound by his promise to Amalie's father to let her wed a man of her own choosin'. She chose me."

"Still, he must have believed without a shadow of a doubt that he could trust you."

"Och, I'm certain he had doubts, but he hoped the marriage would further bind me to him, for he kent I cared deeply for Amalie."

"And you took this young woman to wife after the Catholic manner, even knowing that you would soon abandon her?"

Morgan could see where this was going and knew he was damned. "Aye, sir. And that is why I did not consummate—"

"The truth, Major MacKinnon, is that you never intended to escape!" Hamilton cut across him, his voice raised to a shout. "You planned to live out your life amongst the French and only returned to Fort Edward because you were in the awkward position of having been kidnapped by the Abenaki and then rescued by your own men!"

"That is a lie!"

"Thank you, Major. That is all." Hamilton motioned for guards to escort Morgan back to his chair. "Bring in the next witness."

Dragging his shackles, Morgan sat in the chair that served as a witness box—then came to his feet again when he saw her. Dressed in a green gown he recognized as Annie's, Amalie entered the room, her gaze seeking him out, the dark circles beneath her eyes and the strain on her sweet face telling him that these past days had been hard ones. And still the sight of her was like a tonic, chasing away his weariness and filling him with hope.

She smiled first at him, then at Iain and Annie, who sat behind him, her smile not enough to hide her fear. Then she took her seat, her hands clenched nervously in her lap, the wooden beads of his rosary visible between her fingers.

Och, how he wished he could spare her this! Hamilton was ruthless, giving no quarter, his objective to give Amherst the guilty verdict he wanted. He would not hesitate to mock and abuse her. Morgan had forbidden the court from calling on her, but that rutting bastard Wentworth had refused to heed him.

"Please tell the court your name," Hamilton said.

Her gaze locked with Morgan's, she answered. "Amalie Chauvenet MacKinnon."

"Miss Chauvenet," Hamilton said, ignoring her married name, "please tell us how you came to know Major Morgan MacKinnon and how you came to be with him here, so far from Ticonderoga—what you call Fort Carillon."

And so, her chin high, her accent sweet, she told the story from the beginning. How she'd been asked by her guardian, the Chevalier de Bourlamaque, to help the surgeon care for Morgan so that he might survive to be interrogated. How Morgan had sought his own death, refusing to drink until they overthrew his will with laudanum. How knowing he faced a terrible death at the hands of the Abenaki had sickened her. How she'd persuaded Bourlamaque to offer him sanctuary. How Morgan had pretended not to know French and had won her as his French tutor by shooting at marks.

Then Hamilton interrupted her. "Why did it occur to you to offer Major MacKinnon sanctuary?"

And Morgan saw that Amalie had wandered into a trap. There

was no good way to answer this question—not when the officers acting as jury were ready to seize upon anything at all to justify a verdict of guilty. He tried to reassure her with a smile.

Whatever befalls me, lass, 'tis no' your doin'.

"The Scots have long been allies of the French because we are all Catholic," she said simply, seeming unaware that she was walking into a swamp.

"In fact, Major MacKinnon's grandfather was renowned amongst the traitorous Jacobites for helping Charles Stuart escape to France, wasn't he?"

She hesitated. "So Monsieur de Bourlamaque told me."

"You witnessed Major MacKinnon load his musket and fire it before the assembled French army?" Hamilton asked.

"No man can teach another to strike marks by simply watchin' another do it!" Iain shouted, breaking the rule of silence. "Did you learn to sit a horse by watchin' your daddy ride?"

"Silence!" Amherst bellowed, his shout startling Amalie. "Interrupt again, and I shall have you removed!"

"Answer the question, Miss Chauvenet."

"*O-oui, monsieur.* I saw him fire at marks."

"Please continue with your story."

She told how Morgan had protected her from Lieutenant Rillieux, how he'd spared the life of her cousin, drawing his own blood in an effort to appease the Abenaki's rage. Then she told how Morgan had struck Rillieux for playing with Charlie Gordon's skull, how she'd found Morgan in the graveyard, and how she'd stood beside him, the entire fort watching as he buried Charlie's remains with the priest's blessing. But this did not seem to interest Hamilton.

"Did Major MacKinnon ever wear a French uniform?"

"Not at first. Monsieur de Bourlamaque clad him as befitted the son of a Scottish laird, but feared a uniform would enrage the soldiers."

"But eventually, he did don a French officer's uniform, correct?"

"Yes, monsieur." Amalie's eyes implored Morgan to forgive her. He smiled again, and some of the fear in her eyes lessened.

"Please go on, Miss Chauvenet."

Amalie drew strength from the warmth in Morgan's eyes, from the presence of Iain and Annie behind him, and took a steadying breath, her stomach so full of butterflies that she'd long since quit feeling hungry. "I—I began to feel affection for Monsieur Mac-Kinnon. He told me we could not be together until the war was over. I did not know at the time that he meant to escape."

She told the officers how she'd gone to speak with Morgan one night but had found his room empty. Then she'd noticed that the hall candle was missing and that a faint glow was coming from the door to Bourlamaque's study.

"I found Monsieur MacKinnon there, sitting at Monsieur de Bourlamaque's writing table, reading Monsieur de Bourlamaque's private letters. For a moment I didn't understand how he could be reading the letters when he did not speak French. And then I understood. He had deceived us. He was spying."

She remembered the shock she'd felt, the disbelief, the hurt, the anger. But then she looked into Morgan's eyes and knew that she'd long since forgiven him.

"How do you know for certain that Major MacKinnon was *spying*?" The bewigged man imitated her voice, her accent.

She felt her temper pique. "What else would he be doing, monsieur?"

"Did you tell your guardian what you'd seen?"

She shook her head. "I turned to run and might have told him, but Monsieur MacKinnon stopped me. He put his hand over my mouth and forced me into his room, where we argued. We must have woken Monsieur de Bourlamaque, for he . . . discovered us together. He demanded that Monsieur MacKinnon marry me."

"Help me to understand, Miss Chauvenet. Your guardian found you *arguing* with Major MacKinnon and forced you to marry him?"

The men that made up Morgan's jury chuckled.

Amalie felt heat rush into her cheeks, knowing that everyone in the room saw past her words. But it *had* started as an argument. "While we argued, Major MacKinnon . . . He kissed me, monsieur."

'Twas not the full truth, but she could not bring herself to say more.

"So Bourlamaque discovered Major MacKinnon kissing you, and still you did not tell Bourlamaque what you'd witnessed. Instead, you married a man who you believed had betrayed you, your guardian, and your king."

Amalie looked down at her hands. "Yes."

"Please explain to the court how you could have done such a thing?"

She lifted her gaze to Morgan's, wanting him to hear the words again. "I love him. I could not bear to see him suffer."

"So you were willing to lie to your guardian in order to protect him."

Amalie started to object, but the man cut across her, his voice raised.

"It was *you*, Miss Chauvenet, who first suggested Major MacKinnon commit treason by joining the French, *you* who led him astray! In a moment of weakness, he allowed himself to be lured by *you*. And now that he is facing the consequences of that decision, you are willing to lie to protect him!"

"Non!" She heard herself object, found herself on her feet.

A terrible heaviness bore down upon her, the blood rushing from her head. The room seemed to spin, a swirl of gray, the floor rushing up at her.

"That's enough, Hamilton!"

She heard Morgan shout, felt strong arms catch her.

"I've got you, *a leannan.*"

And then there was nothing.

M organ sat in the hot, stuffy room, awaiting the verdict, his gut churning with helpless rage. 'Twas Hamilton's fault that Amalie had swooned. The whoreson had all but accused her of putting Morgan's neck in the noose! Her face had gone pale as death, her eyes round with fear, and Morgan knew that if he hanged, she would blame herself.

If she'd been conscious, he'd have told her that none of this was her doing, but Amherst hadn't given her time to revive. No sooner had Morgan caught her, breaking her fall, than he'd been dragged back to his chair.

"Rise from your chair again, and I shall have you flogged!" Amherst had shouted.

Thank Mary and all the blessed saints that Iain and Annie had been there. Annie had knelt beside Amalie, Iain behind her. "There's no fever, but we must get her to Dr. Blake."

Ignoring Amherst's objections, Iain had lifted Amalie into his arms and, brooking no challenge, had carried her toward the door, meeting Morgan's gaze as he passed and speaking to him for the first time since Morgan had left the farm. *"Is duilich leam gun deach mo mhealladh cho furast', is nach do chùm mi i sàbhailte bhuapa, ach cha leig mi leotha a toirt air falbh a-rithist, air mionnan!"*

I'm sorry I let myself be so easily tricked and failed to keep her safe from them, but I willna let them take her again, I swear it!

And Morgan had realized he might never see Amalie again. The words spilled out of him. *"Inns do dh'Amalie nach ise as coireach. Inns' dhi gu bheil gaol agam oirre. Inns' dhi gun do chuir mi seachad mo làithean a bu thoilichte comhla rithe, 's nach eil aithreachas orm mu ghin dhiubh."*

Tell Amalie this is no' her doin'. Tell her my love lies upon her. Tell her that the happiest days of my life have been spent wi' her, and I regret no' a one of them.

No sooner had Iain stepped through the door than Amherst, shouting again, had called the court to order and declared the trial ended. The officers who made up the jury had retired to decide Morgan's fate. But there was no doubt in his mind what they would decide. Now there was naught he could do but wait to hear the words spoken.

He didn't have to wait long.

"Major MacKinnon, this court finds you guilty of the reprehensible crimes of desertion and treason. Tomorrow at dawn, you shall be taken from the gaol to the parade grounds, where you shall be hanged by the neck until dead. May God have mercy upon your soul."

Chapter 30

Amalie awoke feeling strangely confused, Iain and Annie looking down at her. *"Où suis-je? Qu'est-ce qui s'est passé?"*

She didn't realize she'd spoken French until Annie answered in French.

"Vous êtes à l'hôpital. Vous vous êtes évanouie." You're in the hospital. You fainted.

Still confused, Amalie looked around and saw that she was in a hospital very much like the one at Fort Carillon.

Annie pressed a cool cloth to Amalie's forehead, her voice soothing. "Lord William said you've no' eaten or slept for two days. Dr. Blake, the surgeon, thinks you're overwrought and famished and need to rest."

And then Amalie remembered, her heart hitting her breastbone with a single, sickening thud. She sat upright. "Morgan! The trial . . . Is it?"

"Aye, 'tis over." Annie set the cloth back in a bowl of water, her face lined with worry. "They found him guilty."

"Non!" The breath left Amalie's lungs in a cry. "But he is innocent!"

"Aye, but that doesna matter to them, lass." Iain's voice was edged with rage, a muscle clenching in his jaw. "He's to be hanged at dawn."

The words left her feeling dizzy, sick, fear coiling through her belly. She met Iain's gaze. "This is my fault! I tried to spare his life, but—"

Iain pressed a finger to her lips and leaned down, his gaze searching the room as if to make certain no one was watching. "I swear to you, lass, that Connor and I willna allow them to kill Morgan while we yet live, nor will we suffer them to take you from us against your will. But you must be ready for whate'er comes, aye?"

Amalie nodded, fighting her tears, knowing she could bear anything if it spared Morgan the hangman's noose. "I love him."

Iain took her hand, gave it a squeeze. "Aye, I ken you do—as he loves you. He gave me a message for you. When I was carryin' you out the door, he called out to me in Gaelic so they couldna understand him. He said, 'Tell Amalie this is no' her fault. Tell her that I love her. Tell her that the happiest days of my life have been spent wi' her, and I regret no' a one of them.'"

Fresh tears spilled down Amalie's cheeks, a bittersweet ache swelling behind her breast. "If only I could see him! If only I could speak with him!"

Iain shook his head. "Wentworth says Morgan's to have no visitors save himself, Amherst, or the chaplain."

"He won't even let him say farewell to his own brothers?" The thought of Morgan alone in his cell facing his own death sickened her. "How cruel! The man has no heart!"

Annie looked troubled. "I had hoped for better from him."

And it struck Amalie that any attempt to free Morgan might well place Iain in mortal peril as well. She and Annie might both be widows ere the sun rose again. She swallowed her tears and met Iain's gaze. "I will do whatever you ask of me."

Iain smiled. "That's our Amalie."

Annie set a small basket of fruit, bread, and cheese on her lap. "First, you must eat."

"The Stockbridge departed this morning, and those Rangers whose terms of service were long ago completed are leaving as well, reducing our strength by more than one hundred and fifty men." William delivered this news with a measure of satisfaction, pouring himself a rare second cognac. "The Rangers now number fewer than four score."

From Ranger Island came the wail of pipes playing forbidden tunes—a farewell to Major MacKinnon from his men and a warning to Amherst and, William supposed, to himself. If Morgan MacKinnon died on the gallows, they'd have a revolt on their hands.

Amherst looked up from his charts toward the darkened window, his long face betraying his rage and disgust. "How can they walk away on the eve of our campaign? Are their loyalties given only to the MacKinnon brothers and not to Britain?"

William swirled the amber liquid, raised the snifter to his nose, and inhaled the heady aroma, answering at his leisure. "I did warn you. Many believe Major MacKinnon's trial was a biased affair with the verdict determined before it started. They believe his hanging will be nothing less than murder."

Amherst glared at William, clearly dismayed to have the truth spoken so plainly. "Fire a few six-pounders over their heads. That ought to quiet them."

"Or incite them to open rebellion." William glanced at the clock.

Ten minutes to the changing of the guard.

Amherst stood, pointed an accusing finger in a display of gauche behavior that William found almost amusing. "This is *your* doing for keeping a company of Jacobite spawn in your service!"

"Until Morgan MacKinnon was sentenced to hang, our relationship with the Rangers was rather cordial." That was an exaggeration, of course. The MacKinnon brothers held William in contempt, but they had fought well for him. "Under my command, their woodcraft and marksmanship have served His Majesty well, helping to turn the tide of this war. In my opinion, such skill excuses a bit of insubordination. I measure loyalty by action on the field, not by obsequious behavior."

"Since you get on with them so well, go and quiet them! At the very least, stop those infernal pipes! I've a long march tomorrow and must sleep tonight!"

"As you wish." This is what William had hoped he'd say. For, although he was certain Governor DeLancey would respond, he was not at all certain the reply would arrive in time to spare Major MacKinnon's life. If DeLancey were traveling or indisposed, it might be weeks or even months before an answer came.

Clearly, it was necessary to take other measures.

William set his glass aside and strode out of his study, calling to Lieutenant Cooke. "Fetch me Major MacKinnon's effects, Lieutenant. I'm going to Ranger Island. I shall return them as a token of His Majesty's goodwill."

"Aye, sir." The lieutenant's eyes went wide, but he hurried to do William's bidding, returning quickly with the major's tumpline pack and broadsword. "Shall I accompany you or arrange for armed escort, my lord?"

"That won't be necessary, Lieutenant." William took the pack and sword and walked out his front door, leaving his lieutenant to stare after him.

His pulse unusually rapid, he walked across the parade grounds, passed through the first gate, and crossed the draw-bridge to the outer gate, where guards snapped to attention when they saw him, the screech of pipes seeming to echo through the fort. Beyond the gate stood thousands upon thousands of canvas tents stretching in long rows, almost eleven thousand soldiers encamped and ready for tomorrow's march north to Lake George. William would wager that not a man amongst them was asleep amidst this din.

He turned to his left and was soon crossing the bateau bridge that joined Ranger Island to the rest of the fort. Two Rangers stood guard on the western end of the bridge, their contempt for him written clearly on their faces. They spoke to each other in Gaelic, clearly recognizing the major's sword. From behind them, the wail of the pipes died down—only to begin anew.

The taller of the two—a lieutenant William recognized as the man whose life Major MacKinnon had saved, the one called Dougie—stepped forward. "Do you see, Brandon? The feckless German lairdie has come to gloat afore Mack and Connor. Shall we let him ashore, or shall we run him through wi' Morgan's *claidheamh mòr* and let the river ha' him?"

William met Dougie's gaze without wavering, certain the man wanted to kill him and just as certain that he would not. "If you value Major MacKinnon's life, you will take me to his brothers at once."

With many a muttered Gaelic curse, Dougie led William through the camp, which fell silent at his approach, its inhabitants watching as William passed, some following him, others racing ahead with word of his presence, the silence broken by strange birdcalls as the Rangers slowly surrounded him like a pack of wolves. By the time William reached the major's cabin, both MacKinnon brothers were waiting for him, Lady Anne watching from the doorway, holding her sleeping baby in her arms.

Iain MacKinnon stepped forward, jerked the pack and the sword from William's hands, and gave them to his brother. "You've got bigger cods than I thought, comin' here tonight alone."

"Or perhaps you're just a bloody fool!" Captain MacKinnon thrust the tip of the sword into the ground.

William met the elder MacKinnon's rage-filled gaze, drums beating out the change of guard in the distance. With any luck, there'd soon be no one at the gate who knew that he'd left the fort alone. "I've taken quite the risk in coming here—"

"Like the risk Morgan took when he saved Dougie's life?" Captain MacKinnon glared at him, his tone of voice implying that the risk William had taken was no risk at all.

William ignored him. "There is little time, so let us dispense with the pleasantries."

Captain MacKinnon opened his mouth to speak again, but his older brother held up a hand to silence him. "Come inside."

"Lady Anne." William bowed his head respectfully as he passed. Even in the candlelight he could see she'd been crying, the grief in her eyes stirring something like guilt in his chest—a curious and unpleasant sensation.

The door closed behind him.

"What in God's good name are you doin' here?" Iain MacKinnon stood before him, arms crossed over his chest.

"I've come to halt whatever ill-conceived plot you're concocting to rescue Major MacKinnon." William held up his hand to still their protests. "In the pack, you'll find your brother's effects, as well as two British uniforms. I suggest you each put one on."

"What?" The elder MacKinnon gaped at him.

Captain MacKinnon opened the pack, staring in disbelief as two complete uniforms tumbled to the floor. "You're daft! I'll no' wear that!"

"On the contrary, Captain. I rather think you will."

* * *

Morgan leaned against the wall of his cage, looking through the iron bars of his window at the night sky. An almost full moon hung in the heavens, sending a shaft of silver light through the window to the straw at his feet. Would that he were *chi bai*. He would climb the moonbeams to freedom, then lift Amalie into the sky beside him and fly away to someplace where this accursed war and its hatreds could not touch them.

"Tha móran ghràdh agam ort, dh'Amalaidh." My love lies upon you, Amalie.

He was not afraid to die, but he did not wish to leave her, could not bear to leave her. For although his brothers would care for her and any bairn she bore him after his death, no man would ever love her the way he did.

She'd endured so much already—the loss of her mother so young, her father's death in battle, Rillieux's assault. Now she was about to lose her husband. Alone and in Wentworth's keeping, she would have only her prayers to comfort her through the long watches of the night. Aye, tonight would be hardest upon her.

And what if Amherst and Wentworth should force her to watch him die?

The thought made Morgan's empty stomach churn.

If only he'd been able to see her, to speak with her one last time, but that *neach dìolain* Wentworth had not permitted it. He hadn't even had the courage to face Morgan himself, instead sending the chaplain, a thin man who'd looked at Morgan through cold, dark eyes and told Morgan he was going to hell. Morgan had sent him away—but not before he'd wormed from him the news that Amalie had recovered and that Annie had been to see her.

"I'm told the silly girl fainted because she'd refused to eat until you were set free," the chaplain had said, as if it were the most absurd thing he'd ever heard.

Morgan had been deeply touched by Amalie's loyalty, and yet she could not help him by hurting herself. She would need her strength in the days to come, the more so if she were with child. "Be strong, *a leannan*."

All was silent now, the last refrain from McHugh's pipes having died away just before the changing of the guard. Had Amherst or Wentworth gone to Ranger Island and forced them to stop playing under threat of punishment? Perhaps they were too drunk to go on. Or perhaps Dougie was singing the newest verse of "The Ballad of Morgan MacKinnon," in which Morgan died not at the hands of the French, but at the end of a rope.

If Morgan looked far to the left, he could see the gallows, a ghostly outline in the dark, its shadow stretching toward him in the moonlight. There was no scaffold beneath, no trapdoor, only a single hogshead. Rather than permitting him to fall and die quickly of a broken neck, it was clear that they planned to kick the hogshead from beneath him, leaving him to strangle slowly, twisting and jerking in the noose—a terrifying sight for any soldier who might be thinking of deserting on the eve of battle.

Dancin' in the winds is better than burnin' alive, laddie.

Aye, it was. He would have to remember that tomorrow when the life was being slowly choked from his body.

Not that Morgan had consigned himself to death. He knew Iain, Connor, Joseph, and the men would do all they could to free him, knew he must be ready for anything. And yet what could two hundred men do with eleven thousand redcoats encamped before the gates? He could only hope that their loyalty wouldn't drive them to attempt something foolhardy. He wanted no one to die on his account.

Morgan heard voices—the guards muttering to each other. He'd already dismissed it from his mind when something bumped against the door—hard. He turned in time to see the unlikely sight of two redcoats entering and dragging two unconscious redcoats with them.

His pulse thrumming, Morgan rushed to the bars, pressed his face against the cold iron, trying to get a better look, trying to figure out who amongst the British Regulars would want to help him.

Then one of the redcoats spoke.

"Och, these bloody breeches are cuttin' into my cods!"

"For God's sake, Connor, you whinge and yammer like a dog! I've seen your cods, and they're no' that big!"

Morgan stared in disbelief as Iain and Connor, dressed as British Regulars, dumped the unconscious guards on the floor and began to search the men's pockets for the key. "Holy Mary, Mother of God!"

*   *   *

Amalie glanced around her, feeling afraid. "How did we get here?"

"Can you no' recall, *a leannan?*" Morgan drew her against him so that her cheek pressed against his bare chest, warm water surrounding them both, the waterfall a shimmering curtain of silver behind him. "We walked, aye?"

And then she did remember. They'd walked together from Fort Carillon. Morgan had made love to her here. She'd been happy here with him. "I don't want to leave this place."

"We'll bide here for as long as you'd like."

A vague sense of foreboding lifted from her, whatever had troubled her seeming to melt in the warm water, contentment seeping through to her bones, his embrace a refuge. This is what she'd wanted—to be with him again. Then he kissed her, clever hands teasing out her secrets, his caress heating her blood until she could not wait to have him inside her. Sensing her need, he settled her astride him and filled her with a single, slow thrust that took her breath away.

"Morgan!"

A sharp knock came at the door. "Miss Chauvenet?"

"Morgan?" Amalie opened her eyes to find herself fully dressed and kneeling on the floor, her cheek pressed not against Morgan's chest, but the bed, his rosary clasped in her hand. Confused, she glanced about, her dream fading—and with it all happiness. *"Morgan."*

She whispered his name, felt as if she were saying farewell, despair forming a hard lump in her throat.

"Miss Chauvenet! I say, are you awake? Are you dressed?" It was the young lieutenant—Lieutenant Cooke.

He'd come to escort her to Morgan's execution.

The realization struck her with the force of a blow, her stomach turning, her heart thumping painfully behind her breast.

She slowly rose to unsteady feet, not noticing how sore she was from a long night of kneeling at prayer, her gaze fixed in horror on the door. She struggled to find the will to speak, to still her trembling, to stop her tears. "Y-yes, monsieur."

The key turned.

The door opened.

Lieutenant Cooke stood there in a state of utter deshabille, no wig to cover his short brown hair, no coat or waistcoat over his shirt, no stock to adorn his throat. He met her gaze, a strange look in his eyes. "Forgive me, mademoiselle, but Brigadier General Wentworth wished me to warn you. Major General Amherst will send for you. He wishes to question you."

As he spoke, there came raised voices from below stairs.

"B-but why? Wh-what did I—?"

The lieutenant's lips curved into the barest hint of a smile. "Major MacKinnon—he has escaped! The morning watch found the two sentries from first watch shackled together in his cell, and the major was gone. Four sentries were found at the postern gate unconscious. We've already searched the fort and Ranger Island and have not found him . . ."

Though the lieutenant continued to speak, Amalie did not hear him, his words drowned out by the rush of her own pulse, hot tears spilling down her cheeks, the terrible fear she'd carried these past days giving way to a surge of relief.

Morgan had escaped! He had escaped!

She raised Morgan's cross to her lips and kissed it. *"Merci, Marie, Reine du Ciel!"* Thank you, Mary, Queen of Heaven!

She heard Amherst shouting from below and felt no fear. So long as Morgan was alive and free, there was nothing that Amherst or Wentworth could do to hurt her.

Chapter 31

Amalie held on to the side of the bateau, its rocking motion leaving her queasy. The late-afternoon sun beat down upon her from a cloudless summer sky, the inconstant breeze her only respite from the sticky heat. In the distance, boats were already going ashore, the vanguard of a fleet of hundreds descending upon Fort Carillon just as the British had done a year ago.

She could not see the fort yet, but knew Monsieur de Bourlamaque had already been warned of the British army's arrival, just as Montcalm had been warned last summer. Soon the forest would echo with the beating of drums, the tramp of boots, and the clatter of swords in sheaths as the British army surrounded the little outpost.

It seemed like only yesterday . . .

If the fort should fall, stay close to Père François. I will come to you if I can. If aught should befall me, Père François will take you to Montcalm or Bourlamaque. They will keep you safe.

Nothing will happen to you, Papa!

Amalie squeezed her eyes shut, refusing to cry. In truth, she did not know how to feel. So much had changed since then. Even *she* had changed.

Now the land her father had died defending for France—the very ground in which he was buried—would fall into British hands, his sacrifice and her loss for naught in the end. And yet no blood would be spilled this time, for, as Morgan had told her, Monsieur de Bourlamaque was under orders to abandon the fort and march northward. She was grateful for that at least.

Her gaze was drawn once again to the shore and the dark wall of the forest beyond. Somewhere amongst those hills, amidst those trees, she had lived the happiest days of her life. And now those hills, those very trees, sheltered Morgan, concealing him from men who would shoot him on sight or hang him from the nearest strong branch.

Perhaps it was just her imagination, but from the moment the army had left Fort Edward, she'd felt Morgan nearby. The night they'd camped near the ruins of Fort William Henry, where Amherst's men had build hasty ramparts, she'd sworn she'd heard the Rangers' special whistle. And today as they'd crossed the wide waters of Lac Saint-Sacrement—what the English called Lake George—she'd felt him watching her.

He was out there. She knew it.

But so did Amherst and Wentworth. They'd set a watch upon her, but not where Morgan could see the guards. Spread out around her, her gaolers seemed to be ordinary British soldiers going about their duties. But their weapons were always at hand and their gazes never wandered far from her, unless to watch the forest. It hadn't taken Amalie long to understand that Amherst and Wentworth were using her as bait.

Amherst had been beside himself with rage that morning after Morgan had escaped, his pride clearly bruised at being bested. She'd been made to wait in Wentworth's study while Amherst finished questioning Iain and Connor, both of whom had challenged Amherst to explain how they could have gotten past twelve thousand Regulars—*and* the sentries at the gates— without being seen.

"No matter what you've heard from the Abenaki, we cannae fly, sir," Iain had said, the grave look on his face betraying no hint of humor.

Amherst had not been amused. "Your men are a disgrace, Captain MacKinnon!"

Connor's eyes had narrowed. "You wouldna say that if you were in the forest and under attack, sir. Nay, then you'd count yourself lucky to have us watchin' your back."

Amherst had ignored this.

"The sentries said they were set upon by *two* men, and though they did not see the men who attacked them, I find it curious that Major MacKinnon happens to have *two* brothers here at the fort, both of whom have served as Rangers and are known for their stealth!"

"They also said the men who attacked them wore British uniforms, sir. Perhaps 'tis your own men you should question."

Amherst glowered at Iain, then turned on Amalie so suddenly it made her gasp. "What do you know of this, Miss Chauvenet?"

Though Amalie was certain Iain and Connor had been behind Morgan's rescue, she'd let nothing of her thoughts show. She'd stepped forward, lifted her chin, and met Amherst's accusing gaze. "I know only that I prayed for such a miracle through the night and that my prayers have been answered."

The pride in Iain and Connor's eyes when they'd looked at her had warmed her heart, and she could almost hear Iain's thoughts. *That's our Amalie.*

The army had left the fort just after breakfast. Amherst hadn't allowed Amalie to bid Iain and Annie farewell, and he'd placed Connor and the Rangers so far in the rear of the column that she'd caught only a glimpse of them. And the overwhelming joy and relief she'd felt knowing that Morgan had escaped had dimmed in the face of her growing fear that he would come for her—and be captured or killed.

Oars now resting in the gunwales, the little bateau neared the shore, hands reaching out to steady it as soldiers clambered out with their gear, splashing as they went.

Lieutenant Cooke appeared beside the boat, his friendly face a welcome sight. "If you'll give me your hand, Miss Chauvenet, I'll help you ashore."

"*Merci, monsieur.* You are most kind."

He carried her through ankle-deep water to the sandy bank, then set her down and led her through the bustling soldiers toward her tent, which had already been set up on the western edge of the encampment. There she found Amherst and Wentworth, their heads bowed together.

"If he comes for her, it will be tonight," Wentworth said. "We must be vigilant."

Amherst nodded. "I've ordered my sharpshooters to open fire the moment he appears."

Amalie's stomach, still queasy, seemed to fall to the ground. She found herself hoping Morgan would not come for her. And yet if he didn't come, if he could not reach her, she would soon be in Monsieur de Bourlamaque's keeping—and she would likely never see him again.

She glanced toward the forested hills, her gaze seeking the shadows, her thoughts winging skyward.

Ô, Morgan, mon cher, méfie toi! Be careful!

Stripped down to his breeches, painted white and black to blend with the shadows, Morgan lay on his belly, watching through the spying glass as Amalie endured another supper with Wentworth and that whoreson Amherst. Her long hair spilling down her back, her sweet face rosy from too much sun, she picked at her meal, her gaze shifting furtively to the west, as if watching for him.

I'm here, a leannan. I've no' forsaken you.

For three long days, he'd shadowed the army, following their progress, keeping watch on Amalie through his spying glass. Everything inside him wanted to cease this endless waiting, charge down the hillside, and carry her away. But he did not wish to take British lives or risk losing Amalie or any of his men in needless fighting.

Soon, lass. We shall be together soon.

Beside Morgan, Joseph spoke in his own tongue. "Connor said they will not let him near her. He said Cooke seems to be watching over her."

"Cooke is a good man." Morgan rolled onto his back, collapsing the spying glass. "It sounds strange to say, but I believe Wentworth might have a heart after all."

Morgan still found it hard to believe that he was here and alive because of Wentworth. He'd have sworn the *neach dìolain* had wanted him to hang. He'd been utterly stamagastert to see Iain and Connor dressed as redcoats, but he'd been even more taken aback to learn where they'd gotten the uniforms.

Joseph grinned, his teeth bright white in contrast to the dark paint on his face. "Somewhere inside Wentworth's body is a man fighting to come out."

"So it seems, brother."

Then Killy and Forbes appeared beside them, both out of breath from their hike up the hill, two of almost forty Rangers who'd left Ranger Island and joined with Joseph and his men, waiting in the forest beyond Fort Edward to aid Morgan and his brothers in whatever way they could. Iain had wanted to join them, but they'd all known that Amherst would set a watch upon him, so he had taken Annie and the baby and gone home, unable to do more for Morgan than he'd already done.

Killy spoke first, his scarred face red from exertion. "'Tis as you said it would be. The Frenchies are fleein' northward."

"And what of Bourlamaque?"

Forbes nodded. "Aye, he's still there. We spotted him on the ramparts. The moment he sets his arse outside his own gates, we'll be ready for him."

Morgan clapped a hand on Forbes's shoulder. "Did you find the falls?"

"Aye, and Captain Joseph's men are in position."

Morgan looked down at the encampment below, his gaze seeking Amalie. "Then there's naugh' to do but wait."

Amalie dipped the cloth into the cool water, squeezed it out, then lifted her hair aside and pressed it to her nape. It was not the sort of bath to which she was accustomed, but after three long, hot days with no bath at all, it felt like heaven. She dipped the cloth again, squeezed it, and washed her face, the water helping to ease the heat of her sunburnt skin. But although she wished to be truly clean again, she dared not remove her gown. Not only was she the only woman in an encampment of soldiers, but she also knew that Iain had meant what he'd said.

You must be ready for whate'er comes, aye?

She washed her face, throat, and hands, then set the bowl of water aside, snuffed out her candle, and lay back on her bedroll, still fully dressed.

If Morgan came for her tonight, she would be ready.

Darkness fell around her, the night borne down by a heavy

silence, the soldiers anxious in their sleep. They remembered last summer's carnage and wondered if they, too, were fated to die before Fort Carillon's abatis. They did not know what she knew—that none of them would die tomorrow, for there would be no battle.

And so, surrounded by the troubled stillness, she waited.

Amalie did not remember falling asleep. She did not know she was sleeping until Lieutenant Cooke's voice woke her.

"Major General Amherst and Brigadier General Wentworth await you at breakfast, mademoiselle. I've come to escort you."

She sat up, glanced about in confusion, and realized that it was past dawn. Morgan had not come. "*Merci,* Lieutenant. I'll be but a moment."

Amalie quickly repaired her braid, her relief that nothing had happened during the night at odds with her rising fear that Morgan would not be able to reach her in time. And then what would she do? She could not bear to think of facing a lifetime without him, the very idea making her feel sick, bringing tears to her eyes.

She blinked them away, then ducked out of her tent, to find Lieutenant Cooke waiting for her. "I am ready."

Breakfast turned out to be a hurried cup of tea and a stale biscuit. Amalie did not care, for she hadn't the appetite for more. She'd barely finished her tea, when Amherst glanced at his pocket watch.

"Let us be off."

And Amalie knew.

They were taking her to Monsieur de Bourlamaque.

Pulse tripping, she stood, grasped Wentworth's hand. "I beseech you, monsieur, be merciful and permit me to say farewell to my husband's brother, Captain MacKinnon. Just a few moments are all I ask. Please!"

If she could but distance herself from the soldiers who guarded her, if she could find Connor and the Rangers, then perhaps . . .

Wentworth gazed coldly down at her. "I'm afraid I can't permit that, Miss Chauvenet."

Heedless of the tears that welled in her eyes, he led her to the meadow where the officers' horses had been picketed through the night, accompanied by Amherst and several soldiers. Then he lifted her onto one of the horses and climbed into the saddle behind her.

"Don't look so glum, Miss Chauvenet." He wrapped his arm about her waist, his voice like velvet in her ear. "You're about to be reunited with your loving guardian—surely a happy occasion."

But it would be anything but happy, for Monsieur de Bourlamaque would take her deeper into French territory, making it almost impossible for Morgan to find her. Not only that, but once she confessed that she'd discovered Morgan spying and had not told him—and confess she must—he would surely despise her.

Amalie said nothing of her fears. Instead, she glared back at Wentworth, rage thrumming through her veins that he should make so light of her sorrow. "Indeed, it shall be happy, for I shall at last be rid of you."

Wentworth merely smiled.

They rode along the lakeshore, then took a path leading northwest through the forest, sunlight piercing through leaves to dapple the trail before them, the forest seeming to hold its breath. And then she saw it—movement amongst the trees.

Amalie's pulse skipped, her breath seeming to catch in her lungs.

But it was only a doe startled from the undergrowth by the horses.

Her heart sank.

Wentworth leaned near and whispered, his lips almost touching her temple. "Do you think he'd be foolish enough to try to take you here? Our men have kept this trail under watch since yesterday afternoon. It is quite free of any presence but our own."

Then through the trees, she could hear it—the rushing waters of rivière La Chute. Soon the forest fell back to reveal a wide waterfall. And on the other side, surrounded by a full military escort bearing the fleur-de-lis, stood Lieutenant Durand and Lieutenant Foucher, Monsieur de Bourlamaque between them.

An unexpected pang of joy, sharp and bittersweet, swelled inside her at the sight of her guardian's familiar face. But if he felt any happiness at the sight of her, it did not show. He stood still and solemn as Wentworth lifted her into a bateau and the entire British party crossed the river.

"It seems your *husband* was not as keen on reacquiring you as you might have believed." Amherst looked down his long nose at her, a mocking smile on his lips. "He saved himself and forgot all about you."

"Then he has eluded us both," she said, gratified by the angry flush that came into Amherst's cheeks.

Yet even as Amalie told herself to ignore Amherst's hateful words, cold doubt clutched at her belly, and her gaze sought the shadows of the forest once again.

Chapter 32

Morgan watched as the British crossed the river in bateaux sent over by Bourlamaque, Amalie seated between Amherst and Wentworth, Amherst's marksmen keeping watch from the far bank. Wentworth helped Amalie ashore, his arm lingering about her waist too long for Morgan's liking.

That's my wife, you mac-dìolain*!*

Time slowed to a crawl as the British formed a line and, leaving Amalie under guard at the riverbank, marched forward to the rat-a-tat-tat of drums to exchange formal greetings with Bourlamaque and his party. Amherst's aide-de-camp was the first to step forward. He doffed his hat and made an outlandish bow. Not to be outdone, Lieutenant Durand returned the extravagant gesture, adding several hand flourishes.

Och, for God's sake!

Did they think they were at court?

Then Amherst and Bourlamaque began to speak. Morgan could not hear what was being said, nor did he give a tinker's damn, his blood as primed for action as the pistol in his hands. But seconds stretched into long minutes, until it seemed the two men could have nothing more under the sun to say to each other.

Bloody hell!

Then at last, Bourlamaque turned to the men behind him and

gestured. Two British officers appeared, impossibly pale and thin, their faces showing both joy and disbelief, as if they could not fathom that they were now free. Amherst's men saluted them, then led them to a waiting bateau.

Now it was Amherst's turn. He looked over his shoulder at Amalie, motioning her forward. Lifting her skirts, she hurried toward Bourlamaque, who opened his arms and embraced her like a daughter, relief plain on his face.

Something twisted in Morgan's gut.

She's your wife now. She belongs wi' you, laddie.

Aye, she did—and yet to stay with him, she would lose so much.

He pushed the thought from his mind, watching as the British took their leave of the French, crossed the river, and disappeared back into the forest.

Amalie stood in silence beside Monsieur de Bourlamaque, watching as the British vanished amongst the trees, her hope disappearing with them, despair threatening to swallow her whole. The tears she'd been fighting since she'd awoken at last got the better of her, spilling down her cheeks.

Morgan!

It was Monsieur de Bourlamaque who spoke first, turning her to face him, his gaze seeming to take in the wrinkles on her gown, her sunburnt skin, and her tears all at once. "Praise God and the saints you are alive and whole! When I learned what that whoreson Rillieux had done, I feared the worst. Did he harm you, Amalie?"

"Rillieux struck me and tried to—"

"Not Rillieux! That bastard MacKinnon! Did he hurt you or dishonor you?"

Astonished that he should ask such a thing, Amalie gaped up at him. "*Non, monsieur!* Why would Morgan harm me? He is my husband!"

Monsieur de Bourlamaque's expression grew hard. "He betrayed me, Amalie! He confessed to me in a letter—written in French! He betrayed me, and he misled you to the altar, taking what he would never have gotten had I known the truth."

Amalie swallowed and met Bourlamaque's gaze. "He did not

mislead me, monsieur. I . . . I knew. Before I married him, I knew that he had stolen secrets. I caught him spying late one night and—"

Monsieur de Bourlamaque's grip on her arms tightened, a look of hurt disbelief in his eyes. "And you did not tell me?"

"I—I couldn't! Forgive me, monsieur, but I could not betray him, knowing that it would mean his death!" She drew a shaky breath, her mind searching for words to explain. "I . . . I love him!"

Bourlamaque's gaze grew cold. He turned her and led her toward a waiting wagon. "Such girlish nonsense! I am sending you back to Trois Rivières to await the end of the war and your annulment. I only pray you're not carrying his child."

Amalie's despair turned to anger. "And I pray that I am! I would have been happy to live out my life with him, but this war will not let us be. You took me away from him, and the British want to hang him!"

Bourlamaque stopped still and gaped at her. "What?"

Amalie told him how Amherst and Wentworth believed Morgan was a traitor and how they'd tried him in a court-martial, found him guilty, and would already have hanged him three days past had he not escaped. "You did not know?"

"No." Bourlamaque drew a deep breath, a look of weariness upon his face. Then he lowered his voice. "Say nothing of your role in this to anyone lest you find yourself in the same predicament. I will do my best to find you a suitable husband—"

"The lass already has a husband."

Amalie whirled toward the sound of that familiar voice. "Morgan!"

But where was he? She glanced about, but did not see him.

Then a shape detached itself from the forest, and what had seemed like dappled shadow took on the form of a man and stepped into the sunlight.

Morgan stood not ten paces away, dressed in dark leather breeches, his bare chest, arms, and face painted with alternating bands of white and black, the dark paint making his eyes seem startlingly blue. His dark hair hung down his back, a warrior braid at each temple, his chest rising and falling with each slow, steady breath. But, though he was clad as a warrior, he bore no weapon.

Lieutenant Durand and Lieutenant Foucher raised their pistols.

"No!" In a rush of fear, Amalie started toward him.

But Monsieur de Bourlamaque held her fast.

Morgan saw the hope in Amalie's eyes, and the doubt he'd carried with him these past days vanished. No matter that he was a condemned man, her love still lay upon him. He met Bourlamaque's gaze, saw the fury that blazed there. "Release her, and tell your men to lower their weapons."

"We do not answer to you, traitor!" Lieutenant Durand spat at him.

Bourlamaque laughed, a bitter sound. "I do not know how you found us, Ranger, but my scouts have you surrounded. They will—"

"These scouts?" Morgan gestured for his men to step forward.

From around the clearing, Rangers and Mahicans stepped out of the shadows in twos and threes, holding a French soldier or Abenaki warrior at the tip of their muskets.

Bourlamaque glanced about, surprise turning to rage. Then he met Morgan's gaze once more. "Try to take her from me by force, and you'll die where you stand!"

Morgan looked into his eyes, saw the man he'd come to admire, and felt a moment of regret. "I dinnae wish this to come to bloodshed, but kill me, and you'll die ere I hit the ground."

"Stop, please!" Amalie cried. "I could not bear it if either of you were hurt!"

Silence stretched taut between them.

It was Bourlamaque who spoke first. "I spared your life! I treated you with honor! I trusted you, and you betrayed me!"

"I had no choice! I couldna fight for an army that sought to kill my brothers and my men!"

"You broke your word!" Bourlamaque's voice was dark with condemnation.

"Aye, I did." It was the truth, and there was naught Morgan could do to change it. "But long afore I laid eyes upon you, my word was already given."

This only served to enrage Bourlamaque further. "Tell me why I should not order them to shoot you where you stand!"

Morgan took a step toward him, and then another, mindful of Durand and Foucher. "Because you dinnae truly wish to see me die. Because 'tis only this godforsaken war that stands between us. Because you dinnae wish Amalie to watch you kill the man she loves."

Morgan dared not look at Amalie, his mind on Bourlamaque and the two officers who still pointed pistols at his chest. He saw in Bourlamaque's eyes the battle that raged within him, watched the old man's anger rise, dark and venomous—and then break.

Suddenly Bourlamaque seemed weary, the fight leaving his limbs. He motioned for Durand and Foucher to lower their weapons. "I would have treated you with honor, kept you at my right hand."

Morgan felt the sharp edges of regret press into his chest. "And I'd have been proud to stand beside you had I been free to make such a choice."

For a moment neither of them spoke, their gazes locked in understanding.

Then Bourlamaque looked down at Amalie and spoke in French. "You must choose, *ma petite,* and from your decision there can be no turning back. Come with me now, and I shall do all I can to free you from this marriage and settle you with a man who can keep you safe and happy, perhaps in France. Or go with MacKinnon and live whatever life he can give you. He is an outlaw, Amalie, condemned by both France and Britain. No matter who wins this war, there will be a price on his head. Ever you shall wander, but I do not believe you will find peace. And when children come, they shall suffer even as you suffer."

"I protect what's mine, Bourlamaque." But even as Morgan spoke, the truth in Bourlamaque's words assailed him. He was a selfish bastard to take the woman he loved from a life of safety into such peril. And if she were with child . . .

She's your wife. She belongs at your side.

Aye, but what life could he give her? What life could he give a child? If he loved her, wouldn't it be better for her if he let her go?

A fist seemed to close around his heart, his tongue shaping words his mind did not wish to speak. "He's right, Amalie. I am a condemned man. I will be hunted wi' no place I can call home. You're my wife, *a leannan,* and I want you beside me, but I wouldna see you suffer for love of me."

Amalie saw the anguish in Morgan's eyes and knew what it

had cost him to speak those words—this proud Scotsman, this warrior. Love for him swelled in her heart, putting tears in her eyes. She wanted to run to him, but first it was time for farewells.

She turned to Monsieur de Bourlamaque, met his worried gaze. "You have done so much for me, monsieur. You have cared for me and protected me, treating me as a favored niece. I am forever grateful to you."

Bourlamaque cupped her cheek and smiled at her, the tenderness on his face enough to break Amalie's heart. "Come with me, and let me give you the life you deserve, far from the frontier. Let me—"

Amalie pressed her fingers to his lips, a bittersweet ache in her breast. "You are most generous, but my place is with Morgan. He is my husband. I go with him."

A look of sadness came over Monsieur de Bourlamaque's face, but he nodded. Then he smiled. "Your father married for love and cherished your mother to his dying day. You are your father's daughter in the end, *non*?"

Nothing Monsieur de Bourlamaque could have said in that moment would have touched Amalie more. She threw her arms around him and held him tight, tears choking back her words. *"Merci beaucoup, monsieur! Je ne vous oublierai jamais."* I will never forget you!

He crushed her against him in a great hug, held her, then set her free. "Go to him, Amalie."

She stood on tiptoe, kissed her guardian's bristly cheek, then turned toward Morgan. He stood only a few paces away, his blue eyes reflecting the same tumult of emotions she was feeling. She took one step in his direction and another, then lifted her skirts and ran to him, his strong arms enfolding her, holding her close.

"Och, Amalie, lass!"

She pressed her cheek against his chest, felt his heart beating strong and steady beneath his breast. "Oh, Morgan! I was so afraid! I thought they'd hang you or shoot you and I'd never see you again!"

And then the tears came in earnest as she wept out the horror of the past week, safe in the sanctuary of his embrace, the familiar scent of his skin, the feel of his arms around her seeming precious beyond imagining, his nearness a miracle.

He kissed her hair, murmuring reassurances, his arms holding her tighter. "Shhh, *a leannan,* I'm here, and I'll no' let us be parted again."

Then he tucked a finger beneath her chin, ducked down, and kissed her. It was a scorching kiss, desperate and brutal—a kiss of death defeated, a kiss of life reclaimed. Her heart soaring, she welcomed the sweet invasion of his tongue, arching against him, her fingers delving into the silk of his hair, even as his fisted in hers.

Someone coughed.

Monsieur de Bourlamaque.

Amalie had forgotten all about the others.

Morgan could have kissed her forever—but not here, not caught between two armies on the brink of battle. He drew back from her, wiped the tears from her cheeks, and couldn't help but chuckle. "You look like you're weepin' ink, lass. See? Your tears are washin' away my scary paint."

She looked at the patch of bare skin on his chest, sniffed, then laughed, the sound bonnier to his ears than the most beautiful music.

Then Joseph spoke. "The hour grows late. It is time for us to leave this place."

"Aye, we must." Morgan met Bourlamaque's gaze. "I speak for the Rangers and for the Mahican when I say that none of us shall fire upon you or steal your wine again. We owe you a life debt. Let there be peace between us at least."

He stepped away from Amalie, reached out his hand.

Bourlamaque seemed to hesitate. Then he stepped forward and took Morgan's hand, his grasp firm. "Nor will my soldiers pursue you."

Then Simon came forward and spoke in Abenaki, Atoan keeping pace beside him. "You are husband to my cousin, and she loves you. Twice you spared my life. I will not make war on you or your brothers again, Mack-in-non."

"Nor will I." Atoan drew out his hatchet and turned the handle toward Morgan, symbolically offering him peace. "Enough blood has been spilled between our peoples, and I would not see your woman torn by further grief. Let us fight no more."

Morgan nodded, took the hatchet, then drew the hunting knife from his belt and turned the handle toward Atoan. *"Wli-gen. Ni-do-bak."* *It is good. Let us be friends.*

Bourlamaque said something to Durand and Fouchet, then

turned to face Morgan once more. "Amalie's belongings are in the trunk in that wagon—her gowns, her rosary, her father's books. Take what you will. My scouts tell me British scouts are still searching for you in the hills south of here. You must make haste. Go with God, Major MacKinnon. And take care of her."

"I will. God be wi' you, old man."

"Adieu, Amalie. I doubt we shall see each other again on this earth. May God and His saints watch over you and your Ranger. I shall keep you both in my prayers."

Morgan watched as Amalie ran to Bourlamaque and embraced her guardian one last time, her voice quavering. *"Adieu, monsieur."*

Durand and Foucher each gave Morgan a nod—and then the French were gone, melting into the forest with their Abenaki allies.

A malie's belongings were quickly removed from the trunk and everything except for her rosary, which she insisted on carrying, was divided amongst the men to stow in their packs. They journeyed quickly upriver to where they'd hidden canoes amongst the reeds, then crossed the river once more, heading southward, Joseph's men scouting ahead, Morgan unable to let Amalie out of arm's reach.

" 'Twill be long ere I can bear to let you out of my sight, *a leannan*," he told her as he lifted her from the canoe.

"Or I you. I was so afraid you would be hanged!" The dark circles beneath her eyes and her grip on his fingers told him just how afraid she'd been. "How did you escape?"

"Och, well, I climbed a moonbeam and floated away on the breeze."

She smiled, the sight warming him to his soul. "I know you well enough to know that you are a man, Morgan MacKinnon, not *chi bai*."

He lowered his voice, savoring the feel of her small hand in his. "Aye, I'm a man, and I thank heaven for it every time I lay eyes upon you."

Her cheeks flushed pink. "So how *did* you escape?"

" 'Twas Wentworth."

"What?" She gaped at him in disbelief. "But Wentworth thought you guilty!"

"Or so he feigned. He secreted British uniforms out to my brothers, using the changing of the watch to bring them within the fort's walls. They overpowered the guards, freed me, then crept wi' me through the shadows to the postern gate. While I concealed myself, they walked up to the sentries and struck them senseless. We left by the gate and made our way back around to Ranger Island, throwin' the uniforms in the river. I gathered my gear and made my way through the forest to where Joseph was encamped. 'Twas a chancie plan, but it worked."

Then Morgan told her how Wentworth had revealed to Iain and Connor when and where she was to be traded for the two soldiers, hinting in his own way that Morgan should wait to retake Amalie until after the exchange was made. He told her how he and Joseph had paced the army day after day, how they'd had their men in position long before Amherst or Bourlamaque had scouted the area around the falls, and how the wait had nearly driven him daft.

"So you *were* watching over me."

He gave her hand a squeeze. "Aye, lass, every hour of every day."

Soon they found themselves making their way up the slope of Rattlesnake Mountain, the ground rocky at their feet. Although Amalie was stronger than she'd been the last time they'd come this way, the climb was not an easy one. As they'd done on the journey to Fort Edward, they moved more slowly, Joseph and his men scouting ahead, giving Amalie and Morgan a wide berth. But no sooner had the crest of the mountain come into view than Morgan heard the blast of cannon in the distance.

Amalie gasped, gave a startled jump. "I thought there was to be no battle. I thought Bourlamaque planned to abandon the fort."

"Those were his orders." Morgan quickened their pace. "Come. Let us see."

On the rocky summit, he lay on his belly and inched forward to the edge, motioning for Amalie to do the same. The valley spread out before them, the shimmering waters of Lake Champlain stretching to the north, Lake George over the hills to the west. And there, on a small peninsula, stood Fort Carillon, about to be swept away in a tide of red, the British army approaching from the south.

There came the roar of cannon, and smoke rose from the ramparts of Carillon.

Amalie gasped again. "The fort looks so small! Why do they not flee?"

"That wylie bastard!" Morgan chuckled. "They are fleein'. See?"

He pointed north of the fort, where he could just make out a band of blue stretching along a forest road. It was the French army. "Do you see them?"

She nodded. "But who is firing the guns?"

"It seems Bourlamaque has left a rear guard to hold the British at bay. He kens I told Amherst that the fort would be abandoned, and he kens Amherst didna believe me, so he's firin' the guns to fool Amherst into thinkin' he's still there. See how Amherst rolls out his artillery? While he wastes his time preparin' for battle, Bourlamaque's army makes good its escape. By the time Amherst is ready to fire, the fort will be empty."

It was a brilliant plan.

But Amalie was not smiling, her face pale as the last French soldiers abandoned the guns, mounted their horses and rode out, deserting the fort at last. Then her eyes filled with tears. *"Adieu, Papa."*

Morgan heard the anguish in her voice, and felt a surge of regret at his thoughtlessness. He'd not thought what this would mean to her. "'Tis sorry I am that you should suffer, *a leannan*. The British willna disrespect the graves, and I've no doubt Connor will seek your father's grave to pay his respects."

She nodded, sniffed, seeming to take comfort in his words.

But now regret assailed him in earnest, the pricking of his conscience impossible to ignore. "Bourlamaque is right, lass. I am a wanted man, welcome neither amongst the French nor the British. I promised you a home, and now I cannae so much as give you a roof to cover your head."

Amalie looked into Morgan's eyes and saw the depth of his remorse. "This is not your doing, Morgan. I do not blame you. Please do not blame yourself."

But she could see her words did not soothe him.

She sat up, traced the line of his jaw with her fingertips. "The night before you were to be . . . hanged . . . I prayed for God to work some miracle and set you free. I would have given anything to spare you, anything at all. Now that my prayers have been answered, why should I worry about something so small as a roof?"

He took her hand, pressed her fingers to his lips, kissed them. "But I promised you a home, lass."

She sought for words to make him understand. "*You* are my home, Morgan MacKinnon."

He watched her for a moment, as if amazed, and some of his regret and doubt seemed to fade. "Life at my side willna be easy, but I swear to you, lass, you'll ne'er go hungry, nor will you want for warmth or a man's protection."

She smiled, a feeling of pure happiness swelling inside her just to be near him like this. "Then I shall want for nothing."

Joseph appeared out of the forest, his men behind him. He said something to Morgan in his mother tongue and pointed to the valley below.

Morgan looked startled, then took Amalie's hand and stood.

And there in the valley not far from the roots of the mountain stood Connor and the Rangers. They were easy to recognize, the only company in the British army not wearing red uniforms. The moment they saw Morgan, they raised their rifles over their heads and let loose a bloodcurdling cry—the Mahican war cry.

And Amalie knew.

This was the Rangers' way of bidding Morgan farewell.

Tears of bittersweet joy streamed down her cheeks as she watched Morgan receive this tribute from his men, his head high, his brow furrowed with emotion, his jaw tight. Then Morgan raised his rifle above his head and returned the cry, Joseph and the others joining with him, until the entire forest echoed with the terrible, wonderful sound.

And then the world fell silent.

Far below them, the Rangers turned and marched on, duty calling to them.

"Farewell, Connor," she heard Morgan whisper, his arm sliding about her waist. "Farewell, lads."

"Will we see them again?"

"God willing, lass. God willing." Then he turned to her, wiped the tears from her cheeks. "We have far to go ere nightfall. We must be certain that no one has followed us. Can you make it, *a leannan*?"

Amalie smiled. "As long as you're with me, Morgan, I can do anything.

Epilogue

Morgan put the heavy iron lid on the pot, settled it amongst the coals, then sat back on his heels, sharing a conspiratorial grin with Joseph. "And now we wait."

He gazed at Amalie as she watched the pot, excitement and anticipation on her sweet face. When he'd heard that she'd never tasted or even seen popped corn, he'd known he'd have to ask Joseph to bring some when next he came to visit. His Muhheconneok brother had not disappointed him, bringing not only popped corn, but also cider, pumpkins, potatoes, corn, apples, dried plums, cornmeal, butter, and cheese from the MacKinnon farm. Joseph had even brought sugar and a wee bit of precious cinnamon, which he'd gotten from a Dutch trader in Albany.

With the plump turkey Morgan would bring down, 'twould make a grand Christmas feast. And Amalie deserved a happy Christmas.

As true and good a wife as any man could hope for, she'd endured these months of exile without complaint, her smile never failing, her love never faltering. Not when they'd journeyed long leagues through the forest to take shelter with Joseph's kin in Stockbridge. Not when the sudden arrival of Amherst's scouts had forced them to flee westward in the dark of night. Not when she, already quickening with his child, had been made to sleep upon pine boughs in a lean-to while Morgan put up this cabin.

Sturdy and warm, it stood near a spring in the heart of Mahican hunting grounds, deep enough in the wilderness to keep Amherst at bay and near enough to Stockbridge for someone from the village to make the journey once a month, bringing the provisions Morgan could not find in the forest and taking peltries in trade. For four months now they'd lived within its thick and sturdy walls, and happy months they'd been. With no fields or livestock to tend, their days and nights turned around the simple rhythms of living—harvesting food and firewood from the forest, bathing in the spring, making love whenever and wherever they chose, as if they were the only two people in the world.

Though he'd not believed it possible, Morgan loved Amalie more today than he had when he'd taken her from Bourlamaque, the joy he'd found with her beyond anything he'd ever known or even imagined. Despite Amalie's fears that he would desire her less as her belly grew big and round, he wanted her all the more. For although some women grew pale and wan when with child, the life seeming to drain from them even as the bairn within them grew, Amalie had blossomed, her feminine curves becoming more lush, her eyes growing brighter, roses blooming in her cheeks.

Yet amidst such happiness, there were shadows. Amalie still had unquiet dreams, stalked in her sleep by a bastard Morgan oft wished he could slay again. And although he'd taught her to shoot, she hated being left alone in the cabin when he went hunting. But most of all she feared what would happen when her time came. She spoke nothing of it, but Morgan knew it just the same. He could see it in her eyes sometimes as she stroked her belly, could see it in the way she sometimes lay awake late at night.

'Twas only natural for her to be afraid. Childbirth was as hard on a woman as battle was on a man—or so Morgan reasoned. Many women suffered for long hours only to lose the bairn ere it took a single breath, and more than a few lost their own lives. Hadn't Amalie's own mother died in childbed? It helped matters not one whit that Amalie's thoughts were filled with the frichtsome ramblings of that gabby old nun.

Morgan wished he could take Amalie home. He knew she missed Annie greatly, knew that now more than ever Amalie needed a woman's company. Annie had already borne one child and was now well along with her second. She would have been able to assuage Amalie's fears both before and during the birthing—and she might have been able to soothe Morgan's worries as well.

Come March, when the deep snows began to melt, he would have to help Amalie bring forth the bairn he'd planted inside her. But although he'd helped cows to calve and horses to foal, he'd ne'er even witnessed childbirth. The nearest he'd come was the endless night he'd sat by the campfire drinking rum with Iain as Annie had struggled to bring wee Iain Cameron into the world, her cries turning Iain's face white and tugging at the heart of every man in Ranger Camp.

Knowing that Amalie must suffer such pain on account of him was hard enough for Morgan. But the thought that she might perish . . .

Nay, neither she nor the child would die. Morgan loved her with every breath in his body. He would not let that happen.

Pop.

The first corn popped. And then the next.

Amalie laughed, gazing up at him in wide-eyed wonder, a bright smile on her face, her happiness making Morgan forget his worries—for now.

Amalie listened as the popping became a frantic tattoo, and had to fight the urge to lift off the lid so that she could see what was happening inside the pot. Soon a warm, delicious scent filled the room. She watched as Morgan removed the pot from the coals, then pressed in close as he lifted the lid.

"Ô, mon Dieu!" She stared in amazement at what looked like fluffy bits of cloud. While Morgan and Joseph argued about what to put on it—butter and salt or butter and sugar—she reached out, picked a piece, and popped it into her mouth. It was strangely crunchy and yet seemed to melt on her tongue.

"I didn't carry this all the way from Stockbridge so that you could ruin it by putting salt on it." Joseph took up the sugar sack, the stubborn look upon his face enough to make Amalie laugh.

Morgan jerked the popcorn out of his reach. "Let's let Amalie decide, for this is her first taste . . ."

Both men fell silent, looked toward the door.

And Amalie heard.

Men's voices. The snort of a horse.

Morgan took up his rifle and drew the cork from the barrel,

his face grave, his voice dropping to a whisper. "Amalie, get in the back room, and bar the door."

Heart thrumming, Amalie hurried to do as he asked, the baby kicking restlessly inside her, as if it sensed her alarm. Joseph moved silently toward the front door while Morgan slipped toward the back door.

Then a familiar voice called to them. "Hallo in the house!"

'Twas Connor!

Joseph cursed under his breath, opened the door, and froze.

Beyond the door in the snow stood Connor. Behind him were a score of redcoats on horseback. And leading them was Wentworth.

Morgan stared past Joseph out the front door, rifle still in his hand, trying to make sense of what he saw. Connor had led a dozen redcoats to their door, Wentworth and Lieutenant Cooke amongst them. But his brother would not betray him. And hadn't Wentworth aided his escape?

He drew in a breath to clear his mind and glanced over his shoulder to where Amalie stood in the door of their room, her eyes wide. "Stay where you are, lass."

Connor and Wentworth and the redcoats dismounted, the redcoats seeing to their horses as Connor strode toward him, a grin on his unshaven face, a bearskin coat wrapped tightly around him. "Surprised to see me, brothers?"

He slapped Joseph on the shoulder, then engulfed Morgan in a crushing hug, his voice dropping to a whisper. "You ken I'd ne'er have led them here if they meant to harm you." With those strange words, he strode past Morgan to greet Amalie and warm himself by the fire.

"Major MacKinnon." Wentworth measured him through cold gray eyes, stamping the snow from his boots. "If my men and I might warm ourselves at your hearth, I've brought news from Albany."

Stomach knotted with fear for Morgan, Amalie filled Lieutenant Cooke's cup with hot coffee, then shifted her gaze back to Morgan, who was reading a letter Wentworth had handed to him, his dark brows bent in a frown.

Morgan lifted his gaze and looked up at Wentworth, stunned disbelief on his dear face. "Pardoned? But . . . *how*?"

What did that mean—*pardoned*?

Her pulse raced.

"Having heard of your military exploits, Governor DeLancey took a personal interest in your conviction and subsequent escape. He conducted his own investigation and concluded that the jury had been less than impartial in your case, perhaps owing to your parentage. He threw out the verdict and issued a pardon. Of course, his decision was heavily influenced by the missives we found at Fort Ticonderoga in Bourlamaque's study—letters from the Marquis de Montcalm berating him for allowing you to deceive him and escape. Odd that Bourlamaque left them behind, don't you think, Major?"

Threw out the verdict? Issued a pardon?

Was Morgan no longer a fugitive?

Amalie's pulse raced faster.

A look of comprehension came over Morgan's face. "This is *your* doin'."

"Mine?" Wentworth raised an eyebrow. "General Amherst would be most distressed if that were the case. I assure you, the praise or blame lies with Governor DeLancey."

A knowing look passed between the two men.

"And what did Amherst say when he heard the news?" Morgan asked.

"He was so angry that he kicked your arse out of the army!" Connor grinned. "You're free, brother."

"What?"

Out of the army?

Amalie could scarce breathe.

"Captain MacKinnon is correct. General Amherst was enraged. He felt that since your loyalties were uncertain at best, you presented too great a risk. You have been discharged." The tone of Wentworth's voice and the hard look in his eyes left Amalie with no doubt that this was not the outcome he'd expected.

Joseph gave a loud whoop and laughed out loud.

Amalie met Morgan's gaze, feeling light-headed. "Wh-what does this mean? Morgan, what is he saying?"

Morgan pushed through the crowded cabin, lifted her into his arms, and planted a kiss on her lips. When he set her on her feet again, there was a broad smile on his face. "It means, *a leannan,* that we're goin' home."

Three months later

The keening cry became a sob, then faded to a whimper and fell silent.

Morgan found himself holding his breath. He'd never felt so bloody helpless—or so afraid—in his life. He exhaled, met Iain's gaze, his belly too knotted for rum. "How much longer will she have to bide this?"

Already, twenty long hours had gone by.

"The first one is always the hardest." Iain's voice held a reassuring tone. "Annie labored for the better part of a day with Iain, but 'twas much quicker with Mara."

How could Iain be so calm? Did he feel nothing for Amalie's suffering?

And then Morgan saw.

Iain might sound calm, but he was holding his cup so tightly that his knuckles were white.

Morgan drew a deep breath. "Aye, that seems to be the way of it."

He glanced at the little cradle near the hearth, where his brother's daughter slept. Only six weeks old, little Mara Elasaid MacKinnon had been born in a matter of hours, Annie's pains beginning in the early morn and her daughter's lusty cry echoing through the cabin ere midday. Amalie had held Annie's hand, and had come away from the birthing less afraid than before and awed by Annie's strength.

"Women are strong, too, but in a different way than men," she'd told him that night as he'd held her, one hand on her belly to feel the bairn move within her.

Och, aye, women were strong, for if giving birth were left to men, there'd be scarce a child born anywhere in the world. From the sound of it, giving birth was worse than being flogged.

Sweet Mary, Mother of God, help her! Dinnae let her or the bairn perish!

Another pain began, Amalie's moan becoming a cry of agony

that seemed to go on forever before fading into silence like the others.

Then he heard footsteps on the stairs.

Rebecca, Joseph's sister, appeared at the foot of the stairs, her dark hair piled atop her head, her face lined with worry. She met Morgan's gaze. "Amalie's womb has opened, but the child is not moving down. I fear the baby may be too big to be born."

Morgan heard Rebecca's words, tried to understand what she was telling him, the floor seeming to tilt beneath him. "Are you tellin' me . . . she's goin' to . . . *die*?"

He felt Iain's hand upon his shoulder.

" 'Tis too early to tell, but I fear for her, Morgan. You are a big man, and she is very small. If the child cannot be born, neither of them will survive." Rebecca took his hand. "But there are ways . . . ways to draw the child out. 'Twould mean losing the baby, but it might save Am—"

"No!" Morgan found himself on his feet, the answer surging from the pit of his gut. "I'll no' choose atween them. Amalie wouldna survive her grief if she kent her child had been killed to spare her life."

Rebecca nodded, looking relieved. "Then help me—both of you. Iain, I need you to help Annie hold Amalie upright on the birthing stool. Morgan, when the next pain comes, I want you to push against the top of her womb to try to force the child down. I'll show you how."

Morgan followed Rebecca up the stairs, feeling more afraid than he'd ever felt going into battle, his mind filled with a silent prayer.

Mary, Blessed Virgin, spare my Amalie! Spare them both!

Amalie felt lips press against her cheek, and opened her eyes to see Morgan beside her. She knew why he was there. She could see it on Rebecca's face.

Something was wrong.

"Morgan!" She took his hand, tears filling her eyes at the welcome sight of him. There was something she needed to tell him. "If I should die, cut my belly open and save the baby. Promise me you'll—"

"You're no' goin' to die, *a leannan*." He gave her hand a squeeze, his eyes filled with sharp determination. "I'm wi' you now."

Clenching Annie's hand, Amalie pushed with all her might, fighting not to scream as Morgan used his forearm to push hard against her belly, the pain unbearable. Teeth clenched, she looked into Morgan's eyes, the strength she saw in them becoming her strength. She would *not* die. She would *not* let her baby die.

"A little longer . . . Feel your body open . . . That's the way," Rebecca crooned. "Your baby has lots of dark hair."

Then the pain passed, and Amalie sank back against Iain's chest, barely able to stay awake, her body trembling from exertion, her mind exhausted by pain.

Morgan bathed her forehead with a cool cloth, murmuring reassurances. "It willna be long now, *a leannan*."

Amalie nodded, then fell into a doze.

Again and again her pangs came, and each time Amalie looked into Morgan's eyes, clinging to the love she saw there, the pain between her legs turning to fire.

"The head is almost out, lass," he said, pushing hard against her womb.

Unable to bear it, Amalie screamed—and felt the pain lessen. And there, between her thighs, was a baby's face, its little eyes open, its tiny lips pressed in a frown.

"*Ô, mon Dieu!*" She reached down, stroked her baby's head, even as Rebecca wiped its face with a clean cloth.

And with one last push, her baby slipped into her hands, squalling.

"It's a boy!" Rebecca helped Amalie lift the baby to her breast.

"And a strong one from the sounds of it," Annie said, a relieved smile on her face.

"Well done, lass." Iain's voice came from behind her, his hands giving her shoulders a squeeze.

Relief and elation washed through Amalie as she held her baby close, his healthy cries the most beautiful sound she'd ever heard. She'd been so afraid—afraid that she would perish, afraid that the baby would be stillborn, the long hours of labor more than it could withstand.

She looked up at Morgan, saw tears in his eyes and amazement on his face. She turned the baby so he could see its little face. "Your son."

He reached out, took one of the baby's hands in his, its little fingers curling around one of his. "He's so . . . so *wee*."

Rebecca laughed, pressing her hand against Amalie's belly to help drive out the afterbirth. "He's a big one and . . . Oh! I think he's got a brother or a sister."

Another pang came, catching Amalie by surprise.

Twins?

The second baby came more quickly than the first, slipping into Rebecca's waiting hands with an indignant wail.

Rebecca held the baby up. "Another boy!"

And the room filled with laughter.

A malie knew when Annie took her babies from her arms. She knew when Morgan gently lifted her and carried her to the bed and kissed her cheek. But by the time he drew the blankets over her, she was asleep.

A malie awoke to find Morgan beside her, rocking the two babies that lay side by side in the cradle he'd carved for one, a look of wonder on his handsome face.

"I think you shall have to carve another."

Morgan glanced down at her, his gaze soft. "You're awake already, *a leannan*? I thought you'd sleep the day away. God kens you need the rest."

She tried to sit, winced at her soreness, her gaze settling on her *two* babies. "Do you know which is which?"

He nodded, smiled. "The one in the blue blanket is Lachlan Anthony."

It was the name they'd chosen if the baby was a boy, a name that honored both of their fathers—Lachlan MacKinnon and Antoine Chauvenet.

"What shall we name the second?"

"I've thought hard on that, and I've wondered how you'd feel about 'Connor Joseph.'" He took her hand, his expression turning troubled. "Iain and I are out of the war now. Iain has a son.

But Connor and Joseph are still fightin'. I thought that if we named our son after them, they would go into battle kennin' that their names live on."

It was a beautiful idea, one that touched Amalie deeply. She, too, hated to think of Connor and Joseph facing the danger of battle, their lives still bound to this war. She spoke the name aloud, her throat growing tight. "Connor Joseph MacKinnon. *Oui*. It is a strong and proud name. Connor and Joseph will be pleased."

Morgan raised an eyebrow. "They'll be insufferable."

They laughed together, both knowing it was true.

Laughter faded into smiles, and they sat in silence, staring in quiet amazement at their two sleeping babies. Then Morgan reached over and took Amalie's hand.

He kissed her fingers, one by one. "There's naugh' I can say or do to repay you for what you've given me. If I could have taken your sufferin' upon myself, I'd have done it gladly."

She drew a breath to speak, but Morgan went on.

"For a time, I was afraid I might lose you, and the thought struck fear inside me such as I've ne'er kent afore—not in battle, not when I was shot, not when I thought I might hang. I cannae fathom my life wi'out you, lass." He drew a deep breath, his expression hardening. "I willna spend inside you again."

Amalie saw the sincerity and resolve on his face and knew he was saying such nonsense out of love for her. She raised her hand to his cheek, felt his stubble against her palm. "Am I to be content to live as your sister? No, Morgan. None of us knows what tomorrow will bring. Whether I die in childbed or Connor and Joseph are struck down in battle, we must take life as it comes."

He ran his thumb down her cheek. "My brave, bonnie lass. Where does a wee woman come by such courage?"

"My courage comes from loving you, Morgan MacKinnon."

He gazed at her as if in wonder, then drew a deep breath. "Then let us take each day as it comes, counting our blessings along the way."

They turned as one and gazed into the cradle and counted— by twos.

The Ballad of Morgan MacKinnon

BY DOUGIE MACMORRAN

MacKinnon arose on an April morn'
Taen his rifle in baith his hands
He ha' bid the lassies a lang farewell
Gaen tae fecht on Carillon's strand

When the lassies they heard o' this
Their hands for dule they wrang
Cryin', "Morgan, bide wi' us awhile
Tae the battle dinnae ye gang."

'Tis far tae Ticonderoga
'Tis far through forest and fen
But 'tis there you'll find Morgan MacKinnon
Bonnie and braw untae the end

We cam tae the walls of Carillon
But the battle had cam tae us
For the French they lay a-waitin'
Wi' their rifles aimed at us

MacKinnon, he ordered the retreat
But he ha' stayed ahind
For one o' his men was doun
And he'd nae leave him tae die.

'Tis far tae Ticonderoga
'Tis far through forest and fen
But 'tis there you'll find Morgan MacKinnon
Feal and true untae the end

"Leave me here," cried his woundit man.
"Dinnae gi' your life for me."
Says Morgan, "I've cam wi' a hundred men
And wi' a hundred I shall leave."

So he ha' taen him on his back
An' he buir him tae the strand
Wi' fire rainin' frae above
An' death on either hand

'Tis far tae Ticonderoga
'Tis far through forest and fen
But 'tis there you'll find Morgan MacKinnon
Stark and strang untae the end

Morgan, he buir him on his back
And sent his men awa'
But he stayed tae haud the French attack
So his men micht get awa'

An' the next shot that the French, they fired
They wounded him in the thee
An' the last shot that the French, they fired
Well, his hairt's blood blint his e'e

'Tis far tae Ticonderoga
'Tis far through forest and fen
But 'tis there you'll find Morgan MacKinnon
Brave and bold untae the end

But Morgan ha' taen his pistol forth
An' he raised it one last time
An' he ha' fired on the sodger
An' killed the man who'd struck him doun

Then Morgan fell upon the sand
An' tae his men he cried
"I am lost. Leave me tae my end."
Then he laid doun and died

'Tis far tae Ticonderoga
'Tis far through forest and fen
But 'tis there you'll find Morgan MacKinnon
Bidin' untae the end

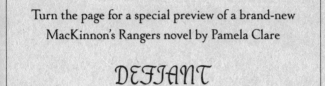

Turn the page for a special preview of a brand-new
MacKinnon's Rangers novel by Pamela Clare

DEFIANT

Coming soon from Berkley Sensation!

Lady Sarah Woodville struggled to keep up with her captor, her lungs aching for breath, a dagger-sharp stitch in her side. Taking no pity on her, he drew her onward, holding fast to the leather cords that bit into her wrists. Her toes and fingers were pinched from cold, her thighs burning from the steep uphill climb. Each step was agony, her feet blistered raw by the wet leather of her new shoes. And yet she dared not ask him to stop nor even slow him.

She knew he would kill her.

She'd been sailing with Mrs. Price, her chaperone, and Jane, her lady's maid, from New York up the Hudson River toward Albany, where she was to visit her uncle William Wentworth ere the summer campaigns called him away, when the captain had encountered ice floes that all but blocked the river. He'd tried to navigate his way around them, but he'd run the ship aground just off the western bank. Apologizing profusely for his error in judgment, he'd sent straightaway for help, assuring Sarah that Albany was not far upriver.

But Mrs. Price's stomach had been unable to tolerate the awkward tilt and rocking of the stranded ship. To help ease her *mal de mer*, the captain had rowed her, Sarah, and Jane ashore, together with a few other passengers who likewise felt queasy.

But they'd no sooner set foot on the embankment than she'd heard a musket fire and the captain had fallen dead.

Then the most terrible screams that could be conceived had come out of the forest, followed by painted men with muskets, knives, and hatchets. And within a matter of moments, everyone who'd left the ship, apart from Sarah, Jane, and a young boy, had been slain, their bloody scalps hanging from beaded belts.

Uncle William will send soldiers. He might even send his Rangers.

Sarah had counted eight attackers, but she could only see three now—her captor and the two who held Jane and the boy. Only rarely did the Indians look back at their prisoners, and then never with concern, their faces terrible to behold, painted in shades of red and black, their heads shaved apart from a single lock of hair that hung from each man's scalp, their bodies clothed in tanned and painted hides.

And to think that only two days ago she'd told Jane she hoped to see an Indian.

How long they walked Sarah could not say. The pain in her feet became unbearable, and yet she had no choice but to bear it, following where she was led. The Indians picked a path through towering pines, avoiding the snow whenever they could, the ground slanting upward, dark forest all around them. And then, in the distance, Sarah heard it—the distant tattoo of military drums.

Soldiers!

The Indians heard it, too. They stopped, spoke to one another in hushed words Sarah could not understand. Jane leaned against a tree, trying to catch her breath, her long red hair having fallen from its pins to hang down her back in a long braid. The boy looked up at Sarah, fear in his green eyes, his face smattered with freckles. Dressed in homespun, he had the look of the frontier about him. How old was he? Nine? Ten? Had his family been amongst those slain?

The poor child!

Then Sarah thought of her own family. What would they do when they got word she'd been taken by Indians? Would Papa and Mama regret sending her away, or would they blame her again? If only she had been the daughter Mama had wanted her to be and not so bent upon her music. There would have been no scandal, and she would be safely at home in London, far from this wild and terrible place.

The boy moved closer to her, as if seeking a mother's comfort. *Do not feel sorry for yourself, Sarah, for shame!*

She smiled, offering him silent encouragement.

Then their captors turned and looked down at them as if noticing them for the first time. The one who held her tether reached out, took a lock of her hair between his fingers, and rubbed it, his dark eyes boring into hers. She felt her heart shrink under his cold stare, but willed herself to meet his gaze unflinching, refusing to let him see how deeply he frightened her.

Then again she heard it—the beating of drums.

As abruptly as they had stopped, the Indians began to move again, dragging Sarah and the others along, faster this time, first uphill, then down, until the pain in Sarah's feet was so excruciating it brought tears to her eyes. Then, at last, the Indians stopped, giving them leave to rest near a frozen stream at the base of the hill, even releasing their bonds, as if they knew their captives were too exhausted to escape.

One of the Indians handed Sarah a water skin and motioned for her to drink. This she did and gratefully. But when she reached to hand the skin to Jane, it was yanked from her grasp.

Her captor knelt down before her, a pair of moccasins in his hands, and she watched, astonished, as he discarded her tattered shoes and torn stockings, bathed her blisters in water from the water skin, then slipped soft, warm moccasins over her feet. His face a mask of cold indifference, he stood and strode off to talk with the others.

And for a moment Sarah was alone with Jane and the boy. She met the boy's gaze. "You're a very brave young man. What is your name?"

"Thomas Wilkins, miss." Thomas gave her a sad smile, his gaze dropping to her moccasins. "I think they're goin' to keep you alive at least."

His words caught her by surprise. "Wh-whatever do you mean?"

"They gave you water and moccasins, but not us." His gaze dropped to her feet again. "They think our soldiers can't track you if you've got moccasins on your feet."

"But what about you, Thomas, and you, my sweet Jane?"

Not much older than she, Jane had been Sarah's most faithful companion since she'd come to New York to stay with Governor DeLancey. Jane hadn't turned up her nose at Sarah like the others, but had shown her sympathy and understanding despite the scandal. Since Margaret's death, she had been Sarah's only friend.

She gave Sarah a tremulous smile. "You shall go on, my lady. But I fear we shall be tomahawked in this lonely place."

A chill that had nothing to do with the cold slid down Sarah's spine. "*No!* Do not say such a thing! They gave me moccasins only because my feet were blistered."

But a glance told her Jane's feet were blistered, too.

Then their captors returned. One hauled Sarah to her feet, while the other two went to stand beside Jane and Thomas. Jane met Sarah's gaze, reaching with bound wrists to hold the boy's hands between hers. "We shall be brave, shall we not, Thomas?"

"No!" Sarah cried, panic like ice in her blood, her knees going weak. "Please—"

A rough hand closed over her mouth, strong arms lifting her off the ground, forcing her to turn away as Jane's voice called after her.

"God bless you, my lady! Don't forget your English tongue!"

For hours, they walked through endless stretches of darkening forest, Sarah struggling to keep up, wolves howling in the distance. But as they went on, a strange thing happened. She became less afraid, as if the bonds on her wrists—and the men who held her captive—were nothing more than a dream.

Surely, Jane and young Thomas would be along soon. Perhaps they were being taken through the forest by a different path. Or perhaps the soldiers had found and freed them.

But night fell, and still she saw no glimpse of them.

Then, through the dark, she could just make out the flickering light of a campfire. As they drew closer, she realized it was the Indians' encampment. Surely, Jane and Thomas were waiting there for her. New vigor filled her weary limbs, and she hurried forward, eager for the fire's warmth and some sign of her companions. But they were nowhere to be seen.

Confused, fighting despair and exhaustion, she sat before the fire, shivering, her woolen traveling cloak offering little protection against the cold, her gown tattered and damp. She drank when she was made to drink and ate when food was placed in her hands. Once, she started to hum without realizing it—Bach's Arioso—only to be struck across the face.

Then her captor draped an animal fur around her shoulders and motioned toward a blanket he'd placed on the ground near the fire, indicating that she should lie down. But she would not lie with him.

And then she saw.

At the edge of the firelight, an Indian sat stitching upon a fresh scalp. Attached to it was a long, red braid.

M ajor Connor MacKinnon gently turned the bodies over— one of the lasses and the lad, both tomahawked, both scalped.

Och, Christ!

He'd warned that arrogant bastard Haviland that sending redcoats after them had been a mistake. War parties often killed captives if pressed. But Haviland, who didn't know his head from his arse, hadn't listened. And now two of the three who'd been taken were lost.

And so young.

Connor crossed himself and whispered a prayer for them, then looked more closely at the lass's face, the features hard to see in the gloaming. But it was not she.

It was not Wentworth's niece. He'd stake his life on it.

Wentworth had shown him a likeness of her. A small locket painting, it had shown a beautiful young girl with hair the color of honey and bright blue eyes, her cheeks pink, a playful smile on her rosy lips. The poor lass lying here on the cold ground was plainer than she with bright red hair. Connor gave her cold, lifeless hand a squeeze, then turned away.

There was nothing he could do for her or the lad now.

Nearer to the frozen stream, Joseph held up a pair of battered shoes and torn stockings.

Connor reached out, touched them. The ties on the shoes were of lace, the shoes themselves of finest leather, the stockings silk. "They must be hers. Such frippery takes coin."

Joseph set the shoes and stockings aside. "The Shawnee think to confuse us by putting her in moccasins."

The trick might have worked had he and Joseph been redcoats or even unseasoned farmers new to the frontier. But Joseph was war chief of the Muhheconneok people, and Connor had grown up beside him, adopted together with his brothers by the Mahican when he was but a stripling lad. They had learnt to track, hunt, and fight together, earning their warrior marks under the stern headship of Joseph's father. They knew this land every bit as well as the Shawnee and could not be fooled by such attempts at cunning.

"She'll be movin' faster wi' moccasins on her feet."

They pressed on, eager to make up for lost time by covering as much ground as possible before darkness fell, following a trail that most others would have missed—a few bent stalks of dried grass, a thread from the lass's skirts caught on a sedge, an overturned rock. They did not need to speak, each anticipating the other's actions, enabling them to move quickly and silently.

For five years they and their men had fought side by side—MacKinnon's Rangers and Captain Joseph's Mahican warriors. Together they'd hounded the French and their Indian allies, fighting them in forest and field, ambushing their supply trains, spending their own blood to turn the tide of this accursed war. There were no fiercer fighters in the colonies, no men more feared by the French and their Indian allies.

If only their men were with them tonight.

But the winter had been long and cold, and the Rangers had not yet mustered. Most of Connor's men were still wintering with their wives and bairns, growing fat and lazy, and Joseph's warriors were warm in their lodges in Stockbridge. None of them were due to report to Fort Edward for a fortnight.

Connor and Joseph had been in Albany to order supplies for spring when a company of grenadiers had marched out of the stockade and down toward the river as if the town were under attack. Connor had learnt that two women and a boy had been taken by Indians about ten miles south of town. He and Joseph had gone straight to the stockade to urge Colonel Haviland to call back the grenadiers and send them instead, only to meet with Colonel Haviland's scorn.

"Do you expect me to believe, Major, that a rustic and an Indian can succeed where His Majesty's trained soldiers cannot?"

Then Wentworth had arrived. In a cold fury, he'd upbraided Haviland, ordering him to recall the grenadiers. Then he'd dispatched Connor and Joseph. "Do whatever you must, Major MacKinnon, but bring the captives back safely."

Connor had never known Wentworth to show concern for captives before, and his surprise must have shown. Then he'd seen something on Wentworth's face he'd never seen before—fear.

"One of the women is my niece," Wentworth had confessed, his mask of ice cracking. "Lady Sarah Woodville—she is young and gently bred. I would not see her suffer harm. Do whatever you must to protect her and return her to me. Do you understand?"

"Aye." Connor understood only too well. Wentworth cared about these captives only because one of them was kin. "For a moment, I thought you'd grown a heart."

He and Joseph had gathered their gear and set out straightaway, but precious hours—and two innocent lives—had been lost thanks to Haviland and his fecklessness.

He's no' the only man wi' innocent blood on his hands, is he, laddie?

Nay, he wasn't.

In the distance, a wolf howled, its call answered by another, a cold wind moving like a whisper through the tall pines as darkness fell.

Daylight gone, they had no choice but to stop for the night. They could not track what they could not see, and if they should miss something and lose the trail, they would waste hours finding it again in the morn.

Without a word, they began to make camp.

Lord William stood at his window staring unseeing into the darkness, the fingers of his left hand worrying the cracked marble chess piece he always kept in his vest pocket—the black king Lady Anne had broken two summers past.

This was his fault.

When Sarah had written to him begging him to let her leave the dreary isolation of Governor DeLancey's home, he'd had misgivings, but he'd ignored them. At the time, he'd been worried about smallpox and measles, both of which had hit Albany hard this winter. He hadn't imagined it possible that Indians would dare strike so close to town with a thousand of His Majesty's troops billeted here.

He'd been wrong.

How he wished now that he had denied her request and admonished her to bear out her exile with fortitude and grace. But the thought of seeing his niece again had appealed to him, so he had relented, arranging for her passage northward. Bright eyed, inquisitive, and talented beyond measure upon the harpsichord, she had always been his favorite.

The last time he'd seen her had been six years ago, just prior to his voyage to the colonies. She'd been but twelve years old and still very much a child. Though her body had shown no sign of approaching womanhood, it had been clear to all that she would grow to become a woman of surpassing beauty. His sister, secretly a severe Lutheran, had restricted her daughters to long hours of daily Bible study and needlework to prepare them for marriage. She'd been openly distressed by her youngest child's beauty and passion for music, deeming both dangerous to Sarah's immortal soul.

But William had found Sarah refreshing and had indulged her when occasion allowed, secretly taking her to hear chamber music, lending her books about history, art, and music theory. Perhaps his sister had been right to restrict Sarah. Perhaps she'd seen something in her daughter that William had not.

Last summer, Sarah had caused such a scandal that her father had sent her away, depositing her in New York with Governor DeLancey, an old family friend. When William had inquired as to the nature of the scandal, his sister had written to say that decency forbade her even to mention it. Even knowing his sister's penchant for exaggeration when it came to matters of sin, William had been intrigued by this, but the summer campaigns had prevented him from inquiring further. He'd hoped to hear the unspeakable truth of it from Sarah on this visit.

But now she was out there somewhere, a captive of men who would not hesitate to do unimaginably cruel things to her.

As second in command of His Majesty's forces in the colonies, William had heard all the tales—accounts of torture, maiming, rape. They'd always just been words on parchment to him, nothing more than the cost of war. This one burnt alive, that one beaten and sold, this one adopted and forced into heathen marriage.

But the thought of Sarah enduring such a fate . . .

In truth, William didn't give one whit what happened to the other two captives so long as Sarah was returned to him alive and unscathed. MacKinnon had probably guessed as much. He'd seen the disgust on MacKinnon's face when MacKinnon had heard that one of the captives was William's niece.

For a moment, I thought you'd grown a heart.

How could William expect a man like MacKinnon to understand that Sarah was worth more than a thousand common frontierswomen?

"Pardon me, my lord." Cooke's voice came from the doorway.

William turned to face him. "Yes, Lieutenant."

Cooke bowed neatly. "I asked local churches to hold observances this evening so that prayers might be said for your niece. Services at St. Peter's begin in half an hour."

"Well done. Thank you." It was then William remembered he was in a state of undress, his wig sitting forgotten on his desk, his coat draped over a chair with his cravat.

"If I may be of any assistance, my lord . . ."

William gave a consenting nod, his gaze drawn back to the window.

"Don't worry, my lord. Major MacKinnon will find her."

Connor took a sip of rum, trying to read the letter Morgan had sent him by firelight. He knew what it said by heart, but still cherished each word, the news it held warming him more than the fire. Morgan was now a father twice over. His bonnie wife, Amalie, had come through a difficult travail and borne him twin sons. Morgan had named one of the wee bairns Connor Joseph in honor of Connor. Och, aye, and in honor of Joseph, too.

"His mother is Indian." Joseph smiled and puffed out his chest like a tom turkey, feathers and all. "He'll be a warrior like me."

Connor lifted his gaze from the parchment. "She's only one quarter Indian. The rest of her is French, aye? He's a MacKinnon. He'll be bonnie and braw—like me."

They'd been having this wee argie-bargie since Morgan's letter had arrived two days ago and were clearly no nearer to resolving their difference of opinion. Knowing it was time to sleep, Connor folded the letter and carefully stowed it with his gear.

Joseph sat on the bed of spruce boughs beside him. "What do you expect she's like?"

"Who?"

"Lady Sarah Woodville. Wentworth showed you a likeness of her."

"She looked like a spoiled princess, unable to do a thing for herself. She'll likely be after us to serve her tea and crumpets on the way back to Albany." Connor lay down, his feet toward the fire, the anger he'd felt all through the day spilling out. "Wentworth never gave a damn when other women were taken. He had Iain nearly flayed alive for savin' Annie. But when his niece is stolen . . ."

Connor let the thought go unfinished. There was no need to explain.

"She is not to blame." Joseph lay down and drew the bear skin up over both of them, his body pressed against Connor's for warmth. "Whatever Wentworth has done—she is innocent."

Connor closed his eyes. "Och, would you let a man sleep!"

A vague sense of guilt stirred in his chest. He quashed it.

The lass's kin had laid waste to the Highlands, shedding MacKinnon blood, and her uncle had enslaved Iain through deceit. What kind of woman could spring from the loins of a clan such as that? Whatever else she might be, it wasn't innocent.

But the image of Lady Sarah, young and beautiful, was there before him and would not leave his mind. And in his dreams she was weeping.

PAMELA CLARE began her writing career as an investigative reporter and columnist, working her way up the newsroom ladder to become the first woman editor of two different newspapers. Along the way, she and her team won numerous state and national journalism awards, including the 2000 National Journalism Award for Public Service and the Lifetime Achievement Award from the Colorado Society of Professional Journalists. A single mother with two sons, she lives in Colorado at the foot of the Rocky Mountains. Visit her website at www.pamelaclare.com.